SARAH HAWTHORNE

Owl of the Pale Moon

To Abby, my biggest fan.

Contents

I   Bixton

1   The Wolf of Bixton   3
2   Doldrums Shattered   20
3   Parting Shots   35
4   Pale Moon   48

II   On Tour

5   Force Vectors   65
6   Culture Shock   79
7   City of Smoke   94
8   The Homefront   106

III   Black Eagle Keep

9   Making Amends   121
10 Calling Card   133
11 Best Friends   144
12 A Wizard's Confession   159

IV   Kahlane Rainforest

13 Sweat and Blood   173
14 Company of Mages   185
15 Another World   199
16 Toad and Frogs   214

V   Bixton Again

17 Long Road Home   233
18 Flying and Festivities   248
19 Fang and Friendship   258
20 Canyon Run   267

VI   House Brandwyck

21 Homecoming   279
22 Mages' Duel   288
23 Heartbare   298
24 Unclear Futures   308

Author's Note   318
About the Author   319

I

Bixton

1

The Wolf of Bixton

Underperforming Subordinates - It Stalks the Streets of Bixton - A Kind of Gasping Murmur - Was that Your Slice of Cake?

A steam whistle screamed out, shattering Cassie's concentration. It startled her enough to cause her to prick her own finger with the sewing needle she had been meticulously threading through a swath of cloth.

"Ten minute break!" A gravelly tenor voice shouted from a catwalk on the far end of the factory floor, in case anyone wasn't already aware.

Cassie threw down the needle and stuck her finger in her mouth to staunch the bleeding. It wasn't the first time she'd pricked her finger on the job, and though she knew she should've been using a thimble, it was such a hassle to find one that fit that she typically preferred to just live on the edge.

Cassandra Mott was a twenty-two-year-old woman with brown skin and raven-black curls that she kept tied up at work. Currently she wore a boring brown work dress and worn leather boots. Her expression was one of exhaustion on a spiritual level. She found everything else about herself completely unremarkable.

The person beside Cassie at the sewing line stretched their arms above their head and turned to her. "Ugh, I'm so tired, Cass."

"Yeah, me too."

This was Jax Dennin, a non-binary Zonan around Cassie's age, who was pretty much her only friend in the world. They had scruffy short-trimmed brown hair, pale white skin, and brown eyes, matching their brown canvas work overalls and once-white shirt.

"Are you okay? Did you prick your finger again?"

"Yeah." Cassie took her finger out of her mouth. Fortunately it hadn't been a deep puncture, so the bleeding had already stopped.

"You should really be more careful, girl. You don't want that to get infected."

"Yeah, yeah. I know, Jax."

"Oh, by the way, did you hear about Cathy?"

"No, what happened to Cathy? I haven't seen her today."

"That's the thing, *nobody knooooooows.*" Jax seemed to be getting a little too much enjoyment out of what Cass deemed to be, at best, none of anyone's business.

"Oh I'm sure she's fine. Probably just exhausted from overwork. Gods know I don't blame her."

Cassie massaged her temples with her palms. The work day was only halfway over, but she was already on the verge of falling asleep. She stretched her sore hands and cracked her fingers at the knuckles before massaging her aching carpals. She sighed. "I gotta get out of this place."

"Mott! My office, now!" The same abrasive male voice shattered Cassie's one moment of calm.

Jax raised their bushy eyebrows. "You sure pissed him off this time."

"I dunno, I'd just say he's just got a *short* temper."

* * *

Thomas Hardden was a man of strict regimen. He arose every morning at four AM sharp, took his coffee black with one sugar, had a nice pre-work cigar, and then arrived at the factory far earlier than anyone had the right to be there, looking for something to be mad about. He enjoyed his job as a factory manager, operating one of a chain of textile factories owned by the Jones & Sons Textile Corporation, a very profitable business. By the end of each workday, he had completely filled his desk's ashtray with cigar butts and replaced every drop of blood in his body with pure dark roast. Nobody knew what he did after work, but ostensibly it involved going immediately to bed.

Hardden had spent ten years serving in the Zonan army, during which time he had risen to the rank of Major, a feat that he would not let anyone within earshot forget. During his tours, he had learned that the only path to success in life was to keep your head down, work yourself to death, do what your superiors told you to do, and kiss ass as much as possible. With this foolproof strategy, he hoped to seize a regional manager position in the company before his fiftieth birthday, a mere eight years away.

One thing Hardden could not stand, however, was underperforming subordinates. It was, as he said to himself with closed office door, his job to whip the no good low-lifes into shape the way his commanding officers had done to him and his generation, lest they reflect poorly on his managerial capabilities. Of all the thorns in his side, none were more frustrating than Cassandra Mott. An underachiever at best, Ms. Mott struggled to keep up with the other women on the factory floor. Perhaps it was those large hands of hers, Hardden often wondered, or perhaps it was just her Abaxian heritage. Every time he looked at her, Hardden thought back to the time an Abaxian mage had roasted his entire squad alive, a snap of their fingers ending the lives of six good men and leaving a nasty burn on the small of Hardden's back. It was this wound that began to itch whenever Hardden had the misfortune of seeing the woman make mistakes at simple tasks.

Today was worse. Today, the wound felt like it was set alight once more as Cassandra Mott walked into Hardden's office. He slammed the door shut, the miniature set of blinds over the door's window swinging behind it.

"Siddown, Mott."

Cassie sat in an uncomfortable wooden chair with no cushion that her boss always kept in his office so that he could yell at whoever was unfortunate enough to sit there. Hardden himself sat in his cushy leather chair behind his desk, ruffled a few papers officiously, and then lit a cigar for himself. Cassie avoided eye contact and stared off into the distance, wishing for Hardden to just get it all out already so the encounter could be over. He took his sweet time lighting the cigar, filling the room with the acrid smoke of tar and pipe weed rolled into one foul package. Cassie guessed he was doing this for dramatic effect.

"Do ya know why I called you in here?"

"No, sir."

"Heh, of course you don't. The only thing worse than your sewing skills is your lack of self-awareness."

"I'm sorry, sir, I'll do better."

"You'd better, if you want to keep this job."

Cassie desperately wanted to tell him how she'd rather be doing just about anything else. The sound of the steam whistle rang from outside the office, signaling the end of the seamstresses' break. The scrape of stools adjusting back into place at the long tables in the next room were only slightly muffled by the thin office walls, blinded windows affording selective privacy to the room's occupant.

Cassie's eyes flicked to the window, but she remained silent.

"You can be replaced, you know. I've got young ladies lining up just on the *off-chance* of a vacancy at this very factory." If the economy wasn't so poor, Cassie would have doubted this was the case. She still doubted it, a little. Sometimes she felt like she stayed at this job just to spite Hardden that much more.

"You know, when I was in the army…" Hardden began a long-winded diatribe about discipline and obedience and general boot-lickery. Cassie exhaled. Though the boss's temper was short and his lectures long, sitting in the cool, shaded office beat the heat of the factory floor, which steamed her alive even in the mid autumn. She could easily tune out the lecture and just daydream for a few minutes, free of fabric that needed sewing.

Cassie was not a woman who aspired to much. This was not due to contentment with her current situation, but more a lack of direction in her life. There weren't many opportunities for an early-twenties woman who didn't come from money. On top of that, many establishments in Zona turned their nose up at applicants of Abaxian blood purely on principle. And on top of *that*, once they found out she was a Changer, most of the remaining establishments suddenly didn't have the time to talk to her. Thus why she found herself sitting in this office on the receiving end of a classic Hardden tirade.

"…Mott, are you listening?"

"Yes, sir."

"Uh huh." Hardden stood up, which actually decreased his effective height. Standing at a towering four foot eleven, what the man lacked in verticality he made up for in bluster. He brushed off his well-cleaned business waistcoat, shirt permanently stained with cigar smoke. "Now get back to work. I'm not paying you to sit around."

Cassie stood up and stepped towards the door, bracing herself for more labor. She reached for the handle, but Hardden stopped her.

"Mott, just one more thing." She turned slowly to face him. "I only gave you this job because of the good graces of your mother. You wouldn't want your performance to reflect poorly on her, would you?"

Cassie would have rathered he fired her on the spot.

* * *

Work was as arduous as ever, though Cassie managed to muddle through by imagining a myriad of horrible accidents she could surreptitiously inflict upon Hardden. Before she knew it, the day ended leaving her exhausted and dejected. As Jax gathered their belongings, they offered her a hand up from her seat at the work table. "C'mon girl, you got this. Good work out there today."

Cassie accepted her friend's help and the two headed off to the dressing room to don their coats and hats.

"Thanks, Jax. Try telling that to Hardden, though."

Jax pulled on their khaki overcoat and donned an old top hat, faded in places, with the stitching coming loose. The rest of the pair's coworkers were already finishing up in the workers' coat room, gossiping to each other. As Cassie was dusting off her hat, a hand-me-down straw affair with a loose bow tied in its fading ribbon, a blonde girl peeked around the corner of the coat room lockers.

"Oh, Cassandra, Jax, be careful out there, okay?"

Jax cocked an eyebrow. "Whaddaya mean?"

The girl donned a mischievous expression. "The Wolf," she said with the quiet ominousness of one telling a ghost story.

Jax sighed. "What wolf, Donna?"

"The Wolf of Bixton. Surely you've heard?"

Cassie had certainly not heard and shook her head.

"Ooooh, sounds spooky," Jax said.

"They say it stalks the streets of Bixton after sundown, preying on pretty young ladies!" Donna was pantomiming a stalking motion, grinning like an idiot. "But you two shouldn't have anything to worry about, then."

"Good to know you'll get gobbled up, instead," Jax teased back. The two laughed, but Cassie didn't think it was terribly funny.

"Are there any victims, then?"

This put a damper on her coworkers' grim fun. Donna looked bashful. "I dunno, but… well, some of the girls have been saying that's what happened to Cathy. That she got… y'know, gobbled up."

Cassie sighed. "I'm sure Cathy is just fine. I'll go by her house tonight and check on her on my way home. Try not to put too much thought into rumors like this. Does you more worry than good."

The company of women and Jax started to disperse as each made their way out onto the chilly autumn streets of Bixton, saying their goodbyes and going their separate ways. The sun was already set, with the last vestiges of light fading beneath the mountains to the west. This time of year, the laborers at the Jones & Sons factory arrived early in the morning before the sun rose and left just as it finished setting. The only hints of sunlight that let Cassie know she was living on the surface of the world were filtered through the dingy frosted-glass tiles of the factory ceiling. Now, it was nearly as dark as the pre-dawn morning, giving a disorienting perspective of time.

Cassie's stomach grumbled, telling her that it didn't give a damn what time it was, it needed sustenance. Knowing there was almost certainly no food waiting for her at home, Cassie frequently took her evening meals al fresco. A local butcher's shop was a favorite, their sandwiches made with local cheeses and cured meats, and with bread from the bakery next door. Luckily, they closed an hour after she got off work, so she had time to swing by on her way home.

The door to the butcher's opened with a light tinkle of its bell, and Cassie was suddenly amidst ham hocks, sausage ropes, legs of unidentifiable origin, and various other cuts of meat. A man's voice called from further in, where she knew the counter to be.

"Izzat you, Cass? Wot'll it be today, love?"

"Hello, Mr. Burton. Do you have any more of that pepper salami? I'd love some slices of that."

Cassie came around the corner of an aisle to see a man behind the shop counter getting something out of a container in the back. Mr. Burton was a broad-set Zonan man with a full beard, bald head, and a warm smile. His highland accent was always as warm and inviting as his manner, and Cassie couldn't help but feel at home in his shop.

"Here you are, m'dear." Mr. Burton turned around with a fully assembled sandwich: salami, turkey, and sharp swysse cheese on a ciabatta roll, all wrapped in newsprint. Cassie tried not to drool. "I added a bit o' spicy mayonnaise. It's a new recipe I'm tryin' so let me know wot ye think."

The lettering on the newsprint was faded and smeared, but she could barely make out a headline to the effect of "Terrorist 'Owl' Strikes Again." Cassie was not one for the news, as most of it was little more than celebrity gossip, political propaganda, and corporate brown-nosing. However, despite her ignorance of current affairs, even she had heard of the Owl of the Pale Moon, a notorious gentleman thief and mage adept. She, like many other young ladies, followed the exploits of the Owl with much interest, finding his bombast and flamboyant nature enchanting. Cassie had already read the story visible on the newsprint, however. It was a pretty dry and dispassionate account of Owl's theft of a royal gem from the Zonan treasury, true to his calling card sent a day prior. Her stomach growled again.

Cassie set two crowns on the counter and took the sandwich, eager to taste Mr. Burton's newest concoction. Biting down, her mouth filled first with the crunch of the bread, then the umami of the meat, the softness and bite of the cheese, and the creamy texture of the mayonnaise. After a second, she felt a tingle on her lips as the capsaicin in the mayo hit, revealing a slightly smoky taste. It was very good.

"Mmmmph." Cassie said, taking another bite.

"That good, eh?"

Cassie cleared her mouth before answering. "Mr. Burton, you've outdone yourself again. Have you considered officially rebranding as a delicatessen? Because this is probably the best sandwich I've ever had."

Mr. Burton stroked his beard, looking thoughtful. "Burton's Butchery and Delicatessen, eh? It's got a good ring to it, aye. Ye know, I only started making sandwiches because of you, lass. When ye first walked into me shop looking haggard and hungry after ye first day of work I figured I'd best offer ye *something*. An' ye kept coming back, so I reckoned I oughta step up me game."

"Well consider the game stepped up. You've made a customer of me for life, sir."

Mr. Burton laughed heartily, clapping a hand to his belly. "The highest compliment, t'be sure. Well lass, I'll have to consider your suggestion now, won't I?"

"If you need some help around the shop just let me know, I'd be happy to work for you."

"Already had enough of the Jones place, have ye?"

Cassie sighed dramatically and took some more bites of the sandwich, wishing she could live in this moment for a while longer.

"Well, as much as I'd love t' hire ye, 'fraid the economy won't allow it. Everything and sundry's getting more expensive by the day, and I'm loath to raise me prices lest I lose me competitive edge."

Cassie understood all too well. The Kingdom of Zona was experiencing a rapid period of inflation, due largely to competition with the Free State of Abaxia, a neighboring nation with whom Zona was currently at war. It was just hard for a largely magically-inept nation to compete with one whose primary export was magical goods and services. Cassie, being racially Abaxian, wished she could have grown up there, possibly attending the Abaxian University for Mages. In her wildest fantasies, Cassie would dream of flying away from the dreary town of Bixton, casting a particularly vexing spell on Hardden as she left. But alas, she had never displayed any magical talent whatsoever, so the dream was shelved for more pragmatic occupations.

Mr. Burton cleared his throat, interrupting Cassie's fantasy as she finished the last few bites of the sandwich. "Well lass, better run ye along. It's getting late, and I'm about to close up shop here, meself."

Cassie nodded to the man. "Thanks again, Mr. Burton."

"Oh, and be careful out there, lass. I hear rumors of some sort of vile beastie roamin' the streets."

"Ugh, not you, too."

* * *

Back out on the streets, a cold wind swept down the main boulevard where Burton's Butchery was located. The sun was well set by this point, and the only light came from the regularly spaced gas street lamps along the main roads. Cassie decided she should probably carry a hand lantern or even a magical light stick in her bag for such an occasion, but all she could do now was to trudge on home as quickly as possible.

Bixton was a modest mountainside town known best for its industry. The town was almost literally owned by the corporations that built their factories here, though bits of the pre-industrial farming town still survived. Cobblestone streets weaved their way between rows of brick houses and commercial buildings, arching over Mellius and Koyan, the two river tributaries that ran through the town on their way down the Brachius mountain range. The streets were mostly empty at this hour, but there were still the occasional few factory workers returning home, and Cassie was passed by a few horse-drawn carriages clopping their way to who knows where.

Cassie crossed the Mellius into the eastern side of the town, remembering to stop by the Bateman household to check on Cathy. The house was a modest brick affair in a row of similar houses along Merrian Way, a side street of the town's main boulevard. The house was painted blue, and aging window frames revealed curtained windows. The inside of the house was dark. Cassie stepped up to the front door and rang the bell. After a minute without response, she rang again to no avail. She was determined to believe that the Batemans were just out for dinner at the moment, though she couldn't help but feel slightly nervous, the image of Donna miming a wolf stalking its prey flashing through her mind.

"Get a hold of yourself, girl. There's no Wolf, and Cathy has not been killed. I'm sure there's a perfectly rational explanation here."

Almost to punctuate the thought, a clattering sound of toppling rubbish bins echoed from a nearby alleyway. Any sane person would have run, but Cassie had the unfortunate insanity of morbid curiosity. She crept forward as quiet as she could to peek around the corner of the alleyway.

What she saw plunged her stomach into ice water and needled her brain with arrows of fear. Hunched over in the mess of spilled rubbish bins was the most grotesque creature that Cassie had ever seen. Like a dog, but horribly long in all the wrong ways, covered in patchy mange-eaten fur, its hands with long spindly fingers clutching at... something. Something red and bloody. She thought she caught a scrap of fabric in the fleshy lump the creature was slowly gnawing at and couldn't stop herself from yelping slightly.

The gnawing stopped and the creature slowly turned to face Cassie. It was the size of a bear, but lean like a greyhound. It stared directly into Cassie's eyes and she could see in the depths of its pitch-black marbles an expression of madness, like the creature had no idea what it was doing, as if it was merely sleepwalking. Its snout was abnormally long, and it opened its mouth, revealing rows of razor sharp teeth and blood oozing down its scraggly chin.

The creature let out a sound that Cassie was not expecting, a kind of gasping murmur, like a human struggling to speak, but that sound quickly rose in both volume and pitch to an otherworldly screaming wail. The hunk of mystery meat in the creature's clutches dropped to the cobblestones with a wet thud and something inside Cassie snapped. She turned as fast as she could and fled, not realizing there were tears in her eyes until she was maybe a quarter mile down the road. She heard the *pa-pat-pa-pat* sound of quadrupedal locomotion on the road behind her, and knew the creature was giving chase, though she refused to turn and look.

In her haste, she sped by two Peace Officers, their royal blue double-breasted doublets and brimmed hats turning to watch her egress. One of the men leaned nonchalantly against a nearby building, smoking a cigarette, and the other fiddled with his mustache. Neither seemed particularly concerned about Cassie, and made no motion to help her. It was pretty much what she expected. Peace Officers avoided helping Abaxians at best and at worst… Cassie had more pressing matters to think about right now and ignored the two men.

Heedless of the proper path, she continued heading east, desperate to escape this creature and be home. She twisted through alleyways, trying to lose her pursuer, but the noise of the chase kept coming. As she pulled herself out of a particularly narrow alley and stumbled onto the main street, she heard that high-pitched wail, like a fox's cry mixed with the squealing of an infant. Knowing not why, she closed her eyes as she ran full sprint down the street, wishing now that she had kept better care of her physical fitness. When she opened her eyes again, she was merely a foot away from the edge of the road as it peered over the Koyan some fifteen feet below. Without time to stop, Cassie jumped, screwing her eyes closed once more and praying for escape.

She felt the sensation of falling, then there was a loud rumbling crack like petulant thunder and her feet impacted hard ground. Cassie rolled, scraping her knees and thoroughly dirtying her dress. She opened her eyes and raised herself to an upright position on one arm, nursing a solid bruise forming on the other elbow. Somehow she was on the other side of the river. The canal was some thirty feet wide, a distance she'd never be able to vault even with the proper training. On the other street she saw something she didn't expect. Instead of the nightmare that was chasing her, she saw three feral dogs baying and barking in frustration on the far bank. The dogs craned their necks in confusion at how the human was able to make it over the river. After a few seconds, the dogs bored and dispersed to find other prey to chase.

Was it really just dogs? Cassie wondered. She slowly stood up, feeling thoroughly bruised and gasping for breath.

She walked the rest of the way home with frightened determination, coming to the Mott household in just a few minutes. In contrast to the Bateman house, hers was a standalone building, still of brick, but plastered over and painted a rusty pink. It was about twice as big as where Cathy lived, and although the house was objectively nicer, Cassie would have rather lived anywhere else.

She pulled her key from her breast pocket, thankful she hadn't dropped it in her panic. She unlocked the door and opened it to a darkened house.

"Hello?" she called, knowing full well she wouldn't receive a response.

Using the scant light from the street, she kindled the fireplace, desperate for warmth and comfort. As the flames slowly heated the room, she removed her hat and overcoat and hung them on the brass hangers by the front door. She kicked off her boots and massaged her aching heels. What she really needed right now was a bath.

Cassie trudged upstairs towards the communal bathroom when she passed an open door to a lit room. Through the door she could see a lavishly dressed young woman sitting daintily on a plush four-poster bed. She wore elbow-length white gloves and her face was adorned with what Cassie thought was a bit too much makeup. Her dress was the latest from the Avalon fall line, a white satin with purple floral stitching with cinched sleeves and a waistline that gently corseted the wearer and made this particular person look like a porcelain doll. Most garish of all was the deep yellow blonde curls atop the woman's head that absolutely did not complement her brown skin.

"I'm home, Feelie." Cassie said.

"Oh, hello, Cass. I didn't notice you there," the woman said back, with a sickeningly coquettish smile. This was Ophelia, Cassie's younger sister. Ophelia was eighteen years old, but as of yet remained unemployed. She held in her hand what at first blush appeared to be a rectangular hand mirror, but was actually a magical memory viewer that Ophelia had received for her birthday and had spent every waking moment using since.

"You could at least have started the fire. It's freezing in here!"

"Didn't wanna."

"And what in the world did you do to your hair?" Cassie stepped into the room and felt Ophelia's hair with her fingers. "Please tell me this is a wig."

Ophelia gave a crocodile's grin. "Nope. It's real. Mama took me to get it magically altered today. And don't touch it! It's still fresh."

Cassie groaned, retracting her hands. "But why this color?"

"I told you, I want to be a princess, and princesses have blonde hair!"

"Zonan princesses do, maybe, but you don't. You should really appreciate your natural hair better."

Ophelia pouted. "Our natural hair is ugly and I want it to be blonde like a princess! Now fetch me my dinner!"

Cassie sighed. Ophelia was a lost cause, having been completely enabled by their mother her whole life. "There isn't any food. You'll have to wait for Mom to get home. Besides, I'm going to go take a bath."

"No! I wanna take a bath!"

"Look, Feelie, I've had a really long day and I just want to get clean and go to bed. I'm not waiting for you to take a two-hour bubble bath."

"I'm gonna tell Mama that you didn't let me use the bath!"

"Tell her, then, see if I care." Cassie left her sister's room before Ophelia had a chance to entrap her further with childish bickering.

Cassie started the bath and locked the bathroom door. She could faintly hear the sound of a memory being played out on her sister's mirror from the other room, but she tuned it out. She slowly undressed, examining her bruised shoulder and skinned knees. They were both sore, and she found she was banged up in many more places besides. Catching a glimpse of her reflection in the fogging vanity mirror, Cassie scrutinized the shape of her breasts. They weren't coming in nearly as quickly as she liked. She'd have to up her dose of Changing Potion if she wanted results sometime before she was old and gray. Unfortunately, the potion was limited, and there was little it could do about the rest of her body aside from redistributing fat to choice locations. Besides, it was expensive.

Trying not to think about it too hard lest she fall into a spiral of self-hatred and dysphoria, she slipped into the hot bath. The near-scalding water felt good on her cold and battered skin and she relaxed in the feeling for a while before washing. She savored the warmth as long as possible before Ophelia announced her presence.

"Cassieeeeeee! Hurry uuuuuup. I wanna take a bath too!"

The water was beginning to cool anyway, so Cassie got out, dried off, shaved her face, and retreated to her room wrapped in her towel. As she dressed into her nightgown, she heard the front door open and close directly beneath her.

"I'm home!" a woman's voice called out from downstairs. The sound of heels on the wooden staircase preceded the arrival of a middle aged woman wearing a finely tailored business suit and shiny black heels. Corinne Mott was Cassie and Ophelia's mother, a career woman nearing her 50th birthday and head accountant to Zona's Magistrate of Defense. She was mostly aloof except for when she was doting on Ophelia. She was always so busy with work and pampering her youngest daughter that she had little to no attention left for Cassie, who was over it at this point. It was the way their family had always been, and she had no hope of changing things now.

"Ophelia, are you here, my love?"

"I'm in the bath, Mama!"

"And where's your brother?"

Cassie winced, feeling like a knife had plunged into her gut. "Sister. I'm her sister, Mom."

"Oh right, of course. You know I can't keep up with all these *changes*. By the way, Ophelia, I brought home your favorite meat pie. It's on the table downstairs."

"Yay! Thank you, Mommy," Ophelia simpered, knowing that her mother would give her anything she wanted.

Cassie emerged from her bedroom and brushed past her mother on the way downstairs.

"Did you get something to eat?" her mother asked.

"Yeah, I ate on the way home. I'm going to go get my slice of cake from the larder."

Ophelia squeaked from behind the bathroom door. "Oh nooooo! Was that *your* slice of cake?"

Cassie gritted her teeth. "Yes, Ophelia. Yes it was."

"I'm so sorry, I ate it this afternoon."

"Gods dammit, Feelie! I was saving that!"

The woman in the hallway stepped between Cassie and the bathroom door. "Don't yell at your sister! She didn't mean to eat your cake, did she?"

Ophelia gave an unconvincing whimper from behind the door. "I didn't know it was yours, I was just so hungry."

This charade of innocence was Ophelia's usual tactic, and it worked on their mother every time. Cassie had no doubt that she had purposely taken the cake, knowing it was hers. Once their mother was involved, however, Cassie was forced into a losing battle. Instead of arguing further she just returned to her bedroom and shut the door, wishing she were anywhere else.

2

Doldrums Shattered

A Great Big Gunship! - Someone Like You - A Wizard, to be Precise - More Important than Gold

The next day at work, everything seemed to be back to normal. If anyone noticed Cassie's bruises, they didn't say anything, which frankly was what she preferred. Cassie was consumed with thoughts of her encounter with what could only have been the Wolf. But the more she thought about it, the less vivid the memory seemed. Did she really see a grotesque nightmare, or was it just some stray dogs digging in the trash? Cassie couldn't make sense of it and it hurt her head to try to force it. Only Jax noticed that anything was different about her.

"Hey, you okay, Cass?" they asked, seeing her lost in thought, having watched her hold a needle and thread in front of her face for about three minutes without moving.

"Oh, uh… Yeah, I'm fine. Got chased by some dogs last night. Must've thought I had food on me or something."

"Glad you're okay, though, hon. That sounds pretty scary. Dogs can be vicious when they're abandoned and hungry. Worse than wolves, even, I hear."

Cassie shivered visibly. The less she had to think about what it was she saw the better.

"But don't worry, you're okay now."

The two talked idly as they worked, but Cassie's heart just wasn't in it. She kept thinking about the fact that she could have died. Her life would have been over and all she would have accomplished would be some dead-end job in a factory. She felt overwhelming depression at this fact for a while before voicing her concerns.

"Jax, what *is* my life right now?"

"What do you mean?"

"Like, what am I doing with my life?"

"Uh, I dunno, you tell me."

"That's exactly it, I don't know, either. I sure don't want to be working here when it's time for me to retire."

"Well, you got any passions? Dreams?"

This sent Cassie into a completely separate depressive spiral.

"Oh, c'mon, Cass. Surely there's *something* you wanna do. Even if it's something silly. You can tell me."

"Well..." Cassie began, knowing deep down what she wanted, but barely daring to allow herself to indulge. "I've kind of always wanted to learn magic."

She had expected Jax to laugh and tell her it was a foolish idea. Instead, they just smiled warmly. "See, that's something. A bit lofty, I'll admit, but I hear anyone can do it if they study hard enough."

Cassie flushed slightly, reinvigorated that someone had taken her seriously. "I'd love to be able to attend the Abaxian University, but it's extremely expensive for non-citizens."

"Well don't let some people here hear you say that." Jax said, looking around the factory floor. There were no supervisors in sight. "Not that *I* care, personally. It'd be cool to be able to wave your hand and shoot fireballs or whatever. Or just teleport to and from work, that'd save me a ton of time every day."

"My mom was actually born in Abaxia, but my grandparents moved here when she was still a kid. If they hadn't done that, I could still go to the university."

"Yeah, well, no point worrying about what-ifs. You could always see if you can find some books about magic in the library and try to learn a bit on your own. Then if you get good enough, you could open a magic shop."

One of the things Cassie liked best about Jax is that they always knew the right thing to say, and offered the most practical advice. She didn't know what she would have done without them. "You're probably right. I'll go this weekend and see what I can find."

The two returned to their work, and Cassie managed to get a fair amount done before she started to notice something odd. There was a faint buzzing sound that she couldn't quite place. At first she dismissed it as some of the factory's machinery, but it steadily grew louder and louder until it almost sounded like a train, even though there was no railroad in Bixton. At this point, other women were looking around, trying to locate the source of the noise.

"Up there!" It was Donna. She pointed up to the nearly opaque skylight. A large dark figure soared through the sky somewhere above the factory, though its precise shape was indeterminate through the murky glass. Some of the girls were pushing past each other to make their way outside to see for themselves. Cassie followed them and made it outside just in time to see some sort of flying mechanical shape disappear into the mountains before the sound of a distant impact shook the ground beneath her feet. Her coworkers were whispering with excitement.

"What do you think it was?"

"...an airship! Definitely an airship!"

"...ours or theirs?"

"A great big gunship!"

From what Cassie could gather, it was some sort of military gunship, though to whose military it belonged remained a mystery. Statistically speaking it was probably a Zonan ship, but Bixton was about as far from the front lines as you could get. The only interesting thing about the town was its proximity to the Zonan capital of New Ozion. The City of Machines, they called it, sprawling across the countryside some fifty miles east of Bixton, visible in the distance down the mountain.

"Back to work! Back to work!" Hardden called, emerging from the building and flapping his arms for attention like a flightless bird attempting to take off. "I don't pay you broads to stand around and rubberneck!" Hardden herded the women back into the building like a chihuahua attempting to play sheep dog.

Needless to say, Cassie's thoughts over the next few days were consumed with the strange goings-on in her previously sleepy hometown. She couldn't stop herself from daydreaming at work, wondering who could have been on that airship. No doubt her productivity similarly slacked, but she found it hard to care. According to word of mouth, the Peace Officers were checking on the situation and working with the Zonan military to identify the cause of the crash and clean up the crash site. There was a good probability that she would never find out what the cause of the crash really was.

Two days later, Cassie received news about the fate of Cathy Bateman when Cathy herself walked into the factory that morning, revealing her fate was that she was returning to work. Truly a fate worse than death. Apparently she had suffered a case of influenza and had to leave town for a few days to recover. Jax looked bored to tears at this perfectly mundane outcome. Cassie was just glad that nothing unfortunate had happened to her. The shop girls crowded around and asked if she had seen The Wolf, but Cathy didn't even know what they were talking about.

About a week later, Cassie was struggling to make her synapses engage. She was trying to stick a threaded needle through a patch of fabric, but couldn't find the willpower. It was one of those days where she was contemplating whether it was worth it to just stick the needle straight through her hand and get the rest of the day off due to injury. It wasn't that she didn't want to work hard, it was just that she couldn't bring herself to concentrate on boring and menial tasks. Besides, working hard at this job got you the same thing that not working hard did: a lecture from Hardden about how you weren't doing a good enough job making him look good.

Almost on cue, Hardden grabbed the back of her collar and scooted her chair back in place. It took Cassie a second to realize what had happened, and she still couldn't believe the short man had the leverage to do so.

"Mott. Office."

Cassie had never seen Hardden so incensed. The man looked like a radish in a suit and seemed to be ready to burst at the slightest provocation. She once again found herself back in that uncomfortable wooden chair in the boss's office wondering how this day could get any worse. Fortunately, she wouldn't have to wait long for an answer. Hardden flung himself into his chair and leaned over on his desk, gripping a half-smoked cigar a bit too tightly, crushing it like paper.

"I've given you chances, Mott. Gods know I've given you chances."

Here we go, Cassie thought, mentally rolling her eyes.

"I've only put up with you for as long as I have because your mother is a very well-respected member of the government and I thought... I *thought* that some of her work ethic and social graces might rub off on you." Hardden slumped back into his chair, looking defeated, an expression of which Cassie did not think him capable. "You came into this job with a surly attitude and it's only gotten worse. I thought a firm hand was what you needed like all the other up-start whelps I've dealt with in my time. What a fool I was. All this time I thought I could fix you, but congratulations. You beat me, Mott. You showed me that you can only lead a horse to water; you can only open the door to success. What was I thinking? What if the regional manager came by and saw that I was employing *someone like you?*" The intonation of 'someone like you' led Cassie to believe he wasn't just talking about her productivity. "But forget it. This business needs hard workers, not slobs who will fall asleep at the needle. I've got career aspirations, and I won't let you make a mockery of me."

Cassie was afraid she knew where this was going. As if to confirm, Hardden reached into a drawer of his desk and pulled out a meager stack of bound banknotes and tossed them across the desk to her. "Here's your final paycheck. You're fired, Mott."

It took a second for it to really sink in. Cassie wasn't sure if she should beg for her job, go down in a blaze of glory, or just leave quietly. Instead she compromised. "Yeah, well you're a shitty boss, anyway. Everyone here hates you." She stood up and snatched the money from the desk and stormed out of the shaded office. She didn't speak to anyone on the way out, though the eyes of the entire factory floor were upon her. Jax tried to say something to her, but her blood was rushing in her ears and she didn't hear what they said. She tore through the front dressing room, grabbing her belongings loosely and pushing through the building's front door with her shoulder. Tears of anger began to fall down her face. She didn't know where she was running, but it hardly mattered at this point.

After wandering aimlessly in fury, Cassie found herself sitting by the bank of the Mellius, down in the canal, boots and socks off, feet splashing in the water like a child. She just sat there for a solid while, watching traffic passing over a nearby bridge and wondering what she was going to do. How was she ever going to explain this to her mom?

Maybe she'd just fake going to work for a little while and instead go to the library to read up on magic like Jax had suggested. She examined the thin fold of bills in her hand. She had some savings in addition to this, but she was mostly trying to save up to try to move somewhere else. Where, she hadn't decided. She could live off these savings for a little bit, but without a proper direction she would just be floundering. She wished dearly that something, *anything*, would happen to give her a sign, but nothing happened. Nobody came by to disturb her self-pity on the riverbank, not even the Peace Officers who sometimes accused people of loitering.

Cassie's anger subsided quickly, and she fell into a haze of daydreaming as she usually did, imagining hopping on the mysterious gunship and flying away to adventure and a new life. It had been around noon when she had left the factory, and she stayed in this escapist reverie for a few hours until the sun was starting to set. She realized she would need to go home at some point, and reluctantly got to her feet.

She was in the process of putting her socks back on when something in the river caught her eye. Flotsam was not uncommon in the town's rivers, with driftwood, branches, garbage, and other refuse from humans and nature alike. However this was none of those things. For a split second, Cassie wasn't sure what it was. It looked like a mass of rags and hair. Then two and two coalesced into four in her brain. It was a body! Yanking off her half-donned socks and pulling her dress over her head, she dove into the river in just her smallclothes. Cassie could never brag about knowing how to swim, but the basic motions were fairly instinctive. She clumsily paddled over to the floating object.

On closer inspection, it appeared to be a person, though unlike anyone Cassie had ever seen. This person had long straight purple hair and a kind of sandy skin that was neither quite Zonan nor Abaxian. But what caught her eye most of all was this person's (ostensibly a woman, but she was loath to assume) outfit. A flowing but now ruined all-around cloak weighed the person down. Cassie hoisted an arm of the body over her shoulder and floundered back to the canal shore. Once her hands gripped solid stone, she lugged the body with all her strength up onto solid ground, following behind it as best as she could. Upper body strength was one of the casualties of Changing, something she had seen as a benefit until this very moment.

Back on land, Cassie rolled the body onto its back. She wasn't entirely sure what to do but she had read a book once where the protagonist, a detective, encountered a similar situation. First she checked under the side of the chin. She felt a weak but discernible heartbeat beneath her fingertips. Good, they were still alive. Next she checked the mouth and nose for breathing. Nothing. This was not good. Starting to panic a little, she remembered what her fictional detective had done. She tilted the person's head back, pinched their nose and administered a rescue breath into their mouth. No sooner had the air gone in than the body began to convulse. Cassie sprang back as whoever this was coughed and sputtered what must have been nearly a gallon of water out of their lungs. Once the coughing fit subsided, she could see that the person was breathing again, but they still weren't fully conscious. She couldn't just leave them there for the Peace Officers to find and throw in a jail cell. There was only one thing to do.

She heaved the body, a few inches taller than herself, up and braced them against her shoulder. This would be a long and awkward walk back to the house, but she could provide better care there. It turned out her assessment was completely correct. She garnered many bewildered looks as she practically dragged the soaking person through the late afternoon streets, but she was able to dismiss most onlookers with a wry smile as if to say "they've had a bit too much."

After about half an hour, Cassie arrived at her front stoop, struggled to unlock the door, then stumbled inside. Her charge was merely soggy now and no longer dripping, but she wanted to dry them completely, laying them down in front of the fireplace. She tried and failed to be stealthy as she went up the stairs; Ophelia was already approaching the landing.

"What's going on? Why are you home early?" Ophelia asked, seeming nervous.

"Don't worry about it. Where does Mom keep the old towels?"

"Uhhhh in her bedroom closet, I think. Why?"

Cassie pushed on past her sister and grabbed three ragged old towels from the master closet. She hurried back downstairs and began alternating between drying the person off with towels and lighting a fire.

"Who's that? Your girlfriend?" Ophelia called from around the stairs.

"I don't know, I just found them floating in the river. They need my help."

"I'm telling mom you brought a bum into the house."

"Really not helpful right now, Feelie."

"I'm serious. You're gonna get in so much trouble."

"Not if you don't tell her."

"And whyyyyyyy wouldn't I?"

Cassie still hadn't forgiven her sister for eating her beloved slice of cake, and really didn't have patience for bickering. "Because if you do I'm going to smash that little mirror of yours into unrecognizable pieces. And then I'll stomp on those pieces."

Ophelia gave a fake cry and fled back upstairs to the sanctuary of her bedroom.

Below Cassie, there was a grunt and then slight movement. The warmth and noise must have woken up the person now laying on the Mott household hearth.

"Wh….where am I?" This person spoke in a deep, smoky feminine voice with a refined, high-class accent. Now that Cassie had a chance to look at them properly, she saw a body that was tall and somewhat muscular, but still feminine. They were wearing a loose-fitting white blouse with a plunging neckline, black pants, and more jewelry than she had ever seen on a single person, and that was saying a lot as her mother's daughter. An amulet around the neck caught her eye, with a gleaming purple gem. The purple all-around cloak had been removed and was hung to dry on the hearth.

Probably safe to assume a woman, Cassie thought, noticing in particular the woman's not insignificant breasts. A strange twinge shot through her stomach, and she wasn't sure if it was attraction, jealousy, or some mixture thereof. At any rate, she was attractive. Cassie tried to suppress the urge to fall into a pure lesbian panic, forcing herself to focus on the task at hand.

"Are you okay, ma'am?"

The woman coughed a little bit and tried to sit up, getting about a fifth of the way there before clutching at her side and collapsing back down. Cassie gingerly lifted the blouse, horrified by what she saw underneath. It looked like a small chunk had been taken out of the woman's side, then blasted with fire. The wound was mostly cauterized, but there were still bits where the flesh was open and blood struggled to coagulate. Plus, there was a pretty severe burn, and it was probably going to scar badly, not to mention the potential for infection from floating in that river for who knows how long.

"Oh gods, what happened to you? What should I do?"

"Bandages… Water…"

"O-okay! Just a sec!"

Cassie flung into action, scrambling to find some bandages in the family's medical kit, and filled a basin with water and grabbed a small towel. Coming back over to the woman, she cooled the burn with the water. The woman on the floor winced at the touch of the towel, but it was clear the water brought her some relief. After cleaning the wound and cooling the burn for a while, she wrapped the woman's side in gauze. The woman seemed to be breathing easier now and was able to prop herself up on her elbows to drink water.

"I was shot fleeing from Zonan soldiers. I used the last of my stamina to conjure flames to cauterize the wound, but it seems in my haste I used too much power."

There was a lot to unpack in that statement. Cassie cut to the heart of the matter. "You're a mage?"

"A wizard, to be precise, yes."

"Couldn't you just… use magic to heal yourself?"

"It's… ugh… not that easy. Biomancy… is incredibly complicated."

"I see. Why were you shot by soldiers? Are you some kind of criminal?"

Cassie's question fell on deaf ears. The woman had already fallen asleep.

* * *

Cassie managed to bargain with her sister to help her carry the woman up to Cassie's bedroom in exchange for not kicking her ass about the stolen cake. The woman must have been out cold because she didn't wake for the entire ordeal.

"Remember, Feelie, not a *word* about this to Mom. Got it?"

"Whatever, Cass, you're such a bitch." Ophelia said, in a rare moment of clarity away from her babydoll act. "I know you won't smash my mirror, you're too much of a softie. I'm just going along with this because I want you to get in more trouble when Mom finds out."

"*I'm* the bitch, huh?"

"Just hurry up and move out already. Mom said I can have your room for my stuff when you're gone."

"*Stuff*? Your room is already filled to bursting with *stuff*."

"Yes, precisely why I need your room."

"What *you* need is an intervention, but it won't be from me."

"Whatever, Mom likes me better, anyway. She's always talking about how much of a failure you are." Cassie wasn't sure if this was true or if her sister was just making this up to hurt her, but regardless it worked. She retreated to her room and slammed the door.

A few hours later, Cassie woke up on the rug in the center of the floor of her room. She couldn't quite remember how she got there, but vaguely recalled lying prostrate on the floor and crying for a good while. Apparently a good cry and a good nap was what she needed, because she rose feeling refreshed. It was fully dark out at this point, and she couldn't see very well, but suddenly she felt like she was being watched.

The entire day suddenly flashed back to Cassie and she whipped around. Behind her on her bed, the woman she had rescued was sitting up, hands quietly folded on her lap, and looking down at Cassie with enigmatic serenity.

"Oh, good evening," the woman said. "I was wondering when you'd wake up."

Cassie suddenly felt very awkward. "Uhh... yeah, sorry about that. Didn't realize I was so tired." She fidgeted with her hands, not really knowing what to say. "Um... I guess you're feeling better? I hope?"

"Yes, thank you very much. A good night's rest and I should be back on my feet again and out of your hair." She gave a polite nod to Cassie. "You have my thanks for saving my life, despite the obvious amount it has put you out."

"O-oh, no, it's fine. I couldn't just let you die. Umm... perhaps I should change your bandages?"

"A good idea. I will remain here to avoid upsetting the already tenuous social order in this household."

"Yeah… sorry again."

Cassie crept from her room, hoping to avoid speaking to either of the other women of the house. As she passed her mother's bedroom, she heard Ophelia's voice.

"…she really threatened me, mama! She said she was gonna smash my mirror!"

Cassie grimaced. She wasn't sure how much her sister had told, but she wasn't going to wait around to find out. She swept down the stairs, grabbed the bandages from the medical kit, and ascended the stairs again. As she was coming into the upstairs hallway, the door opened and Corinne emerged.

"Oh, *there* you are, #####," Corinne spat, Cassie's deadname sounding like painful static in her ears.

"That isn't my name, Mom."

"Whatever. If I have to have another talk with you about being nicer to your sister, you're going to have to start finding a new place to live, do you hear me, child?"

Cassie rolled her eyes. "Yep, I'll be just as sweet with her as she is with me."

"Don't give me that! I mean it, child. You know what I always say. 'Family is more important than gold.'"

That particular catchphrase never made any sense to Cassie in a family where nobody seemed to listen to each other or think of each other as adult humans.

"Okay. I'm going back to my room now."

"We're not done here!" her mother called, but Cassie had already closed the door in her face. Once her mother had returned to her quarters, Cassie looked around the dark room, suddenly not seeing her mystery woman anywhere. With a sound like the faintest wind in one's ear, the woman reappeared on the bed.

"Figured I'd make myself scarce while you were out."

"You were just… invisible?"

"Yes, it's one of the spells I have memorized. Comes in handy more often than you'd think."

"That's so cool…" Cassie realized her mouth was hanging open, and she shut it again. "Sorry, um… let's get your bandages changed."

"You needn't worry about the noise, I've placed a sonic ward around this room. No sound in here will be able to make it out shy of a dragon burning the place down."

Cassie was very impressed. She had never seen magic before, at least not in person. There used to be a potion shop in town when she was a kid, but that had closed a long time ago. As she changed the woman's bandages, she tried to remain calm. This woman was *very* attractive. Cassie had seen plenty of pretty women before, and was very gay for them, but this woman was on a completely different level. She seemed to be a few years older than Cassie, maybe mid-to-late twenties at most. She stood with perfect posture despite her injury, and barely even reacted to Cassie's medical care, staying cool and impassive.

"Um… so what's your name?" Cassie said, trying to make conversation.

"You would dare to ask a lady her name without first offering your own?"

Cassie blanched, terrified that she had upset her guest.

"Uh… n-no… I'm sorry. Um. I'm Cassandra Mott. Oh, b-but you can just call me Cassie… if… you want."

There was a twinkle in the woman's eye. "I was just kidding, Cassie."

Cassie felt herself blush hard.

"You may call me Gwynne. That's with two N's and an E."

"Okay Wizard Gwynne-enn-ee," Cassie joked back. "What brings you to the sleepy town of Bixton? And with a gunshot wound, no less."

Gwynne clicked her tongue as Cassie finished wrapping the bandages. "Secrets, darling."

She wasn't sure how she felt about being called 'darling', but it kind of made her stomach turn upside down.

"Sorry for asking, I guess. I'll just assume you're some kind of spy or secret agent. You don't seem like you mean me any harm, though, so that's all that really matters."

"Good girl."

If being called 'darling' made Cassie's stomach flip, being called 'good girl' made her heart stop and be shocked back to life for a quick second, the cold feeling of resuscitation tingling through her extremities as she tried to keep her cool.

"I must say, you are *very* easy to tease, Cassandra Mott."

"Yeah, well..." Cassie wasn't sure where that sentence was heading, so she just stopped talking.

For the rest of the night, the two conversed about various matters. Cassie tried to ask about magic, but Gwynne would give her vague answers, or just say "secrets" again. In turn, Gwynne asked many questions about Cassie herself. Cassie had never had someone pay this much attention to her, and she couldn't help but feel that it was a bit intoxicating.

3

Parting Shots

Nothing Better to Do - The Broadside of a Barn at Twenty Paces - Wicked, Rusted, and Jagged Blades - Didn't I Tell You?

The next morning, Cassie awoke to the sun streaming in through her squat bedroom window. She had gotten some old blankets out from the closet and spread them on the floor, letting Gwynne take the bed. The wizard herself was already awake and was just finishing wrapping up fresh bandages.

"Good morning, Cassandra Mott. Not in a hurry to go to work, I see?"

Cassie had a miniature heart attack before she remembered the squalid truth. "I got fired yesterday."

"Oh, fantastic."

"Fantastic, yeah." Cassie rubbed the sleep out of her eyes and stretched. "Wait, why is that fantastic?"

"Well, if you've nothing better to do, I thought perhaps you could help me with a bit of an errand."

"I guess if you put it that way, I really *don't* have anything better to do."

"Excellent. I would like you to escort me to the gunship crash site."

"You know about that? Were you involved with that?"

"Perhaps. There's something there that I need."

Cassie didn't need convincing. Gwynne was by far the most interesting thing that had ever happened to her, and she was hungry to know more about her. Plus, maybe she could pick up a tidbit or two about magic from a real-life wizard.

Once Cassie had made sure that her mother was gone and her sister was asleep, Cassie and Gwynne left the house, Cassie dressed in her most comfortable clothes. The loose-fitting blouse and skirt were by no means elegant, but if she was going hiking it beat wearing a work dress. The pair stopped at various stores to stock up on supplies for their trip. Gwynne estimated it would take the rest of the day to get up there, and if need be they could camp out overnight. Lastly, they stopped at Burton's Butchery to pick up meat. When the pair entered, Mr. Burton looked at Gwynne then at Cassie and cocked an eyebrow. Cassie just shrugged. "She's passing through town and we happened to run into each other yesterday. I'm helping her stock up." It was the truth, save a well-buried lede.

"I'm from the capital," Gwynne told the man, as if that explained everything. Judging by Mr. Burton's expression, it told him everything he needed to know.

At the start of their shopping trip, Gwynne had pulled a tiny burlap sack from an interior pocket of her cloak. With a bit of stretching and a few muttered incantations, the sack expanded to the size of a small backpack. Gwynne had been placing all the food inside as they went along, and now she was adding beef shanks, huge slabs of pork belly, and whole chickens to the bag, all wrapped up in waxed paper. Cassie wasn't sure exactly how all of this food was fitting inside, but suspected arcane workings.

"Just a bit of space-stretching magic." Gwynne told her as they left the shop. "It'll keep everything nice and cold, too. I enchanted this bag a long time ago, so now I only need to maintain the spell on it every so often."

The two eventually decided they were full on provisions and started to walk out of town. Cassie was mentally calculating the amount of money she was missing out on by not working. It was less a matter of missing the job and more a matter of being scared of losing her financial stability. Fortunately, Gwynne seemed loaded, and she was able to purchase all the supplies for their trip as easily as a kid buying bubble gum from the general store. Right when the road transitioned from cobblestone to dirt, Cassie stopped. This would be the first time she had really left her hometown as far as she could remember.

Gwynne slowed to a stop beside her and put her arm on Cassie's shoulder.

"Don't move or look around," she whispered, gesturing as if she was talking about something completely different. "We're being followed."

Cassie focused her hearing as hard as she could and detected the faintest sound of gravel under a boot. "Who is it?"

"I suspect your town's Peace Officers. They're in cahoots with the army, of course, and I'm a pretty big target."

Cassie gulped. She had heard tell of what happened to other Abaxians who had run afoul of the disgustingly misnamed Peace Officers.

"When I say 'go', we're going to run, okay? I'll cast a spell on you to make you move faster." Gwynne started muttering under her breath, making odd hand motions. All of a sudden, Cassie felt her heart rate double. "Go!"

The two women took off running, sending puffs of loose dirt up in their wake. Cassie could probably count on her fingers the number of times she had properly run since ten years old, and two of those times happened within the span of the past week. Unlike before with the wild dogs, however, the ground flew by beneath Cassie's feet. It felt like she was running as fast as a horse, maybe faster.

A sharp *pa-CRACK!* ripped through the late morning air as someone now distantly behind them loosed a bullet from a firearm. A fraction of a second later, an accompanying *thwipp!* impacted the dirt somewhere to the right of Cassie.

"They're shooting at us?" Cassie squealed, chancing a glance back for the first time. She saw two uniformed Peace Officers standing at the edge of the town, one with rifle raised.

"Oh don't worry, those pigs couldn't hit the broadside of a barn at twenty paces, much less a moving target two hundred feet away."

Truly, the town of Bixton was vanishing behind the pair at an alarming rate, and as the officers vanished into blue pinpricks, Cassie began to slow involuntarily.

"I can't… *huff*… run any more…"

"That's okay, I was releasing the spell anyway. Better save my energy for later."

At this point, the two adopted a more leisurely pace. Cassie had been scared by the rifle shot, but it was nowhere near the worst thing that had happened to her in the last twenty four hours. Strangely, she felt invigorated and excited for what felt like the first time ever.

"So how much further to this crash site?"

"Hmm, I'd say about ten miles up the mountains."

Cassie had never been so far in her life. "I don't know if I'll make it."

"Don't worry, we'll take breaks. I'm not a slave driver."

They walked for what felt like days, but judging by the sun had really been more like two hours, before taking their first break. Cassie pulled a canteen from the enchanted bag, surprised at its depth. She took a hearty swig from the canteen and passed it to Gwynne, who sipped daintily, clearly not feeling the exertion as much as Cassie was.

"Chin up, girl, we're only about a third of the way there."

Cassie's feet already felt sore, and she didn't want to imagine how they would feel after two more lengths of what she had already walked. "I don't suppose you'll tell me what you're after, then?"

"Maybe when we get there."

Despite how aloof Gwynne seemed, Cassie couldn't help but be fascinated by her. Thus, she kept walking.

About twenty minutes later, Gwynne put out an arm to stop her. "There's something up ahead."

The top of a hill obscured the path forward, but Cassie could see the top of a gnarled tree sticking up over it.

"By that tree?"

"Yes. Whatever it is, it hasn't noticed us and I hope to keep it that way."

Gwynne crouched down and walked silently up to the top of the hill. Cassie followed suit and peered over. Three squat figures stood over something on the ground. Cassie couldn't see them very well, but they couldn't have been more than three feet tall. She could just make out green skin, jagged ears, and bulbous heads.

"What are they?" she whispered to Gwynne.

"Goblins, I believe." Cassie had heard of goblins before, but always thought they only existed in fairy tales or made up to frighten children into going to bed on time. "A nasty race of creatures. All they know is how to inflict pain and misery on others. That and light things on fire. The two really go hand-in-hand if you think about it."

"Aren't there any... you know... *nice* goblins?"

Gwynne shook her head. "Not as such. Good goblins... well, as good as humans, generally, split off from the evil goblins in the olden times. The good ones are called trasgo. They retained their looks and reason. The bad ones... well you can see here. They're as ugly on the inside as they are on the outside."

The gang of goblins parted, and Cassie could see a fox laying on the road. It looked bruised and hurt. It struggled to stand, but one of the goblins kicked it and it yelped, falling back to the ground. The goblins laughed like the deplorable bullies they were.

"Gwynne, we simply must stop them. This is horrible."

Gwynne's expression was hard as stone. "I don't want to waste valuable energy on an avoidable conflict."

"If you don't do something, I will." Without knowing what she was doing, Cassie picked up a rock, stepped up and pitched it at the green monsters. There was a split second where the rock simply disappeared. Then with a familiar crack, it appeared again at a much higher velocity and caromed off the oversized skull of one of the goblins. They fell face-first into the dirt and didn't move.

Gwynne winced. "Oh, you've done it now."

It took a few seconds for the other two goblins to stop laughing, the molasses thought of their comrade being incapacitated percolating through their peanut brains. At once, they drew weapons. Wicked, rusted, and jagged blades appeared in the goblins' hands. They shouted something in a language Cassie could not understand, if it was a language at all.

"Interesting fact, some people think goblins actually let their weapons rust on purpose so that their blades inflict tetanus on their victims. Fascinating, isn't it?"

The goblins were charging on their stumpy legs, spittle flying from their mismatched teeth. Cassie thought she might wet herself on the spot. "Um Gwynne? Help?"

Gwynne stood up with casual nonchalance, dusting off her pants. "You got yourself into this mess. Perhaps you can negotiate with them?"

"Not funny! They're really gonna kill me!" Cassie took a step back. The goblins were only about ten feet away now and closing fast.

"Oh all right. Who could say no to that face?" Gwynne closed her eyes and snapped her fingers. From nowhere a licking ring of fire sprang into existence between the goblins and their prey. The creatures shrieked and backed up, beady black eyes fixated on the blaze. Their proportions were so far removed from humans that Cassie almost likened them to dolls. Creepy, malicious, and bloodthirsty, but still dolls. The head slightly too large for its body was almost comical had they not been about to separate hers from her shoulders only moments before.

Gwynne stepped up and through the crackling flames, which parted ever so slightly to allow her passage. "You will go now" she said, pointing back the way the goblins had come. Cassie wasn't sure if they had understood her words, but they gulped, then sheathed their weapons and fled, leaving their unconscious friend sprawled in the dirt.

With another snap, the flames went out as if they were never even there. Gwynne walked over and picked up the goblin that Cassie had felled under her arm. The cold-blooded murderer looked like a child in the woman's grasp, and she chucked them effortlessly into the grass beside the road.

"I don't envy the headache he'll have when he wakes up. That was a pretty neat trick, Cassie. I didn't know you had it in you."

"To be honest, neither did I. What happened with the rock?"

"Hmm, what indeed." Gwynne crouched down over the whimpering fox and examined it. "Luckily, the poor thing is only bruised. It looks like it sprained a leg running from the goblins, but otherwise it looks alright."

Cassie could have cried from relief. Both for the fox and for herself. This was entirely too many life-threatening experiences for her comfort. But the way Gwynne had willed that fire into being… Just seeing that was worth the risk.

The pair carried on, with few distractions after that. At one point

Cassie saw a herd of wild horses galloping across an alpine field of long grass and wildflowers. She wondered why she hadn't ever come out into nature like this, goblins aside. It was like a whole new world out here, and this was just the immediate vicinity of her hometown. Suddenly she felt very small in the grand scheme of the world.

Gwynne was leading the way through a thicket of pine trees as Cassie's stomach rumbled, and they decided to stop for a meal. She had completely forgotten to eat dinner the previous night in all the hubbub, and was dying for something to eat. Gwynne had pulled a cast iron skillet from the magic sack and made a small fire. She had roasted some cuts of beef in the skillet over the fire and added some large brown mushroom caps she had picked up at the greengrocers. A dash of wine and a magically diced aromatic root combined with the meat and mushroom juices to make a fragrant sauce. All of this took Gwynne about ten minutes to assemble, all the while Cassie stared on in wonderment at her companion's culinary skills.

"It's pretty simple, really. The key is in the aromatics."

The two women dug into the meal, sharing the skillet, and Cassie's taste buds exploded. She had never had something this delicious. The dark flavors of the beef and wine combined to create something even richer than the two on their own, while the aromatic root shot savory smells up her nose as she chewed. Most surprising of all, the mushroom tasted exactly like meat. She had always found mushrooms to be rubbery and tasteless to the point of inedibility, but these not only absorbed the flavors of the meat and sauce, but added their own layers of umami.

"How is it?"

Cassie felt tears welling up in her eyes and she turned away. "It's very good, Gwynne, thank you."

"Just wait until you try a *real* steak. This isn't bad, but this is cheap stuff. I don't cook too often except out of necessity, but I've always thought that man, woman, or otherwise, everyone should be able to prepare their own food."

After they finished eating, Gwynne packed up the incredible bag once more and they began walking anew. Cassie's feet felt like they were going to fall off, but Gwynne assured her they were almost to their destination. An agonizing thirty minutes later, Gwynne stopped Cassie once more and pointed ahead. "There's the crash site. With any luck, it will be abandoned."

Before them, a crater about a hundred feet wide split the mountain open. Twisted metal wreckage was still smoldering at the far side. Bits of scrap metal littered the area. The crater otherwise seemed quiet.

"There we go. Just as I left her."

"*You* did this?" Cassie asked, both surprised and not.

"Yes, didn't I tell you? I crashed this ship."

"'Secrets' is how you phrased it, I believe."

"Ah, right. Well don't tell anyone."

Cassie motioned her arms around, gesturing to all none of the people she could possibly tell. Gwynne wasn't even looking. She had already descended into the crater, a look on her face like a kid in a candy store. She went over to the largest mass of junk metal and yanked a steel panel off its last remaining rivets. Behind it, a mass of machinery seized and smoked.

"Ah yes, this will do nicely."

Cassie watched as Gwynne repeated this process about sixteen times, finding various parts of what ostensibly had once been a military gunship, gathering them up in her arms and throwing them into a pile near Cassie's feet. When she was quite satisfied with her pile of junk, Gwynne crouched down, donned a pair of leather gloves pulled from some previously unseen pocket, and looked up at Cassie.

"Well, ready to get to work?"

"Surely you don't expect *me* to do anything with this junk?"

"What, you've never built a flying machine from scratch before? What are they teaching kids in schools these days?"

"In my defense, I'm *quite* good at math. I was top of my class, even."

"That's nice for you." Gwynne was already elbow deep in the junk pile, grabbing motors, gears, belts, and many other contraptions of which Cassie could make neither heads nor tails. She had come to understand that this sort of dismissive response was Gwynne's way of saying "I'm focusing, conversation over."

As grandiloquent and intimidating as she seemed at first, it seemed Gwynne wasn't the most charismatic conversationalist. No, Gwynne was far too absorbed in her own schemes and machinations to maintain a long conversation. Cassie didn't really mind, though, she saw a bit of herself in that.

After some twenty-odd minutes of work, Gwynne had assembled what looked like some kind of machine engine. "Great!" she exclaimed. "We're nearly there. Now I just need…" She trailed off again, looking around the clearing. She grabbed a number of steel panels, rods, and some strange propeller blades.

"I'm going to cast a spell, so you're going to want to stand back."

Gwynne used one of the rods to trace a circle in the dirt around the engine, finished it with geometric flourishes and strange runes, then threw the remaining parts on top. They *clang*ed in a way that Cassie thought was probably not promising.

"Hold on, I just need to do some calculations."

Gwynne pulled a piece of parchment and a pen from yet another pocket and began writing down numbers and performing advanced math that even Cassie couldn't understand. A short while later, Gwynne replaced the writing implements and rubbed her hands together in anticipation. Cassie had been about to doze off, but snapped back to attention.

"Alright, I think I'm ready." Gwynne clapped her hands together and started reciting an incantation. This one was much longer than the ones Cassie had heard her use before. As Gwynne was casting, Cassie heard voices in the distance. Whipping around, she saw the capped heads of soldiers peeking over the rim of the crater.

"Whatever you're doing, please hurry up!"

One of the soldiers spotted the two women and shouted to his comrades. They began to trot into the crater, drawing their service rifles and struggling to load them. The ranks parted and a soldier with a red coat stepped through. He did not carry a rifle, but had a soldier's saber on his belt. He cleared his throat and called out. "Owl of the Pale Moon. By order of His Majesty King Aberforth Quintus, I hereby place you under arrest, or will shoot you dead in trying. We have you surrounded, Owl. Surrender now or we'll shoot you and your assistant."

"Assistant?" Cassie said with incredulity. "Wait, *you're* Owl? *The* Owl?"

Gwynne ignored everyone around her and finished the incantation. With another snap of her fingers, blue light glowed from the geometry drawn on the ground, and the pile of metal began to twist and mold into a new form. In a few seconds, the crude engine and pile of scrap had transformed into a sort of buggy. Two small seats were bolted onto a metal rack with wheels, and metal bars above them led up to a propeller. The engine Gwynne had assembled sat behind, and began sputtering and coughing to life of its own accord.

"Yes, didn't I tell you?"

The soldiers scrambled to load their rifles, but the technology just wasn't there. In the meantime, the whirligig contraption began to rise slowly off the ground, its propeller whipping the loose dirt up and causing Cassie's hair to flail around. Gwynne hopped into the right seat of the contraption and grabbed at a hitherto hidden lever. The soldiers were finishing up their loading process, ramrods thrusting with fervor to murder the young woman before them. All Cassie could see was Gwynne's striking yellow eyes. She yelled out to Cassie amidst the localized gale. "That's not a problem, is it?"

"N-no."

"Then what are you waiting for? Get on before they shoot you."

Cassie needed no second bidding. With little grace, she clambered up onto the left seat of the contraption. The soldiers were beginning to aim the rifles at the absconding outlaws, seeming to be waiting for an order.

Their commander rolled his eyes. "What are you waiting for, dimwits? Fire at will!"

With that, Gwynne thrust the lever in her hand down into the frame of the machine and Cassie felt the ground drop out from under her. She tried to scream, but the wind was sucked from her mouth as the flying contraption soared up into the air. She saw the soldiers fire, their helpless bullets flying low, and in a few moments the soldiers looked like ants on the pavement. She thought she might be sick.

"It helps not to look down."

"Oh *now* you tell me."

"It seems there are a lot of things I haven't told you."

"I'll say. When were you going to tell me you were Owl? I always thought of the Owl as a man."

"That's what the newspapers think, and I'd like to keep it that way. Keeps them guessing."

"Anything else you'd like to confess to me while we're a mile up in the air?"

"This isn't really the place. Perhaps you'd like to come back to my manor?"

"Manor? You have a mansion?"

"So to speak."

"Where is it?"

"In the sky."

"Of course it's in the sky. Might as well be, after the day I had."

"I'm not kidding. Let me show you." Gwynne thrust another lever forward and the contraption shot forward with alarming speed. Cassie really was sick this time.

4

Pale Moon

A Particularly Low-Hanging Cloud - Hair Concoction No.2 - The Forest of Literature - A Spark of Talent for Magic

Cassie eventually got over her motion sickness, but not before horking half of her prior meal over the side of the flying machine.

Gwynne grimaced. "Do try to keep it in, dear. I've made us invisible, but I'm afraid the same enchantment does not extend to any… expulsions we may produce."

"Sorry… I've never been in a vehicle before… I didn't know it would be so physically upsetting." Speaking of upsetting, Cassie really wished there was some sort of safety bar or buckle keeping her in place. It seems in Gwynne's haste to be off she had neglected certain safety standards. Down below she could see the ground like a patchwork quilt flying by, the sense of scale making her face tingle with nausea.

"Oh, you'll be fine," Gwynne said when Cassie voiced her concerns. "As long as you stay beside me you'll be as safe as you can possibly be." Judging by the day's statistics of danger, Cassie wasn't sure what to think about this.

Conversation was difficult aboard this craft. The engine alone roared and coughed in Cassie's ear, not to mention the violent swinging of the propeller blades above her head. She thought she might go deaf before they arrived at their destination. Gwynne seemed unphased, letting her hair flutter in the breeze. Cassie had to settle for side-eye admiring the wizard as they traveled. It's not like Gwynne would have answered her plethora of questions anyway.

At one point, they sailed through a particularly low-hanging cloud. Cassie braced for impact, but the cloud only lightly brushed her face, like morning dew upon a spider web. They emerged from the other side of the cloud moistened but unharmed, thoroughly startling a flock of geese that were passing by.

From this high up, the petty squabbles and tribulations of those down below seemed insignificant, as if Cassie was on the opposite end of the existential realization she had experienced earlier on the Brachius steppe. It would explain a lot about Gwynne's aloof and disconcerted personality if she lived way up here.

At some point, the exhaustion of the day caught up to her and her eyelids began to grow heavy. Despite the noise of the engine and propeller, the gentle rocking of the craft somehow started to feel relaxing. Without really meaning to, Cassie fell asleep.

In the world of her dreams, Cassie was somehow back in school. She was in the middle of class, but there was a test she had forgotten to study for. In the midst of panic, she realized that she was actually twenty-two and her mother was forcing her to redo school because she hadn't done it well enough the first time. At the same time, if anyone found out she was a grown woman she would surely be in trouble, whatever that meant in this context. Suddenly, Peace Officers burst through the classroom door, led by her former boss Hardden. Hardden arrested her for being an accomplice to a heinous criminal. Behind the officers in the hallway stood Ophelia, looking very smug.

"I'll just go ahead and start moving my stuff into your old room, Cass-Cass."

* * *

Cassie woke up with a start, bolt upright in bed. For that fleeting moment as sleep gave way to lucid wakefulness, she thought she was back at home and the past day was all a dream. Her first clue to the truth was that she was in a completely different room than her humble quarters at her mother's house. For starters, the bed was not the stiff twin mattress of which she was accustomed. This was a plush and luxurious queen bed, and whatever material stuffed the mattress made Cassie feel like she was back in that cloud, only dry. She threw a fluffy white comforter off of her and stretched. Her feet were more sore than they had ever been, and she massaged her soles. There were blisters forming on the back of her heels from where the boots had rubbed them. It was at this point that Cassie realized that she was not wearing the blouse and skirt in which she had left the house, and was instead clad in an ultra-soft white nightgown.

Turning her gaze up to the room around her, she found that she was in a room about twice the size of her old bedroom. The bed was situated with the head against a wall, flanked by nightstands with ornate lamps, their polished bronze bodies twinkling softly in the morning light. The light spilled in through a long but squat row of windows, through which Cassie could see naught but bright light. Beneath the window was a workbench currently devoid of materials. A simple cushioned wooden chair was tucked beneath the desk, already looking much more comfortable than her old workstation at the factory. A bookshelf was on the far wall, but its shelves were only partially filled. Most strange of all, there was no rug in the center of the floor, but instead there was a painted white circle with minor geometric patterns. Against the right wall was a dark wood dresser, on top of which sat Cassie's clothes in a crumpled pile.

Aghast at the thought that Gwynne had undressed her, she leapt out of bed and removed the nightgown. Fortunately, she was still wearing her smallclothes underneath. Her calves and glutes ached at the effort of standing, and she decided a nice hot bath was in order. She walked to the door, the polished wooden floor cold beneath her bare feet.

She opened the door to find a large ginger cat sitting patiently in the hallway beyond. "Oh, hello there," she said.

The cat meowed at her and came to rub on her legs. Cassie petted the cat, scratching it behind its ears.

"What's your name, kitty? You're so sweet and handsome."

As she scratched the cat's back, it twitched its tail in enjoyment. She could see that it was a male cat. "What a sweet boy. Were you waiting for me to get up?"

The cat only purred in response, standing on his hind legs slightly to rub his cheek against her kneecap. After a minute the cat had decided that he had had enough. He gave Cassie's hand a slight nibble and trotted off.

The hallway contained five other doors at intervals. Though she tried their handles, four of them were locked. The hallway itself had dust and dirt around the floorboards and cobwebs could be seen hanging forgotten by their spiders from the edges of the ceiling. The last door on the left was already open, and a glazed tile floor could be seen beyond.

Cassie stepped through to find herself in a luxurious bathroom. There were three toilets in stalls like you would see in a public restroom, but much nicer. On the opposite side of the room was a long counter with three vanities. An archway in the back wall opened up to a deeper chamber, and she was thoroughly impressed by what she saw within. There was quite a large tub along the left wall. It was set into the floor and must have been about ten feet wide and five feet long, almost a small swimming pool. On the other wall were three stall showers built into the wall with opaque glass sliding doors. Lastly, at the back of the bath area was a single chamber with a mechanical grille in the floor and some sort of knobs on the wall. The whole room was lit by a white light embedded into the ceiling, though Cassie couldn't tell exactly what was powering it. The light didn't flicker or waver like fire, meaning it must have been some sort of mechanical or magical light source.

All in all, this was the nicest bathroom Cassie had ever seen, and she wondered if it was okay for her to use it. As far as she could tell, there didn't seem to be anyone else around. She decided she was going to use it anyway, consequences be damned. There was a curtain that could be pulled out to section off the toilet area from the bath area. Cassie did so and turned on the multiple taps. Hot water immediately shot out, filling the tub in mere minutes.

Once the tub was filled, Cassie removed her clothes and slipped in, feeling the steam rising from the water's surface and opening the pores on her face. The water was very hot, just how she liked it, and it did wonders to relieve her aching feet and legs. Her elbow was also still a little sore from where she had fallen on it over a week ago now. There were glass bottles of strangely colored liquid on the side of the tub. One was marked "Hair Concoction No.1", the other "Hair Concoction No.2" and the third "Body Cream". Cassie tried all of them in turn, working the first through her hair, building up a nice lather and massaging her scalp, then rinsing it off and repeating with Hair Concoction No.2. Concoction No.1 did a good job of cleaning out all the dirt and grease from her hair while Concoction No.2 restored her natural oils. As she was washing her body with the ominously named Body Cream, she noticed that her hair was starting to change color. It went from its natural black to a sort of teal blue, then settled on bright bubblegum pink. As much as she loved her natural hair color, she could live with saccharine gay pink for a while. This may as well happen when you use a wizard's shampoo.

After washing off and soaking for a while, she drained the sudsy water from the tub and got out. The bath products had left her smelling slightly of coconut oil and lavender, the precise smell of Gwynne. This made her feel a certain way that she wasn't sure about. Looking around, the alcove with the grille floor caught her eye. She could make out some sort of fan beneath the grating at the bottom and decided to check it out. Stepping inside, she could feel the holes of the grille pressing into her feet, but not enough to make her uncomfortable, like standing on a drain. There were two knobs on the wall. One seemed to be a temperature knob, ranging from "Cold" to "Lukewarm" to "Hot," currently set to maximum. Beside it, a knob seemed to control some sort of intensity, currently on "Off", and ranging from "Low" to "High". Curious, Cassie turned the second knob up to "Low" and was shocked when a blast of torrid air came from beneath her, whipping the moisture right off her body and blasting her hair upward in a comical cone. She quickly shut off the fan and blinked in surprise. Out of curiosity, she turned the fan up to maximum intensity and felt herself almost lift off the ground, her lips flapping from the wind pressure. She then turned the intensity back down to low and let the fan dry her off. It even got her hair, but left it poofed out in a curly afro.

From there, she returned to her room and dressed once more, wishing she had a clean change of clothes, but making do under the circumstances. Now that she was clean and freshened up, she decided to explore the rest of the house she found herself in, ostensibly Gwynne's manor. This time, she started by looking out of the bedroom window. There was nothing but blue-white sky and grey-white clouds as far as she could see. *Well, she wasn't lying about her house being in the sky.* As she focused, she could faintly make out the sound of some sort of engine humming in the distance. The hall outside the bedroom turned by Cassie's door and led to a staircase that went upward. At the other end of the hall, near the bathroom, another staircase went down. She decided heading down was her best bet, hoping to find an entrance or some sort of central room and orient herself from there.

The staircase was cramped and twisting, but eventually it came out to a modest foyer, about ten feet square, that led to a large mahogany door carved with intricate patterns and symbols. It was set into a frame of large flagstones that gave it a front-door feel. There was a complicated series of locks along the side of the door, all seemingly engaged. Archways cut out of the side walls, leading off into various rooms and hallways.

From here, Cassie could see a luxurious sitting room with armchairs and a sofa upholstered in a coarse red fabric. The stitching around the edges of each cushion was embellished with soft gold-tinted rope that gave the lounge a ritzy and glamorous appeal. A large flat hearth was built along the far wall with bright stones to match the front door. The faintest embers of a fire still smoldered here, indicating it had been in use up to a few hours ago. Various trinkets, paintings, vases, plants, and ornaments decorated the room, but shattering the elegant vibe was bits of refuse all about the floor. To her dismay, Cassie saw the remains of what must have at one point been a chicken leg left on the arm of the couch. She also saw a rip in the back cushion of the chair that made her hurt on a spiritual level. That on top of the amount of dust and cobwebs all around the interior gave the impression of a place that had not been properly taken care of in a long time, and was in desperate need of cleaning.

She walked through another door in this sitting room to find a kitchen. A large wooden island table first caught her eye, though it was covered in what looked like onion skins, potato peelings, old bones and bits of fat from trimmed meat, and a dirty corkwood cutting board with the knife stuck in it at its point. The counters were similarly neglected, and dirty dishes stacked up both on the counters and the sink. A very nice cast iron range was starting to rust in the corner, and was covered in flecks of oil from a long-past meal. The kitchen counter turned at an angle, with a bar-style counter on the other side, and beyond that was a kitchen table covered in bits of parchment and books. The whole room stank like garbage, and Cassie wondered how anyone ever was able to eat here, much less cook. She left as quickly as she could.

She found a few other rooms, including a lavish dining room, tablecloth covered in a thick layer of dust from disuse; a few more sitting areas; and finally a workshop. It didn't look like this workshop was currently in use, but there were potion materials, a large black cauldron, and scrolls littered everywhere.

Cassie started to feel a bit lost, and opened a door that she thought might take her back towards the foyer. Instead, it opened into a huge room filled with tall book shelves fit tight with books of many different colors, sizes, and thicknesses. She craned her neck upward, but she couldn't see the tops of the shelves; they seemed to stretch up infinitely into darkness. Likewise, the rows seemed to stretch infinitely away from her. The effect was quite dizzying. As she was trying to make sense of it, a creature appeared before her, as if from nowhere.

"Aaahk!" Cassie shouted, gracelessly. The creature almost looked like a small person, about two feet in height, but hovering in the air on translucent insect wings. They had bluish-white hair swirled up above their head, bright blue eyes with, most grotesque of all, two pupils arranged diagonally in each eye. The creature wore a fancy maroon dress with frilly white lace, and their feet seemed to disappear into unused points at the bottom of their legs.

The creature spoke, a dam of words bursting. "Who are you? Are you an intruder? I ought to alert the Mistress. Unless… you are a guest? In which case, welcome! Welcome to the House Brandwyck library! Please identify yourself such that I might identify your presence as welcome or otherwise. Huh? What's your name? Who are you? Where'd you come from? Why is your skin so dark? Are you a human? Or are you fey? I've never seen hair that color, not even from the Mistress, who has quite the taste for pretty hair colors. Am I talking too much?"

Cassie tried to process everything that had just happened. "Um, Hello."

"Gwaaaah!" The creature fluttered back. "It speaks!"

"Yes, it does, though I prefer 'she' to 'it'. And my name is Cassandra Mott. I believe I am a guest here."

"Oh yes, you humans and your pronouns. What a shame your languages have to develop an obnoxious fixation on a concept as useless as gender. You may call me Tibberwyx of the Silver Stream, though just Tibb if you're short on breath. I do not ascribe to your human 'gender', and the closest thing to my pronouns in your tongue would be 'ze' and 'zir'. Though if you insist on forcing my identity into your language, I insist that you desist from besmirching me with gendered language."

"Nice to meet you, Tibb," Cassie said, giving a short bow. From zir roundabout speech, Cassie assumed that ze was some approximation of non-binary, though approached from a completely different angle than her friend Jax. "I have never seen someone like yourself before. Pardon me for asking, but what race are you?"

"Not a surprise that a human doesn't know much of the fey courts. I am what your people refer to as a 'forest nymph', though the name is much more eloquent in my tongue."

"I would love to hear the native pronunciation."

Tibberwyx made a noise that is completely irreproducible in human writing. It was sort of a chitter and a wail at the same time.

"That's a very beautiful name, though I understand why we chose something a little easier for our inferior human mouths to pronounce."

"Quite. Now, have you business in my library, Cassandra Mott?"

"Ah, so you're the librarian?"

"Yes, the Mistress has bound me here to serve as the bookkeeper for House Brandwyck until the end of her days. As much as I despise serving a human, the Mistress does have a way with words and magic."

"Well I apologize for interrupting your important clerical work, Tibb. I was just looking around and stumbled into the library. But now that I'm here, might I ask what manner of books you keep here?"

Ze chuckled to zirself. "A little bit of everything, really. Mostly magical tomes and scientific reference, but plenty of fiction as well. But this room itself is an extradimensional space and is much too large for someone with a human lifespan to comfortably browse. Allow me to show you how our system works."

Ze led her through aisles between bookshelves near the entrance to a clearing of sorts in the forest of literature. A large circular counter had four tomes the size of flagstones evenly spaced on its surface. Tibberwyx gestured to one of the books and it opened of its own volition. The pages inside were blank, though as she approached a table of contents resolved itself into murky form on the left page. Instead of showing chapters of a book, it showed broad literary topics, categorized under either Fiction or Nonfiction. At the bottom of the page was a disconnected line that just said Search.

"Just tap your finger to one of the genres to browse or tap the Search line and think real hard about what you want to find."

Cassie pressed her finger to the Romance genre, curious to see what would come up. On her touch, the black ink of the words were highlighted in shimmering gold for a second before the whole page of print disappeared and both pages began to fill with a list of book titles. *The Beauty and the Boggard: The Croak of Love* caught her eye and she laughed.

"You can flip through the pages to browse the results and tap on any that catch your fancy."

Cassie tapped on the boggard love book and there was a soft chime like a nearby silver bell. In a few seconds, a blue-cover book soared out from the tangle of shelves, sparkling with silver magic, and flew down to alight on the desk. Cassie picked up the book.

"Would you like to check that one out?" Tibb asked.

Cassie's penchant for morbid curiosity was too strong. "Yes, I would."

"Perfect! Just place your thumb on the page."

Cassie did as ze bid, leaving behind a thumbprint in the same murky black ink.

"There you go! Simple enough. Now, you'll have two weeks to read this book, after which time it will be automatically returned to the library if it is still in the manor, elsewise we will send the book troll after you to recollect. Of course if you want to return it early, just bring it back here and leave it on the counter. It's my job to see to returns."

Cassie wasn't sure if she wanted to meet the book troll, so she vowed to return the book on time. She bid zir farewell and exited the library, sultry frog-folk smut under her arm. She eventually found her way back to the foyer by means of an expansive greenhouse containing some of the most bizarre and unusual plants she had ever seen. As she walked into the foyer, she almost ran into Gwynne, who was barreling down the stairs.

"Oh, Cassandra Mott, there you are. You weren't in your bedroom so I was afraid you might have gotten lost. I see you found the library. Are you acquainted with Tibberwyx, then?"

"Yes, I am. I'm quite impressed by this place. This is all your manor?

How do you afford all this?"

"A story for another time, I'm afraid. Suffice it to say I am quite the prolific wizard and purveyor of magical goods in many places around the world. However, I do not believe I have formally introduced myself, despite the situation. I do hope you'll accept my apologies." Gwynne bowed low. "I am Gwynne Circe Brandwyck, also known as the Owl of the Pale Moon, or just Owl. I humbly and heartily welcome you to my abode, House Brandwyck, situated aboard the wonderful flying craft the *Pale Moon*."

"The pleasure is all mine, Miss Brandwyck," Cassie returned, giving her an equally low and silly bow. From this position, she noticed two cats winding their way around Gwynne's legs. One was the same ginger boy as before, the other was a male gray tabby.

"Oh, it's Mr. Ginger again." Cassie said, scratching the cat behind its ears again.

Gwynne leaned down and scooped the cat up in her arms, holding him over her shoulder. "I see you have already met one of my children. This is my son, Baal. This one down here is my other son, Belial."

"Oh hello, handsome Mr. Belial," Cassie cooed, reaching out to pet the grey-and-white cat. He hissed at her before curling his tail around Gwynne anew.

"Don't mind him, he's not too fond of new people. Would you care to hold Baal?"

"O-okay." Cassie had never held a cat before, but Gwynne showed her how to support his torso and hindquarters. Baal purred in her arms and started licking her cheek. "Aww who's a good boy? Thank you for the kisses, Mr. Baal." Eventually the cat squirmed and Cassie set him down.

"By the way, I must congratulate you on your new hairstyle, Miss Mott. I didn't know you had such abilities."

Cassie had completely forgotten about her pink afro. "Oh gods, no,

I just… uh… used some of the hair product in the bath and it turned this color."

"Ahh, that would be Hair Concoction No.2. An excellent conditioner, especially for natural hair like yours, but it has the side effect that it dyes the user's hair as well. Been trying to work out that kink. It's funny, the color actually varies from person to person. Never been able to figure out why. Maybe I can market that as a gimmick."

"Sorry, I should have asked before using the bath."

"Oh you're fine. Make yourself at home. Now, would you like to meet the other resident of the House?"

Gwynne led her through a hallway and down a flight of stairs. Below the ground floor of the House the construction changed from lavish wood to steel plating. Cassie was led through a number of rooms filled with metal piping, pressure gauges, valves, trundling engines, and large metal tanks. At the end, they came to a chamber lit by a small white light in a caged enclosure. There was a control panel laid out against the wall, and various panels of glass showed different shots of what must have been the exterior of the flying machine. From the outside, it mostly looked like an enormous metal bird, floating without flapping in the clouds. Various embedded propellers provided lift, and rudders at the tail and flaps on the wings allowed directional control. A gloved hand shot into view from behind a tall-backed chair interposed between Cassie and the control panel. It reached up and pulled down a lever, causing a puff of steam to escape the flying machine on one of the glass views.

Gwynne cleared her throat. "Hello Horatio, my good man. We've a new guest aboard."

The chair swiveled around and Cassie was surprised to see what at first looked like one of the goblins from the previous day. On closer inspection, however, this person didn't exactly look like a goblin. The head was proportional to the body, and the face was less grotesque, more of a proper man's face. They still had long pointy ears, but their eyes were not the beady black shark eyes of the cavemen goblins. This individual must have been that goblin off-shoot race that Gwynne had mentioned.

"Ach, an 'hoo izziss, 'en, eh?" The man had a deep highland accent similar to Mr. Burton's but much thicker.

"May I present to you Cassandra Mott. I have decided to take her as my apprentice."

This was the first Cassie had heard of this, and she wasn't sure what to say.

The man nodded to Cassie. "Pleasure, gal. Me name's Horatio. No surname. I'm th' engineer on this bloody hunk a' junk." Then turned to Gwynne. "Yer apprentice, aye? Did'ja even ask th' wee lass first? Wot if she dun want t' be yer apprentice?"

Gwynne smiled and turned to Cassie. "Cassie, would you like to become my apprentice? You have a spark of talent for magic, and I would like to teach you what I know. I warn you that I'm not a great teacher, and it may take a long time to see proper results. Plus, I'm a wanted criminal, and life here means a life on the run from the crown. But in exchange, you'll have free room and board, and of course direct tutelage from one of the most gifted wizards this world has ever seen. What do you say?"

Cassie, feeling very put on the spot, thought about this for a minute. She was nervous to decide, but it really wasn't a hard decision when she thought about it honestly. What else was she going to do? Go back home and try to find a new factory job? Keep living with her mother and become a complete spinster?

"I accept."

Gwynne smiled warmly and Horatio rolled his eyes. This was the beginning of a new life for Cassie, who was suddenly wondering what exactly she had gotten herself into.

II

On Tour

5

Force Vectors

Exertion of Will Upon the Universe - In War, Nobody's Right - The Elder Tongue is Obnoxiously Literal - Arcane Capital of the World

Cassie's lessons began immediately.

"I think we'll use the ground floor workshop," Gwynne had said, leading her off to the room with the cauldron she had passed through before.

Cassie chased after Gwynne, almost tripping over a discarded flower pot left in the hallway. The wizard seemed to have already made up her mind. It seemed once she decided on something, there was little to be done about the matter. "But… why do you want me to be your apprentice? I can't do magic."

"Are you sure? Remember the fight with the goblins? You threw that rock, which by all means shouldn't have made it halfway to its target with those flabby arms of yours."

"Hey!"

"Sorry, you know what I mean."

Cassie didn't mind her lack of upper body strength, but *flabby*? That comment stung, even if Gwynne hadn't meant to offend.

"My point is, as soon as the stone began to fall, it blipped out of existence, then reappeared at startling velocity. This is just my personal opinion, but it seems the rock teleported to another universe, one where time moves faster than here, fell until it reached terminal velocity, then was teleported back. All in the blink of an eye. That's not something that anyone can do."

"But… I didn't mean to do that."

"Well that's why you must learn. See, even if I *hadn't* seen you do that, you've got something much more important than latent magical energy, and that's determination. See, theoretically *anyone* could do magic if they put their minds to it, it's just a lot of work."

Cassie just listened, eyes wide. Nobody had ever accused her of having a good work ethic, or any work ethic really. But it seemed like Gwynne believed in her, so she wanted to prove that conviction worthwhile.

Cassie started idly picking things up in the workshop. It seemed there was more detritus here than she had realized. Stacks of worn books were nestled into a desk and she hadn't realized that there were strange instruments like wind chimes hanging from the ceiling. She thought she saw a real human skull in a jar on top of one of the tables. "I mean… I'll do my best. I've never really been able to concentrate on stuff for long periods of time."

"Oh don't worry, I'm the same way. Attention span of a goldfish, my tutors used to say, but when I decide on a task myself I'm unstoppable. I suspect you are likely the same way." A more obvious statement has yet to be made.

Cassie had never felt motivated to do anything in her life. She had no hobbies or interests aside from idly daydreaming. "Mayyyyybe…"

"Good enough for me." Gwynne moved over to a wall behind the cauldron and pulled down a retractable blackboard. She picked up a length of chalk and began writing. "Before I can teach you to use magic, however, I first have to explain to you what magic *is*, and more importantly, what it *is not*. Your first lesson begins now.

"Magic is simply the exertion of will upon the universe. You provide the universe with an explicit list of commands, and it executes them. The keyword here is *explicit*, because like making a to-do list and then handing it to an idiot, the universe will only do *exactly* what you have commanded. It makes no assumptions and provides no assistance. It is *not* a matter of just waving your hand and thy will be done. If you mess up the instructions, the magic will sometimes fail, or execute in unintended ways.

"Additionally, magic is not an unlimited font of power. Every magical command issued takes a toll of energy on the body of the caster. Generally speaking, the more energy required to execute a command, the more energy is taken from your body. If you attempt commands that are beyond your endurance level, you could cause harm to yourself or even die. This is true even if you intended only a small effect, but through careless casting caused a much stronger effect to execute. Think of it as a burning flame. You only feed the flame just enough oil to do what it needs to do, but if you are careless with fire, it can get out of hand and cause harm."

Cassie was listening intently. She didn't realize that magic was so difficult. She thought back to the times she had unintentionally used magic, first to cross the river, the second to propel the rock at the goblins. It was true she felt tired after each encounter, but she had assumed that was due solely to the stress of each situation.

"Thus, before I will allow you to scribe your first scroll, brew your first potion, or even recite your first incantation, your assignment is to build up some stamina. The best way to do that is to have you doing daily exercise, focused mostly on cardio."

"Nooooooo," Cassie whined. "My worst enemy, physical exertion!"

Her calves were still sore from the previous day's hike, and the thought of more running made her wilt internally.

* * *

With that, Cassie began her training as mundanely as possible. Gwynne showed her to a gym aboard the manor that contained many different types of workout equipment, as well as a running track laid out around the room. According to Gwynne, the track was an eighth of a mile in length. Cassie's blisters started to ache just looking at it. Gwynne lent her a set of boring brown exercise clothes and found her some worn shoes that were at least more comfortable than her usual boots. She spent a week in the manor, waking up each morning to run at least a mile followed by strength training for her whole body. All the while Gwynne alternated between heckling her and cheering her on. The first day, she completed the mile in a miserable fifteen minutes, lungs on fire and legs about to buckle. Gwynne shook her head, saying it made for a good benchmark but at that pace she'd lose to even Horatio in a race.

In the afternoons, Gwynne instructed Cassie on various fundamentals of magic.

"There are actually different kinds of mages, you know. For example, I am a Wizard, arguably the best kind, but there are others as well.

"Wizards are mages that study the workings of the universe, flows of energy, and ways to manipulate that energy. Wizardry is the most difficult school of magic since it requires extensive study to really get right and extensive fine-tuning of the spell development process, but the possibilities are endless.

"Most similarly to wizards, we have Bards. Bardic magic requires study like wizards, but instead of a scientific approach, bards take an artistic one. Their spells are less about fine-tuned calculations to produce the exact effect desired and more about using emotion and intuition to feel out their spells. Most bards channel their magic through music, but other forms of artistic expression also work. As such, bardic spells tend to be less focused on a specific time and place and more about creating widespread and lasting effects, albeit to less powerful degrees.

"Next up is Witchcraft. Witches draw their power from nature, using crystals, herbs, and animals to produce magical effects. Many witches employ the aid of a Familiar, a sort of magical muse that can assist them in their craft as well as help them channel spells. They are often skilled in Biomancy, a discipline that other schools of magic find difficult. Witches are usually secretive, so little is known about the intricacies of their craft.

"Finally, we have Warlocks. Warlocks bypass the careful study that other mages undergo by forming a pact with a magical creature such as a demon, faerie, nature spirit, or Elder god. This creature, called their Patron, supplies them with spells that they can cast at will, but they are normally limited to the personality and species of their patron. Plus, you're essentially selling your soul to a magical creature in exchange for quick and easy power. It's cheating, really, and not a craft of which I approve, but there have been many powerful warlocks throughout history."

"Which am I?" Cassie had asked, overwhelmed with information. She was struggling to write notes in a leather-bound notebook that Gwynne had given her. She had taken to drawing spiteful little doodles in the margins, mostly of Gwynne as a horned and winged demon making her do more exercise.

"Well that's up to you. No one is born a Wizard or a Bard or anything. I am biased, but I believe that wizardry is the most versatile and rewarding school of magic, if you're willing to put in the work."

"Wizard it is, then. Funny, I always thought Wizards were men and

Witches were women."

"A common misconception. While there are many male wizards and many female witches, the titles refer only to how their magic works. There is no hard reason that a woman cannot become a wizard or a man a witch. It is my belief that societal expectations and stereotypes drive this de facto segregation of magical schools by gender, and with better education we might be able to break down these barriers. But that's a discussion for another time."

* * *

A few days into training, Cassie, Gwynne, and Horatio were taking their evening meal in the front sitting room. Horatio had roasted up some manner of meat and Gwynne had thrown together a salad with bitter greens, sweet pears, crushed pecans, and a sort of crumbly white cheese that Cassie did not recognize. She had since twisted Gwynne's arm into picking up the sitting room at least, and had convinced her to use a spell to repair the rip on the armchair.

There was silence in the room for a good while whilst the company ate their food. Eventually, Cassie spoke up. "So, how come Tibberwyx never eats with us? Does ze eat at all?"

Horatio was the first to answer, through a mouth of meat and salad all mashed together. "Tha' wee pixie? Aye, they jus' subsist on moondust, methinks."

Gwynne finished her mouthful of salad and set her utensils down on the plate in her lap. She wiped her mouth with a napkin, the picture of noble grace. "I don't know too much about the fey folk, but from what I have been able to tell, Tibb does not require food in the same way as the rest of us. Ze mentioned once that ze eats insects and drinks magic, but I don't know if that was serious or not. At any rate, I have extended my warmest invitations to zir on multiple occasions, so ze may choose to join us if the fancy strikes zir."

Cassie nodded and set about finishing her meat. Once her plate was clear, she asked another question that had been weighing on her mind the past few days. "So… uh, where are we going? I mean, this is a flying craft. Surely we must be flying somewhere."

Cassie looked at Horatio, who looked at Gwynne, who was picking a bit of meat out from her teeth, completely betraying her earlier grace. "Very sharp, Cassie. Currently we're on our way to Abaddon."

Cassie knew that name. "You mean *the* Abaddon? As in the capital of Abaxia?"

Horatio rolled his eyes "Ach, no lassie, we're 'eaded to Abaddon, Murkolin." Cassie had never heard of a nation called Murkolin, but interpreted the trasgo's words as sarcasm.

"One and the same," Gwynne said. "There is something that I need to pick up from the University there. Something I left during my studies."

Cassie nearly choked on her own spit. "*You* studied at the Abaxian University?"

"Of course, that's where I learned wizardry. Where else?"

"I don't know… I always just thought of you as this self-taught genius."

Gwynne scoffed. "Well, I won't argue with 'genius', but no, I am certainly not self-taught. I received the same education as every other mage to come out of that nation. I just didn't join the Mages' Corps like most of the native students."

"What's the Mages' Corps?"

"Bunch'a bloody spell-slingers is wot!"

"Well, that's certainly a big question, but essentially Abaxia's military is less based on riflery and hard-working non-magical folks like Zona. Zona has the numbers, but Abaxia realized long ago that just one competent mage is worth a hundred soldiers, and requires much less upkeep and training. So the nation subsidizes scholarships for the University for Abaxian residents, provided that they serve at least seven years in the Mages' Corps after graduation."

Cassie thought about it. She hated the concept of military, and found wars to be pointless masculine squabbles, but if it meant getting to fulfill her dream of attending Ab. U.?

"A very enticing offer, then."

"Yes, indeed. Though not all who begin their scholarship end up finishing it. At least half drop out before graduation, and maybe ten percent of those who graduate stay in the military for the full contract. But still, it has meant that Abaxia has a steady stream of mages to hold their own against Zona, and for much cheaper."

"So… I take it you're Zonan, then, Gwynne?"

"Begrudgingly, yes. Though my mother was racially Abaxian, much like yourself, Cassie. But my father… well he only permitted me to attend the university such that I might be more useful to him. I was not thrilled at this part of the deal, so I did not follow through with it."

She could sense a lot of baggage behind that statement, so she didn't press the point. Instead, she tried to change the subject. "So as someone who's seen both sides of the war, what do you think about it? Who's in the right?"

This was the wrong question, apparently. Gwynne had a faraway look in her eye and she stared into the fire. "In war, nobody's right."

Cassie only knew the publicized reasons behind the war. Eight years ago, the crown prince Abneel of Zona went missing. Three years later, the King of Zona issued a public statement exclaiming that Abneel was dead, and that Abaxia had assassinated him. Abaxia officially denied this accusation, but it hardly mattered. Zona then invaded and Abaxia struck back. Thus, war. This narrative was heavily propagandized in Zona, with a national holiday being declared for remembrance of Prince Abneel. People sure seemed awfully sad about his death, despite the fact that nobody seemed to know him personally or even any details about the man.

Horatio butted in. "Ah don' believe none o' th' rumors. It's all propaganda. Just humans lookin' for war fer selfish reasons."

Gwynne still looked distant. "Selfish, aye."

Cassie waited a while before speaking again, allowing Gwynne to move past whatever was troubling her. When the mood lightened a bit, she proffered a new line of conversation.

"Gwynne, I thank you for offering me your tutelage and opening your House to me, but I must say, this place is a mess."

Gwynne looked up. "You think so? I keep meaning to get around to cleaning, I just get… busy."

"I know how you get. There are a million things that demand your attention around here, least of which being me. Why not leave it to a professional?"

"What do you mean?"

"Well this is a manor, isn't it? Why don't we hire a maid?"

Gwynne stroked her chin in thought, a twinkle flashing across her eye. "You know, that's a good idea. I'm hesitant to trust anyone to allow them unsupervised into the House, but I trust your judgment, Cassie. When we stop in Abaddon, I'm hereby charging you with the task of hiring a maid for the manor."

Cassie was surprised by this sudden expression of trust, but suspected that Gwynne just could not be bothered to do the task herself.

* * *

At the end of that first week, Cassie was able to run her daily mile in twelve minutes. Nowhere near proper fitness times, but leaps and bounds above the condition in which she began her training. Gwynne was impressed, and decided she was ready to cast her first spell.

"Nothing amazing, mind you, just something to show you how the process works."

Cassie was sitting at one of the desks in the workshop where she had her daily lessons. Gwynne was explaining the spell she was to perform.

"Applying force is one of the simplest ways to affect the world around you. Think of it as an invisible hand pushing or pulling on things." Gwynne had given Cassie a crash course in rudimentary physics, and she now at least understood the concepts of kinematics. "Hell, even magical flight is just simply applying a constant force vector on your body to counteract gravity." Gwynne leaned down and set a green apple on the floor in the middle of the room. "Your first task is to lift this apple up to eye level and no further."

Cheekily, Cassie reached down and picked up the apple with her hand. "Doesn't seem too hard to me."

Gwynne rolled her eyes. "Without touching it, smartass."

Cassie picked up a scroll she had written and read over the lines of magical instruction on the page. Most of the lines involved establishing an exact point in space to effect, specifying the object to affect, the exact amount of force to apply, and the duration. She struggled with the pronunciation of the eldritch words, which she had only recently learned how to scribe and speak.

"Good," Gwynne said. "Now close your eyes and visualize the effect. Think of the apple rising from its place on the floor up to eye level."

Cassie did as she was bidden, and opened her eyes to see that her desire had become manifest. The apple was slowly levitating off the floor. She could feel a slight soreness in her elbows and her heart rate accelerated as the apple kept moving. It rose up to eye level but did not stop.

"Cassie, dismiss the spell!"

Cassie closed her eyes and muttered a single word of cancellation.

The apple, which had now almost reached the ceiling, thumped to the ground. Cassie felt out of breath and leaned over on her knees.

Instead of checking on Cassie, Gwynne was examining the apple. "That was a close one. I think you slightly flubbed the pronunciation for the duration."

The two argued about pronunciation of the Elder Tongue before Cassie realized her mistake. "Oh, damn, you're right Gwynne. I modified the vowel sound slightly."

"Luckily you have me here and that I taught you the proper cancellation technique. Remember that you are a conduit for magic, and can cinch that conduit at any time. It may just save your life someday, or more importantly, mine."

"Why do we have to do incantations in the Elder Tongue, again, Gwynne? Can't we just use our normal language?"

"You could, in theory, but it'd be tricky. See, human language is riddled with connotations, insinuations, innuendo, inconsistencies, assumptions, and ambiguities. If I were to write a spell to transform me into a bat, for example, would the spell make me into an animal, or into a wooden stick used for sport?"

"I see."

"In all honesty, the spell would probably fail when it encountered an ambiguity, but you can't assume that. What if it went haywire and sapped all your energy in an instant? In contrast, the Elder Tongue is obnoxiously literal. The Elder Gods never invented poetry or deceit, and their language was created in a hive-minded unison. Thus their language is more like math, something unambiguous and universal. Of course, that means you need to study a whole other language, but who doesn't learn a second language these days? It's much easier to spend a year learning the Elder Tongue than to spend your whole life contorting and twisting your existing language to be as certain as you possibly can that you've ironed out all the questionable meanings, praying that you haven't missed some double entendre that might endanger yourself or others."

* * *

When Cassie wasn't exercising or learning magical theory, math, or physics, Gwynne assigned her books from the House library on the Elder Tongue to study in her room. Tibberwyx was delighted to assist her with this study, and ze offered a bit of tutoring on the subject.

"Love the Elder Tongue!" Ze said. "No useless pronouns in that language. Though I suppose the closest thing is the topic particle that can be used in place of the most recently established subject of discussion. And it's perfectly genderless, too! You know, the fey tongue is derived from Elder. And through many iterations, the various human languages as well, though they're so far removed as to be unrecognizable."

Cassie enjoyed Tibb's company in the short term, but she had never met someone who talked as much or as quickly as zir. The library was never fully quiet with zir around.

As for the Elder Tongue, Cassie found it a bit hard to pronounce, and it took a while before she was really comfortable with all the different tenses, cases, conjugations, and vocabulary. At the end of that week, she was able to speak basic commands, feeling the heavy consonants click through her throat and teeth. She thought the language sounded more like a cat trying to cough up a reluctant hairball, but she wouldn't argue with its benefits. The language was very well broken down, with clear distinctions between different meanings of words and phrases. Cassie had never studied another language before out of lack of necessity, but she enjoyed the process of switching her brain into a whole other mode where everything had an exact name and description. It also taught her a lot about her own language as well, and she quickly found many different phrases she was saying incorrectly out of habit.

In her spare time between all that and eating and sleeping, Cassie read any books she could get her hands on. She devoured *The Beauty and the Boggard*. While not particularly fond of the pairing in the story, she still enjoyed herself. She returned it within two days and picked out a new stack to read, which she put on the lonely bookshelf in her room.

As far as Cassie could tell, there was room for four other occupants on her hallway, and perhaps many more beyond. She had ascended the stairs to the third level one day and had come across Gwynne's room. If she thought the sitting room was a mess, Gwynne's room was a disaster. It looked like an entire antique store had exploded in her room, every available surface covered in ornate clocks, twinkling crystals, illegible measuring devices, abstract art, bizarre sculptures, forgotten books and writing implements, dirty clothes, and used dishes. The woman was a living portrait of mania. She thought she saw a stack of blueprints and diagrams of a building on a table inside the room, but Gwynne shut the door quickly and dismissed Cassie's inquiries.

At times, the House felt like an ocean, and Cassie had only explored its shallows. She felt like if she took a wrong turn or went too far she could find herself hopelessly lost in an infinite expanse of hallways and empty rooms. But surely that was just an illusion, right?

Almost two weeks had passed since Cassie began her training at House Brandwyck. She was just finishing up breakfast, a meager plate of scrambled eggs she had made herself, when Gwynne burst into the kitchen.

"Cassie, c'mere, quick! I want you to see this!"

Gwynne grabbed her by the wrist and yanked her away from the kitchen table, where Cassie had shoved piles of parchment out of the way and onto the floor. She dropped her fork onto the plate with a clatter and tried to keep up with Gwynne. She was led up to a doorway on the third floor that she hadn't gone through before. Or perhaps it had never been there before? It was hard to tell in this place. At any rate, Gwynne burst through the door, her pupil in tow, onto a sunny terrace. Cassie could see potted plants and a full size planter in the center with a small tree growing out of it. Around the terrace were lounge chairs that looked like they had seen better days, sun-bleached and dirty.

Gwynne let go of Cassie's hand and walked over to the railing, leaning over to behold the view. Cassie walked up beside her and brushed the wisps of hair out of her face that were whipped around by the gale force winds. Beyond, Cassie could see a massive city down below. They were still quite high up, but she could just barely make out streets teeming with movement, like ants forming a line across cracks in the road. In the center of the city was a great crystal palace, sparkling in the morning light. Various dirigibles floated above the city, and a large tower provided an airship dock that buzzed with activity.

Cassie's jaw dropped. "It's... beautiful."

Gwynne grinned and said "Welcome to Abaddon, crown jewel of the Free State of Abaxia, and arcane capital of the world."

6

Culture Shock

Discreet, Experienced, and Personable - Human Lives Before Money - A Featureless White Mask - Useless Lesbian Brain

As opposed to the Kingdom of Zona, which was home to rugged mountain ranges and high steppe, the Free State of Abaxia was almost all plains leading down to the Aubrine Ocean on its east side. Abaxia had one solitary mountain peak, the high point of a brief range, known as Mt. Kilano. According to the history books, its peoples were once disparate nomadic tribes, but after a bitter tribal war they had all decided to band together to form one nation for the good of all their peoples. This was thousands of years ago now, and today Abaxia was a relatively advanced nation of magic, technology, and strong heritage.

Gwynne had taken the two of them down to the ground in the flying contraption with which they had entered the manor, leaving it under an invisibility spell outside of the city limits. The wizard herself had disguised herself as a middle aged Abaxian woman with bland and forgettable clothing and appearance. She split up with Cassie upon entering the city, warning her not to get lost and to meet her back at the same gate at sundown. She had also given Cassie a generous purse of coin to spend, and she intended to make good use of it.

The city of Abaddon looked even more magnificent from the ground. The buildings were all clean and tall, and the streets were packed with foot traffic, horse-bound carriages, and some manner of mechanical carriages that Cassie had never seen before and which powered themselves through an engine. Those were awfully loud, and they belched acrid clouds of smoke behind them as they drove.

Her first order of business was to find a maid. She had no clue how she was supposed to do that in this city, but with a bit of asking was able to find a job board near one of the many guild offices. She borrowed a piece of parchment and a pen and had drafted what she thought was a good help wanted ad. It read:

Live-In Maid Wanted
Looking for young housekeeper for manor employ, preferably female. Must be discreet, experienced, and personable. Must be okay with travel and chaotic conditions. Pay negotiable. If interested, please meet Ms. Mott at the southern gate at sundown. Today only!

After posting the ad and dating it, she went about her business. She spent a few hours just browsing through the town and shopping for clothes. She specifically wanted clothes that would facilitate physical activity, as well as her own garish and ostentatious outfits like the ones which Gwynne always wore. The amount of clothes she ended up purchasing would have been impossible for her to carry under normal circumstances, but Gwynne had lent her the wondrous bag, and she stuffed it full of bags and boxes filled with clothing and other home goods.

One clothing store in particular had caught her eye. Gaudy dresses and loose-fitting outfits were displayed in the store's window on black mannequins. A minimally-detailed skull patterned a black background in the display, giving the whole affair a macabre and dramatic air. She entered the building, a low bell note sounding to signal her arrival. Someone that Cassie assumed was a man strutted out from the back rows. He was very tall and wiry thin, wearing a tight-fitting cropped white top with a high neck above a pair of high-waisted black pants, covered in buttons. Lastly, he was wearing a pair of high-heeled shoes and was wearing bright eyeshadow and other facial cosmetics that made him seem a bit like a peacock showing off. This was by far the most avant-garde fashion that Cassie had ever seen and she was loving every inch of it.

"Welcome to Devón's," the man breathed with the utmost gravitas. "Don't say a word, darling. I can tell, first time." Cassie just blinked, which the man (ostensibly Devón) took as a response. "That dress, ugh! So last decade. Let me guess, Zonan? Oh, you poor thing."

Cassie liked Devón already, and could tell that she had come to the right shop. With nary a word from her, he had already sauntered over to a rack of dresses at the back and had pulled out something deep black with white lace. "Hm, what do we think about this? I'd say too gothic." Cassie wasn't sure if there was such a thing, but went with Devón's suggestions. After a few failed picks, which she was sure must have been part of some sales act, Devón had picked out a black and white dress with a light amount of corseting and no straps to speak of. It was something that would have made her mother faint to see her wear it, which spurred Cassie on all the more. She tried it on in the dressing room and it made her feel like a proper wizard. Devón cheered her on and she blushed a little, being the star of her own private fashion show. She bought the dress on the spot, along with a few other choice outfits that made her feel like a bad bitch. She left with many boxes in the wondrous bag, which even with its increased capacity was starting to bulge a bit. Cassie decided she'd have to come back to Devón's when next she was in town.

Cassie also spent a fair amount of time dawdling around fancy magic shops in the main boulevard. She had seen some youths gallivanting through the streets on a sort of small flying device that hovered a few feet above the ground. Apparently the shops here sold them, but they were way outside of her budget. She imagined that Gwynne could probably make something better than that, anyway, and she mostly just window-shopped to get ideas for different spells she wanted to learn.

At a popular local apothecary where gooey candles completely failed to illuminate the caliginous aisles, she made sure to pick up a good supply of Changing Potion. A small crate of bottles would be enough until she could figure out how to make it herself, she reasoned. It was vastly cheaper here in Abaxia, perhaps a third of the price in Zona. Plus, nobody batted an eye at this purchase, aside from the taciturn glare of the iguana familiar of the store's clerk who seemed to be the only employee, which led her to believe that such a purchase was fairly normal here.

Beyond the differences in shopping opportunities, life in Abaxia seemed much different from that in Zona. For starters, the vast majority of the population were Abaxian. It felt nice not to be the only person in every room she entered that didn't have pale white skin, and on Abaddon's busy streets Cassie could feel herself blend into the crowd with a sense of belonging. She was glad that her accidental hair experiment had since faded back to its natural midnight shade. The other thing that surprised Cassie was just how much art there was for sale everywhere. She ended up buying an artisan necklace at a stall in a huge bazaar that seemed entirely devoted to local craftspeople.

"It's amazing how much pure creativity there is in this city," she had remarked to the jeweler.

The jeweler was a tall man with a bald head, a clean-shaven and wide-set jaw, and a warm smile on his face. "You must be from out of town. Here in Abaxia, everyone gets Basic, so people who wanna work a day job can, and those who wanna follow their passions can as well."

"What's Basic?"

"Wow, you must *really* be from outta town, hon. Every citizen gets a basic amount of money each month in order to survive. It ain't a fortune, but it's enough to make sure you're fed and you got a roof over your head. You can work if you wanna get money on top of that, but you ain't never gonna starve even if you do nothin'. Most people ain't content with just sittin' around, though. The human mind gotta have something to do, you know?"

Cassie's mind reeled at the concept. "You mean… you don't have to work to survive? But what if you get sick?"

"We got the best hospitals in the world right here in Abaddon, honey. And it's all free for citizens."

"I'm from Zona and that'd never work over there."

"Heh, that's because your economy is built on the rich gettin' richer. Here, it's about human lives before money."

"Surely there's a downside. How does the government pay for it all?"

"Eh, I dunno the proper details, but it helps that our military is much smaller than Zona, though just as powerful, and we make a lot of money exporting magical goods and crystals. I guess the infrastructure and support for smaller towns could be better, but it sure as hell beats people starving in a pretty capital."

This economical concept was very new to Cassie, who had lived a miserable life under capitalism, forced to work terrible jobs just to have the money to afford the privilege of survival. She only had a place to live all those years because her mother didn't have the heart to kick her out at eighteen. She knew it was better for some than others, but she found the system to be inherently heartless and inhumane. She had never before considered that poverty didn't *have* to exist. She thanked the man for his time and wisdom and left, wondering what she would have done if she didn't have to slave away under Hardden for so long.

Cassie had spent a few hours in the city at this point, but had not yet seen the University of which she had long dreamt. Deciding that it would be a complete waste to visit the most magical place in the world without seeing whence said magic was made, she caught a trolley that ran on rails through the main streets of the city, powered by who knew what and packed with people. Cassie hopped on with a crowd of pedestrians, paid her fare, and was lucky enough to grab a seat on a cushioned row along the window as another passenger was leaving. Her feet were sore from prior days on the track and today's gallivant around town. She was glad to be off her feet for a while, at the very least, especially while the aisle of the tram was filled with men on their feet, wearing smart business suits.

Cassie had barely had any time lately to think about the recent change in her lifestyle. It seemed one day she had been stuck in that inevitable rut of a soul-sucking day job, and the next she had been whisked away to a life of magic and fancy of which she could formerly only have dreamt. She still pinched herself each morning to make sure it was all still real, but her skin hurt just as usual from the pinch. Even if it was a bit lonely in that flying manor what with everyone keeping to their own devices, it was still the best Cassie's life had ever been. Gwynne was a wonderful master, even if she was always aloof and self-centered at times. Horatio was alright, too, in his own way. Tibberwyx… well Tibb was a lot to handle, but she still appreciated zir. She hoped that with the addition of a maid that the House would feel more lively and homey.

Occasionally, she'd wonder what her mother and sister were up to and perhaps if they worried about her. She found it hard to care what they thought, as poorly as they had treated her all her life. The one person she did feel bad about leaving behind was Jax, who had been nothing but kind to her from her first day at the factory. She thought she ought to send them a postcard or something to let them know she was alright and not to worry, but then she realized that she didn't know their address. How stupid she was to have been friends with them all this time and never asked for their mailing address! Cassie wondered if she had really been a good friend to them after all. She hoped she could visit Bixton again someday soon to drop in on them.

Cassie could feel a prickle on the back of her neck whilst she daydreamt, and couldn't shake the feeling that someone was watching her. She peered around the cabin of the tram and found that there was a figure sitting on a bench at the far back that seemed to be gazing upon her. They were wearing the finest black suit she had seen all day and bore a featureless white mask upon their face. Altogether, they were completely devoid of any physical description onto which Cassie's memory could latch. She couldn't even make out the color of their skin, as their hands were covered in black leather gloves. *The kind a serial killer might wear*, her subconscious decided. But before she could think too long about the subject, a bell tinkled and the tram slowed to a stop.

"University Crossing. That's University Crossing. All disembarking please rise. Once again, University Crossing." The voice of the conductor snapped Cassie back to attention and she stood up and briskly exited the vehicle. She supposed in a city this large there must be plenty of weirdos abound and promptly forgot about the encounter.

In front of her was the crux of her every daydream. The sidewalks were brick here instead of their usual flagstone, which the locals said was the only way to tell the campus apart from the rest of the city. Truly, the uninitiated would have just taken the tall buildings to be offices or residences, but a careful eye could see that each had a name that belied their true purpose, such as "Bringford Hall" or "Pindleworth Dormitory". All around, Cassie could see young people milling about, making their way to a lecture or laboratory session, no doubt. From what she could tell, they were mostly around her age, but some were older and there were even a few that seemed no more than mid teens in age. Truly the university attracted all types. She caught snippets of conversation as she mingled with the crowds of students.

"Did you finish your transmutation homework?"

"…ugh, I've got Professor Crimbs next. His lectures are always so boring."

"Can you help me study this spell? I can't quite…"

"What'd they have for lunch in the caf' today?"

"…you coming to the party this weekend?"

Altogether, Cassie felt a strange hollow emptiness where she was as close as she had ever been to her life's dream, but somehow the furthest she had ever been. It kind of hurt a little, but in a strange melancholy way that made her want more. She followed a pack into one of the large buildings and found herself in a gigantic lecture hall, a veritable indoor amphitheater with fold-out wooden seats with built-in desks. Cassie sat at the back and listened as a very short man magically magnified his voice and gave a lecture on the flow of energy during a conjuration spell. The presentation was a little dry, but she found it very informative. She was aghast to find that some students were hardly paying attention at all and were instead doing homework, practicing other spells, or just chatting quietly. Surely they ought to show more respect! The professor didn't seem to mind, though, and Cassie figured it wasn't any of her business.

She left the lecture hall with the emotional abscess still aching in her chest. She walked through the campus quad where a booth was set up by the Abaxian army. It informed students about employment and scholarship opportunities funded by the government. No doubt this had something to do with the Mages' Corps of which she had recently learned. She gave the booth a wide berth. As she was walking past a weathered bronze statue of a robe-clad woman with wand held high, she almost bumped into an extraordinarily plain-looking woman.

"Oh, there you are, Cassie. Didn't think I'd run into you here."

She had completely forgotten that Gwynne was incognito, and still didn't quite recognize the form she had taken, but supposed that was the point.

"Oh, Gwynne. I didn't recognize you. How was your business? Did you find what you were looking for?"

Gwynne shot furtive glances around the quad. "Not here. We'll talk when we get back to the House. Suffice it to say my mission was a success."

The sun was getting low in the sky, so the two women decided to return to where Gwynne had parked the flying craft. On their way, they picked up a local street food consisting of flatbread wrapped around flame-roasted rotisserie meats and aromatic vegetables, all smothered with a creamy-yet-tangy white sauce. There were even bits of fried potato stuck into the foil wrapper. It was delicious.

"What did they call this again?" Gwynne asked, intensely examining the dish and all its myriad components. "Yee-row or something, wasn't it?"

Cassie just nodded, experiencing culinary rapture all over again.

"By the way Cassie, how did it go with finding a maid?"

They were getting quite close to the south gate at this point. Cassie had forgotten all about the wanted ad she had placed earlier in the day, the thought blown away in the bustle of the day's activities. As they approached the gate, she saw something she hadn't been expecting, but really ought to have, given the circumstances. A young woman stood near the gate, attracting the attention of everyone around with her curly blonde hair, porcelain skin, and an entirely too revealing maid outfit. Cassie nearly spat out a mouthful of gyro.

The woman curtseyed to the pair, oversized breasts jiggling with the effort. "Good evening, I presume one of you must be Ms. Mott?"

Cassie's useless lesbian brain struggled to speak. "U-uh, yeah, that's me. Um, are you here for the maid ad?"

The woman bowed low, making Cassie go bright red. "Yes, mistress. I'm eager to please you."

Clearly this woman had the wrong idea. "Um… There must be some sort of mixup. We're looking for a… a professional maid. Not necessarily a… um… performer."

The woman stood up again (jiggle jiggle). "What do you mean? The ad specifically said you were looking for someone *discreet, experienced,* and *personable*." Cassie hid her face in embarrassment. She hadn't considered the innuendo in the words that was all too obvious now.

"Gods, Cassie, I'm trying to run a manor, not a *brothel*," Gwynne chided, a smile on her face.

The woman turned to Gwynne and looked her up and down. "Ooh, now *here's* an interesting subject. I must commend thee on thy glamer, madame."

Gwynne just nodded. "Takes one to know one, I suppose. Though I must ask what one of your kind is doing here."

The woman blushed. "Y-you can tell? I thought I was so careful!"

"I am a *very* powerful wizard."

"Whew, well *you* I'd be happy to serve any time."

"Cassie, I've changed my mind. I'm hiring this woman."

Cassie felt a twinge of something in her gut. Sort of a sadness when she saw this woman fawning over Gwynne. What was it? She had never felt something like that before.

"O-okay…"

The woman bowed low. "Let's walk and talk, shall we?"

The three women exited the city gates and made their way back to where Gwynne had hidden the flying craft. At once the two women dispelled their illusory forms. Gwynne was back to her flamboyant self, but where a buxom blonde once was, a thin young woman now stood. Her lack of curves in this form went almost unnoticed when compared to her other defining features. She was taller even than Gwynne, well over six feet tall, though wiry as a vine. Her skin burned a warm burgundy, and two stubby horns sprouted from her forehead, parting her short black hair. She had a thin swishing tail nearly as long as her body that ended in a barbed point, but most striking of all were her eyes. Black sclera surrounded blood red irises, and slit pupils like lizard eyes bored a hole into Cassie's soul. Lastly, her outfit was something Cassie hadn't even seen in Devón's shop. The woman was wearing a close-cut black shirt with minimal material and short sleeves with a pair of long, faded blue trousers made of a rough fabric and seemed to be cut for utilitarian purposes. This woman gave Tibberwyx a run for zir money in the bizarre department.

The woman bowed to Gwynne and Cassie. "The name is Feckalia Damzael, but you can just call me Feck if you like. As you can clearly see, I'm a demon." Cassie had never seen a demon before, or really heard much about them other than snippets of fairy stories that said that demons were rampaging brutes of pure evil that sought to corrupt mankind. Feckalia seemed obnoxious, but not necessarily evil. She resolved to ask Tibb for some books on demons when she got back.

Gwynne and Cassie introduced themselves and Feckalia kept her eyes on Gwynne the entire time. Cassie found this a bit rude, but didn't say anything. "I'm actually traveling to the human world to study your culture. It's so archaic here! I love it. You just barely discovered airplanes and don't even have telephones yet. I don't have any custodial experience, but I know my way around a broom and mop, so I'd be happy to tag along for a while and help you all out."

The three ladies crammed themselves onto the flying craft's bench, with Feckalia insisting on sitting in the middle, much to Cassie's chagrin. The whole way, she hung onto Gwynne's arm, discussing various matters of compensation and duties. Cassie was grumpy. She had had a nice exciting day in the city, but the listlessness of seeing the university on top of a feeling she could only now place as jealousy left a sour tinge to the otherwise happy day.

* * *

When they returned to the manor, the sun had already set, but lamps were already lit inside the foyer and beyond. Cassie had no clue who lit the lights around here, but decided they must be on some sort of magical timer. Feckalia gasped and gaped at the interior of the manor, playing up the kid-in-a-candy-shop act. She grimaced at the mess, however, which made her and Cassie of like mind.

"I'll get myself situated and then see what I can do," Feckalia said, dancing up the stairs, ducking slightly to avoid hitting her head on the ceiling, and into one of the empty bedrooms. "Oh, this room will do nicely. Can I have this room, Gwynne?"

"It's yours, Feck. Welcome aboard."

Gwynne had never welcomed Cassie aboard.

After getting settled in, Feckalia got to work sweeping the halls. She even hovered up to the ceilings and swept the cobwebs out of the rafters. When Cassie was going to bed, she saw that Feckalia was scrubbing the floors with a sudsy mop. Gwynne passed by and complimented her on the work, and Cassie felt quite forgotten indeed.

And so the days passed. Cassie continued to exercise each morning and receive magical tutelage in the afternoon. After another week of study, she was able to lift the apple with no problems, and had moved from simple kinematic spells to more difficult control spells. Gwynne had set her to master a spell to make a broom animate and sweep by itself, something Gwynne claimed was a staple of magical apprenticeship. Cassie asked why Gwynne couldn't just animate an army of brooms to clean the manor herself, but Gwynne dodged the question. Occasionally, Feckalia would interrupt the lessons to dust the workshop, which was now immaculately tidy and had plenty of space for Cassie to study. For as obnoxious as Cassie found Feckalia to be, she couldn't deny the demon's work ethic.

At dinner one evening, in which Feckalia nearly inhaled an entire ham hock on her own (a feat at which Horatio was gaping in awe), Cassie asked her a question.

"Feck, how is it that you're able to clean so quickly? It would take me ages to get this place as clean as you have in only a week."

Feckalia swallowed a mouthful of pork and belched loudly ("Wha' a woman!" Horatio gawked). "Unlike you feeble humans, I don't need nearly as much sleep. A mere two hours a night is more than sufficient for my needs." Somehow she had managed to turn an innocent answer into an insult. Cassie did not take the bait.

Gwynne seemed to be enjoying the catty relationship between the two women, thinking it little more than healthy rivalry. "Yes, aren't magical races fascinating, Cassie? Why, if I only needed that little sleep…"

"I'd be happy to show you a spell for that," Feckalia simpered. It was like living with Ophelia all over again!

Cassie checked out a book from the library at Tibb's recommendation, all about current understandings of infernal races. It turns out that there were many different races of demons, from the lowly Imps to the high-born Rex, there was an interesting social order that was largely irrelevant in current demonic society, but had long ago determined a bitter and bloody caste system. From diagrams and descriptions in the codex, Cassie determined that Feckalia was likely of the Rex race, known for their imperious personalities and predilection towards magic. They often thought themselves better than other races, as their kind had once ruled the demon world.

Cassie was in the middle of reading this book one night, tucked comfortably in bed with a candle flickering on her nightstand. She often liked to read in bed, but sometimes she would read at her bedroom work desk, looking out on the starry night sky. She had snuck herself some cookies from the House pantry, and was nibbling away happily at a crumbly one that contained dried fruits. A knock on her door jolted her up from her concentration. She shoved the rest of the cookie in her mouth, brushed the crumbs off the comforter, and swallowed her treat as she went to the door. She opened the door to see Feckalia's towering form beyond. Her expression fell.

"Can I help you, Feck?"

"Hey, Cassie, can I come in? I figured we should have a heart-to-heart as girls."

Cassie would rather have jumped out of her bedroom window, but figured talking it out with the woman was the mature thing to do. She motioned for Feck to come inside, and she sat on Cassie's desk chair backwards. She was wearing a gaudy maid outfit that she had conjured for herself with a high skirt and fishnet stockings. Cassie wasn't sure if Feck still thought she was being employed as an exotic dancer or she just dressed like this normally.

Cassie didn't say anything for a minute, so Feckalia spoke up. "I know you have your eye on Gwynne."

Cassie erupted into a coughing fit. "What- *hack* what do you mean?"

"Oh come on, Cass, it's *so* obvious. The only reason Gwynne hasn't noticed, herself, is because she's too caught up in her own little world to think about other people's feelings."

Cassie nodded. That *did* sound like Gwynne. "Okay, suppose I *do* have a thing for her. What of it?"

"Well, I've seen the looks you've been giving me since I got here. I know how I must seem, and I know what humans tend to think of demons, but I just want you to know that I'm not here to get in the way of anything."

This was uncharacteristically kind of Feckalia, and Cassie began to wonder if she had misjudged her.

"That and I think it's just more fun to watch you awkwardly fawn over her." Never mind, the woman was a fiend. "I'm just kidding, hon! You're *so* easy to tease!" This was not the first time someone had said this, but it seemed less warm and more self-serving coming from Feckalia. "So here's what I'm gonna do. Gwynne is all yours, but I'm gonna tease the hell out of you. That alone is worth it. So… truce?"

"Truce." The two women shook hands, leaving Cassie feeling more confused than ever.

7

City of Smoke

Sweating Workers and Dangerous Machinery - Godsdamn Miracle Workers - A Generous Bordering on Philanthropic Tip - Thrown from Cruising Altitude

The *Pale Moon* took its time heading back from Abaddon, and Cassie learned that their next destination was New Ozion, the Zonan capital. She was nervous about being so close to home, but it would be a good opportunity to compare the two nations' capitals.

Cassie had walked into the workshop one day to find Gwynne tinkering with a large compass on one of the desks. It was a hand-sized brass instrument with a black needle against a white backdrop. The compass had no cardinal directions, instead it just had a black diamond shape at the top where North should have been. The needle swung wildly, refusing to land.

"What's that?" Cassie asked.

Gwynne looked up from the desk, clearly having missed Cassie's entrance. "Oh, this? This is what I picked up in Abaddon. It's a device I worked on during my university days. It's *supposed* to point you towards any enchantments that are targeting you, but I can't seem to get the damn thing to focus."

Cassie's curiosity was piqued. "Oh, you have enchantments on you?"

"Lest ye forget, o apprentice mine, I am a renowned criminal. I have a great deal of enemies." Gwynne put the compass away and began the lesson as normal. Cassie spent the rest of the day absentmindedly thinking about what magic could concern Gwynne so much that she'd fly all the way across the continent to get a broken device to track it down. Certainly she wasn't telling, the woman kept as much as she could hidden. Why was she so worried about opening up to Cassie? She already knew that Gwynne was a notorious thief, what else could she possibly be hiding?

Before too long, the city of New Ozion came into view, a dark and murky stain on its valley compared to the shining beacon of Abaddon. Cassie could just barely make out towns dotting the mountainside around and wondered which of them was Bixton. Unlike before, Gwynne would not be accompanying Cassie into town. She said that there were too many watchful eyes in the capital and even her best illusions wouldn't be foolproof. Thus, Cassie went alone. If she didn't have the benefit of the magical bag, she would have been very cross with Gwynne for making her lug all the supplies herself.

In the days hence, Gwynne taught Cassie how to fly the whirligig contraption, though she didn't feel very confident in its operation. It was a gut-wrenching journey down to the ground, but she fortunately didn't crash land so much as just thud to the ground in a copse of trees a mile outside the capital. Gwynne had given her a magical powder to sprinkle over the craft that turned the thing invisible. It was a short walk to the exterior of the city, but Cassie's feet were used to the strain of long walks by now.1

Even before she entered the city gates, the difference between New Ozion and Abaddon was clear. Or not clear, rather. The air was filled with a smog that made it difficult to breathe, and even from a distance everything smelled like smoke. People in the streets of the city wore all black, their clothes patched up multiple times from wear and tear. Many children traveled in packs and harangued passersby for handouts, bare-footed and soot-faced. The streets were damp with what Cassie hoped was just rain water, but the murky fluid pooled in spots where the cobble road sunk in. In addition to the people, carts, and horses, various machines trundled through the streets. Roughly humanoid automatons clunked and clanked as they went about various tasks, belching thick exhaust from pipes on their shoulders.

Cassie hurried her way to the more industrial district, where she saw all-too-familiar sights: factories filled with sweating workers and dangerous machinery. Various workmen crossed her path and gave her eyes, that familiar gaze of being the only brown person in eyesight. Cassie had forgotten how much she loathed this feeling.

The largest factories were emblazoned with names that she knew well, including the Jones & Sons brand. These corporations thrived in the capital, where the impoverished populace thronged, hungry for work such that they might feed themselves and their families. The factory conditions were abysmal here, even worse than her repugnant former occupation in Bixton. She had heard rumors of people losing fingers or even whole limbs from insecure machinery, which most dismissed as an occupational hazard. Meanwhile, people were paid the legal minimum nearly everywhere, and constant inflation meant that even those employed struggled to provide for themselves, much less their families. All this meant that the big corporations just kept getting bigger and wealthier, a single CEO making more each year than one of their employees would make in a lifetime. Defenders of this system claimed that all that money would "trickle down" to the common man as the rich pumped the money back into the economy. However in practice, the wealthy just hoarded all the cash or spent it on hefty bribes to the crown to pass more favorable laws that perpetuated the status quo and silenced the corporations' snuffing out of any potential union activity. Still, what was the common folk to do? It's not like they could afford to move anywhere else.

Cassie tried to put these thoughts out of her mind. They just made her more depressed with the state of the world. She had avoided New Ozion in the past for its ugliness and notoriously high crime rate, and she wasn't chuffed to be here now. As she walked, she made sure to keep an eye on her surroundings and her pockets while avoiding eye contact with the locals.

Eventually, she came to her destination. In the midst of the smoky industrial district was a factory branded with the T.H. Bradley Firearms logo. She entered a front door reserved for customers and looked around the entranceway. It was a small office room, much like Hardden's miserable lair. Cassie rang a smudged bell on the counter and a middle aged woman emerged from a back room, holding a lit cigarette. She was round, with a tired expression, as if the cigarette was the only thing keeping her going. The woman looked Cassie up and down.

"Ya lost, kid?" She had a thick, smoky Ozion city accent, which Cassie had rarely heard.

Cassie bristled at being called a kid, but kept her cool and said her lines as Gwynne had instructed. "I represent his lordship Trevor Zepforth. My lord requires ten new cannons that he might better repel the Abaxian scourge." This was one of Gwynne's many aliases that she used to do business across the world to avoid revealing her true identity.

The woman raised her eyebrows, somehow looking more tired than ever. "Ohhh, Mista' Zepforth, eh? Looks like the man's gots himself some new help, too. Much betta' trained than his last servant, I tell ya."

It took all of Cassie's self control not to unload every spell she knew on the woman, which admittedly wasn't many, and just nodded. "Yes, he hopes the job will be done within the week and delivered to his townhouse as per usual."

The woman took a long drag of her cigarette and gave a coughing laugh. "Oh that man, whaddas he think we are, godsdamn miracle workas?"

Cassie set a large sack of coin on the counter. "My lord offers his condolences on the rush order, and has included a little extra for the hassle."

The woman placed the sack on a nearby trade scale, seeming impressed by the amount. "Very well, then. I'll have the boys get sta'ted on it roight aways. Youse is dismissed."

The woman took the sack back into the offices, and she heard a steam whistle toot twice, making Cassie flinch, remembering the sorrow such a thing had brought her in the past. She couldn't have left that shop sooner, the woman's attitude thoroughly rubbing her the wrong way. She wondered how Gwynne was going to get ten huge cannons onto the airship that never seemed to land, and was afraid it would involve manual labor on her part. She also assumed that Gwynne owned a townhouse here in the city, and wondered what it looked like.

Before she went about the arduous task of grocery shopping for the manor, Cassie made her way to the commercial district of the city and sat down at an out-of-the-way cafe in the backstreets called the Nestled Nook. The cafe had indoor seating, which did wonders for the air quality, and it seemed the establishment was filled with books of all description.

Tibb would love this place, she thought, just admiring the full shelves. *Or then again, maybe not. This place is probably far too busy and dirty for zir. Hell, it's almost too much so for me, and I only grew up a few towns over.*

Cassie ordered tea and sandwiches, glad to have a moment of respite. As she rested her feet at a table, she overheard a patron at the counter having a hushed discussion with the cashier. It seemed the cafe was having financial trouble, and procuring their tea leaves was getting more and more expensive on top of the rent always increasing. Cassie felt genuinely bad for them, and wished there was something she could do to help. She felt guilty traveling the world in a luxurious flying manor with one of the wealthiest people in the world but couldn't do much to improve the life of people like her. Perhaps when she became a powerful wizard, too, she could use her magic to make some real change in the world.

Before long, her food and drink arrived, and she devoured the little sandwiches. They contained roasted ham and a sharp cheese, complemented perfectly by lettuce and tomato and finished off with a creamy mayonnaise. The tea itself was slightly spicy, which Cassie appreciated. She was in her own little culinary world again, delighting in a meal that someone else had prepared.

All of a sudden, she began to feel that itch again. She looked up and all around, but there was nothing amiss in the cafe. She strained her vision, and finally saw something outside in the street. It was that same masked individual standing across the road from the shop amidst a crowd of shoppers. He, for his proportions and stance implied masculinity, just stood there perfectly still gazing at Cassie. She felt wholly uncomfortable and moved to another table where the window was not in view. How could this man have followed her from Abaddon to New Ozion? The journey could only have been made in this amount of time by air or by magic. Cassie felt nervous now and decided the sooner she was back in the manor the better. She finished up her tea, left a generous bordering on philanthropic tip, and was on her way.

Once she was outside, there was nothing to be seen of the masked man, which made her even more nervous. But there was nothing to be done. There was no trace of the man anywhere.

Cassie went about her shopping, picking up pounds and pounds of meat, knowing that Horatio and Feckalia could devour tons of it between the two of them, as well as enough vegetables and other sundries to keep the House until they reached their next destination. She had just enough money to purchase everything she needed, and got it all into the wondrous bag. With this, her business in the city was finished, and she decided to head back early, as she only had a few crowns left in her pocket.

On her way out of the market, she passed the royal palace. The castle was very old, centuries old, they said, and made out of dark stone brickwork. The wall around the palace grounds was many times Cassie's height, and the dark wooden gates were guarded by attentive soldiers, standing with rifles in hand. Cassie didn't want to get too close to them after her encounter in the mountain crater. Who knew if they knew her face or not. There was a large billboard in front of the palace walls with posters that decried the viewer to remember the tragedy of Prince Abneel and to keep the late prince in their prayers always. Various other propaganda covered the billboard. It was the same nonsense that the Peace Officers had plastered up around Bixton to try to instill some fledgling nationalism. It hadn't worked on Cassie before, and was somehow less effective now. She decided to make herself scarce from here.

The quickest route from the market district to the gate where she had entered unfortunately passed through the bad side of town, which was saying a lot by Ozion standards. She passed through a long and winding alley that she was sure would take her right to the front gates. The alley wasn't even paved, muddy ground sticking to Cassie's boots and making her upset with her decision. She turned a corner in the alleyway and found herself at a dead end up against the wall of a building. As she was trying to orient herself, a voice came from behind her.

"Don't move!"

Cassie moved anyway, turning around to face her assailant. Her blood pounded in her ears, but she was confident that the few spells she had learned would be enough to get her away from petty thieves. Behind her were three men of varying heights. They wore ragged clothes and looked positively emaciated. The one in front brandished the most pathetic knife that Cassie had ever seen.

"I mean it! Don't move! P-put yer hands up and gimme yer money!"

Cassie did neither, and cocked her head at the man. He must have been in his mid thirties, with hair starting to recede and a few teeth missing. "I don't understand, sir. How am I supposed to give you my money if my hands are up?"

The man turned to his colleagues and they muttered to each other. The man turned around again, looking pleased with himself. "Give us yer money, *then* put yer hands up!"

"Or what? You're going to tickle me with that rusty bread knife?"

The man looked back at his partners, who shrugged.

"I-I-I-I mean it. I'll cut ye!"

"With that stance?" Cassie gestured to the man's legs, knees knocking and footwork all wrong. The man relaxed his stance, arms akimbo.

"Well, what do ye want from me? I'm bloody starving, I am. Ain't that right, brovvas?"

One of the brothers, tall and muscular, nodded. "Absolutely famished, we are." His voice was a booming baritone.

The other brother, short and stout, corroborated with a nod and a grunt.

"Haven't you all got jobs? What's with all this?"

The man in front, clearly the middle brother, looked down. "W-we was engineers at the royal mechanics. Me brovvers an' I was the best the crown 'ad ever seen. But then Lecton Corp. came in and offered our bosses a better price fer th' same labor. Next thing ye know, me an' th' boys is out on the streets, we is. We've only got the one skill, an' nobody in this city'd hire us when they can just outsource the labor to bloomin' Lecton. We was starving!" The other men nodded, the tall brother starting to tear up a bit. "Please take pity on us, lass. We never meant ye no 'arm, 'onest. We jus' needed the coin fer our dinner."

Cassie narrowed her eyes at the group. She had heard sob stories before.

"And this is true? Every word of it?"

"Every word, aye! Jimmy, show 'er yer device. Th' one ye've been workin' on all 'is time."

Jimmy, the tall brother, wiped his eyes and pulled a mass of metal and clockwork from his ragged jacket pocket. He held it out in his hand and pressed a button on top. With a whirring and a clicking, the lump flew to life, taking the form of a small bird. It hopped around Jimmy's palm and fluttered a bit in the air before the servos seized up and the thing fell back into the man's palm. "I's not finished yet, miss." He said, sheepishly.

Cassie thought for a minute. She had an idea that would benefit everyone, but she'd have to be careful.

"Have any of you lot had experience with airship engineering?"

The three men raised their hands like schoolboys.

"Very well. I might, and that's a generous *might*, be able to offer you all work as mechanics aboard one of the best airships in the world."

The talkative man dropped to his knees and began bawling openly. "Oh praise ye, miss. We'll do anything fer a living wage and roof over our heads, won't we, lads?"

Cassie knelt down to meet the man's eye level. "But I must warn you. My master can tell when people are lying, and if you are found to be blackguards or scoundrels, you will be thrown from cruising altitude, have I made myself clear?" The men gulped in unison, even the short one who had yet to speak. They all nodded in turn.

Cassie felt very much like Gwynne ordering these men around. It felt good, almost, to be on the other side of executive orders for once. Now that she had a proper look at these men, they all looked like they might once have been respectable, but had been down on their luck for a while. She made them swear an oath that they were telling the truth and they would be on their best behavior. She ended up learning their names as well. They spoke in a highland accent, not anywhere near as thick as Horatio, but there was a definite similarity there, even if the dialect was technically different.

"The tall bloke is Jimmy, as ye know," the talkative man said. "I'm Bimmy, and this 'ere is li'le Havershank." He gestured to the short man, who only nodded. "Havershank can't talk on accoun' o' 'im suffered a proper bad accident in th' fact'ry an' his tongue is all screwed up-like. An' togevva we're the Ranklin Brothers, at yer service, miss." The men bowed in unison, removing ratty hats in salute.

Cassie introduced herself and led the men out of the city gates and to the hiding place for her flying machine. As she dismissed the invisibility, the men hooted and hollered at the magic, clearly enjoying themselves. The ride back up to the ship was a long and awkward one, with Havershank sitting on Jimmy's lap the whole way, and Cassie trying to touch the filthy and stinking men as little as possible in the cramped seats.

Finally, they arrived in the spartan hangar of the *Pale Moon* to find Horatio working on some contraption. He looked up with abject horror on his face as Cassie flew into the hangar and deposited three dirty humans onto the ship.

"Oh, no no no, lass. Whaddaya think yer doin' bringin' this lot onta me ship? An' wot would th' mistress say?"

Bimmy Ranklin bowed low to the short trasgo. "A pleasure t' be makin' yer acquaintance, t'be sure. Me name is Bimmy Ranklin, an' these are me most esteemed brethren, Jimmy and Havershank."

Cassie smirked. "You should be happy, Horatio, I've brought you some apprentices."

Horatio looked like Cassie had just told him she was pregnant and he was the father, despite the physical and logistical impossibilities preventing such an occurrence.

"I-I don' want no apprentices, lass. I can 'andle the ol' gal jus' fine on me own!"

Something clanked and spluttered from within the mechanical workings of the ship. Before Horatio could say or do anything, Jimmy spoke up.

"Soun's like a busted radial valve, guv'nor. I recommend a replacement, but not before shuttin' off the main pressure flow. From th' sound ov it, could do wi' a spot o' oil as well."

Horatio's jaw hung open, but a twinkle flashed across his eyes. Cassie could tell that he had found his people and was starting to get excited. "I'll... jus' go check in wit' th' mistress real quick. If ye lot can fix up that valve, ye've got me stamp o' approval."

Gwynne seemed unconcerned with the presence of three new members aboard the ship, saying only, "Looks like our little family just keeps growing, huh, Cassie?" Cassie blushed at 'our little family', but felt like she had done the right thing.

Horatio spent most of the evening showing the Ranklins the lay of the ship, finally coming to dinner with a big grin on his face. "Ohh, they're fantastic, they are. Wherever'd ye find 'em, Cass?"

"Well... they tried to mug me."

Feckalia coughed and spit out a bit of the wine she was drinking. "They tried to shank you and you *hired* them?"

This was pure teasing from Feck, and Cassie pouted. "They weren't that bad, they were just down on their luck. The damn empire threw them out of their jobs when a cheap company came around and replaced them. They didn't have anywhere to go and they were starving. I figured Horatio needed assistance, and I thought I had a chance to help everyone."

Feckalia rolled her eyes. "Well, just be careful that naivete doesn't turn around on you. If you keep picking up stray dogs, one of them is sure to bite you."

Cassie considered herself a better judge of character than that, and at any rate, the three brothers had washed up, been given proper clothing that made Cassie wonder from whence such garments came, and now had been given a hot meal. The brothers cried into their food, taking breaks from eating only to praise Gwynne and Cassie. The House would certainly be a lot more lively from here on out.

8

The Homefront

**A Madame Marqz's in Bixton - Gods Bless His Majesty - Always
Said that Lot Weren't Right - A Volcano of Emotion**

True to her estimation, the following days were much more active, giving the House a proper community feeling. The Ranklin Brothers spent most of their time belowdecks tuning the *Moon*'s inner workings under the careful instruction of Horatio. When they graced the upper floors with their presences, they were always polite, appreciative, and gentlemanly. The three had cleaned up well. With a proper shave, haircut, and outfit, one would scarce believe that they had only recently been out on the streets. Jimmy blushed whenever he saw Cassie, and she was afraid the man might have a crush on her. She'd hate to break his heart with the news that she just wasn't into men.

Cassie had been making great strides in her fitness routine and could now run her daily mile in only ten minutes, which was practically bordering on physical aptitude. She had also built up some muscle mass from her strength training, her arms no longer the wimpy noodles they had once been. She was by no means chiseled, but she admired her muscle definition in the mirror at bath times. During her lessons, Cassie had convinced Gwynne to begin teaching her teleportation magic.

"Normally this would be a more advanced topic, but I believe you have some aptitude for the subject, and also I think it might come in handy for you. But don't get complacent because I said you had some modicum of proficiency. Teleportation can be extremely dangerous and physically demanding. Never attempt to teleport more than one hundred yards for now, and never somewhere that you cannot physically see. Teleportation takes roughly twice the amount of energy of running to the same destination at a full sprint, so keep that in mind. Additionally, if you teleport somewhere where there is solid matter and you do not include a contingency clause, you could become fused with that object. I've heard the horror stories, and I can promise you it is every bit as gruesome as it sounds."

Gwynne taught her the incantation for teleportation, as well as the aforementioned contingency clause for an occupied destination. This spell was one of the longer ones that Cassie had heard thus far, and there were many Elder words she did not recognize. After a few attempts, she was able to recite the spell, causing her form to jolt across the workshop with a familiar crack, stopping just shy of the wall. This must have been the magic she had accidentally performed back in Bixton when running from those dogs.

"Good work! You're a natural, Cassie. Keep at it for a few years and you might almost be as good as me."

Cassie rolled her eyes at this uniquely-Gwynne back-handed compliment. She asked a question that had been on her mind for a while. "Gwynne, how is it that one is able to use spells on a whim, like how you conjured fire that one time? You did it without incantation."

"Ah, good question, Cassie. See, all spells require instruction for how to execute, but one thing I haven't taught you yet is that those incantations can be recited ahead of time, left partially completed in the caster's mind. That way, all you have to do is define the variables and execute the spell when you wish to cast it proper. It is very useful, but is dependent on one's short-term memory. If you don't finish the spells before you sleep or go unconscious, the preparation is lost. Still, it can be useful to get in the habit of preparing general-use spells in memory each morning, just in case."

Cassie decided that she would start preparing a short-range teleportation spell each morning, just in case. If nothing else, she could use it to get to the bath quicker after dinner. She had little time to rest after her foray into New Ozion, however. Within a few days, the *Pale Moon* flew over a small town in the mountains northwest of the capital. Gwynne instructed her to head down to the ground to investigate a specific building.

"It's one of my magic shops that seems to have been offline for a while now. I'd like you to see if you can figure out what's wrong with it and report back."

"What exactly do you mean 'offline'? How do you manage all these magic shops?"

Gwynne pointed to a door in the wall of the workshop that Cassie had never touched. She was pretty sure it was locked anyway. "See that door? I've magically linked it to a number of doors around the continent. That means when I open it, I can choose to have it connect to any linked door. I use that as the front door for a number of magic shops that I run. For example, it's linked to a townhouse in New Ozion belonging to one Trevor Zepforth, Wizard Extraordinaire."

Cassie's mind reeled. "So how come we have to fly everywhere for transportation, then? Can't we just use your magical door?"

Gwynne shook her head. "I'm trying to lay low. The Owl is planning his next big heist, so I don't want to attract undue attention by blasting a powerful magical signature right in the middle of the king's capital."

That would explain the blueprints and plans strewn about Gwynne's room. The thought of grand larceny being committed to someone so close to her made Cassie nervous, so she decided to change the subject. "How many of these shops do you run? Just how many people do you pretend to be?"

"Well, let's see. My most profitable chain of shops are the Circe Jones line of potioncraft. I also run a few smaller shops under the name of Madame Marqz. For those I pretend to be an old mystic who tells fortunes and sells spells. It's quite good fun, though I admit I haven't had much time to engage in my businesses of late due to the Owl's activity."

"Wait a minute, that name sounds familiar. There used to be a Madame Marqz's in Bixton when I was a kid."

"Was there? I don't remember all of my locations over the years."

"But that couldn't have been yours, it closed when I was still a kid."

"How old were you?"

"Hmm, I must've been around eight. I remember I used to just sit outside the shop after school, too nervous to go inside. But one day I went by and it was just gone."

Gwynne thought about this. "So if you were eight, I would have been twelve…" She was quiet for a second, before her face resolved into a sly grin. "Yep, that was me."

"At *twelve*?"

"Yes, I was pretty terrible at magic back then, but in those days it didn't matter. People were enchanted by the *idea* of magic alone. I made a killing before my father made me shut it down."

"Got any more life-altering bombshells for me?"

"Not right now, Cass. Perhaps when you get back from your mission I'll fill you in on the plan for my heist."

* * *

With that, Cassie flew down to the small town of Ultan. It looked just like Bixton, but without the defining waterways to give it any sort of character. Walking through its quiet, cobbled streets, she had an uncanny feeling of being at home in an unfamiliar place. People here gave her the gaze that one might give to a potential foreigner, but didn't get in her way. She was used to such looks, even from back in her hometown, and ignored them with ease. She supposed that her new garish outfit did make her look rather fantastical and flamboyant, but gods forbid someone mistake her to be heterosexual.

Ultan seemed to be somewhat poorer than Bixton. While the town hall and corporate factory buildings were as shiny and new as ever, the streets were potholed and rough, and Cassie was saddened by how many abandoned shops she passed in the main boulevard. Nearly all had pitiable handwritten "Out of Business" signs in their front windows. It wasn't long until she saw the cause of the economic collapse, however. In the town center was a giant department store with a luminescent sign reading 'Joy Mart'.

Joy Mart was a chain of corporate stores that were sweeping Zona, popping up almost overnight in small towns the kingdom over. Cassie had heard rumors that Bixton was soon to receive their own Joy Mart as well, but nothing had yet to materialize as of her recent departure. The chain was infamous for their shockingly low prices, far lower than any nearby businesses could hope to match. Because of this, the arrival of a Joy Mart often meant the death of the local economy in favor of cheaply-made and cheaply-sold sweatshop goods from many different departments all in one place. Cassie had also heard that their employees got paid a pittance, which didn't surprise her a bit. The founder of Joy Mart, one Hector Joilen, was a fabulously wealthy entrepreneur who was famous for extravagant parties at his lavish mansion outside of New Ozion. The whole concept made Cassie sick, so she gave the superstore a wide berth.

Eventually, Cassie found her way to a worn building with faded red paint. A sign hung loose in its fittings that read 'Circe Jones Spells and Potions'. Most notable of all, however, was the broken front door. A sign was plastered to the wall beside it, reading:

CONDEMNED BY ORDER OF HIS MAJESTY

For aiding and abetting known criminal 'Owl of the Pale Moon', this establishment has been condemned and all persons found within are subject to immediate arrest. This edict is final. Gods bless His Majesty.

Well it was obvious why the spell wasn't working. The building was run down, and the interior was thoroughly ransacked, though there was little inside save for a few barren desks and papers. The sight scared Cassie, and she didn't want to linger overlong in this shell of a building, lest she be identified as an accomplice.

A man turned to her as he walked by and noticed her attention on the house. "You from out of town, miss? Magic shops like this all over are being shut down by the crown, they say. A shame, but apparently they're connected to that wicked man Owl. I used to get a cream for my joints from this very shop, you know. And Ms. Marckle over on 5th street was always coming 'round to get powder to turn her hair funny colors."

"You don't say. So how do they know if a shop is affiliated with Owl?"

"Nobody knows. But you'd best run along before the soldiers catch you gawking. They might take you in for questioning."

"Thanks, but I'll be fine, sir."

The man shrugged and continued on his way. "Suit yourself."

Cassie still wanted to examine every inch of the building for some sign of who Gwynne was in the past. She didn't know why she thought she would find something here, but nothing turned up. The whole place was either picked clean or completely bare to begin with. As she was picking through the rubble, a rough hand grabbed her shoulder and jerked her upright. Cassie came face-to-face with a royal soldier.

"What do you think you're doing? Can't you see this building is condemned?" The soldier barked in her face. She could see that there were three other soldiers near the entrance, holding rifles and glaring at her. Cassie was afraid she recognized this man, his soldier's saber bringing back memories of that day in the crater near Bixton. She prayed he didn't recognize her.

"Wait a minute, you're that 'baxer that runs with Owl. You're coming with us."

"N-no, wait! You've got the wrong person!"

It was no use. The man thrust Cassie out into the street by her lapel and she staggered to her hands and knees on the stones. The three other soldiers just stepped back and pointed their rifles at her. The captain emerged from the building and put his boot down on Cassie's back, forcing her prone and causing her chin to crack against the stone.

"You will tell us where Owl is and what he is planning next."

Cassie spluttered, her lip cracked and bleeding. "I'm telling you, I don't know anything. You've got the wrong girl!"

One of the soldiers struck the side of her head with the butt of their rifle. Her vision swam for a moment and she thought she might pass out.

"Fool, don't knock her out yet, we still need information," the captain hissed at his man. Instead, he drew his saber and pressed the point lightly into Cassie's back. She could feel its deadly tip prickle her skin and her head started pounding with fear. Discovering that she was a Changer meant that she had accepted the possibility of one day dying under the heel of a Peace Officer or soldier, but it didn't make the reality any easier.

"Now, dog, you will tell me everything I want to know about Owl. If you do, I will grant you a swift death. If you resist, I will make your passing slow and painful."

Cassie spat blood onto the road, trying and failing to hit one of the soldier's boots. "I already told you, I don't know anything. I can't help you pigs."

Cassie felt a cold pain as the captain's saber was thrust through her shoulder. She screamed at the top of her lungs, earning her a kick in the ribs from one of the lackeys. Cassie focused her mind as hard as she possibly could. She couldn't afford to pass out. She only needed focus…

She muttered a few words in the Elder Tongue.

"Stop that, this instant!" the captain yelled. "Knock her out, you fools. She's using magic!"

But it was too late. Cassie shouted the execution phrase to her memorized spell and a now comforting crack split the afternoon air. Next thing she knew, she was lying face down in an alleyway. She wasn't sure exactly where she was or how far she had gone, but she had broken line of sight from the soldiers at least.

She tried to contain her coughing and whispered to herself. "Sorry, Gwynne. I broke one of your teleportation rules. But it really was an emergency." She struggled to sit up and examined herself. The stab wound had avoided any organs, but had pierced straight through her left deltoid. She wouldn't be using that arm for anything substantial anytime soon. It was bleeding quite profusely, though, and she had little choice but to rip up her skirt and tie swaths of cloth around the puncture. The blow to her head would likely concuss and her ribs ached from the kick, but those would heal on their own. Right now she had to evade the soldiers and get out of town. Her head swam from the trauma but she resolved not to rest as she knew well enough that if one slept too soon after a concussion they would likely not wake.

In the distance, she could hear shouting. "…can't have gone far! Split up and find the dog!" Hurried bootsteps tramped past Cassie's alleyway from somewhere out of sight. Once they faded out of earshot, Cassie lumbered to her feet, clutching her wounded shoulder, and hobbled low out onto the main avenue. On top of the stress of the trauma, she was also drained from the spell. Gwynne was right, teleportation really took a lot out of you. Still, her life was on the line, so she summoned a second wind and ran as fast as she could. As she ran, she took stock of her options. She had only memorized the one spell, and had not brought any scrolls to town, so casting something else was out of the question. As she turned a corner onto the main street, she felt in her pockets, hoping for something that might save her. She eventually grasped at a paper packet that she had completely forgotten about in a back pocket. It was the invisibility powder that Gwynne had given her to hide the landing craft. Cassie could have cried from joy. She wasn't sure if it worked on living beings, but what had she to lose? She tipped the contents of the packet over her head and crossed her fingers. She began to feel a tingle start at the crown of her head and spread down her body. When she looked down, her limbs were swirling and swaying into nothingness before her eyes. She was invisible!

Relaxing her caution a bit, she staggered towards the road via which she had entered Ultan. At the exit, a number of Peace Officers were already stationed. They had erected crude barricades and the officers were leaning against them nonchalantly. Word must have traveled fast. Fortunately, they could not see her, so she was able to creep by. As she passed, she overheard their chatter.

"So who is this dog we gotta catch?"

"I dunno, some 'baxer that apparently works for Owl. The crown is really intent on catching this one."

"Do we have an ID on the bitch?"

"Yes, apparently goes by Cassandra Mott, from over in Bixton. Kid of the defense minister's secretary, I hear. The mom gave 'em up immediately. How sad is that?"

The officers laughed.

"Oh, and get this, they're a filthy Changer, to boot."

The officers wrinkled their noses in disgust. "Always said that lot weren't right."

"I heard one of our boys in Plintford beat up one of those nasty Changers just 'cuz they looked at 'im funny. Don't worry, we shushed it up proper."

Cassie wasn't sure if it was the blatant bigotry or the head trauma, but she wanted to vomit listening to these pigs talk about her like some beast. As she crept by, she tripped the one who seemed to be their leader. He fell face first onto the pavement, and Cassie distinctly heard his nose crack. The other officers rushed to help the man, but Cassie was long gone at that point. She ran up the dirt path out of town, feeling tears streaming down her face.

Her mother had always told her that the Peace Officers thought of Abaxians as second class citizens and went looking for excuses to accost them. But somewhere deep within Cassie's naive heart she had thought that *surely* they couldn't be *all* bad. But no, even the ones that didn't actively seek to commit hate crimes covered up for those that did. Cassie swore many vengeances that day.

It was a long trek to where the landing craft was stashed. Cassie was sure she left bloodstains behind on the particularly thick heather clumps as she dismissed the invisibility spells. She almost passed out trying to lug the thing out with one arm and get it started, but she managed to make it back to the *Pale Moon* a few hours later, almost crashing the landing craft into the hangar before collapsing onto the floor.

Horatio rushed over to help her. "Lass? Lass, are ye alright?"

Cassie felt groggy and couldn't give a coherent answer. The shock of the day was catching up to her.

"Ohhh, bless, this isnae good." The last thing Cassie remembered was Horatio dragging her across the hangar with his short arms. "Lads, get ye out 'ere! Th' young miss is in a right spot o' trouble!"

* * *

Cassie's mind floated in and out of consciousness. She thought she saw visions of Gwynne flash across her mind, but everything was spinning and undefined. She remembered thinking how nice it would be for Gwynne to hold her and fuss over her wounds. While she slept, she dreamt of flying. She soared through the sky above who knows where, just her arms and her magic keeping her aloft. Gwynne glided up next to her and the two embraced. Gwynne seemed warm and soft in this dream and Cassie went to kiss her. To her horror, Gwynne had transformed into her mother.

"See, Cassie? I always said you'd never be able to take care of yourself properly."

Cassie woke up shouting. She was in her bed in the manor, tight bandages wrapped around her wounded shoulder and a modest slip around her midsection. She looked around at her empty room before the pain of her wound bubbled to the surface. She laid back down and nursed the damaged muscles, gently feeling where the blade had pierced her. The pain lessened a bit, but still persisted. She tried not to focus on it.

A few minutes went by, and Cassie's door opened. In walked Gwynne, with the rest of the House's occupants looking in through the doorway. "Alright, you nosy louts, back to work. Give the poor girl some privacy!"

Feckalia, Horatio, and the Ranklin Brothers all slunk away, but not before giving their wishes of good health to Cassie. Gwynne shut the door once they were gone and she came over and sat on the foot of the bed. Cassie remembered the dream she had just experienced and tried not to blush. Gwynne put her hand on Cassie's ankle above the sheets, which made keeping her composure even more difficult.

"Cassie, please, tell me what happened. Is my shop okay?"

All the warmth and affection Cassie felt disappeared in an instant. She clenched her teeth and her breath caught in her throat. A volcano of emotion began to boil up from within Cassie, coming to a fever pitch before erupting. She couldn't stop herself from lashing out at this tactless comment.

"Your shop? Your bloody shop? Is that all you care about? Your shop is destroyed, Gwynne. The army found out that it belonged to Owl and ransacked it. There, you happy?"

Gwynne ignored Cassie's outburst and stroked her chin. "Hmm, must be my father's doing. I might need to create some new aliases."

"Never mind that I'm dying over here!" This was an exaggeration, but Cassie was too annoyed to care. "I was nearly killed by a pack of rabid soldiers just on the *off chance* I had information about you. Don't you care?"

"Cassie, I…"

"You sent me into this dangerous town knowing that I might be hurt or killed. And when I come back bloodied and on the verge of death, all you can ask me about is your stupid shop?"

Cassie was crying at this point. Gwynne looked flabbergasted at her words, seemingly not understanding.

"You're so selfish, Gwynne! All you care about is your own schemes and your own squabbles. I could have died and you don't even care."

Her master looked sheepish now. She got up from the bed and left the room without a further word. Horatio was still standing out in the hallway, shaking his head.

"Absoluteleh bloody clueless, th' both o' ye." The trasgo did not explain what he meant and walked off, leaving Cassie behind in her tears of hurt and self-pity.

III

Black Eagle Keep

9

Making Amends

Slithering Around on Your Belly - A Temper Like a Dragon - A Grumble of Settling Gravel - We're After a Spell

Cassie remained alone in that quiet and empty room for a matter of days, waiting for her shoulder to heal. The wound was quite clean, but it still required her muscle to repair itself. Cassie worried that it might leave a scar until she realized that a scar would probably be pretty badass and she fantasized strutting about some small town in her lavish outfits and showing off her scars to the local maidens. She almost thought *like Gwynne*, but stopped herself. She was still mad at her and refused to speak to, speak about, or think about the woman until she received an apology. Fortunately for her temper, Gwynne did not come by at all during that time. Feckalia brought Cassie her meals at midday and in the evening, but Cassie mostly only picked at the food on her plate, listless and depressed. Feck also helped tidy up Cassie's room from the used bandages and other refuse that had accrued during Cassie's infirmity.

Feckalia would float weightlessly around the room and wave at piles of dirty laundry, causing them to rise into the air and float themselves out to the laundry chute. Cassie watched the maid's use of magic with great curiosity. "I've been meaning to ask, Feck, but what kind of mage are you?"

"I'm not," the demon replied. Cassie waited for her to elaborate, but she kept right on with the cleaning.

"Okay, what do you mean, then? You're obviously quite proficient in magic."

Feckalia sighed and relaxed her arms. A feather duster that she was telekinetically animating fell to the desk. "Unlike feeble humans and other races of this world, I need not beseech the universe to rearrange itself in my favor. Demons, such as myself, are what humans refer to as 'magical creatures'. We are born with the ability to manipulate aetheric fields to make our magic work. Only we don't call it 'magic' because it isn't particularly special or remarkable. It'd be like if a snake asked you what kind of stilts you wear to walk upright instead of slithering around on your belly."

Cassie pondered this metaphor for a while. She knew that demons, fey, dragons, and the like had innate magical abilities but she didn't realize just how natural it must seem to them and how primitive humans must seem by comparison. It was a chilling thought to consider oneself so low on the arcane food chain.

Eventually, the floor and desk were clean, and Feckalia brought up another subject as she straightened the bedsheets and collected Cassie's dirty dishes. "You really shouldn't be so hard on Gwynne, you know. I know she didn't mean anything by what she said."

Cassie's eyes narrowed. "It doesn't matter. Now I know that she thinks of me as no more than a mere servant."

"You *are* her apprentice, correct?"

"Well yes, on an official level, but I always thought we were friends, too."

Feckalia shook her head. "A rapport does not a friendship make, human. You should take better measures to establish expectations in your relationships."

"Look, Feck, if I wanted a rundown on everything I'm doing wrong, I'd just ask my mother." Cassie immediately felt bad about snapping at Feck, who was just trying to help in her own way. "Sorry, I'm just… I'm just frustrated. I feel like I don't matter around here."

Feckalia just shrugged, unphased. "I get it. Feelings of community and belonging are important for humans, especially adults of your age." Her clinical tone made Cassie feel like she was being looked down on, but at this point she had realized that this was just the way Feck was. "I don't know Gwynne all that well, but I *do* know that she's headstrong enough that if she didn't like you or value your presence, she wouldn't keep you around."

Cassie didn't say anything. She just stared at her hands as she fiddled with the pages of a book she was reading on her bed. She knew Feck was right, but it didn't make her feel any better at the moment.

"Anyway, Cass, food for thought. I'll be back later with dinner. Speaking of food, I hear tonight Horatio's making his interpretation of beef stroganoff. I can't tell if I'm excited or mortified to find out what he thinks that is." Feckalia shook her head as she left the room. "Hells below, we really need a proper cook."

Cassie was left alone and decided she did not feel like entertaining the company of her thoughts at this present moment. She opened the book on her lap again and began reading. Gwynne had obviously not given her any training since she had returned but that did not stop her from engaging in a bit of independent study. She had convinced Jimmy Ranklin, who visited her every day, to take a note to Tibberwyx to request books about specific magical topics. She felt bad taking advantage of the man's feelings but there wasn't much choice in the first few days as she hadn't the energy to leave the bed save for laborious treks to the lavatory.

This particular book was a study of forms of arcane instruction, presenting to the reader ways that they might trim the fat of their incantations and thus produce more elegant spells and save casting time and complexity. Cassie's mind sponged up these books, and she even allowed herself to practice spells that she already knew with more precise diction and obscure-but-efficient syntax.

One night, as Cassie was studying, she heard a thud and muffled swearing from somewhere above her. She thought about going to see what the matter was, but reconsidered when she heard Gwynne stomping through the hall outside of the closed bedroom rattling off every vile word she knew.

"Horatio!" she shouted from entirely too close by.

A minute later, the head engineer trudged up the stairs on his short legs, huffing and puffing. "Wot ye want, woman? Cannae ye see I'm busy runnin' yer ship?"

The conversation muffled through the door at this point. Cassie could only catch bits of what was said.

"How am I supposed to…… don't have enough information!"

"Well whaddaye want me t' do…… it yerself!"

"That's too dangerous! You know they're looking for me…… about *instead* if I were to…"

"Ye cannae be serious, miss! Jus' think o' how ye already…"

"Fine. *Fine*! I'll…… don't worry about it!"

The two parted then, each grumbling off to separate parts of the House. A snag must have presented itself in Gwynne's heist planning, but Cassie could not imagine what, and refused to let her curiosity venture down that path.

* * *

Cassie was astonished with the rate at which her wound healed.

Within a week, she was able to get back out of bed to attend to her exercise (albeit without afternoon lessons), and after two weeks she could, very gingerly, use her left arm without it erupting into pain. It was more of a gurgle of pain. This was no doubt due to a special powder that arrived each morning in an inconspicuous paper envelope amidst Cassie's brunch and had instructions written to apply lightly to the exterior of the wound. This was probably Gwynne's attempt at an apology, but Cassie would accept nothing less than the full verbal deal.

Cassie occupied her afternoons with further study by working through some spells that Gwynne had left incomplete in the workshop as extra practice for her weeks ago. Each was a scroll of increasing incompleteness where lines to entire blocks of instruction needed to be filled in by the reader in order for the spell to properly function. For someone who regularly had depressive meltdowns about homework as a child, Cassie took to these problems with admirable aplomb. Many of them required multiple iterations to produce anything more than a puff of smoke or a jolt of force that flung unattended objects around the room. The first spell she completed allowed the caster to conjure a bouquet of flowers, wild and clashing, which disappeared into a puff of loose petals minutes later. After that, she completed a spell for conjuring fire, though her current stamina would only allow her to produce enough thermal energy to light a candle before she had to take a break.

While she was tackling the next problem, who should walk into the workshop but Horatio. The trasgo man was covered in smudges of grease and his mop of brown hair was tied back into a minuscule ponytail between his long green ears. Cassie had not seen him in the workshop before, and rarely saw him above decks aside from meal times. Clearly he was here to speak with her.

"G'day t' ye, lass. Good t' see ye oop an' aboot." Watching the otherwise blunt man fumble his way through small talk made Cassie smile.

"What can I do ya for, Horatio?"

He wrung his hands, clearly feeling awkward. "Well, I jus' wanted t' apologize on accoun' o' the Mistress. I kno' it's no' a proper apology an' all, but I've known 'er the longest o' anyone 'ere, and she's… well she's been alone fer a long time, Cass. Pretty much 'er whole life, I reckon, up until ye came along. Not countin' me, of course, I'm no' really one fer conversation, ye ken."

Cassie set down her pen and smiled at him. "I appreciate the thought, Horatio, but I'm really just looking for Gwynne to swallow her pride and apologize to me proper."

Horatio sighed. "I kno', I'm no' askin' ye to forgive 'er proper-like, jus' try to understand where she's comin' from. Ye don' kno' th' 'alf o' 'er life, s'jus' try t'go easy on 'er 's'all."

If Cassie wasn't so used to Horatio's accent, she would have found that last sentence nigh unintelligible. The highland accent had grown on her, though, and she could understand the vernacular with ease at this point.

"I'm not responsible for her emotional intelligence, but I can at least be the mature one in this situation and talk to her, does that work?"

"Aye, lass, ye havnae seen 'ow she gets when she gets upset. To'ally isolatin' and with a temper like a dragon."

"Does she get like this often?"

"Only when she gets rejected by a maiden."

"Gods, okay. Let's go have an intervention."

* * *

Horatio accompanied Cassie up to the third floor to the master bedroom. The door was closed and Cassie knocked. "Gwynne, are you in there? We need to talk."

There was no response. A strange scent wafted from under the door, acrid and smoky.

"Okay, I'm coming in." Cassie turned the handle, expecting the door to be locked, but it swiveled obediently in her grasp and creaked open. At least, it creaked partly open. A pile of pure refuse blocked the door halfway. The acrid smell billowed out in wispy clouds. Something was burning, possibly some kind of incense. It made Cassie's eyes water, but she pushed herself through the half-open door anyway into Gwynne's room.

She had previously seen glimpses of the room, but being inside it was a completely different experience. It was like the whole room was screaming at her from the clutter, tacky design, and burning smell. Some sort of dangling set of glass baubles clinked softly from above Cassie's head, and a device on a shelf beside her whirred and spun with magical energy. She saw the source of the smoke on a far table: an incense burner filled with what must have been six or seven different sticks of incense, their scents clashing and counteracting until all that was left was the smell of smoke. On a large table along the right wall lay rolls of large parchment. One was weighed down across the center of the table and seemed to be a blueprint of sorts labeled "Black Eagle Keep - 1F" depicting a large building with many rooms.

Most curious of all, there appeared to be a stone statue laying face-down on the bed in the room's center. Belial the cat sat curled up atop the statue's butt and squinted at Cassie and Horatio as they looked on. The cat's tail flicked up and down, warning the two bipeds not to come any closer. Upon inspection, the statue looked familiar, and Cassie assumed this must be Gwynne.

"Is she okay? What's wrong with her?"

Horatio just rolled his eyes. "She's jus' bein' dramatic. Turns 'erself t'stone when she's upset. She can turn back whene'er she likes."

"Can she hear us?"

He shrugged.

Cassie figured she should at least try to address the petrified woman, elsewise the conversation would never begin. "Gwynne, are you in there? We need to talk."

No response.

"Gwynne, hello?"

Silence.

"Okay, well then I guess you won't mind if I put out this wretched incense so a girl can breathe in here."

There was a window above the large table, and Cassie pushed it open. Air rushed in, sweeping out the milky white smoke and clearing the air. She walked over to the incense burner and blew out the smoldering sticks. The air was finally breathable again and Cassie took a deep breath.

"There we go, much better. We really should let Miss Feck in here to tidy up. Has anyone ever told you your room is a pigsty? Because it is."

A grumble of settling gravel came from somewhere beneath the statue.

"Oh, finally a response, eh? Has the mistress of House Brandwyck deigned to grace us with her presence?"

With a flash of light, the stone statue on the bed was replaced with the familiar form of Gwynne Brandwyck, still face-down. At least de-petrification was progress. Cassie pulled up a chair near the bed, kicking over a pile of unidentifiable garbage in her way.

Cassie decided to swallow her pride and just get things over with. "Gwynne, I'm sorry I snapped at you. I was really scared, and I guess I expected you to comfort me, but I apologize for overstepping your boundaries. I know I shouldn't have expected that of you, since we're not really that close."

Gwynne rose to a sitting position, facing away from Cassie. Belial waited until the absolute last moment to stir and climbed into Gwynne's lap instead. She scratched him behind the ears and he gave a faint purr, leaning into the touch. Gwynne's voice was hoarse and scratchy from the autopetrification spell as she spoke to Cassie for the first time in days.

"I… I'm not very good with emotions. Myself or others'. When other people are hurt or upset, I find it difficult to relate to them and feel empathy. My instinct is to just avoid them for my own protection. When I feel hurt, I can't help but recoil and push everyone else away. I'm… sorry… that I did not respond appropriately to your pain, Cassie. I apologize that I gave the impression that you are not a valued member of the House. I will… try to be more sensitive in the future."

"I've never 'eard 'er apologize to any'ne 'efore," Horatio whispered. Cassie saw out of the corner of her eye that his eyebrows were raised in surprise as he leaned against the doorframe. Clearly this was the most mature he had ever seen Gwynne.

Cassie responded. "It's alright, Gwynne. Let's just put this behind us, okay?" She thought back to the advice that Feckalia had given her. "And if possible, I'd like for us to be friends."

Gwynne looked down at her cat and petted him down his spine. He arched his back out and stuck up his butt and she patted it. "It's been a long time since I had anyone I could call a friend, and the last time didn't end well. I hope you understand that it's hard for me to open up. However, I would very much like to be your friend, Cassie, just please be patient with me."

Cassie gave Gwynne a hug, something Gwynne clearly had not been expecting because she squeaked slightly as Cassie touched her. Gwynne patted Cassie's back awkwardly, and refused to meet her eye when she pulled away.

"Sorry, was that too much?"

"No, you're fine. I just… wasn't expecting that."

"Well that's what friends do when they make up. You gotta hug it out."

"Ye never been hugged 'efore, lass?" Horatio chuckled.

"Not since my mother was alive, no." This cast the room into an awkward silence for a beat before Gwynne changed the subject. "At any rate, while you're here, Cassie, I've got a job for you."

Cassie sighed. It seemed that in the face of complicated emotion, Gwynne reverted to a task-oriented mindset. There were worse defense mechanisms.

"I assume this is related to your heist? Are you stealing something from the Black Eagle Keep?"

"Very observant, Cassie." Gwynne leapt out of bed, startling Belial who had been trying his best to go to sleep in his mother's lap. The cat batted at Gwynne's feet in frustration as she strode over to the planning table, but she didn't seem to notice.

"So what are we after? Gold? Jewels? Fine art?"

"None of those things, we're after a spell. Though I may swipe some valuables as well to cover my true target."

"A spell? What do you mean?"

Gwynne's expression darkened from one of mischief to a stormy visage. "You see, Cassie, I'm cursed. There's a spell that's been on me for years and I finally found out how to break it."

Cassie wondered how Gwynne had managed to find herself on the receiving end of a curse, but did not ask.

"You see, Cassie, while short-term spells use energy from their caster, some spells can be greatly extended by transferring their focal point from the caster to a certain type of crystal that resonates with arcane energy. Thus the spell can slowly burn through the crystal's energy instead of the caster's. You may have heard of these crystals before in Abaddon, since the majority of the world's supply is mined in Abaxia.

They're very useful, as you can imagine, but the process of transferring a spell to a crystal is quite difficult without interrupting the casting, so only skilled mages can perform such a spell with any reliability."

Gwynne gestured to herself when she said 'skilled mages', as if the act was child's play to her.

"So we have to steal this crystal? Why is it in the Black Eagle Keep? What *is* the Black Eagle Keep, anyway? Who lives there?"

Gwynne leaned over the blueprints. "All good questions. The keep belongs to one Roger Ackerman, retired Royal Magician and all-around bastard. My father is the one who requested Ackerman put the curse on me many years ago, and Ackerman has kept the crystal with him ever since." Cassie didn't have time to unpack that baggage, or even think about the questions that raised about Gwynne's upbringing. "But I recently learned that the normally reclusive and paranoid Ackerman is holding a party at his keep, and the date is only a few days away. This is the perfect chance to sneak in and snatch the crystal out from under his crooked nose. The only problem is, while I was able to swipe the blueprint of the keep from the Royal Treasury, it tells me nothing about the magical defenses of the building, or where people are going to be. I need someone on the inside to case the building for me. I'd do it myself, but I'm very well-known, and any disguise I wear could be very easily stripped away by Ackerman's spells. The man may be retired, but he's still a sharp wizard."

Cassie had a bad feeling she knew where this was going. "Let me guess, I'm the canary in this coal mine?"

"Great minds, Cassie. That was my idea exactly. You are relatively unknown and as a fellow human you'd attract the least amount of attention of anyone here. We're still a few days away from the Keep, but the plan is to arrive in the vicinity the day before. You slip in disguised as a maid. Nobody in the Keep will think twice about an Abaxian being part of the help, as racist as that is. But we can use that racism against them as blindness. I'm pretty sure the crystal is being kept here," Gwynne jabbed a finger onto a room marked 'Trophy Room'. "Ackerman is nothing if not a braggart, and there should be plenty of goodies there."

Gwynne went into further detail on what Cassie was to do. She felt nervous at being put back in danger, but Gwynne was adamant about this, and promised there would be almost no risk involved. She wasn't sure when exactly she became a phantom thief, but supposed it beat factory work.

10

Calling Card

The Name's Molly Jones, Sir - Oil on Canvas - Aphrodite Scorns the King - A Bolt of Green Energy

True to Gwynne's word, the *Pale Moon* arrived at the rendezvous point for the Keep in two short days. The House was high up in the Zonan mountains at this point, and it got quite cold in the manor, particularly at night. Gwynne had enchanted some spare crystals to radiate heat to warm individual rooms, and Cassie slept with one beside her bed.

From where the craft hovered, Black Eagle Keep was not visible for stealth purposes. Gwynne had refused to fly any closer for fear of detection. Fortunately for Cassie, Gwynne volunteered to teleport her near the Keep.

"I'd zip you right inside, Cassie, but no doubt that'd trip all kinds of detection spells that Ackerman has on the place. No, you'll need to go in as mundanely as possible. I can get you near and you'll need to enter the servant's door, change into a servant's outfit, and then begin reconnaissance." Gwynne handed her a small notebook. "Here, I've prepared a spellbook for you. There should be a few helpful bits and bobs in there for you. Just avoid casting any spells unless it is an emergency, as no doubt that will set off alarms as well."

A few hours later, Cassie found herself walking a rocky mountain trail, bundled up against the cold as wind howled through the mountains' peaks. She did not enjoy the conditions but was at least thankful she didn't have to fly that rickety landing machine in all this. Before long, a large stone castle came into view. It was perched atop a peak with imposing drops around its sides. A gargantuan gate was built into the front as a decoration piece. According to the blueprints, this was merely for show and reasonable-sized doors were cut into it. There was a small plateau nearby where a single dirigible rested, anchored down to steel moorings set into the stones. This was likely Ackerman's personal craft. There seemed to be plenty of space around the plateau for additional craft to dock if need be, which was where party guests would be arriving in only a day's time.

Cassie made her way along a precarious trail around the side of the castle to an inconspicuous door at its rear. She recognized it from the blueprint as the servants' entrance. As she approached, the door opened and a man stepped out to light a cigarette. He watched Cassie approach with little interest. As she came up to the door, the man stopped her.

"Pretty cold out, isn't it? What business you got out here? An' how come I've never seen you before?"

Cassie was prepared to lie her way in. Gwynne had given her a crash course on deception, the key being to act like you belonged there and that your presence was perfectly normal. She affected a highland accent, saying "Th' name's Molly Jones, sir. I'm with the house staff. The master asked me personally to attend to a matter with his airship, and now I'd very much like to get inside and out of this cold."

The man shrugged, clearly not paid enough to care. "Okay, Miss Jones. Don' freeze your bum off."

Cassie nodded to the man and pulled open the door. Her desire to warm up was not a lie, at least, and she was happy to be out of the elements. Immediately inside the door was what appeared to be a short hallway leading to two changing rooms. Cassie slipped into the women's side and looked around. There were a few lockers against one wall, and an alcove against the other where racks of uniforms were kept. The room was empty of people at the moment, no doubt the entire staff was busy with preparations. She sifted through uniforms on the rack until she found a maid's uniform that seemed as if it would fit her. She got changed in a hurry and stuffed her previous outfit into the wondrous bag. *I've really got to get one of these for myself instead of mooching it off of Gwynne every time I go out*, she thought as she stuffed the bag into the miserably small pocket of the dress. The outfit was by no means flattering, and the size that was large enough to accommodate Cassie's hips left a bit of slack in the chest area, but the goal wasn't to make an impression here.

She made her way through the door at the far side of the changing room into a chaotic kitchen. There must have been fifteen people in that room all shouting, mixing, chopping, stirring, carrying, tasting, and nearly but not quite tripping over each other. Nobody paid Cassie any attention, which made her cold sweat subside a bit, though she almost ran into a tall woman carrying an oversized platter of some sort of hors d'oeuvres on her way out of the kitchen.

"Watch where you're going, kid!" The woman shouted, not even looking at Cassie. Cassie didn't even bother to apologize. She pushed her way through a swinging door into a lavish dining room, a mahogany table stretching out with room for some twenty people. It occurred to her that the House did not have a dining room, and decided to talk to Gwynne about it when she got back.

In preparation for this day, Cassie had memorized the layout of the Keep, and knew that just beyond the dining room was the Keep's ballroom. Gwynne had ordered her to become familiar with that room, as she might be needed to keep lookout there during the heist proper. Cassie had picked up a feather duster in the changing room and used it to dust off silver vases and fine portraits of same-face Zonan men, trying to look nonchalant as she made her way over to the door to the ballroom. She stopped as a particular portrait caught her eye. As opposed to gray and dignified men, this painting was of a young boy. He seemed no more than eight or nine years old and had a tired look on his face, as if sitting for this portrait was the most boring thing he had ever done. Cassie sympathized. The boy had perfectly curled blond hair, striking blue eyes, and wore a stuffy collared shirt. The caption read "Gregory Yance, *Prince Abneel Quintus, 8*, oil on canvas". So *this* was what the tragic prince had looked like. Cassie thought he looked a bit of a spoiled brat. The label did not include a year of publication, and it struck her that she had no idea how old Prince Abneel had been at his time of death. She doubted the Abaxians had any involvement in the prince's death, but it was still sad that he had died, especially if he had been a child at the time.

At that time, the door to the ballroom opened beside Cassie and a middle-aged woman in a similar maid's uniform emerged. She had grayish brown hair tied up in a bonnet, but strands had fallen loose and framed her face like a lumpy egg. She looked at Cassie. "What are you doing standing around gawking at paintings like that? There's mountains of work to be done. What's your name again?"

"Molly, miss. Molly Jones."

"Miss Jones, I'm going to be talking with the steward about your salary later. I haven't the time to berate you now, I've got a million other things to be doing."

Cassie tried to play the part, hoping there wasn't an *actual* Molly Jones on the staff to take the fall for her poor acting. "So sorry, miss. It won't happen again, miss."

"Good. Now go dust the ballroom, it seems to have filled again with dust since yesterday."

Cassie laughed internally, being sentenced to do something she was already going to do. The angry woman left through another door, beyond which Cassie could see a lavish parlor, putting the one in the House to shame with its leather furniture. Cassie slipped out through the ballroom door and found herself in the largest room she had ever been in. It was bigger even than the factory floor at Jones & Sons, though it was largely empty. Similar decorations lined the walls, and there was a slightly raised stage where an orchestra might serenade guests while they danced. The tile floor was polished to a sparkling luster, and every step clacked against it. Cassie surveyed every corner of the room, looking for good hiding spots and blind angles. There was a sitting area in one corner with white cloth chairs. Cassie dusted them, lest anyone else accuse her of not working. It was dull work, and she didn't know how anyone did this every day. She made her way over to another corner where there were a few marble statues and busts, figuring this would provide the best cover once the ballroom was full. She attended to a few other places around the room for good measure before leaving through the back door. She already knew the route she wanted to take, and it was a short walk through carpeted hallways, dusting ornaments as she went whenever someone else came by, until she found herself before a set of closed white-painted doors. If her memory was correct, this was the Trophy Room.

Cassie took a deep breath to calm her nerves and opened the doors. The room was about the same size as the dining room, filled with strange curios in glass cases and littered with trinkets. She saw medals, trophies, weapons, suits of armor, piles of gold coins and gems, and various oddities. One was what first appeared to be a human skull, but had three eye sockets and two horns. Another was some sort of unidentifiable organ floating in a jar of formaldehyde. Lastly, she saw a set of fangs on a crimson pillow in one of the cases, labeled as dragon fangs. Cassie wasn't sure if dragons were even real, and if they were they surely must have died off long ago, but these teeth looked immaculately preserved, as if they had been plucked from their jaws mere minutes ago. Towards the southwest corner, Cassie saw the target of her mission. Inside one of the glass cases was a white crystal pulsing with yellow light. The label made no mention of the crystal's true purpose, but this had to be it.

Looking around, Cassie tried to determine what the most flashy bit of finery in the room was. Then something caught her eye. On the far wall was a gigantic painting, probably seven feet tall by five wide, depicting a beautiful Abaxian woman looking coy, her hand balking a bearded and finely-dressed Zonan man on his knees, pleading with her for something. Crowds of onlookers covered their mouths in shock. The title read *"Aphrodite Scorns the King"*. *Good for her*, Cassie thought. Remembering her purpose, Cassie took out a piece of paper cut into the shape of a stylized owl. Gwynne had instructed her to leave this calling card on the most auspicious and gaudy object in the room, and Cassie couldn't think of anything flashier than this painting. She tucked the note into the frame and backed up to examine some of the other items in the room.

Suddenly the door to the trophy room opened. Cassie grasped at her feather duster and tried to make herself look busy and unassuming. Someone walked in on heavy leather boots. She spared a glance through the case she was dusting to see a sight that made her stomach freeze. Standing across the room, hands clasped behind their back in a proper stance of waiting, was the masked man that had been following her over the past month. She looked down again in a hurry, hoping he hadn't recognized her.

"Sorry, sir, I'll be out of your way shortly. Just let me finish dusting this case."

The man slowly walked up to Cassie and admired the object inside the case. This was the strange skull with three eyes. She could feel her heart trying to burst free from her chest, but kept about her work, silently pleading for the man to leave.

"Do you know what this is?" The man asked, his voice like smooth whiskey. Cassie almost screamed with shock at hearing him for the first time, but managed to maintain her act. She didn't know what she expected him to sound like, but she was almost relieved that he sounded normal, almost amiable. The only thing that marred the pleasant voice was the muffling from the nondescript white mask.

"No, sir. I'm just here for the cleaning," Cassie said, giving a cute laugh. It sounded stilted, but she hoped he didn't notice.

"Really? You're looking history in the eyes, girl. This happens to be a troglodyte skull. I assume you know not of troglodytes?"

Cassie just shook her head.

"Long ago, in the days of creation, when the Elder Gods still graced us with their presence, the lands were not ruled by men but by beasts. The first intelligent race to emerge called themselves the Gorki. They built cities, advanced technology, and discovered magic while humans were still cowering below the ground in caves and banging rocks together to make fire. Nobody knows why, but the Gorki civilization fell, and man came into power. The Gorki that were left retreated underground, regressing to a primitive state before nearly dying out altogether. Meanwhile, man filled in the niche the Gorki left behind, taking their technology as their own. These days, the remnants of the Gorki are little more than cavemen that want nothing more than to retake the surface. We call these remnants troglodytes."

"That's very interesting, sir."

"Yes, but nowhere near as interesting as *you*."

Cassie wasn't sure if he was on to her or *coming* on to her, but either way it made her want to barf.

"I'm sorry sir? I'm afraid I don't understand. Is there something I can do for you?" Cassie backed away, feeling that any maid would be right to be afraid in this situation. The man removed the glove on his right hand, revealing a twisted scar that ran up the back of his hand and between his middle and ring finger.

"Something you can do? Just stay right there and don't scream." In a flash, the hand was around Cassie's arm. She tried to jerk it free, but the man's grip was like iron.

"Sir, this is most improper-"

The man was muttering something, his head lolling back enraptured. Cassie had no time to react before her mind suddenly felt like it was being stabbed. There was a screaming like nails on a chalkboard and her body seized with pain. It felt like a hot dagger was being stuck into her brain, wiggling and probing for information. She mustered every bit of willpower she had to resist, and suddenly there was a sound like breaking glass. Cassie's mind and vision both cleared, and she saw the man stagger backwards, his grip and concentration broken.

The man coughed and steadied himself. "Urgh... I should have known you'd be warded." The magical protections that Gwynne had placed on her ahead of time rejected the man's attack and saved her life.

Cassie did not give him time to try again. She turned and fled the room at top speed, fumbling in her pocket for the small spellbook that Gwynne had lent her. Before she could make it into the hallway, the floor beneath her turned black and a mass of grasping besuckered tentacles emerged. They tripped Cassie, and she found herself grasped in their embrace. The man walked slowly up to her, hand outstretched to maintain the spell.

"You may have been warded, but I was at least able to get one thing from that mind of yours. Your name is Cassandra."

Cassie did not like this one bit. She flipped through the pages of the spellbook with her thumb and found one she liked. With a bit of incantation, the tentacles burst into flame, sizzling away into ash. Cassie felt like she had just run a mile on the track, but she was used to this feeling by now.

The flames did not touch Cassie, but the dissolving tentacles dropped her to the floor on her elbow, fortunately her right. She scrambled to her feet and bolted once more. As she ran, she found the page for long-distance teleport. She began the incantation, but it would take almost a minute to complete. In the meantime, she burst out into the ballroom, the man chasing behind her. An electric crackle shot past her ear, and she saw a bolt of green energy whiz past her and slam into one of the ballroom pillars, sending debris and dust flying. Cassie maintained concentration, picturing the foyer of the House vividly in her mind. She was starting the final verse of the spell as she tore across the ballroom when she slipped on the polished floor. This time she did land on her wounded arm and it sent new waves of pain across her back. Yet still she maintained concentration.

The man stood nearby, showing no signs of exertion. "Cassandra, I know you work for Owl. I have my suspicions about their identity, but I need you to tell me who they are. You can either do it willingly, or I can force you to do so."

Cassie did not rise to the provocation and finished her spell. The man tried to bring forth more tentacles to hold her in place, but it didn't matter. She vanished with a crack and reappeared on the floor of the foyer of House Brandwyck, thoroughly startling Baal the cat who had been licking his butt in a sunbeam.

In a few seconds, Gwynne was thundering down the stairs and helping Cassie up, who with that spell felt like she could sleep for a few days.

"Cassie? What happened? Are you okay?"

She struggled to remain conscious. "M-masked man... been fol-

lowing me… since Abaddon. Knew I worked for you… is a mage…
"

Gwynne hoisted her up and set her down on the sofa in the sitting room. She was dazed and exhausted from the exertion of the spell, but otherwise was uninjured. Gwynne called to Feckalia who brought Cassie a glass of water. Once she had taken a few sips, her vision started to return to normal and she felt herself begin to stabilize. Gwynne was sitting at the far end of the sofa, unsure how to approach the situation.

"I think I'm okay, Gwynne. He mostly just scared the hell out of me."

"Describe him."

Cassie recounted her entire interactions with the man, from first seeing him on the tram in Abaddon to glimpsing him outside of the cafe in New Ozion, and every detail of the encounter in the Keep. Gwynne looked concerned, but not afraid.

"Well it seems like he is after Owl specifically, but does not know my identity. How odd. What concerns me most is that our masked friend seemed to know I would be coming here before I even arrived. Perhaps if he's studying my past escapades he realized that the Keep blueprints were stolen during my last heist. But that wouldn't explain why he keeps appearing to Cassie. I have some hunches, but nothing definite yet."

"What does this mean for the mission?"

"Oh, the mission is still on. I've already sent the calling card, so I can't rightly back out now. I wish you had left it on something easier to carry, but that's why we have magic, isn't it?"

Gwynne got up from her seat and walked out of the room. "I must think on this some more. Until tomorrow night, please try to rest and recover your strength, Cassie. It will be doubly important for you to run interference tomorrow. You'll need to be able to cast that spell again, and perhaps more besides." And with that, the Owl had retreated to its roost to plot and scheme.

Cassie took the rest of the evening easy, taking a bath and having a hearty dinner. By the time she was ready for bed, she felt perfectly normal, at least physically. Mentally she was scared out of her wits, imagining every way the mission could go wrong the following night. She wasn't sure if she was scared more for herself or for Gwynne, but then decided that it was definitely for herself. Gwynne was the most powerful wizard in the world, right?

11

Best Friends

Enough Hetero Energy to Power a Small City - Determination and Knowledge - It's Definitely a Look, Honey - Those Foul Abaxian Magics

At dusk the following day, Cassie snuck back into the servant's door of Black Eagle Keep. If she thought the kitchen was a mess the previous day, this evening it was a disaster. Yet somehow a coordinated disaster, as every person dashing through the room and performing various tasks seemed to be like cogs in a well-oiled machine. Needless to say, they didn't have time to pay attention to every servant girl that came and went.

Tonight, the maid uniforms had been replaced with more formal servant wear, and Cassie found herself wearing black pants into which a black shirt was tucked. This was more masculine than she felt comfortable being, but seeing other women in the same outfit made her feel a little better. The event wasn't even scheduled to start for another hour, but already the ballroom was a pleasant buzz of conversation and chatter as Ackerman's VIP guests had arrived earlier that day to do whatever it was that rich people did in their ample free time. Cassie busied herself carrying platters of fizzy drinks in thin glass flutes, which the guests seemed to enjoy. Apparently it was a good vintage or something. At least this job didn't require Cassie to talk, at which case she feared she would immediately be revealed to know nothing at all about whatever kind of special champagne was being served. She thought that Feckalia would get a kick out of this, and she could imagine the demon in a skimpy black dress flitting from group to group and seducing everyone in the room.

Fortunately, Feckalia was not here, and neither, it seemed, was the masked man. This brought Cassie some relief, and she found herself settling into the serving role quite naturally. She figured that she could be quite good at this job if she didn't find the existence of the fabulously wealthy to be fundamentally abhorrent. It seemed that Ackerman himself had not yet made an appearance at the party, either. The guests assumed he was waiting to make a dramatic entrance. Knowing he was a wizard, this was almost certainly the case, and she wondered between Gwynne and Ackerman who was the most showy. *It's gotta be Gwynne,* she thought.

The hour of the main event rolled around, and guests were pouring in via the main gate. Cassie caught glimpses of the landing plateau outside and saw that there were no fewer than five dirigibles parked outside, with another drifting in for a landing. Attendants at the front gate were greeting everyone by name and she was impressed that they could remember them all. Each guest was dressed in the finest clothes Cassie had ever seen. Luxurious ball gowns, fitted dresses, and archaic bustled dresses filled the hall, with the men each in nearly identical black tuxedos, holding onto the arms of their dates. The noise level steadily rose from a dull conversation to a full on roar as the room packed with people, all eager to get tipsy and dance.

A discordant whine came from the direction of the stage, and Cassie saw that a string quintet was warming up and tuning their instruments.

After a few minutes, they started with a chamber piece with a modest tempo that allowed for dancing, and the crowd cleared at the center of the room to allow couples to waltz to and fro. Cassie didn't have the slightest clue about the discipline, but she found herself drifting off into a daydream about Gwynne leading her around the dance floor. Her fantasy was interrupted when a guest asked her if they had any more of the shrimp fritters, to which she gave a dismissive answer and made her rounds again.

When she reached the corner with the statues, she heard a whisper in her ear. She was startled for a second before she remembered the jeweled earring that Gwynne had given her earlier. It was a silver hoop with a small pearl set into it. According to Gwynne, when one pinched the pearl, their voice could be transmitted to the wearer of the other piece.

"How's the party, Cass?" Gwynne asked, her voice sounding tinny and distant.

Cassie tucked herself surreptitiously into a corner behind a statue. "Loud, crowded, enough hetero energy to power a small city. Ackerman hasn't shown yet."

"I suspect he has a grand entrance planned. And then a speech. And then a grand exit."

"How are things on your end?"

"Good. The glider works perfectly. I'll be at the window of the trophy room in just a few minutes. Let me know if Ackerman shows up."

Before they arrived, Gwynne had used her technomancy to fashion a sort of bar attached to a horizontal sail. Gwynne claimed it would catch the winds, and called it a 'glider'. Cassie was just glad she hadn't plummeted to her death on the cliffs with that thing.

"Roger."

"He's here?"

"No, like 'roger,' 'confirm,' or whatever. That's what detectives say."

"Oh, right. Well, good luck, Cassie. Requesting silence."

Cassie imagined that Gwynne looked ridiculous soaring towards the keep on her death glider in her gaudy Owl costume. Cassie would have killed for a painting of such a sight, but tried to keep her mind on the task at hand.

A particularly rowdy group of guests had taken up spot on the opposite side of the statue from Cassie, and she couldn't help but overhear their conversation.

"Yeah, we're planning to open up another five Joy Marts by the end of the year, or at least that's what my financial guys tell me, anyway."

The group laughed. Cassie blanched at the idea that she was five feet away from Hector Joilen, the founder of Joy Mart.

"That's all well and good, Hector," another man said, confirming Cassie's suspicions. "But what are you going to do about the protests? I'd hate to think of what might happen to your profits if any more of your stores decide to join in."

"What am I gonna do? Um… nothing? Even if one or two stores go on strike, I'm still making millions. They'll tire eventually and come back to work. And if they don't, I'll just replace them."

The party laughed, making Cassie feel sick.

"Oh, that reminds me, have you all got your money in on the new Labor Standards Act? I've been playing croquet with two of the magistrates, and I think I can get them to vote against it."

"Excellent," a woman's voice said. "The last thing we need is for those rats to start demanding *rights*."

It took all of Cassie's self-control to stop herself from going on an anticapitalist rampage right then and there, but decided that was a problem for another day. She relocated for her own mental health. As she was walking to the lounge area, the lights in the room began to magically dim. Conversations finished and the room fell quiet. The band finished their music with a flourish and a spotlight clicked on, illuminating the grand staircase at the far end of the ballroom with an isolating glow.

There on the landing stood a very unremarkable man. He must have been about fifty years old, with neatly trimmed hair and beard, and with a robust and athletic build. He wore a black tuxedo like all the other men in the room. He gave a roguish grin to the audience and waved his hand. Everyone cheered.

"How ya doin', everyone?" He asked, voice booming out with magical magnification and a thick Ozion accent. "I just wanted to say thanks for coming out tonight. You all know I'm not one for grand entrances." The crowd laughed. "Oh, who am I kidding. Let's get this party started!" With that, jets of sparks flew from the walls around the room, creating an indoor pyrotechnics display. Ackerman, for this was certainly he, rose up in the air and waved his hands, causing clouds of colored smoke to billow forth from his sleeves. The smoke filled the vaulted ceiling of the room, and lights shimmered and danced across the fog. Eventually, the fog cleared to reveal a perfect representation of the night sky. Cassie was thoroughly impressed.

"He's here," she said into her earring.

"I can hear the bombast from here. I'm about to start working on the lock to the trophy room window. Anything amiss on your end?"

"Everything seems fine here. Still no sign of the mask."

"Good, let's hope it stays that way. Lemme know if anything changes."

"Roger."

Ackerman had been flying around the room at this point, shaking the hands of various people from the air and doing all sorts of flips and spins. The crowd was eating it up. After a minute, he landed back on the landing of the staircase.

"But seriously, folks, what a party, huh? The guy who put this on must be a real stand-up guy, eh?"

Laughter.

"Anyway, lemme bend ya ears for a few minutes. I wanna talk about a little something called hard work. Right? Because honestly that's what got us all here. That's right, take a second to give yourselves a pat on the back. You earned it, ladies and gentlemen."

Cassie could feel her bile rising. She doubted anyone in this room had worked hard a day in their life.

"Naysayers may say that we're *lucky*. Right? But we're not really lucky, are we? It's about cultivating a mindset of success."

Cassie tried her hardest to tune the man out at this point, but he was still very loud due to the magical magnification.

"I remember when I used to be a young kid and I didn't have nuthin'. My dad used to tell me, 'Son, there's something more important than money out there, and that's *knowledge*'. And I took that to heart. I really did! I worked hard under the apprenticeship of the late Wizard Vandradamus- yeah, some of you have probably heard of him."

Cassie hadn't, and wasn't convinced he was real.

"He was a wacky old coot, I tell you what. Had a thing for the dream powder." Ackerman gave a gesture to imply that Vandradamus was completely off his rocker. The crowd hooted and laughed. "But despite all that, I really had it 'ard, ya know. I didn't have the fancy keep, the private dirigible, or the tenure as Royal Magician under my belt. No, back then all I had were my two best friends: *determination*, and *knowledge*."

Cassie didn't know how much more of this self-aggrandizing waffle she could take. She slipped from the ballroom into a hallway to catch her breath. Two men were against the wall here locking lips. They turned when the door opened, but went right back to it when they saw it was just a servant. Cassie felt uncomfortable and went into a nearby washroom. She could still hear Ackerman's speech in the distance, but it was much easier to tune out here. She just needed a minute to decompress before she went back out there. She made faces in the mirror, mocking Ackerman's self-righteous speech.

"Oh don't do that, what if it sticks that way?" A voice said in reply. Cassie's mind flicked through the possibilities. Gwynne? No, too masculine. The masked man? Not smarmy enough. "Oh don't be afraid, darling, it's just me," the voice said again, and she realized that the mirror above the sink was talking to her. *It may as well just after the couple of days I've had,* she thought. A white face appeared in the corner of the mirror, like the masked man's mask, but much friendlier.

"Why are you talking?" Cassie asked it.

"Why are *you* talking?" The mirror mocked back. Cassie just left it at 'magic mirror'.

"Anyway, magic mirror, while I'm here, can you tell me if you've seen someone?"

"Oh, I've seen many people, and far too much of some." The mirror's face did not have eyes, but it somehow seemed to roll them all the same. "I was created by Ackerman for the express purpose of giving compliments to those who use the bathroom, but fortunately for me he got the intonation wrong, and so I get to be *sassy*. Somehow he still likes me too much to redo the spell. Anyway, who are you looking for, love?"

"A man, wearing all black-"

"Oh, plenty of those here."

"-black leather gloves and a mask. A sort of white mask like your face, except scarier."

"You know, I've never actually *seen* my own face? Funny, for a talking mirror, the only thing I can't see is my own reflection!"

"Yes, yes, it's very ironic. Have you seen him before or not?"

"Hmmm, let's see, honey, scary mask, leather gloves. Scary mask, leather gloves. You know, I believe I saw someone like that this morning. Didn't wash his hands for the gloves, and I shudder to think what *that* implies for his wiping habits."

"Seen him since then?"

"No, I don't believe I have, honey. Now I'm exhausted from all this talking, so I'm going back to sleep."

"Well that's no help."

"Hey, would a compliment make you feel any better? Because you are looking…. Well it's definitely a look, honey, I'll give you that."

"What is that supposed to mean?"

"Sorry, darling, best I can do." And the face faded out of the mirror's reflection, leaving Cassie feeling gobsmacked, but at least it had made her forget about Ackerman for a minute. As if on cue, she heard his voice ringing across the Keep.

"…oh, and before I forget, guys and gals, we've got a very special guest tonight!"

Cassie hurried back out to the ballroom, the couple in the hallway fortunately moved on at this point.

"That's right, yesterday we got a calling card from one Owl of the Pale Moon. Ah? Ah? A name you've all heard, no doubt." The crowd began to erupt into worried murmurs. "Oh don't worry, ladies and gents, because I was prepared. Owl says he wants to steal a painting of mine, but that's all a farce. I know what he's really after."

Cassie had made it out into the ballroom at this point, but had trouble seeing Ackerman due to the crowd of people.

"He knew you were coming," Cassie said into her earring.

"I know, I sent a calling card."

"No, I mean before that. Explains why the mask guy is here."

Cassie managed to elbow her way into a gap in the crowd where she could see the landing where Ackerman was standing. He had something about the height of a person covered in a cloth. The something had a square top with sharp corners. Cassie was afraid she knew what this was. Ackerman grabbed a corner of the sheet and yanked it down, revealing the white crystal she had seen yesterday in the trophy room.

"Just finishing the lock now," Gwynne said.

"Uh, Gwynne, there's a problem."

"What?"

"The crystal."

"Yes, I know, I'm almost in the room."

"No, I mean it's not there. It's here."

"Are you sure?"

"Looks like it. Ackerman's making a big deal about it."

"Check to see if it's an illusion. Use the detection spell in the book."

"But you said…"

"Don't worry about it, this one should be low enough power that it won't be picked up."

Cassie flipped through the notebook and found the page for the detection spell. It had only a few lines, so she recited it quickly enough, causing the room to change to a pale gray, while the crystal stood out with an aura of bright yellow.

"It looks yellow."

"Shit! Okay, he's moved it, then. I'll have to improvise. Hold tight."

Ackerman had paused for dramatic effect, allowing the audience to wonder what this crystal was. He grinned at them before filling them in. "See, this is a magical crystal. Magical crystals contain perpetuating spells. And the particular spell on this crystal is currently affecting Owl. And boy does he want to get his hands on this. You see, I'm the one that cast this spell." Ackerman looked out over the audience, and Cassie felt like he locked eyes with her, but his gaze passed. "Would you all like to know what this spell does?"

The audience cheered.

"Oh? I can't hear you."

Louder cheering.

"Alright, alright, we're having fun. This spell is one of protection. It prevents Owl from raising a hand against a certain someone. Anyone wanna take a guess at who?"

"You?" someone asked.

"Nope! Good guess, though. Thank youse for lookin' out for me. Alright!"

Hector Joilen raised his hand and said, "Me?"

The audience laughed.

"Who's that? Oh, ol' Hector J. What a man. Can we get a round of applause for Mister Joilen? You all know him, you all love him. What a jokester, I've always said."

The chatter died down and there was one last suggestion.

"The king?"

Ackerman opened his mouth to speak, but before words could come out, all the lights in the room cut off. The house lights were nearly out already, but the subtraction of the spotlight dropped the ballroom of the Black Eagle Keep into near pitch blackness. Cassie could hear Ackerman shouting from the stage, his voice amplification removed. "Alright, alright, stay calm everyone!"

With a *clunk*, the spotlight turned on once more. It was no longer focused on Ackerman on the landing but up at the top of the stairs where a black cloaked figure now stood, their clothing looking almost like wings wrapping around them. A half-mask covered the figure's eyes and nose, protruding out into a long beak-like point.

"Good evening, everyone," the figure said, their voice having stolen Ackerman's magnification. This sounded like Gwynne's voice, but modulated into an affectatious masculine. It sounded unnatural to Cassie, and she didn't much care for it. "Hate to crash the party, but I must say, I *did* send my regards."

"Owl! It's Owl!" guests were shouting. A few women screamed.

"Now now, be ye not afraid," Owl continued. "I mean no harm to the gentlefolk of the party. I have already taken what is owed to me by the capitalist pig who owns this place and then some. If you don't want the same fate to befall you, reconsider your ways. Live your life to serve your fellow man and not your own interests. Now, if you will permit me, I'll take my leave."

"Hey, hey, not so fast, Mr. Owl." Ackerman had restored his vocal spell. "Like I said, I knew youse was coming, see. And I've got a special friend here who's dying to say hello."

With another clunk, a second spotlight turned on, illuminating the other side of the split staircase. On the eastern split, the masked man stood. He looked identical to yesterday, only now he had a glittering longsword drawn, pointing it at Owl.

Owl scoffed. "I've heard of a masked man who has been nipping at my heels. Identify yourself, you coward."

"Oh there's no need," came the voice like smoke and honey. "You know who I am. Just as I knew who you were by the sound of your voice."

There was a *clang* of metal as both shapes disappeared from their spotlights. The lights struggled to keep up with the pair as they clashed swords. Owl had drawn a rapier from within their cloak. Cassie didn't even know that Gwynne knew how to use a rapier, but here it was. The two met in an exchange of blows and a shower of sparks. The masked man's longsword was much heavier than Owl's rapier, but the smaller sword was faster. With deft movements that wasted no energy, Owl parried the blows from the larger weapon, deflecting it away. The two were in the air, their sword fight becoming a full-on mages' duel. The exchanges of steel were too quick for Cassie to follow, and she just focused on getting closer to the scene of the fight. With any luck, she could maybe teleport Gwynne out of there.

The spotlights tracked the two fighters through the air, the whole thing looking a bit like a stage production or a circus show at this point, but judging by their grunts of exertion this was very real. Cassie watched as the masked man lunged at Owl, who raised their arm to parry, only for the masked man to adjust his grip, snap his fingers, and appear behind Owl. They could barely get the rapier up in time to block as the longsword crashed down on them. Owl shot down to the ground and crashed into the staircase. The crowd gasped for breath, and began cheering as the notorious criminal staggered to their feet.

The masked man hovered down to the ground and relaxed their stance. "Figured it out yet?"

Owl spat on the rug of the stairs and stretched. "Mordecai. It's been a while."

Cassie was a mere fifteen feet from the conflict now, and could hear everything. Who was Mordecai? Gwynne had never mentioned them before.

"That's right, *old friend.* I've been looking for you for a very long time." Mordecai spat the words 'old friend' like a particularly virulent venom.

Owl seemed unfazed. "How's my father doing, by the way? Enjoying being his lapdog?"

Mordecai snarled, not helping his case. He lunged out at Owl again with his longsword, this time purple flames crackling off its blade. Owl didn't even try to parry this one, they just hopped to the side and let the blade impact on the floor.

"I would do anything he asked of me. He's the one that took me in when I had nowhere to go and raised me as his own son. You were born into that gift and threw it back into his face."

Whatever the purple magic was, Owl wanted nothing to do with it. They ducked and dodged, not even allowing their blade to make contact. "He got what he deserved. He only cared about us insofar as we were useful to him. Surely you've realized that."

"I don't care! I owe him my life and I want nothing more than to be useful." Mordecai, enraged, made a powerful overhand swing. Owl seemed to have anticipated this and whipped around behind him, jabbing him in the kidney with the rapier's tip. Mordecai roared, his proper honeyed voice turning to hot gravel with rage and pain.

"Curse you, Owl! You were corrupted by those foul Abaxian magics and twisted into something disgusting."

"Aww, jealous, much? Turns out, that's not how it works, Mordy."

What was Mordecai talking about? What was Gwynne supposed to be twisted into? Cassie's mind was racing as she broke through the last line of the crowd and scrambled up onto the staircase landing that served as the fighters' stage.

"And who are you to talk, anyway? I see you've learned some magic of your own. With what kind of fiend did you bargain to obtain these dark powers?"

"I'll show you if you like."

There was a wavering sound in the air, and a shape appeared on Mordecai's shoulder. It was like a giant octopus, but where the body should be, there was only a bloodshot eyeball that whipped its gaze across the room. The tentacles were nearly four feet long, and wrapped around Mordecai's torso. It dripped with a purple-black ooze. The sight of the creature alone sent waves of panic over Cassie's brain. There was something about it that just didn't fit with her perception of the universe, and looking at it felt like everything she knew about reality was wrong. She fell to her knees and gripped her head to make the ringing and fear stop. There were similar reactions from the crowd, and people seemed to be on the verge of panic. Owl seemed immune.

"An Elder spawn, *really*? Put that thing away, you're going to make the guests go insane."

The sound vibrated out again and the creature disappeared. The room stopped spinning and everyone seemed to calm down again.

"I'll do whatever it takes to bring you back. I *will* make you see the light, Abneel!"

Abneel...? The name barely had time to register in Cassie's mind before Owl vanished and reappeared with blade at Mordecai's throat.

"That's not my name anymore!" Cassie had never heard Gwynne this angry in all the time she had spent in her home. The level of fury matched Mordecai's own, and he grinned.

"Oh, have I hit a sore spot? I see I've made my way past that pretentious facade of yours. Tell me, does that 'baxer that follows you around know that *you're* the reason the kingdom is at war?"

Owl gritted their teeth. "Shut up! The propaganda my father puts out is no responsibility of mine. Everything he does is purely for his own greed. He couldn't control me, so he made use of me the only way he knew how, as a scapegoat for his petty dreams of war."

Mordecai shook his head. "When will you see the light? You can still be His Majesty's right-hand man or at least his Royal Magician, if only you'd give up this silly little rebellious phase. Gods, His Majesty has even agreed to drop the charges of grand larceny."

"I have no desire of returning to that prison you call a palace. I will forge my own life and become the greatest mage the world has ever seen!"

"You have no right. Your place is on the throne. Come back and be my brother again. Come back, Prince Abneel Quintus!"

Owl screamed in fury and drew back their rapier, ready to pierce Mordecai's throat. But Mordecai was counting on this and sliced upward with his longsword, thrusting it by the pommel. Owl hadn't been expecting this, and the sickly purple fire bolted across their body. The mask was rent in twain, clattering to the ground, and leaving a gash across Gwynne's face. She fell to the ground and convulsed as the purple fire pulsed over her form.

Mordecai sheathed his sword, very proud of himself. "I hope this curse gives you something to think about, brother."

Gwynne could do nothing but scream, the curse racking her body with what must have been the most intense pain. Her head jolted back, revealing her face and her lustrous purple hair for the world to see. Murmurs started to spread through the crowd.

"Prince Abneel is alive?"

"Owl is Prince Abneel?"

"What's going on?"

"Owl is a woman?"

Cassie could just barely make it to Gwynne, finishing up an incantation. She grabbed Gwynne's shaking form and the two women vanished from the ballroom of the Black Eagle Keep and reappeared in the workshop of House Brandwyck. Cassie rolled as they hit the ground, trying to interpose herself between Gwynne and the floor, succeeding only in jolting her wounded shoulder yet again. Gwynne rolled out of her grasp and curled into a fetal position on the wooden floors. It seemed the convulsions had stopped, and Gwynne was still. Cassie scrambled over to check on her. It seemed the blade had sliced her face open from chin to forehead, leaving an awful gash. The only grace was that the cursed fire had instantly cauterized the wound, meaning it was no longer open, but still just as grisly. For the first time since Gwynne had met Cassie, she began to cry.

12

A Wizard's Confession

Quite Literally the Worst I've Ever Been - My Father's Strongest Memories - Spacial Recursion is a Powerful Magic - It's to Her that We Now Fly

The *Pale Moon* beat a hasty retreat from the Black Eagle Keep. Gwynne did not disclose their next destination, but told Horatio only to head south. The mountains disappeared from beneath the craft within a day, and eventually the airship was soaring above grassy plains and then the glittering ocean. Cassie had never seen the sea before, and this much water made her nervous. She also had no clue where this was, but clearly it was somewhere far to the south of Zona.

The night of the heist, Gwynne had retreated to her room and locked the door. As far as Cassie could tell, Gwynne's only injury was the gash across her face, but it was clean and closed, so there wasn't much to do for it. The curse that Mordecai's blade had channeled was another matter altogether, and the wound to Gwynne's emotions was far deeper besides.

The ramifications of that night weighed heavily on Cassie's mind, but she decided not to think about it. Regardless of how Gwynne had been born, it had no bearing on the woman she was today, and Cassie left it to her to decide how to address the elephant in the room. Feckalia was intensely curious to know what happened, but Cassie convinced her that it was Gwynne's business to talk about it and not hers to gossip. Besides, Cassie was well acquainted with feelings of dysphoria and knew that sometimes you just needed some time alone to feel right in your own skin again.

A few days later, Cassie found herself out on the terrace near Gwynne's room for no particular reason other than a desire to look at the ocean. Even at this altitude, the air was filled with a smell of wet salt. Gwynne was there, finally out of her room, and was leaning against the railing looking pensive. It seemed she had cut her hair short and her usual bombastic purple had been replaced with a moody raven black. She didn't stir when Cassie came out, and Cassie leaned on the railing beside her.

"You know, I've never seen the ocean before. Seems kind of silly to admit next to everything you've done. I guess I never expected it to be so… *big*."

Gwynne spoke for the first time in days. "There's a lot of world out there. Zona and even Abaxia are just a small part of it."

"I'm sure you've seen things that I couldn't even imagine."

Gwynne gave a weak smile, her face still split by the wound. "That and then some."

The two women stood in silence for a few minutes, just watching the roiling blue pass far beneath them. Cassie wasn't sure what exactly to say to Gwynne. What *could* she say? Her stomach churned and her heart pounded at this state of emotional vulnerability. Even with the grotesque scar, Gwynne was very beautiful. Cassie's dumb gay brain fumbled for words, before finally sputtering out, "A-are you okay, Gwynne?"

Stupid, is that really the best you can do? Cassie's mind berated her. *Tell her how you feel!*

Gwynne's brow furrowed slightly. "I'm twice cursed, my masterfully crafted face has been split open, my career as Owl is in shambles, and I was embarrassed in front of the most important people in the kingdom. This is quite literally the worst I've ever been."

Cassie tried to inch closer. "Do you... want to talk about it?"

Gwynne looked at her with perplexion, as if the concept of talking about one's feelings was foreign and unusual to her. "Why?"

"It'll make you feel better. Have you... never talked about your feelings before?"

Gwynne looked aghast, as if she found the idea horrifying. "No... I... Nobody's ever offered to listen to me before."

Cassie couldn't help but feel sorry for Gwynne and the lonely life she must have led.

"I understand, Gwynne. I... never had any real friends growing up. I mostly just tagged along with groups of boys from school out of some misguided sense of obligation, but I never really belonged. It wasn't until a few years ago that I figured out why. The only person I felt any kind of connection to was Jax, one of my coworkers at my old job. We weren't super close, but they were always kind to me. I kind of feel bad about leaving them behind so suddenly."

Gwynne just stared ahead. Cassie wasn't sure if she was listening, or even why she was saying all this, but kept talking anyway.

"I know it's not the same as what you went through. I couldn't even imagine. I just... wanted to let you know that... I'm here for you if you need me, and... I know all too well about certain things."

Gwynne just nodded. "Thank you, Cassie. I think I just need to be alone for now. I will keep your offer in mind."

* * *

Later that day, Cassie was working on spells in the workshop. She was trying to puzzle her way through an incomplete illusion spell when Gwynne entered as if nothing had happened. "Cassie, I need you to break one of my curses."

"You need me to do *what* now?"

Gwynne set the glowing crystal down on her work table. "I'm going to instruct you how to pull the magic out from this crystal into yourself and then cancel it. Dispelling magical effects is an important skill for any mage to have."

"Is that safe? Why do I have to do it?"

"Because…" Gwynne looked troubled for a beat. "It will be good practice for you, and there are a lot of unpleasant energies in that spell that I don't feel like touching right now."

"Well you'll have to wait. I'm right in the middle of this illusion spell and I want to finish what I'm doing before I even think about anything else."

Gwynne peered over the desk at the parchment. "Oh, that's simple. You need to do this…" she grabbed the pen from Cassie's hand and wrote over a line she had already written, "…and this," and added a phrase to the end. "That should do the trick."

"Wow, great, thanks," Cassie was irritated that she had not been able to solve the spell herself.

"You're welcome," Gwynne said, either missing the sarcasm or deliberately ignoring it. "Now you have plenty of time to help me."

Cassie rubbed her temples. To some degree, Gwynne was back to her usual self. Perhaps lifting one of her curses would improve her condition somewhat. "Ok, fine. What do I have to do?"

"Put your hands on the crystal and close your eyes. In Elder, tell the crystal that you accept ownership of the will imbued within."

Cassie spoke the words and instantly felt a cold rush shoot through her hands and up her arms.

"That's it, just a bit longer and it'll be fully transferred."

Images began to flow into Cassie's mind. She saw a courtyard walled in black stone with patches of grass finely tended between brick paths. On one of these patches of grass, two young boys played together with wooden swords, one with curly blond hair and the other with messy brown. The brown haired boy ducked under an overextended swing from the blond boy and deftly disarmed his opponent. He bonked his partner on the head with the wooden sword and the blond boy fell to his knees and began crying. He seemed a bit too old to be crying at something so trivial. Cassie's perspective approached the two boys and she could see arms extending, revealing that this was someone's point-of-view. Two rough and hairy hands extended down to pick the blond boy up from the ground. The three spoke, but there was no sound in this vision so she couldn't tell what they were saying. It seemed the blond boy was being scolded, and he pouted in frustration. The brown-haired boy stood with arms akimbo looking exasperated. The man whose perspective this was guided the blond boy's arms and showed him how to strike properly without wasting so much effort and leaving himself wide open.

The vision faded and Cassie saw the boy again, a young man now, a few years younger than herself. He was dressed in tight-fitted clothing that gave him a feminine feel. She could tell at this point that this was a younger Gwynne, pre-transition. Young Gwynne was using magic to make various stationary hover in the air. She had an expression of pure wonder on her face, one that Cassie had never seen her wear. She could see the same hairy arms cross in front of her below her perspective, and the view shook side to side in disapproval. Young Gwynne's face became crestfallen and the stationary dropped to the desk again. Cassie could hear distorted voices, as if coming from underwater.

"...news about Mother?" young Gwynne asked, in the same voice she used when portraying Owl.

A deep male voice came from Cassie's perspective. "None yet, Abneel. I promise…"

Images flashed in Cassie's mind of a beautiful Abaxian woman, as if the person she was inhabiting was recollecting various memories. This must be Gwynne's mother.

The vision shifted to a dark room where a slightly older and now very feminine Gwynne was having a shouting match with the person whose memories Cassie was occupying, ostensibly King Aberforth Quintus, Gwynne's father. Fortunately, this memory was also muted, though the look of pure heartbreak and rage on Gwynne's face made Cassie hurt inside. Suddenly, there was an explosion where Gwynne stood and moonlight filtered in through a now gaping hole in the wall, Gwynne nowhere to be seen.

"Cassie, are you still with me?" Gwynne's voice shot through the reminiscent reverie, quite clear.

"Y-yeah. A lot of visions just came into my head."

"No doubt some of my father's strongest memories of me. Please do your best to disregard them and focus on my instruction."

The memories were brief and foggy now. There was a flash of a small baby with a single lock of curly blond hair being held by the same woman from before. There was a flash of Gwynne as a child at the dinner table, looking miserable in a stuffy royal outfit and pushing a head of broccoli around the dinner plate.

"Concentrate, Cassie."

"I'm trying. What do I do now?"

"Remember your cancellation phrase? Same one as always."

Cassie uttered the words a bit louder than she had intended, as the rush of mental images was deafening, despite being silent. In an instant, everything stopped and she was back in the workshop once more. She hadn't realized that she was sweating, and wiped her brow.

Gwynne was looking over her.

"Good, I knew you could handle it. If it had been too much for you, you would have been torn apart as soon as you accepted the spell from the crystal."

"You couldn't warn a girl first?"

"You handled it with aplomb. What's the issue?"

"Maybe still work on that sense of empathy, girl. Now, what about this other curse? The one our mutual enemy hit you with? And what's it doing to you, exactly? You seem okay to me."

Gwynne picked up some odds and ends from a nearby desk. "That one is more complicated. Breaking a curse is much more complex than dismissing one. Mordecai is maintaining the curse himself, meaning the only way to remove it is to either kill him or force him to dismiss it, both daunting tasks indeed. Still, it will be sapping some of his energy each day, so we at least have that satisfaction." Gwynne sat down and Cassie walked over to her. Looking over her shoulder, Cassie could see that Gwynne was playing with a set of bones, possibly some sort of knucklebones.

"What are we going to do, then?"

Gwynne rolled the knucklebones like dice and they clacked across the table. "We're going to need some outside help. But for now, please round up the rest of the residents. I would like to make an announcement."

* * *

It took Cassie the better part of an hour to track down everyone. Tibberwyx was easy to find, always hovering about the library. Horatio and the Ranklins were entangled in piping and vents deep within the inner workings of the ship, and it took Cassie about twenty minutes just to figure out where they were. They promised they would be along as soon as they finished their current tasks. Feckalia was the tough one. Cassie checked everywhere, before finally finding the demon woman upside down on the ceiling of a large sort of theatre room that Cassie had never seen in the House before.

"Feckalia? Could you come down, please? I have something to tell you."

She floated down, flipping upright as naturally as one might stand up from a chair. "Have you seen this room before? I swear it didn't exist until just a few minutes ago when I entered it. The further I go into this house, the more I'm convinced that it's infinite."

"Is that likely?"

"I don't put anything past a wizard. Spatial recursion is a powerful magic, but Gwynne is something of a special case. You know, I've never seen a human with nearly this much magical ability? Don't tell anyone, but I suspect our mistress may be a dragon in disguise."

"Mmmmm I don't think so."

Feck gave a quizzical look.

"Gwynne wants to talk to everyone in the parlor. Can you come by, please?"

"Okay, I was done here anyway, but I bet you five crowns that this place disappears when we next try to look for it."

The two made their way down to the parlor where everyone else was already waiting. The Ranklin brothers were taking up the couch and Horatio one of the armchairs. Tibberwyx was floating in the air in the corner, zir iridescent insect wings buzzing. It was strange to see zir out of the library, and it felt wrong somehow, like ze belonged in an entirely separate reality. Cassie took the last armchair and Feck threatened to sit on her lap, but at a scathing look decided to sit on the chaise lounge by the front window instead. Gwynne was standing at the fireplace, composing herself. This couldn't be easy for her. Coming out was a difficult and emotional process at the best of times, much more so for someone who was as emotionally neglected as Gwynne.

Everyone eventually fell quiet, waiting for Gwynne to speak. She cleared her throat and looked into the middle distance. Could Gwynne be nervous? Where was all the bravado that Owl had shown at the party? Though Cassie supposed this was a more intimate setting and a much more personal topic.

"So, before someone gets ahold of a newsprint, I'd like to clear up some things that I may not have communicated to you all yet. Please hold your questions until the end. First, you may have heard of the notorious criminal Owl. I'm sure everyone here knows that said criminal is actually me."

Jimmy gasped and Havershank rolled his eyes.

Gwynne smiled. "That's really only the least of it. I've spent the last… oh four years or so stealing from the rich. I've snagged many priceless gems, chests of gold, and impressive works of art. However, these thefts were a mere coverup for my true objectives. You see, every target that Owl has hit had information about something greater. My true goal is to take down King Aberforth Quintus of Zona, AKA my father."

Jimmy's jaw dropped at this. Bimmy piped up. "Yer a princess, miss? T'would explain a lo' t'be sure."

"No, I have renounced my royalty. You all may have heard of… of a certain Prince Abneel who has officially been declared dead. That was my birth name. I was brought up in the King's court and sent to Abaxia to study magic that I might steal the Free State's secrets and become a mage to serve the King. As soon as I graduated the Abaxian University, I ran away from my family, found someone who could alter my body to my specifications, and then was reborn as Gwynne Brandwyck, the woman you see before you. In a way, the propaganda is right."

Jimmy looked like he was doing some rigorous mental gymnastics. "Bu' tha' means…"

Bimmy elbowed him hard in the ribs. "Ge' it togevver, mate. Can' ye read th' room?"

Two and two finally added up to four in the man's brain. "Ohhhhh-hhh…."

Bimmy rolled his eyes. "Well that don' mean naught to us, does it, mates? We've no love fer the crown no more, and we don' pry into others' business. Ain' that right, brovvas?"

"Yeah, we're wit' ye t' the end, boss." Jimmy was beaming now. Havershank just gave an enthusiastic thumbs up.

"I knew all that already," Feckalia scoffed. "A few of your hairs and a little divination magic told me everything I wanted to know. I just want to say, and I mean this in the most positive way, that I genuinely don't care. I'm more interested in your magic by far."

Tibberwyx buzzed up to Gwynne. "You brought me out here to talk about *gender*, human? I'll be in the library." Ze left the room in a twinkling flash.

Horatio chuckled from the armchair where he looked comically small. "Heh, I suppose ye got yer answer, there, lass. We're all par' o' th' crew an' if ye say to damn the crown, then we'll damn it wit' ye."

Cassie got up, finally deciding to speak her piece. "As a fellow Changer, I at least appreciate the effort it took to talk about all this, Gwynne." She tried not to meet Jimmy's gaze, who was staring at her slack-jawed. "And I want to reiterate that you have my support as well. Your enemies are mine."

"Wai' a mo'" Jimmy interrupted. "I always 'eard 'at Changers were icky child-snatchers."

Bimmy buried his face in his hands in embarrassment. "Mate, listen. Ye can' believe all tha' gossip."

"Bu' tha's wot I'm sayin', innit? 'Ere I was, finkin' all me life tha'

Changers were bad, but I'm jus' now findin' out tha' two o' the mos' amazin' people in the world are Changers. It's jus' right sad, it is..." Jimmy began to tear up, ever the softie.

"Oi, get it togevva, will ye?" Bimmy chided, starting to sniffle, himself. "'Ese gals don' wan' ye sympathy, ye goon."

Gwynne smiled. "Yes, things are quite grim out there for us, but your support is very much appreciated."

"My only question," Cassie said, "is what the hell kind of Changing Potion have you been taking? Because damn, girl, you look good."

It might have just been Cassie's imagination, but Gwynne seemed to blush a bit at this affirmation. "That's an excellent segue, Cassie," she said, again distracting from heavy emotions with pragmatism. "I haven't needed the potion in years. When I ran away from the palace after graduation, I hired the services of an expert who sculpted me a new body."

"But... wouldn't that be Biomancy? Isn't that supposed to be impossibly difficult?"

Gwynne's eyes twinkled. "Not for a witch. I have something of a business relationship with a very powerful witch named Beatrice Eldegrand who lives in the middle of the Kahlane Rainforest, though she goes by a different name to the locals. It's to her that we now fly."

"To repair your face?" Cassie asked.

"That and to remove the curse placed upon me by my former friend-turned-dark crusader Mordecai. I've divulged the basics of the battle that took place that night in Black Eagle Keep, but I must now disclose the nature of this curse. It seems that the curse has severely limited my capacity to perform magic."

Cassie couldn't help but gasp. "But... without your magic..."

"That's right, Cassie. Without my magic, I'm just your everyday gorgeous and fabulous woman, albeit one in ownership of a magical flying mansion and with a badass scar on her face. While Cassie was able to dismiss the curse that Ackerman had cast on me since we stole the crystal, this one will require force to break, and there's only one other mage that I trust to do that. Friends, we're going to pay a visit to Baba Yaga."

IV

Kahlane Rainforest

13

Sweat and Blood

A Carpet of Death - A Veritable Rite of Passage - Remember Your Vector Addition! - Scarlet Flames Blossomed

Before Cassie knew it, she was up to her armpits in thick undergrowth. It was sweltering hot and thick humidity filled her lungs. Insects nipped at her skin and thick vines tripped her step. On top of everything, it threatened to rain. The climate was a complete shock compared to the frigid peaks where the Black Eagle Keep was located, but Cassie wasn't sure this was any better. Gwynne, on the other hand, seemed to be relishing the hostile environment.

The two had come alone, as Gwynne had said the witch would not take kindly to too many unfamiliar faces. Unfortunately without her magic, Gwynne could not pinpoint the witch's exact location.

"Her home moves, you see," Gwynne had said, "so she's never in the same spot twice. Normally I'd use magic detecting spells to narrow it down, but in my current state, this isn't an option."

After a round of discussion, Cassie had convinced Gwynne to let her attempt some of the divination. She wasn't able to do anything large-scale, but after a bit of experimenting, she was able to detect two distinct magical signatures in the jungle, but couldn't distinguish their strengths. In the end, Gwynne made the executive decision to start with the signal to the south, as it was near a large lake. Apparently the witch liked to stop by bodies of water, and it was a distinct landmark besides.

Gwynne had forbidden Cassie from teleporting them down, as teleporting somewhere unfamiliar was a recipe for disaster. As such, they took the trundling landing craft once more, clunking through the air and puffing smoke, targeting a rare clearing in the canopy. From here, the *Pale Moon* looked like a gigantic gray bird soaring above the rainforest but below the ominous gray clouds. Cassie still couldn't tell exactly how the sprawling manor fit aboard the craft, but suspected magic was at play.

Eventually, the wizard and her apprentice touched down in the clearing, which they could now see was filled with stumps of once mighty trees. Gwynne looked concerned.

"This forest is supposed to be sanctioned. Who the hell has been logging here? Curse that blackguard Mordecai. What I wouldn't give to cast some spells right now and find the ones responsible. No doubt a Zonan company."

The ground crunched beneath Cassie's feet. It seemed the undergrowth had been burned away, leaving a carpet of death in its wake. She tried not to think about all the animals that had no doubt perished as part of this destructive operation.

The two had decided to move on before they got too worked up, and now found themselves in the thick of the jungle where Cassie was dripping with sweat and swatting bugs left and right.

"Gwynne, this is miserable. Isn't there a spell that can make things a bit more hospitable?"

"Oh, absolutely there is. I don't know it, personally, but you're a bright young woman. You could figure it out if you really want."

"What's the catch? I was expecting you to tell me that it was impossible."

"You mean besides the fact that you'd have to maintain it all day? Or the fact that I have no clue what the Elder word for 'insect' is? No, no catch at all."

Cassie rolled her eyes. "You could have just said so."

Eventually, the pair came to a rough dirt path that wound its way through the trees. It seemed to be headed in the general direction of their goal, so they decided to follow it.

"We should be wary of the inhabitants of the jungle, Cassie. There's no telling what they'll do."

"Do you mean… natives?"

"Oh, no, the people who live here are perfectly harmless, quite lovely in fact. I stayed with them for about a month when briefly I studied underneath Miss Eldegrand. They make the *best* coffee, Cassie, you have to try it. Oh, and their folklore is absolutely fascinating. I really must take you there sometime."

"Then who are we watching out for?"

Gwynne's eyes narrowed. "The fey."

"What, like Tibb? How bad could they be?"

"You have no idea. Let's just say that Tibberwyx is uncharacteristically agreeable for fey. Mostly they just want to trick you into falling for what they see as pranks, but to us is really cruelty. Some fey are perfectly nice, however, but the difficulty of it is that you can never really tell, and at the very least they all follow a set of rules and laws that are quite counter-intuitive for us humans."

"Sounds like a headache."

"You don't know the half of it."

At this point, there was a sound of rushing water in the distance that heralded a waterfall. In course, the trees opened upon a rocky gorge through which white water surged, whipping around jagged rocks to form churning rapids. The dirt path led up to a worn rope-and-plank bridge that dangled with creeping vines. Gwynne's eyes lit up with excitement at this staple of jungle adventure.

"Look, Cassie, a rope bridge! I don't remember this from my time here before. We simply must cross it."

"Oh no, there's no way you're getting me on that rickety thing. I've read enough books to know what happens next."

"Oh don't be a *spoilsport*, Cassie. It's a veritable rite of passage as an adventurer to cross a perilous rope bridge."

"Yeah, and it's a veritable *cliché* when the rope bridge snaps halfway through and the dashing heroes must scramble for their lives."

"We *are* quite dashing, aren't we?"

Cassie crouched down to rest a bit. "Ugh, you're not even listening to me, are you?"

"Attention span of a goldfish, my tutors used to say."

"Aye, and selective hearing like an old maid."

"Hey, I resent that! I'm not *that* much older than you, Cassie."

"You're twenty-six, which may as well be eighty for all I care."

"Then you should do well to respect your elders, young one!"

Gwynne and Cassie looked at each other before breaking out laughing at their own banter.

"No, but seriously, Cassie. Let's cross the bridge."

Cassie massaged her temples. "Can't we just fly over it?"

"Do you have access to a fly spell?"

"I prepared one, yes."

"Ahh, now that's using the old noodle. Better save that for a sticky situation, though. Wouldn't want you falling to your death."

"Which is precisely what will happen if I try to cross that decrepit bridge!"

"Then you've got your fly spell ready, so what's the problem? Besides, I wouldn't go so far as to call it *decrepit*. Perhaps *derelict*, or even *disused*, but these ropes are still in working condition." Gwynne twanged one of the ropes, causing a rain of dirt and dust to dislodge from the length of the bridge and snow down on the river below.

Cassie sighed. Clearly Gwynne had cornered her logic, but she didn't want to give her the satisfaction. "Okay, fine. We'll cross your death bridge, but if I fall and have to save myself with a flight spell, I *will* give you hell about it later."

Gwynne beamed, a big fan of cowing others with her ballista of a personality. "See, it's just like I told you before. As long as you stick by me, you're the safest you'll ever be." Without waiting for a response, she stomped out onto the wooden planks of the bridge. The rope creaked under Gwynne's weight, but showed no sign of rupture.

Cassie followed with utmost reluctance. "Big talk from the wizard with no magic."

"Yes, well, we're working on that, aren't we?"

Every step on the bridge felt like the planks would shatter at any moment, plunging Cassie into the roiling drink beneath where she would certainly meet her end upon the jagged and piercing stones.

"Stop looking down, Cassie," Gwynne warned. "You're only going to scare yourself further."

Cassie blushed. "I'm fine! An ounce of caution is perfectly reasonable in this situation."

"Just keep looking ahead and you'll be fine."

Cassie gripped the rope railings tightly. There was barely more room than for one person abreast, and Gwynne's movement ahead was making the whole bridge sway beneath her feet. She wasn't sure if her nerves could handle *not* looking down, but just as she was steeling herself to look ahead, something erupted from the rapids below. A lithe, scaled form breached the spray and rocketed up towards Cassie.

"Gwynne!" Cassie barely had time to shout before the creature impacted the bridge. Gwynne began to turn on her heels, but it was too late. The creature split the bridge between the two and Cassie began to fall. In that split second, Gwynne was able to grab hold of the frayed ropes as her half of the bridge sailed towards the opposite cliff. Cassie wasn't so lucky, and her feet slipped out from under her, sending her sailing into thin air. She may have been taken by surprise, but she was ready for just such a scenario. Closing her eyes and muttering the completion chant, she finished the flight spell she had prepared earlier in the day. While one second she felt the sickening stomach drop of falling, she was now suspended in the air. She opened her eyes. Circling towards her on leathery wings was the glistening serpentine form that had rent the bridge asunder mere moments hence. It was roughly the size of a human, and resembled what Cassie suspected a dragon to look like, only it had hooked bat-like wings instead of forelegs and various ichthyan fins spurred off its form. It screeched at her like a bird of prey and swooped towards her with rear talons extended.

"Get out of there, Cass!" Gwynne shouted. Cassie spared her a side glance, and saw that Gwynne's bridge had fallen to rest against the north cliff face. Gwynne was hanging on for dear life, but still was looking back to aid her.

Wasting no time, Cassie willed herself forward, shooting towards Gwynne at speed.

"No, not pure horizontal, Cassie! Remember your vector addition! You still need to counteract gravity if you wish to stay aloft."

She was right. Cassie was quickly losing altitude. She took a split second to recalculate and managed to slow her descent. The whole matter of the spell was quite counter-intuitive, but she managed to balance the forces on her and accelerate forward. The creature corrected out of its dive, confused by its prey's evasive measures despite the obvious lack of wings. This didn't stymie it for long, and it glided around to follow Cassie.

"What do I do? How do I lose this thing?"

Gwynne was starting to climb, now that Cassie had gained control of her spell. "Just keep it busy for now. Once I'm back on solid ground, we can retreat into the foliage. It won't be able to follow us in there."

Once again Cassie found herself Gwynne's scapegoat, but there wasn't anything for it. Gwynne was completely exposed and defenseless in her current position. Cassie looped around the gulch, quickly mastering the art of flight by force vectors. She visualized an arrow overlapping her body that pointed in the direction she thrust herself, though turns were a little tricky, especially in three dimensions. Additionally, her magical flight was not very fast, and the naturally airborne creature was swiftly catching up. Cassie dove down to the water line, hoping to lose it amidst the rocks, but instead the creature dove straight into the river with only the lightest splash. She tried to look for the beast as she wove between shark tooth rocks, but it was invisible beneath the water. Suddenly, a flash of color appeared beneath Cassie. She rolled to starboard as the creature shot out of the water once more, but not before its claws drew a line of blood on her arm. The wound was shallow, though, so she kept flying. Clearly water was its natural habitat. Gwynne was almost to the top of the cliff, and Cassie had an idea. She flew up to the opposite cliff and waited against its craggy embrace. The creature charged towards her through the air, thinking her cornered. At the last second she kicked off from the wall, narrowly avoiding another kiss of the monster's claws. The creature itself slammed into the cliff face, dislodging stones and gravel on impact. This disoriented the beast, but did not render it inert.

"I'm good now! Let's go, Cassie!"

Those were the words she had been waiting for. She poured all of her energy into a straight charge towards the north cliff. The creature had recovered by the time she reached Gwynne, but by that time the two had already shot into the trees. Cassie could hear the beast's screeching bays in the distance as she landed in a bush and breathed deeply to steady her overworked heart. She gave Gwynne a smug look.

Gwynne rolled her eyes. "Okay, to be fair, it wasn't the bridge's fault."

* * *

Now that the gorge was behind them, they traveled east along the river towards the lake.

"What was that thing, anyway? Was it a dragon?"

Gwynne shook her head. "Sort of, but not exactly. I suspect it was a river drake. Drakes are sort of an offshoot of dragons that lack the intellect and magical prowess of their draconic kin. Drakes are typically little more than just wild animals, though they share blood with the much more intimidating creatures."

Cassie decided she never wanted to meet a proper dragon.

They traveled on this way for what felt like hours. It was difficult to tell the time in the jungle as the sky stayed the same overcast gray with no hope of a clear view of the sun. Cassie was beginning to run out of steam and decided to petition for a break when the sound of something moving through the undergrowth caught both women's attention and they stopped in their tracks. Something quite large was making its way through the trees, trampling underbrush and audibly sniffing the air. It was hard to get a proper look at the thing. It was much larger than the drake, but its true mass was still indeterminate.

Gwynne bid Cassie crouch behind a bush and they watched the creature pass. As it lumbered past their hiding spot Cassie could see a roughly humanoid shape that stood about ten feet tall but would have been taller if it would only improve its posture and stop hunching its back. The creature was covered in a fine green-and-brown fur and wore a primitive cloth around its nether regions. As it tramped it sniffed around, revealing an elongated snout like a crocodile, but covered in coarse fur and with beady black eyes. Altogether the thing looked like a gigantic goblin crossed with a very unpleasant dog. It huffed the humid air through a gnarled and dripping nose and chipped tusks rose from its lower jaw like a boar. The creature spoke in a booming voice and in a guttural language that Cassie didn't understand.

"It smells us, but hasn't seen us," Gwynne whispered.

"What *is* it?" Cassie whispered back.

"Troll."

The troll took a couple steps forward then realized the smell was getting weaker and turned around. It spoke again in a singsong tone that made it all the more horrifying.

"'Come out, come out, wherever you are, tasty man' is what I gathered from that."

"Just let me know if it says anything useful."

"They rarely do."

"Just shut up, for once, Gwynne!"

It didn't seem like the troll could hear them over the cacophony of jungle life, but Cassie didn't want to take any chances. It was gradually honing in on their position via scent, and would be upon them in moments.

"We need to run," she hissed.

"It would easily outpace us in this environment. You saw how it trampled the thickets."

"Then what do we do?"

"Hope for it to lose interest, and then fight if we have to. Got any fire spells?"

Cassie pulled out the notebook Gwynne had given her back at the

Keep. "Yeah, there's one in here."

"Good. When we get back, you're making your own spellbook, got that?"

"Not the time!"

The troll now plodded within feet of their hiding spot, and its putrid musk assaulted Cassie's nostrils. It reeked of unwashed man, feces, and flesh decay. It was all she could do to stop herself from gagging. Its saliva oozed down its jowls, quivering with anticipation of a meal of man-flesh, then plunged to the ground, sizzling where it fell.

"Ooo-man!" the troll bayed from above Cassie, in a pitiable approximation of human speech. Its crusted proboscis gulped down gallons of humid air as it honed in on the two women. Suddenly the snout thrust through the brush right between Cassie and Gwynne. With a *clink* of steel, Gwynne drew her rapier and stabbed the beast in its nose. It roared in pain and reeled back, taking Gwynne with it.

"Now, Cassie! Start the spell!"

Gwynne yanked the rapier free, causing floods of gooey brown blood to gush forth. She stabbed again and again, one blow piercing through one of the creature's runny eyes. But it was merely a nuisance to the troll, for as soon as the sword was retracted, its wounds began to steam, closing up within seconds. Cassie was trying her best to concentrate, reciting the spell for fire. Fortunately she already knew it was a short incantation, and she finished before the beast was able to buck Gwynne into a tree. Scarlet flames blossomed on the creature's chest and spread across its matted fur like kindling. If the creature smelled bad normally, the filth and decay on its form was now properly charred and aerosolized, and this time Cassie did gag. The fire seemed to be properly hurting it, though, and the burns it left across the troll's flesh did not heal over. But it was far from dead or even dissuaded. In its pain and fury, it turned its attention away from Gwynne and thrust a tree-trunk arm at Cassie. She had no time to dodge and the four-fingered fist slammed into her chest, ripping her breath from her lungs and sending her sailing into a patch of thorny brambles. It was hard to breathe, and her skin was scratched up and bleeding in many places. She couldn't move.

"Cassie!" Gwynne shouted, still furiously stabbing at monstrous eyes. She was saturated in the thing's blood, as if she had fallen in mud. The creature reached up its other meaty arm and swiped above its head, knocking Gwynne to the ground where she grunted in pain and struggled to rise.

The troll grinned now, a disgusting display of rotted and broken teeth. The flames had extinguished, and after a few seconds, its burns began to heal along with the stab wounds. It lumbered over to Gwynne and readied an arm to crush her spine. Cassie screamed, but suddenly there was a flash of light and heat. At first, she thought that she had cast more fire, or Gwynne somehow overcame her cursed limitations, but she saw multiple figures charging the beast, each pelting it with rays of scorching immolation. There must have been about six of them, all dancing around the troll as it squealed and roared in pain. One of the figures was holding a guitar, and was playing a spirited song.

The troll succumbed to its burns and collapsed to the jungle ground, but the people around did not stop burning it.

"Don't stop 'til naught but ash remains!"

Cassie thought this was a bit cruel against a creature that could no longer fight back, but she had little sympathy for it, and there wasn't anything she could do, anyway. The forest was dark at this point in the twilight, but the flames lit the vicinity like daylight. Once the gathered figures were satisfied, their spells ended. All that was left of the troll was a vaguely troll-shaped pile of ash on the jungle floor, undergrowth burned away where it lay.

One of the people helped Gwynne to her feet. "You didn't sever anything from it, did you?"

Gwynne shook her head. "I'm not… that foolish."

"Good, because the smallest cutting of flesh or bone could have regenerated the entire troll."

Gwynne didn't respond and just pointed in Cassie's direction. The rest of the group were able to extricate her from the brambles. "Can you two walk?" Someone asked. Gwynne nodded, but Cassie could barely move. Her breathing was labored and her head was spinning.

The voices around her began to grow faint. "Conjure a stretcher! Retzel, begin a healing chant. Let's get these ladies back to camp. Move out!"

Cassie could feel herself being lifted onto a stretch of cloth, then raised from the ground and carried through the dark trees. Gwynne walked ahead of her, leaning on one of the people of the group. Guitar music floated through the air and Cassie thought she was hallucinating. "Haha… Gwynne I can see your butt…" Cassie chuckled in her delirium before passing out.

14

Company of Mages

The Guitar is Real - A Mean Shrimp Boil - The Luxuries of Modern Living - Defensive Formation

Cassie clawed her way back to consciousness, no stranger to doing so under Gwynne's watch at this point. Her whole body ached as if she had rolled down a particularly rocky hillside. She sat up to find that she was laying on a crude cot in a canvas tent. It was dark save for the flickering light of fire from outside. She remembered being punched by the troll and her ribs creaked in response. She felt herself and realized she was in her smallclothes, but that all the superficial scratches and cuts from the brambles had healed, though a few scabs remained behind. Furthermore, while she was still sore, her bruised chest felt a bit clearer than before.

She rose from the cot, found her clothes and bag nearby, and exited the tent after dressing. She wasn't quite sure where she was, but there were four other tents all around a central camp fire. She saw Gwynne sitting here with five people she did not recognize. They looked Abaxian, and wore what were possibly military uniforms, though the most well-designed and good-looking uniforms she had ever seen.

They looked more like fancy suits in deep colors, with many pockets and straps. She assumed they must be soldiers, and from context she realized they must be from the Abaxian Mages' Corps. One soldier sat a distance away from the campfire, quietly strumming a guitar.

Oh good, the guitar is real. I could have sworn I hallucinated that detail, Cassie thought. She waited politely outside the circle of people for an opening in the conversation. Gwynne seemed to be the center of attention, her favorite place to be, describing their trek through the jungle up to the troll encounter.

"Oh, there you are!" Gwynne said, ushering her to sit beside her. "This is my associate Cassie that I told you all about. She's a bit of an aspiring wizard." The group laughed, a bit mean-spirited, Cassie thought. "I only hope I become as talented as her someday." Okay, now Gwynne was making fun of her, but she didn't say anything about it.

"Nice to meet you all. To whom do I owe this pleasure?"

A man with closely-shaved hair nodded to her. "Major Jep Hanz; 24th ranger's company of the Mages' Corps of Abaxia. We've also got Captain Moira Kant…" a woman with a tight bun saluted, "Sergeant Mick Stevens…" a tall man with a wide smile gave a cheeky wave, "Corporal Lin Hastings…" a woman with a completely bald head and a cold expression gave an upwards nod, "and lastly over there with the guitar is our resident bard, Private Ollien Retzel." The man with the guitar gave a flourish by way of greeting. His hair was closely trimmed in a neat fade, and he had a thin mustache growing on his upper lip. Upon closer inspection, he seemed to be younger than Cassie, and couldn't be older than twenty.

"Pleasure to meet you all. I'm sorry you had to meet us in the midst of battle with that troll, we're usually a bit more refined than that."

"That thing nearly had you for dinner, heheh!" Sgt. Stevens said, with a laugh. Cassie didn't think the possibility of their imminent demise was so funny.

"It's just a good thing we came along when we did, then," Cpt. Kant said, trying to cut off Stevens's irreverent comment. She had a warm and relaxing voice that Cassie quite liked.

"The real question," Gwynne cut in, "is what in the blue hell was a troll doing here?"

Mjr. Hanz cleared his throat. "Well I was hoping you could tell us that. We were under the impression that the worst we'd have to deal with is some resident fey."

"Oh, they're still an issue to be sure, but the presence of a troll raises quite different concerns. They are not natural creatures, of course, and usually only spawn in areas of extreme negativity. We only came upon it by chance, but it seemed to be following the scent of humans. Perhaps it was tracking you?"

The soldiers exchanged glances. "We need to cover our tracks better, then," Kant said. "But fortunately we should be moving from this camp come morning. We've a mission here."

"A mission?" Cassie asked.

Kant and Hanz looked at each other and shrugged. "We're looking for a certain someone," Hanz said. "There's apparently a witch in this region who the locals know as Baba Yaga."

Gwynne's eyebrow cocked. "What do you want with her?"

Hanz started to speak, but Kant cut him off. "We could really use her help for the war."

"Hah! I don't think she'd be willing for that, but you're welcome to try," Gwynne scoffed.

"Whaddayou know about her, anyway, fancy boots?" Stevens said, giving her a quizzical look.

Gwynne just smiled. "Oh, we've met. She helped me out once years ago. We hope to seek her aid again."

Stevens laughed, "I would too, with that split face of yours."

Gwynne's lip quivered into the hint of a snarl, but maintained her composure.

"Knock it off, Sergeant," Kant barked, her warm tone replaced with an officer's bite.

Stevens just shrugged. "I'm just callin' it like it is, Captain."

"Well stop it. We're not trying to scare our friends here away."

'Friends' was a bit generous, but Cassie gave a polite smile anyway.

"At any rate," Hanz said, trying to steer the conversation back on topic, "it sounds like we share a common objective. What say you to traveling together? It'd certainly make any further trolls much less deadly."

Gwynne appeared to consider the offer, but Cassie could tell that she had already made up her mind. Gwynne lived for the attention, and even Cassie could not deny that she felt safer with five highly-trained mages around.

"Very well, I suppose we can work together," Gwynne said, coyness not fooling anyone.

Hanz stood up and dusted off his pants. "Well, let's go ahead and eat, then, so we can tuck in for the night and set off at dawn."

"Oh, I can handle the cooking," Gwynne said, seizing an opportunity to flaunt. "Cassie, can you hand me our bag?"

Cassie handed her the knapsack that she had brought with her. Gwynne extracted the wondrous bag, and plunged her arm elbow deep in its contents. She first pulled out a cast iron pot, setting it on a rack the soldiers had laid over the fire. "I'm thinking… paella? Sound good to everyone?"

"What the hell is that?" Stevens asked.

Gwynne grinned. "Oh, then you're in for a treat. Can I get a table?"

Hanz ordered Stevens to drag a small collapsible wooden table out from one of the tents. Gwynne produced a cutting board and a sharp chef's knife. She chopped up a number of vegetables and began sauteing onions in the pan. When those were cooked, she added the other vegetables, then sliced-up chunks of chicken, dry rice, a splash of white wine, some water, then a sort of crumbly brown powder from a paper envelope, and then finally a bunch of different herbs and spices. Everyone looked on in confusion and amazement, but the scents wafting from the pot were rich and fragrant, making Cassie's mouth water.

After about half an hour, the soupy consistency had reduced down and was absorbed by the rice, leaving behind a flavorful mixture of rice, meat, and vegetables. There was enough for everyone in the camp to have two servings. Everyone told Gwynne how good it was, except for Corporal Hastings, who just gave Gwynne a nod of approval before saying, "Didn't suck."

Stevens rolled his eyes. "What are you *talking* about, Hastings? This is the best damn meal I ever had, shy of my momma's home cooking."

Hastings just shrugged. "I dunno, food all tastes the same to me."

"I'd like to meet your mother, then," Gwynne said.

"Oh, she can make a *mean* shrimp boil, I tell you what." Stevens then went on a fifteen minute tangent about his mother, to which Cassie only half-listened. She was content with eating Gwynne's cooking, and she thought back to the remark that Feckalia had made some weeks hence. A cook would be welcomed at the House, but they'd have to compete with Gwynne's ego and need to be in control of everything. Still, Gwynne seemed to acquiesce to Cassie's recruiting decisions, if the precedent set by the Ranklin brothers meant anything.

Stevens was wearing down Hastings's patience. "Alright, fine," she said. "The food is good, I'll admit. Better than rations at any rate."

After everyone finished eating, Private Retzel performed a song for the group that the soldiers all knew well, singing along in off-key unison. They sang of friends back home, lovers left behind, and the noble sacrifice of duty. Cassie had never heard this song before, and although the distinctly nationalistic lines failed to resonate with her, she felt the musical style awaken some sort of cultural homesickness the likes of which she had never before felt.

After the song finished, Major Hanz bid them all to sleep. Everyone milled about, finishing their nightly preparations. Gwynne took the bag from Cassie and told her to wait while she set up their tent. Cassie was a bit worried about Gwynne's wilderness survival skills, so to take her mind off it she decided to talk to Private Retzel. He was a little ways away at the river near where it met the lake, much calmer and drake-free here, washing his hands and face.

"Hello," Cassie said, walking up by him. "I really enjoyed your playing earlier. Um… do you think maybe you could tell me more about that kind of music?"

Retzel turned to face her, looking her up and down with an expression of shock on his face. It seemed he didn't know what to say.

Cassie kept talking to fill the awkward silence. "Um… sorry if that's weird. We didn't have much music in my hometown, save for a single gramophone in the local tavern, and I uh… didn't spend a lot of time there."

Retzel didn't say anything for a second, with the expression of one who thought they were in trouble.

"Sorry, is now a bad time? I didn't mean to disturb you."

"The guitar… been playing it since I was a kid." Retzel spoke for the first time that night. His voice had the high and soft quality of a teenager, despite his age. "My dad used to make 'em, see. Didn't make much money off 'em, but we had Basic, so we survived. As soon as I was old enough to reach the top fret he put a guitar in my hand and taught me chords. Ever since then I could… I could make things happen when I played. Made people happy, made the wounded heal, made bullies change their mind about punching me, y'know. Started performing when I was fourteen and got banned from a lot of taverns for charming tips right out of people's pockets." He gave a quiet but youthful laugh. "So it only seemed right that I study. Get better, y'know. Only way I could do that was on a military scholarship, and here I am. Graduated the University at twenty, and now I'm here."

Cassie blinked, not expecting this deluge of information. "Wait, how old were you when you enrolled?"

"S-sixteen, ma'am."

"Oh gods, I feel old."

"H-how…" Retzel started.

"Barely older than you now. Gosh, they're really starting them off young these days."

Retzel gave a bashful smile. "I'm a bit of a… a special case. Had the gift all my life. Plenty of people enroll who are… y'know, older than you."

He was trying to reassure her, Cassie realized, but she still felt quite inadequate.

"Cassie! Tent's finished. Come see!" Gwynne called from back at the camp. Cassie bid goodnight to Private Retzel and found her wizard standing in front of a small, plain canvas tent looking very proud of herself. "Had to put it up the old-fashioned way, you know. I've had this baby in storage since I was last here, so I hope it still works." She pushed aside the flap and disappeared into the tent. Cassie braced herself for cramped quarters and dismal sleeping conditions, and was thus shocked when the inside of the tent completely defied her expectations. The interior must have been five times larger than the exterior in floor space alone, with a canopied ceiling that rose almost ten feet above them at its apex. The floor of the tent was the same canvas as the rest, but it was almost entirely covered in fine plush rugs with intricately woven patterns. In the very center was a stone-ringed firepit equipped for rotisserie as well as grilling. It reminded Cassie a bit of the gyro stand they had visited in Abaddon, but more compact. Many cushions sat around the firepit, and two lavish cots bedecked with furs and fluffy feather comforters were blocked off by paper screens. At the very back was another screen that sectioned off a large wooden washtub complete with a variety of soaps, hair tinctures, washing implements, and perfumes. Two large white towels stood stacked beside it. Best of all, the cacophony of jungle life was extinguished inside the tent and it was completely silent.

"What in the world is this?" Cassie gaped.

Gwynne grinned. "Picked this baby up from a traveling merchant years back when I was still in university. It was a fierce battle, haggling it off him. This tent can support up to eight people, determined when it's set up, is fully equipped for a luxurious night's stay, fully climate-controlled, and with adjustable sounds. I can make it sound like a thunderstorm outside if you want." She hopped over to a set of dials near the entrance and turned one. Thunder rocked the air and lightning illuminated the canvas. Raindrops like falling gravel pounded on the top of the tent. "Oops, maybe a bit too loud." Gwynne turned another dial and the sound became quieter, as if the storm was moving away. "What do you think, Cassie? I've been dying to learn all the spells that go into this thing, but haven't had the time just yet."

Cassie sat down on one of the beds and began removing her boots. It felt like sitting on a cloud, and she would know, having been through a few on that devil of a landing craft in her time. While the tent exceeded her every expectation, she was used to miracles at this point.

"Could do with a proper bath," she criticized. This drove Gwynne crazy.

"Oh come *on*, Cassie! We're in the wilderness. You're going to have to do without some of the luxuries of modern living."

"Just some, though."

"Well we're not *barbarians*. You think *I* could sleep on a bedroll on the ground? Gods forbid bathe in a *river*? Have you any idea how many parasites live in that water? Yuck!"

Cassie laid down on the bed, her exhausted feet and aching muscles finally finding some relief. She barely had the energy to undress behind the screen before she fell into a deep sleep, hearing the illusion of rain all around her.

* * *

When Cassie awoke in the morning, it really was raining. It was to be expected, given the climate, but it still made her dread their trek that day. She dressed in haste and looked out of the tent flap. To her amazement, the ground was completely dry. The rain seemed to be parting somewhere above the camp and falling around it instead. The faint sound of plucking guitar strings interwove the staccato percussion of the precipitation. The soldiers were already dressed, packed, and ready to go.

"Oh look who's finally awake," Major Hanz said. "It's already after dawn, you all need to be quicker to pack camp."

Back inside the tent, Gwynne snored. Cassie roused her, aghast to find that she slept in the nude, modesty preserved by messy blankets. Cassie tried her hardest not to look as she shook her awake. "Gwynne, c'mon, we gotta go."

"Jus' five more minutes," Gwynne murmured, rolling over and drooling on the pillow a bit.

"Either you get up now with dignity or I rip those blankets off you, you spoiled baby. The soldiers are going to leave us behind."

At this, Gwynne promptly prepared herself and exited the tent. With a snap of her fingers, the tent collapsed into a folded pile of canvas that she tucked into the wondrous bag. It was like they had never been there.

With that, the seven people set off into the jungle. The rain deflection spell followed the group, centered on Private Retzel's location, and Cassie found that the spell was also layered with a climate ward and insect repellent.

Just the thing we needed yesterday, she thought. *So this is what bardic magic is like. Perhaps I can learn a thing or two from him.*

As they walked, Gwynne produced mixes of nuts, dried fruit, dried meats, and little bits of chocolate in individual paper bags. She handed one to Cassie. "Horatio prepared this. Called it 'trail mix'. Hope it makes for a good morning snack."

The two women munched as they walked. Judging by their trajectory, Hanz was leading them directly to that other magical signature that Cassie had detected so long ago in the manor. She hoped she could trust these people. They had already saved her life once before, which lent them major credibility.

Speaking of which, Major Hanz was leading the group, parting the thick undergrowth in swathes with waves of his hands. A small red-scaled winged serpentine form perched on his shoulder, reeking of magic. Cassie assumed Hanz must be a warlock who had formed a pact with a young dragon. The dragon paid no attention to any of the other humans, and communicated with Hanz in a strange guttural language she did not recognize.

"So Hastings, how long you got with the Corps?" Stevens asked.

Hastings's answer was typically stiff. "Six years still."

"An' then what? Got any big plans? Got someone waitin' for ya at home?"

"No."

"No? Nothing at all?"

"The Corps is the only place I can properly practice my craft." Hastings ran her palm over the pommel of a curved saber sheathed at her side.

Private Retzel fell in step with the two civilians, continuing to strum as easily as he breathed. "Corporal Hastings is a specialized kind of wizard called a magus. Basically they study both spellcraft and swordplay, channeling spells through their blades."

Gwynne's curiosity was piqued, and she asked many questions about various spells and areas of study. Hastings clearly wasn't used to the attention, and seemed a bit uncomfortable by the barrage of inquiries.

"Look, civvie, I can recommend some books if you want to know more. I don't have time for a magic lesson right now."

"If you don't mind me asking one last question," Cassie finally spoke up, "what made you decide to specialize in something so focused on combat? Seems like it might not have many applications outside of fighting."

Hastings shrugged. "The Corp's my home. I'm fine being a weapon, not that I expect a civvie to understand."

Cassie couldn't understand this mindset, being such an anti-nationalist herself, but supposed it took all types.

The party entered a clearing and decided to stop for a quick break. "What about you, then?" Gwynne asked Stevens.

"Me what? Oh, you mean like aspirations. Well, I'd always wanted to open up my own restaurant. Spread my momma's coastal cooking style across the country. It's dumb, I know."

"No, I think that's actually quite wonderful. Consider us customers."

Stevens smiled. "Y'know what? Y'all are alright. Weird, but alright."

The group finished their break, having made sure to stay hydrated. The humidity of the jungle was oppressive, even with Retzel's climate warding, and Cassie was sweating buckets. As everyone began to move out again under Hanz's orders, Cassie decided to try talking to Retzel again. She walked beside him as he plucked out an arpeggiated pattern on his guitar.

"So, what's bardic magic like?" she asked. "I've only studied wizardry so far."

Retzel thought about this before answering. "I… only know the basics of wizardry. Had a 101 class about the different styles. It's a lot of the same thing in that we both study the Elder Tongue, but I've always felt like the words have just come naturally to me. There's a sort of flow that you get to bardic incantations where you just start playing and the rest just kind of comes out naturally. Also the structure of a song can really affect the outcome of the spell. Like, too many key changes can get really overwhelming, or if your verses are too long, an effect might be spread too thin. Does that… make sense?"

"I've never studied music before, so unfortunately not really, but I sort of get what you're saying. At the very least, your guitar playing sounds very good and I am thankful for the ward spell you've been casting over us. I was *dying* from the heat and insects my first day here."

Retzel just gave a nervous smile. "T-thanks…"

* * *

The crew proceeded like this all day, and then again the next day. Cassie was very tired of walking, and as comfortable as her boots were, they were starting to rub blisters into her heels. By the afternoon of the second day with the Abaxian mages, the group was passing through a valley that cut deep into the jungle's floor. The valley was a few miles long but only about a thousand feet across, steep cliffs covered in vines and creepers walling it in. According to Hanz's calculations, this was a significant shortcut that would get them to Baba Yaga's location by the next day.

Thick shrubs grew down in the valley and the noise of jungle life was much quieter here. Everyone was on edge, but couldn't place exactly why. Gwynne had bent Private Retzel's ear, and was asking him about the Corps' mission here. She seemed to think he was the most likely to be intimidated by her and blab.

"But seriously, you think Baba Yaga will help Abaxia just because you *asked*?"

Retzel looked uncomfortable. "Look, I dunno, I-I'm just following the Major's orders."

"Surely there's more to it than just a diplomatic mission. Why couldn't you talented spellcasters just fly straight there? Why the long walk on foot?"

"The Major said the witch can detect us miles off, and an aerial approach would look like an attack. We want her to know that we're approaching peacefully."

Gwynne looked skeptical, but didn't have time to think about it before there was a loud *crack*, then a sound like something thick whipping through the air, punctuated by a sickening squelch of impact on flesh. In an instant, the soldiers snapped to attention, readying combat spells. Looking around, however, Major Hanz was missing from the formation. It wasn't hard to find out where he had gone, as the underbrush parted ahead, leading to a thick tree where the shape of a man was pinned, impaled through the shoulder by a crude wooden javelin. He was bleeding around where the implement had pierced him and was unconscious from the shock and impact, but seemed to still be breathing.

"Battle stations, fellows!" Kant shouted. "Defensive formation. Civvies and bard to the center. Protect the noncombatants and don't let anyone near the Major."

In perfect practiced discipline, Retzel grabbed Cassie's wrist and pulled her towards the tree where Hanz was pinned. Gwynne followed close behind, and the other three soldiers backed up around them, Hastings in the center, flanked by Kant and Stevens, blades drawn all.

There were a few tense minutes while nobody moved. If anybody or anything was out there in the thick shrubs and vines, they weren't moving. While the soldiers kept their gaze trained on their surroundings, Cassie examined the javelin. It had a thin translucent thread attached to it that reminded her of spider webbing, but seemed stronger than normal thread.

"I think," she said, startling the soldiers from their intense concentration, "that this may have been a trap."

As she said this, Cassie noticed a very fine powder snowing down on the group, barely perceptible save for its glisten in the afternoon sun. She looked above and thought she saw a large butterfly with a humanoid body, but she didn't have time to think about it as the powder made her sleepy and she completely lost consciousness.

15

Another World

**The Membranous Wall Oozed Closed - Simple Rescue Op -
Suffering. Starvation. Cruelty. Ignominy. Avarice. Gluttony. -
Black Slime from Every Orifice**

Cassie snapped awake, finding herself unable to move. Around her, her companions were also awake and looking as confused as she felt. She seemed to be tightly bound by thick green vines to a gigantic tree trunk. Each person was bound separately beside her, the vines sprouting directly from the bark of the tree through some unknown magic. The soldiers struggled against their bonds to no avail. Cassie looked over and saw Gwynne looking nervous.

"Everyone, listen to me, quickly." Gwynne took charge of the situation. "We've been captured by fey. No doubt we've been taken to one of their cities. If you want to get out of this place, you have to abide by very specific rules. Don't accept any offers or anything given to you, don't eat or drink anything, always bow back when someone bows to you, and under no circumstances give out your names. If in doubt, just keep quiet and do what I do, understand?"

Even Stevens understood the gravity of the situation, and everyone nodded. Cassie finally got a chance to look around the room. They were inside a chamber made out of a smooth white substance with one wall open to allow a colossal tree to grow through. Tall, thin windows were set into a far wall, but all that could be seen through them was a swirling blue and green light.

After a few minutes, the wall opposite Cassie parted into a circular orifice and a strange creature hovered through. It was a vaguely humanoid form about six feet tall and emaciated, its limbs like matchsticks. No clothes could be seen, and its body was the same pale white all over. It had pointy and chitinous insect legs suspended inches above the floor. Its eyes had the same dual-pupils as Tibberwyx, but they were much larger, giving the creature the appearance of compound eyes. Where hair might have been on another humanoid creature, this creature had a hard beetle's carapace opened to expose gossamer wings that buzzed to keep it aloft. Lastly, it had two twitching antennae that were covered in short pale hairs. The creature opened uncanny lips and spoke. "Greetings humans. I am Voxxinquill, but you may call me Vox. May I please have your names?"

Before anyone else could answer, Gwynne spoke up. "We come in peace. You may call us Joe," nodding to Stevens, "Haley," Kant, "Amanda," Hastings, "Abneel," Gwynne nodded to herself, "And Molly."

The creature stared at Gwynne for a tense few seconds; Cassie thought it must have seen through her lie, but it merely waved a hand in front of them and into a bow. The vines around each member of the party slunk back into the bark of the tree as if they were never there. Cassie saw that everyone was missing their weapons. She tried to surreptitiously cast a spell, but the Elder words would not come to her, blocked off by a mental fog.

"Very well, then. Joe, Haley, Amanda, Abneel, and Molly. I take these names and welcome you into the Court of the Butterfly King. Please follow me."

Gwynne bowed back and gave everyone a look urging them to bow as well. Cassie felt a little silly bowing to this weird insect person, but she didn't question Gwynne's judgment, and the anxiety on Gwynne's face impressed the gravity of the situation on her. Without another word, Voxxinquill flew backwards out of the room. The group followed with Gwynne in the lead, and the membranous wall oozed closed behind them.

Beyond the holding cell was a bright yard, the same swirling cyan light illuminating the sky. Cassie could see large trees blurred in the distance; something in the air impaired the visibility. Formless lights floated at various distances giving the appearance of stars. In the immediate vicinity teal grass grew at her feet to a height of over a foot and various twisted and colorful mushrooms the size of trees were being cultivated around the yard. One let off a puff of spores which dissipated into the atmosphere. There were few other individuals around, but Cassie could see solid shapes flying through the air in groups in the distance, flitting between various extrusions on the colossal trees that glowed with warm light like distant skyscrapers. There was no trace of the Kahlane around, and Cassie wondered if they had slipped into another world.

Across the yard, another building rose high above the ground: chambers extruding from a tree whose canopy disappeared into the mist above. The part that could be called a building seemed to be made out of gigantic mushrooms that were growing out of the tree. She turned around and saw that the chamber from which they had just emerged was also a fungal growth.

Voxxinquill ushered the group across the lawn and to the tree building. It had an entrance of high arches formed in the mycological structure leading to an atrium that put Ackerman's party hall to shame. Rows of tables lined the floors and, shockingly, the walls as well. Insect fey creatures sat at seats around these tables at ninety degree angles eating grotesque meals of multicolored slop as easily as if they were upright.

"Please friends," Vox said, "Eat and drink to your heart's content. You may see the King shortly."

Gwynne led the group over to a table and gave them a warning shake of her head. They were not to touch any of this food. Cassie didn't mind, as the bowls full of lukewarm mush and sizzling cricket legs the size of turkey legs looked repulsive, and she doubted whatever sustenance it could provide would be worth the twisted consequences it bore.

"So, uhh, where the hell are we?" Stevens asked.

"Don't you remember the briefing… uh… Joe? There are fey in the jungle." Kant said.

"I may not've been paying attention to that part."

Hastings rolled her eyes.

Kant continued. "The Major was supposed to be our fey liaison on the off-chance we were to stumble across them, but he's not with us at the moment."

"Where is he?" Hastings asked.

Kant shook her head. "I don't know, Corporal. We can only hope that the folks here have given him medical attention. They do not seem hostile, but I am worried about what might happen if we break the rules."

"As you should be," Gwynne said. Cassie was surprised how nervous Gwynne looked. She was normally unflappable in the face of danger, but something here made her turn pale. "They won't hurt you, but the fey have a very different sense of hospitality than us, and you could find yourself trapped here for a very long time. Not to mention time is a little funny between the fey world and the human one. We need to keep our heads down, find the Major, and get out of here ASAP."

Stevens was reaching to grab what looked like an abstract artist's impression of a ham hock, but Hastings swatted his hand away. "Simple rescue op, got it," she said.

Sound flooded the hall, like trumpets but without any trace of enunciation to the notes. Vox stood at the far end of the room, having emerged from the wall. "The human guests may come forward for audience with the king."

Gwynne rose and led her companions over to where Vox was hovering. They bowed to her and everyone bowed back in response.

"Please, follow me and do not stray."

Vox buzzed through an opening in the wall at quite the clip, and the party had to jog to keep up. On the other side was a staircase that curved upwards at an angle that made Cassie's brain hurt. She carried on anyway and somehow as they made their way along it, the angle in their local vicinity seemed normal, as if the room was twisting around them as they walked. Eventually, the stairs gave way to a flat floor, which she believed led them straight up the interior of the tree trunk. They passed many openings into chambers of varying description, such as rooms filled with flowers, a room entirely full of water that somehow didn't fall through the archway, a library that reminded Cassie of the one in the House, and one filled entirely with gold and shiny gems. Kant had to push Stevens along at the latter, much to his disappointment.

"How in the world does anyone around here know where they're going?" Kant asked.

"Space is a mere formality to the fey," Gwynne explained. "They can project themselves into higher dimensions, so simple three-dimensional geometry is elementary to them."

Hastings was looking a bit green about the gills as they climbed higher and higher.

"Everything okay, Corporal?" Kant asked.

"Yes, Captain. I just… I feel a little off in this place."

Gwynne put Hastings's arm over her shoulder and helped the woman forward. "That's to be expected. You're in a different world that doesn't resolve easily into our understanding of reality. A little nausea is normal and will pass."

"I dunno what you mean, I feel great!" Stevens said, skipping along through the hallways.

"Good for you then, twinkletoes," Hastings said, giving Stevens her signature squint of disapproval.

"Hey guys?" Cassie interrupted. "Where is Vox? I'm afraid I lost sight of them."

Gwynne blanched. "Oh no, please tell me you're kidding."

"Sorry… no." Cassie felt stupid. She was trying to keep an eye on the fey creature, but all the antics of the soldiers had distracted her and they had vanished.

Gwynne sighed. "Well, that was bound to happen. I think they were trying to lose us on purpose. This must be some sort of game or test. Let us see if we can find our own way to the throne room."

Something had been tickling the back of Cassie's mind the entire time she was here, like there was something she was trying to remember. The thought finally bubbled up to the surface as she did a headcount of the group.

"Um… I think we're missing someone."

Kant's eyes narrowed. "…Are we? I… can't remember."

Hastings and Stevens shared confused looks.

"Oh, I remember now, it's the Private! Where's the Private?"

"Right where ya left 'em, lady!" Stevens burst out into a hysterical laughter and even the unflappable Kant began to giggle a bit.

Cassie could remember now, Private Retzel had not been with them the entire time since they arrived, and she had no idea what had happened to him.

"It's this place, it messes with your mind," Gwynne said. "I've been here before, so I'm used to it a bit, but even I was thrown off until you mentioned it, Ca- I mean, Molly. You'll need to keep that sharpness of mind about you, because I'm afraid the oddities are only just beginning."

Kant and Stevens were now singing and dancing together, the enchantment of the place capturing their senses in a rapturous glee. It would have been very funny were the circumstances not so dire and were it not so embarrassing.

"Get ahold of yourselves, soldiers," Cassie said, snapping her fingers to catch their attention. The Captain and Sergeant were attempting to dance a rhythmless flamenco, and doing quite a bad job of it. At Cassie's voice, they blinked and looked around, as if they had lost themselves. Then they looked at each other, still locked in a dancing embrace and quickly stood to attention, their faces trying to hold back their embarrassment.

Gwynne smirked. "Don't worry, fellows. What happens in the fey world stays in the fey world, as they say."

Cassie turned to face down the hallway. "Right, and I don't know about you all, but I'd like to find our missing friends and get the hell out of here. And as the person with the clearest head here, I'm taking charge." She wasn't quite sure what had possessed her to assume command like this, but someone needed to, and she couldn't rely on Gwynne to lead her around by the hand forever.

"But… uh, where are we going?" Stevens said, still looking sheepish.

"I haven't the slightest clue. We'll just have to look around and see if we can get some directions."

Cassie opened the nearest door, which looked like a proper wooden door painted white. It swung open to reveal a small room where a fey creature with a wide jaw was gulping down golden nectar that was oozing from the ceiling.

"Do you *mind?*" the creature gasped, before slamming the door shut in Cassie's face.

"...Okay, not *that* way."

She tried another door and found it led to an identical hallway. It seemed as good a path as any. This hall had no doors except for at its very end, where an asymmetrical door opened into a vast room where narrow staircases wrapped around each other at various orientations in non-euclidean geometries. Without any better course presented to her, Cassie pushed on into this room. She soon found herself quite lost in the twisting and turning passageways, not sure which way was up or down anymore. She turned a corner to find a horse quite impossibly sitting in a fine wooden chair by a tea table elegantly sipping from a porcelain cup, despite having no fingers with which to grip. It just stared at Cassie until it was out of sight. Fortunately, Gwynne and the soldiers were right behind her. They stopped once when Hastings was violently sick over the side of one of the staircases. The puke fell for about five feet before it began to circle back around the room and hurtled right towards the nauseous soldier. She was barely able to duck out of the way before the vomit whizzed past her and splattered on a wall beside the group.

"Do not litter," a voice boomed out from everywhere and nowhere.

"S-sorry about that," Hastings said, wiping her mouth.

A few more flips of perspective later, Cassie watched aghast as a ten foot tall skeleton with a deer skull creaked around a corner and began to charge at the group. Everyone except Gwynne attempted to use magic to ward off the specter, but nothing happened.

"Don't look at it!" Gwynne shouted. "It can't hurt you if you can't see it."

Cassie shut her eyes and the creaking of bone and the chattering of teeth disappeared. After a minute, she opened them again to find that the beast was gone as quickly as it had appeared. Hastings was almost sick again, but managed to suppress it to a gag.

"What the hell was that thing?" Cassie gasped.

"I don't know," Gwynne said. "Some sort of apparition, I think. Everything here is either a spatial warp or some sort of illusion. Illusions lose their power if you can't perceive them. Do you all feel that, though? There's something… heavy nearby."

Gwynne's words made no sense at face value, but somehow Cassie could tell what she meant. There was some sort of pressure coming from nearby that made the hairs on her neck stand on end. "I think we're getting close to something."

The space around them was becoming more and more distorted as they progressed, and eventually they came to a circular chamber around a large glass tube containing a disembodied brain the size of a cow.

Pain. Pain. Pain. Pain. Pain. Pain. A voice blasted into Cassie's mind, clearly not her own. *War. Pain. Death. Nonexistence. Violence. Misery. Greed. Oblivion.*

Hastings looked like she was going to pass out, Kant and Stevens were giggling again, and Gwynne looked like her mind was in a fog. Only Cassie maintained her sanity, despite the troubling torrent of thoughts from the terrifying brain.

"Um…" Cassie said, who had no idea how to process the situation.

"Hello? Is someone there?" A calming and refined voice called from somewhere nearby. Cassie looked down to see a small fey creature dressed in a proper white gentleman's suit standing before her. They looked like Tibberwyx, only dressed differently, and actually standing on their legs instead of flying. The creature bowed to Cassie and tipped their miniature top hat. It took her a second before she remembered she was supposed to bow back.

"I hope you are friendly," Cassie said. "We've had a hell of a day."

"Yes, I am. This is the Silver Stream, the core of the fey world. You humans should not be here. I fear it is harmful for your neural health."

"We're… a bit lost. We were supposed to have an audience with the King, but our guide left us."

The creature shook their head. "Really, how disrespectful. I keep telling those cads to treat guests with more reverence, but they insist on their silly games. Was it Voxxinquill? Seems like something they'd do."

The name was familiar, but Cassie's memory wasn't working so well. "I… think so? Might you be able to help us out of here?"

The creature nodded. "You may call me Pytt. I shall not ask your names, for I fear in your compromised mental state you might just give me your true names and I do not wish to take on such a responsibility."

Pytt led Cassie and her struggling companions over to one of the walls of the circular chamber. A door opened back into that original twisting hallway.

Suffering. Starvation. Cruelty. Ignominy. Avarice. Gluttony.

"What… is that thing?" Cassie asked, looking at the brain.

"Oh, don't mind the brain," Pytt said. "It's one of the central nexi of the reality mesh. It's a little depressed right now because it's contemplating the state of the human world."

"I thought that attitude sounded familiar. Y'know, speaking of familiarity, I feel like I've heard of the Silver Stream. You wouldn't happen to know a forest nymph by the name of Tibberwyx, would you?"

"Oh, Tibb? Ze's my sibling. Say hello to zir for me, will you?"

And with that, Pytt ushered the humans through the orifice and out into the hallway. As soon as the opening closed behind them, everyone breathed heavily. Cassie's mind cleared once more, and it seemed the others were feeling the same way.

Pytt's voice spoke into her mind. "Just go left down this hall and that should take you to the throne room."

"Thanks, Pytt." Cassie said out loud, not sure if they could hear her. She helped gather her comrades and they made their way to where an ornate wooden door stood, carved with frescoes of incomprehensible scenes. The slab was too heavy to budge without everyone pushing together, but with a team effort it creaked open to reveal a carved chamber somewhere near the top of the tree. A crown of leaves formed the ceiling, and branches made windows in the walls. In the very center was a pile of bones arranged into a crude throne atop which a figure sat. It was impossible to properly perceive the figure's form and to Cassie it looked like a humanoid mass of shadows with oversized elk horns on top of its head.

To the side of the throne, a weary human form strummed at a guitar. It was Private Retzel, who was smiling widely, but upon closer inspection had a tired and frightened expression in his eyes.

"Humans!" The same disembodied voice from the Silver Stream boomed through the boughs of the tree. It must have been the voice of the Butterfly King. "What business have ye in my court?"

Cassie cleared her throat and spoke for the group, despite Gwynne's prior warnings. "Your majesty, we are peaceful travelers passing through the Kahlane Rainforest in search of one who might aid us. A fellow human. We enter your court simply by accident and wish only to reclaim our friends and return to our world to bother you no further." She bowed to the King for good measure, hoping this was enough.

"The injured one," the King intoned, ignoring Cassie's request. "What is its name?"

Gwynne tried to speak up. "Y-you may call him-"

"I care not what you deign to allow me to call it. I am asking for its *name.*"

"Why do you need it?" Cassie asked. "Is he okay?"

"We require use of the creature's name in order to heal it. It loses too much ichor and faces consumption. Give us the name if you wish for us to help."

"He means the Major is bleeding out," Gwynne explained. "I think they should be able to heal him, but giving up his name may trap him here."

Kant shook her head. "Better than having him die. As the acting commanding officer, I hereby approve the release of the Major's name in exchange for his life."

The King did not move. He had not moved since Cassie had first laid eyes on him. "You who professes authority, may I have the injured human's name?"

"His name is Jep Hanz."

There was a crack in the air and Major Hanz appeared in front of the group, seeming perfectly uninjured.

"C-captain," he gasped. "What happened? I remember taking fire and then… nothing." He looked around and beheld the Butterfly King. "Oh. Oh no. I was afraid of this."

"Jep Hanz, we are good for our word. You have been healed of all injury, however your name is now mine, so by the laws of the Fey, you may never return to the human world."

Hanz fell to his knees.

"But that's not fair!" Cassie shouted. "He belongs in our world with us!"

The room began to shake and leaves dislodged from the canopy and fell into Cassie's hair. "And who are *you* to tell me what is and isn't fair?"

Gwynne spoke up. "Umm, maybe we should just cut our losses…"

"No! I'm tired of people like you who think themselves above everyone else just because of how they're born. You make me sick. Give us back the Major and the Private!"

The room began to turn dark and shadows from the tree dripped down. A screaming she had only heard once before when she beheld the form of Mordecai's patron tore through her mind.

"You dare to speak to the Butterfly King in this way! Perish, foolish humans!"

"Time to go," Gwynne said, grabbing Cassie's wrist and pulling her back through the doorway. The soldiers followed, even Hanz and Retzel. In the King's rage at Cassie, he seemed to lose focus on his captives. They tore back through the impossible hallway, much shorter this time, as legions of winged fey thronged into the chamber on their buzzing wings. Somehow the group found themselves back in the entrance hall, where the once orderly fey diners were oozing black slime from every orifice and throwing the now decayed food at each other. Stevens was screaming in terror, and Hastings was pulling him along by the collar, her face taut and impassive as she focused only on the mission. Kant was helping Retzel, who seemed drained of energy from his servitude to the King.

The group made it to the courtyard where a twenty foot vertical circle of branches interwove and a swirling portal emerged. Cassie couldn't remember if this was here before, but at this point didn't care.

"Into the portal!" Gwynne shouted, dragging Cassie.

The two women were about to run through when a voice shouted out.

"Wait!" It was Major Hanz. Everyone skidded to a stop. Hastings let go of Stevens, who was having difficulty moving closer to the portal and he fell backwards to the grass. In the distance, the King's castle, if you could call it that, was a hive of activity as the fey swarmed and buzzed in fury.

"What's the matter, sir?" Kant asked. "We're at the extraction point. Let's go already."

Hanz shook his head. "Negative, Captain. You all can go, but I physically can't go any closer. The King was telling the truth; I don't think I can leave. I'll stay behind and try to fix things here. You all go ahead."

Kant was distraught. "Sir, I can't-"

Stevens stood up from the grass and gave a wry grin. "Same here, sir. I couldn't stop myself and ate a bit of the food earlier when no one was looking. Looks like we'll have to split up into two fireteams from here."

Kant gritted her teeth, knowing they were right. "Major Hanz, Stevens, I'll be back for you."

Hanz clapped her on the shoulder. "Complete the mission, Captain. The nation is counting on you."

Kant just nodded and turned away. Hastings gave a salute, her eyes glazed over with the look of someone who had seen much worse in the line of duty.

"C'mon, Cassie, let's go." Gwynne grabbed Cassie anew and they jumped through the portal. It felt a bit like doing a front flip from a standing position as the world spun around Cassie and her stomach felt like it was dropping. Then the ground resolved itself beneath her and she fell into the dirt as the sound of the jungle flooded her ears once more. Her head hurt, and she looked around to see Gwynne, Kant, Hastings, and Retzel all staggering to their feet. Retzel was starting to tear up a bit. Kant went to comfort him, and Gwynne stepped a few paces away, looking pensive.

Cassie wasn't sure what to say, so she went over to her. "Everything okay, Gwynne?"

Despite everything, Gwynne was chuckling to herself. Cassie was afraid she was still under the charm of the fey world until she spoke. "Cassie, what's my deadname?"

She wasn't sure why Gwynne was asking this, but answered all the same. "That's easy, it's… it's…" she realized that she had completely forgotten Gwynne's old name. "I can't remember for some reason."

Gwynne laughed and cheered, eliciting glares from the Mages' Corps crowd. "I knew that would work! I don't have a deadname anymore! I gave it away to the fey! And of *course* it didn't let them control me, because it's *not my name* anymore! Gods, I'm a damn *genius*!"

The soldiers looked confused, but despite everything Cassie couldn't help but laugh. In the distance, something caught her eye. "Gwynne, everyone, look!" She pointed to the sky above the trees directly in front of them. There was a wispy trail snaking its way up into what was now the morning sky.

Gwynne laughed anew. "Well I'll be, it's smoke! Well done, Cassie. You've found Baba Yaga."

16

Toad and Frogs

Three Green and Brown Frogs - The Interior of the Toad - The Thing Most Important - Why Do You Have a Frog?

It really was morning, Cassie found. The sun slowly climbed through the sky as they made their way towards the smoke. She didn't think it had been that long, but who could say when it came to the fey world. At any rate, while she was tired she was also eager to get this trip over with so she could go back to the House and have a proper bath. Gwynne's wonder tent was nice, but even the nicest outdoor accommodations were still outdoor.

The group came to a tacit consensus not to talk about the events that transpired in the fey world, and the soldiers were quiet as they marched. Even Retzel didn't feel like playing, meaning the mosquitoes were eating Cassie alive once more. She plodded forward, each step feeling like a mile, until eventually there was a large knot in the underbrush ahead of her.

"This is it!" Gwynne exclaimed. Everyone else looked at her like she was crazy. She rolled her eyes. "The witch obviously wards her location. We have to break through this ward to get in."

"Stand aside," Kant said, the warmth long gone from her voice.

"Be my guest."

Kant investigated the knot, a twisted ball of vines and roots that reminded Cassie of the brain in the Silver Stream. This particular fleshy mass was psychically mute, however, much to Cassie's relief. Kant closed her eyes and recited an identification spell, working her hands over the meaty vines. She finally opened her eyes and turned back to the group.

"There are many different layers to this ward. I'm impressed."

Gwynne nodded. "Yes, I would expect no less."

"But there seems to be a way to bypass it all entirely."

"Let me guess, a riddle?"

"Yes, how did you know?"

Gwynne smiled and shook her head. "The witch is very fond of riddles. Likes to ask vague questions and see how people respond to them, too. Very well, what is this riddle?"

Kant looked back at the vegetative knot. "There seems to be a few phrases embedded in the Elder instructions that are written in the human tongue." Kant cleared her throat and recited the riddle.

In the morning I have no legs, at night I have four.
In the day I bathe, in the evening I must scream.
Touch me not, lest ye contract my scourge!
A pearl necklace, I lay upon the stream.
What am I, I implore?

Everyone was quiet for a beat.

"Do you want me to tell you all the answer?" Gwynne said, looking very smug indeed.

"No, I want to figure it out myself," Cassie responded.

Kant rolled her eyes. "Well don't take too long, we've got business here."

Cassie thought hard about each line, puzzling out the hidden meanings in each word. "I think I've got it."

"Go on, then. What is it?" Gwynne smiled at her.

"I believe the answer is a toad."

Hastings looked shocked. "A toad? Why a toad?"

"Well," Cassie began, "the first line refers to the amphibian life cycle. The 'morning' refers to the beginning of its life when it is but a tadpole, when it has no legs, and then 'at night' is when it is fully grown and it has legs. The second line refers to the fact that they enjoy soaking in the water, but scream out in the evening, trying to attract mates. We've heard it the whole time!"

Gwynne was just beaming.

"All the lines except the third could apply to any amphibian, or at least a frog, but the third line makes reference to the myth that touching a toad can give you warts, though calling it a 'scourge' is a bit of an exaggeration. And then the 'pearl necklace' in the last line is their eggs."

At this, the knot twitched and began to unclench. A gap in the vines opened up, revealing a clearing beyond.

"Well done, Cassie," Gwynne said. "Always knew you were smarter than you looked."

Cassie just rolled her eyes and pressed into the clearing. A root caught her foot and she stumbled forward through the gap in the jungle growth. Looking up from the dirt, she found herself beside a large pond. Frogs and toads croaked lustily in the morning sun, but this area of the rainforest seemed to be different somehow. There was no undergrowth here and instead a dirt forest floor spread around like in the logged area. In contrast to the burn, however, the ground here was not covered in ash and was instead neatly kept and pruned into a deliberate yard. In the distance, though, something amazing caught her eye. A mahogany-skinned toad the size of a house sat in the water just off the shore of the pond. It seemed to be sleeping, breathing slowly with its glassy eyes closed.

Cassie's companions entered the glade behind her and looked around.

"This where the old hag lives?" Hastings asked, seeming unimpressed.

"You ought to mind your manners, missie," a mischievous voice called from an indeterminate location.

The soldiers immediately went into a battle stance.

"Who's there? Are we addressing Baba Yaga?" Kant called.

An old woman appeared from behind a nearby tree, as if she had just walked past it. "There are those who call me by that name, yes." She looked to be around sixty years old, with wrinkled white skin, braided silver hair, and walked with a hunch in her back. She wore a red shawl over a green dress and her gait was aided by a carved walking stick.

Kant turned to face the woman, still in her battle stance. "Baba Yaga, by order of the Free State of Abaxia, you are hereby under arrest and sentenced to military aid of the Mages' Corps. Please do not cast any spells or we will be obliged to detain you by force."

Cassie couldn't believe what she was hearing. *Arrest?* But Hanz had told her that they came in peace!

"You lied to us!" Cassie shouted at Kant. "You're no better than that damnable Butterfly King!"

Kant's expression was hardened. "We're doing what we have to do for the sake of our nation."

The old woman just chuckled and casually waved a hand. "Oh, I don't think so, dearies. Here, take some time to cool off." There was a faint wobbling sound and where Kant and the two other soldiers were once standing, three green and brown frogs were now hopping amongst the fallen leaves in confusion.

Gwynne laughed. "Amazing! Just as powerful as ever, madame Eldegrand."

"And *you*, Gwynne Circe Brandwyck. How dare you show your face here again! Though, now that I look at you, what happened to that pretty young face I crafted for you? Don't tell me you broke it!"

Cassie was stunned. Gwynne was finally the one cowed. She looked bashful, like a child being scolded by their mother. "It… wasn't my fault. Mordecai cursed me."

"It was too your fault! I told you running around playing cops and robbers would get you in trouble, child! And yes, I could smell that disgusting Elder Spawn curse a mile away. I suppose you've come to beg me to help you once more."

Gwynne bowed low. "I would be most humbled to receive your aid, Madame Eldegrand. Please consider assisting your foolish former pupil once more."

"Foolish indeed." Eldegrand screwed her face up, looking down on Gwynne shrewdly. "You'll owe me big time for this, you know."

Gwynne did not raise her head. "Name your price. I am truly at my most desperate."

"That's what you said last time, too, whelp. I'm starting to think every inconvenience puts you at your most desperate."

Cassie couldn't stifle her laugh. The witch had cut straight to the heart of the matter and laid a bullseye on Gwynne's ego in a way of which Cassie could only dream.

"And who's this hussy you dragged along with you, hm?" The witch ambled over to Cassie and looked her over. "She's got a spark of magic to her, I see. Tell me, girl, has Gwynne been teaching you?"

Cassie curtseyed to Eldegrand, knowing it would make Gwynne's eyes roll. "Yes, ma'am. My name is Cassandra Mott, and I am Gwynne's humble apprentice."

Eldegrand gave a bark of a laugh. "Gods, the toddler thinks she can take an infant as an apprentice does she? Well, come along. Let's get this started."

Madame Eldegrand walked away with her stick, but many times more sprightly and energetic than she first appeared. Gwynne followed, shaking her head in bemused exasperation. "Really, Cassie, a curtsy?"

Cassie wasn't sure what to do about the three soldiers-cum-frogs that looked very miserable indeed. She was about to ask Gwynne when Eldegrand looked back over her shoulder. "You can leave those louts. The curse I put on them will wear off in a few days and they'll be back to normal. That ought to teach them to accost a poor old woman like that. Ha!"

The witch led the two wizards over to the gigantic toad. With a wave of her hand, a doorway opened in the toad's side and a long platform of dubious material emerged like a gangplank to bridge the way to the shore. She walked along this platform as if it was the most ordinary thing in the world and Gwynne and Cassie followed with trepidation.

The interior of the toad was very clearly somewhere else. The entire structure was carved out of a tree much like the Butterfly King's throne room, but much more welcoming. A brick fireplace was set into a far wall and filled the room with a warmth that made Cassie sleepy. The air was clouded with incense like Gwynne's room, but the particular scents had been chosen more carefully and with better harmony; clearly this was where Gwynne had picked up the habit. The room was filled with potted plants and a large wooden table in the center was surrounded by cushioned log chairs currently housing clothes, plants, and various odds and ends. Eldegrand cleared off some chairs for her guests and scuttled off into the kitchen.

"Make yourselves at home, girls. Would you like some tea? I'll put the kettle on."

Gwynne looked anxious. "I'd really like to get on with breaking the curse, if you don't mind."

Eldegrand was humming to herself in the kitchen. She came out with a tray of various cheeses, crackers, pickled vegetables, and dried fruits. "Not that simple, dear, and you know it. I'll need some time to analyze the different layers, so stay here a while." Cassie was very hungry and helped herself to some snacks, realizing she hadn't eaten in some time now. "I see your apprentice has not been well fed."

"Unfortunately we paid a visit to the Butterfly King before stopping by."

"Ah, that explains it. Can't stand that lot. Don't know how you managed to get one to work in your house, Gwynne."

"Well they're not *all* bad."

"You say that now until you have something they want! At any rate, at least you made it out in one piece. Now, Miss Cassandra, I'd like you to go gather some things in the jungle for me. It will help me with my work here. Plus, I need to have a serious chat with Gwynne here."

"O-okay…" Cassie said, who had been looking forward to relaxing for a while.

"Nothing too bad, just a few plants that grow around here, okay? I'll make you a list."

With that, Cassie set off into the jungle once more with a scrap of parchment on which were the names of various flowers and short descriptions thereof. She didn't approve of being kicked out, but there wasn't much to be done. It took her about half an hour to find all the flowers described. While she looked, she thought back on everything that had happened to her. It seemed like only yesterday that she was slaving away in the Jones & Sons factory in Bixton, even though it was weeks, or perhaps even months ago now. She wondered what things were like at home, and realized that everyone must be preparing for the harvest festival. As much as she loathed her hometown, the festival was an annual highlight and she particularly enjoyed tasting tons of local foods.

She also had time to reflect on her relationship with Gwynne. She felt like after everything that had happened the two had grown quite close. Cassie's stomach did a little shudder at this. She supposed there wasn't much point in denying it any longer, she really liked Gwynne. Like, a lot. She was incredibly beautiful, wicked smart, fun to be around, and wealthy and powerful to boot. Hell, Gwynne had even managed to learn a bit of caring and empathy. Cassie felt herself flush warm when she indulged in these thoughts. It was certainly true that they got along well together and really understood each other. But... surely Gwynne didn't feel the same way? A woman like that could have anyone she wanted, but Cassie was just... plain old Cassie. No boobs to speak of, still growing facial hair every other day, and with a voice, she thought, like one of Eldegrand's toads. No, there was nothing there to impress anyone, much less woo the most powerful wizard in the world. Still, she enjoyed being around Gwynne and resigned herself to the idea that that alone was enough.

She had a good cry about it for a few minutes, feeling sorry for herself amidst the steaming and screaming jungle. She felt a little better now that she had gotten her emotions out, and realized she had everything for which the witch had asked. Following the smoke once more, she made her way back into the witch's clearing and over to the toad. The gargantuan beast was awake now and blinked at her with bedsheet eyelids.

"I don't suppose you could open up and let me in? I have some things for Madame Eldegrand." The toad gave a croak like thunder and extended the gangplank, allowing Cassie entrance.

Back inside the witch's house, Gwynne had sat down on an old sofa at the back of the room, resting her eyes. Cassie went into the kitchen where Eldegrand was cooking something. There was a towering cauldron at the back that was boiling and an oar-sized spoon seemed to be stirring all by itself. It smelled like herbs in there.

"Madame Eldegrand? I brought the plants you require."

Without even looking up, the witch held out her hand and accepted the bundle of stalks and flowers. "Thank you, dear. You are dismissed."

"If you don't mind me asking, what did you need these plants for? Was it for some great spell?"

Now she looked up, giving Cassie a bemused look. "No, they're seasoning." She dropped the plants into a mortar she was using and ground them up into paste.

Cassie was too tired to care that she had been used for grocery errands and just walked back into the living room. Gwynne seemed properly asleep now, and snored a bit with her head lolled back onto the top of the sofa cushion. Cassie sat down beside her, rousing her a bit from her nap. Only half awake, Gwynne leaned over and rested her head on Cassie's shoulder, falling back asleep. Cassie decided she was alright with this and fell into slumber as well, relishing the touch and smell of her favorite person.

* * *

When Cassie awoke, a rich smell filled her nostrils. The messy log table had been cleaned up and covered with a quilted tablecloth. In the center was a large pork roast, dripping with juices. Despite the snack she had earlier, Cassie's stomach roared in protest.

"Dinner's ready, dearies. Go wash your hands now. I didn't want to wake you up, you were so cute there, snoring away."

Cassie blushed. "I do not snore!"

The witch gave her a look, as if to say *'you sure about that?'*, but Cassie roused Gwynne and did as she was bid. They then sat down to dinner, eating juicy and rich roast pork, fluffy mashed potatoes, and a refreshing wild greens salad. Cassie surprised herself with how much she ate. On top of being absolutely famished, Gwynne's campfire cooking couldn't compare to a home cooked meal. Gwynne herself was also putting away the food, and Cassie had never seen her eat this much. They washed the food down with a sweet wine made from wild blackberries. There were no words for a long time while the two hungry women ate. Madame Eldegrand seemed happy to watch them enjoy her cooking and she smiled warmly at them.

Once Cassie had eaten enough that she could slow down a little, she began to make conversation.

"So Madame Eldegrand, why do they call you 'Baba Yaga'? What does that mean?"

The witch sighed. "I keep telling the villagers to call me 'Granny Witch', but apparently that's how it translates in their language. Sounds a bit more frightening than I'd like, but I'll admit it keeps away the looky-loos who might bother my garden. You can call me Granny, if you like, dear."

Cassie blushed, but agreed that she would very much like that. She didn't know her biological grandparents, so she wondered if this is what it felt like.

"I hope Gwynne has been treating you well, dear," Granny continued. "She's... a bit new to opening up to others, but we've made it work."

Gwynne looked away. Could she be embarrassed?

Granny smiled, seeing something between the young women that Cassie could not. "I understand."

Gwynne finished a mouthful of food and cleared her throat. "Granny, when can we break the curse?"

"Such an impertinent child! Learn some patience, already. You're far too old to be nagging at me like a hungry puppy."

Gwynne rolled her eyes. "Okay, I apologize. But still, I'm very eager to get this curse off of me. It's blocking my magic, and that's making me itch."

"I thought as much. It's a doozy of a curse, dear. I've determined the catalysts needed to break the enchantment, but I'm afraid you're not going to like it."

Gwynne stood up from the table with a start and slammed her hands down on it. "It doesn't matter. I must know!"

"Well I certainly won't tell you with manners like that. Who raised you, child?"

"I did. But manners be damned, we're talking about a matter of life or death here."

Granny sighed deep and began cleaning up the table. It was a minute before she responded. "You really shouldn't have let yourself be hit by that fool Mordecai. He's put some wicked conditions on this one."

"Knowing Mordecai's motivations, nothing good for me."

"No." She took the dishes into the kitchen, avoiding Gwynne's gaze. She called from the kitchen, "There are two conditions, one is trivial and one is difficult. I shall tell you the difficult one first. In order to satisfy this condition, you must destroy the thing most precious to you."

Gwynne looked troubled, then pulled a pendant out from her shirt. On it was a locket that opened, revealing a miniature portrait of an Abaxian woman in noble dress with a sassy facial expression. "I've been carrying this portrait of my mother with me ever since I was a child."

"And you're sure that's what's most dear to you?"

"I'm certain." Gwynne threw the locket to the floor and stomped it to pieces, rendering it no more than scraps of gold and silver on the wood. "Now what?"

"My child, I did say this would be *difficult*, did I not?"

Gwynne looked angry, clearly having destroyed a beloved keepsake for naught. "Well then, what is it? What could possibly be more precious to me than the memories of my mother?"

Granny didn't say anything, leaving it up to Gwynne to decide. Gwynne looked confused for a moment, checking her person for anything else of value, but couldn't find anything that made sense. After a second she froze, gaze slowly rising to look at Cassie.

"No... There's no way."

"I'm afraid so," Granny said, still out of sight in the kitchen. That woman had an impeccable intuition.

Cassie was very afraid of what was happening.

"I have to destroy... *kill* Cassie?"

"Only if you want to break the curse. Your heart has decided that she's the most precious thing to you, so go on. Destroy her. You can do that much, right?" Granny emerged from the kitchen and thrust the handle of a long kitchen knife into Gwynne's hands.

Gwynne just stood there, staring at the knife, then at Cassie, then back to the knife. "But... but I..."

Cassie reached out a hand to Gwynne to comfort her, but Gwynne yelled out in frustration and threw the knife. It whipped across the room and embedded itself in the wall above the couch.

Granny stood in the archway to the kitchen and just watched with neutral expression. "What's the matter? Can't kill one girl?"

"No, of course I can't!"

"And why not?"

"Because that's murder!"

"Since when did you become such a goody-goody? Are you sure that's the reason?"

"I... Yes!"

"You don't sound so sure."

"Look, just not Cassie, okay?"

"And why not? Why couldn't you hurt Cassie?"

Gwynne looked like she was about to explode. "Because I care about her, okay!"

There was a moment of silence in the room. The toad croaked from somewhere outside.

"And… why do you care about her?"

Gwynne was starting to cry now, and Cassie could feel that tears were also leaking unabated from her own eyes. "Because… she's the only person who's ever really cared about me. She helps me all the time, but sees through my bullshit when I'm being dramatic. She's saved my life more than once and is one of the smartest people in the world."

Granny smiled. "Why are you telling me this? Tell *her*, the poor girl."

Their eyes met and Gwynne walked over to Cassie. Before Cassie knew what was happening, Gwynne had flung her arms around her, holding her tight in an emotional hug.

"Cassie, you're my best friend. I don't want to kill you. I could never hurt you. When you were injured by those soldiers in Ultan, I didn't know what to do. I tried to play it off all blasé, but that was so stupid of me. I was beside myself worrying about you, and when you yelled at me - and you were right to do so - I felt like I lost everything I cared about. I couldn't stand to face you. And yet, you helped me through some of the most important and dangerous times of my life after that, risking your neck for my selfish whims day after day. I really have mistreated you. I'm so sorry."

Gwynne sobbed into Cassie's shoulder. Cassie didn't know what to say. Her subconscious was screaming at her, *Tell her you love her!*, but the words wouldn't come out. "Gwynne… I… I feel the same way. I forgave you for all of that ages ago. You're my best friend, too. I'd do anything for you because I care about you as well."

Granny cleared her throat. "I must apologize as well. I may have told a teeny little lie just a minute ago."

Gwynne composed herself in an instant. "What did you say?"

Granny feigned innocence. "Oh, I may have lied about the difficult curse condition. Sort of."

Gwynne dropped Cassie and stormed over to the witch. "You sly, conniving old hag!"

Granny laughed openly. "But if I just told you the truth, you'd never have done the difficult part just now! Or started to, at least."

Gwynne stopped. "What do you mean? Speak clearly, Granny."

Granny sat down on a nearby armchair and picked up crochet needles and yarn. "Okay, okay, I'll explain. So from what you told me about this Mordecai, he's suffering under the misconception that *you're* the deluded one; that you're just pretending to be a Changer and are doing all your wizard business solely to rebel against your father. So when he crafted this curse, it seems he made the difficult condition that you must abandon your facades and 'see the light' as it were. Be honest with your feelings and accept them. Oh, but that fool! That misguided fool! He plays at knowing your true emotions but couldn't be further from the truth. His condition has turned around and bitten him. By acknowledging your feelings for Cassie and getting over your own hoity-toity act, you are doing exactly what he wants you to do, but in exactly the wrong way. But of course the curse doesn't care! Mordecai was too vague in effort to reduce the energy cost."

"So… the curse is broken?" Cassie asked.

"No, dear. Remember, there were two conditions. The difficult condition was that Gwynne be honest with her true feelings, which she has only started to do tonight. That will require more work on her part. Additionally, there is an easy condition, but one that might prove more difficult than it seems."

"What's the second condition?" Gwynne asked.

"Oh, nothing much, just an intact werewolf fang."

"Where in the world would we get one of those?"

Granny just shrugged and continued with her crochet.

"What's… what's a werewolf?" Cassie asked, a dread growing in her stomach.

Gwynne looked thoughtful, thinking how best to describe it. "Werewolves are humans that are cursed to turn into grotesque wolf-like creatures at night when the moon is strong. They say that while transformed they are completely consumed by madness and bloodlust. But they're incredibly rare, so I wouldn't be surprised if this was an exaggeration."

Cassie felt her blood run cold. "I… I think I might have seen one."

Gwynne whipped around to look at her. "Where, Cassie?"

"In Bixton. There was a wolf creature that was supposed to be eating people in the streets, and I saw it once." The memories of that night came rushing back. She had long since convinced herself that it was an illusion or some false memory she had constructed when running from the feral dogs. "It had these horrible beady black eyes and gangly limbs. Gods, it was the scariest thing I've ever seen."

Gwynne beamed. "That's Cassie for you, always helpful, if only by accident."

Cassie blushed. Gwynne stood up and straightened her outfit. "Sorry to dine and dash, Granny, but I'd like to chase down this werewolf with all haste."

"Oh you young people, always rushing around. Why not stay for a while? I've got cookies…"

"Gwynne, cookies!"

"No, I'm afraid we must be off at once. I've got that itch to get things done, Cassie, and it can't wait for cookies."

Granny sighed, set down her crochet, and stood up. "At least give me a hug before you go blasting off." She hugged each of them in turn, and said in Cassie's ear, "You keep that girl in line, you hear me? She's a mess! And if you ever want a little *resculpting*, just let me know, okay?"

"Thank you, Granny."

* * *

Cassie really was sad to leave. She had such a good time with Madame Eldegrand, and the idea of cookies sounded too good to pass up, but Gwynne was a woman possessed, and Cassie knew how that went. Gwynne danced out into the dark jungle clearing, eager to be back aboard the ship.

"C'mon, Cassie, start the teleportation spell already! I want to be moving!"

Cassie pulled out the miniature spellbook from her back pocket, which was heavily worn and water damaged at this point. She was about to start the spell when a small voice interrupted her.

"H-hey, don't leave me! Please!"

It was dark outside, so Cassie couldn't see anyone around.

"I recognize that voice," Gwynne said, looking down at the ground. "Private Retzel?"

A small green tree frog hopped up to Cassie. "Please! I didn't know they were going to capture the witch. I don't want anything to do with the Corps anymore. Please take me with you!"

"And why should I believe you?" Cassie asked, still stung by the Corps' earlier actions.

Gwynne scooped up the frog. "Aww, Cassie, look. He's just a widdle froggie. Isn't that adorable?"

Cassie rolled her eyes. It was decided then. With former Private Retzel in hand, she grabbed Gwynne's hand and completed the spell, yanking the three of them out of the middle of the dark Kahlane Rainforest and into the parlor of the *Pale Moon*, thoroughly startling a lounging Feckalia.

"Shit! You're back! Holy hell, stop doing that! You gotta warn a girl fir- hey, is that a frog? Why do you have a frog?"

V

Bixton Again

17

Long Road Home

He Almost Sounded Cool - You'll Always Be My Dearest Friend - Morning Star - Fodder For The Fungus That Grows Upon The Great Trees

Things were awkward back at the House as the *Pale Moon* sped back to Zona towards Bixton. Part of it was that Cassie was returning to her hometown, a place she hadn't expected ever to see again. She couldn't help but think of her mother and sister and wonder how they had handled her disappearance. She knew that her mother had given her up to the authorities, but she couldn't help but wish that there was some level of remorse there as well. Who knew what Ophelia felt about it, though Cassie was sure that her baby sister was delighted to get a new junk room so soon. Cassie found herself daydreaming about her relatives distraught about her disappearance, if only out of spite for how poorly they had treated her all her life.

There was something else that nagged at Cassie's emotions in those days. Despite the intimate discussion that Gwynne and Cassie shared in Granny's hut, she couldn't help but feel like things weren't quite right. Sure, the two were now officially best friends and were emotionally closer than ever. This was great, but without the werewolf fang Gwynne's magic had yet to return. Besides, Cassie felt sad somehow when she thought of Gwynne as her best friend, and could not explain the emotion. It seemed like nothing had really changed since before they entered the jungle. Surely she was just being selfish, though.

Finally, there was a new member of the crew. Ollien Retzel, or just Ollie, as he came to be called, spent the first few days as a frog. Tibberwyx was completely taken with him and enjoyed flying him around the library and feeding him dried grubs that ze kept in a jar. Ollie hated every minute of this, but fortunately for his sake the curse wore off two days later. Unfortunately, it did so in the midst of a faerie flight, causing him to crash to the library floor under his weight.

"Well this is a disappointment," Tibb said, glaring at Cassie. "I liked this one better as a frog."

She, for the record, could not stop laughing at the hilarity of the timing. Ollie rose to his feet and dusted himself off. His guitar and other gear had been melded into his cursed frog form, and all his belongings were now strewn across the floor, the body of the guitar cracked. With a sigh, Ollie picked it up and sang a quiet song to the broken instrument. Words flowed from his mouth and Cassie could hear soft creaking and cracking sounds as the broken guitar reformed, good as new.

"I hate frogs," he grumbled.

Tibb flitted down to examine the instrument. "What is this device, human? What manner of weapon is this? Might thee grasp it about its slender extrusion and swing it like a club? Or perhaps the wiggly strings might be used for launching projectiles?"

Ollie tuned the strings and strummed a few chords. "It's not… a weapon. Not like… as such. It's a guitar, and it's a musical instrument. But… uh… music *is* a kind of weapon to me. Or something…"

He almost sounded cool there, Cassie thought.

From then on, Ollie played songs for the occupants of the house, which made mealtimes much more lively. Additionally, his pieces had rejuvenating effects, and Cassie's bruises and fatigue vanished in no time. Gwynne sang along with songs as well, and Cassie was delighted to learn that she had a wonderful singing voice. Horatio's singing voice, on the other hand, was not as graceful, and the Ranklins' was more of an out-of-sync warbling howl. Feckalia, who refused to sing, was probably the most happy with the new addition, finding a new target to bully who was even more bashful than Cassie. Ollie would cover his face when Feck teased him, making him even more of a target.

Ollie had claimed a bedroom upstairs, and the hallway was now filled with occupants. Horatio had one room, the Ranklin brothers shared another, Feck had the room nearest the bathroom, and Ollie took the one remaining room. Cassie was sure that Gwynne could have created more if she really wanted to, but everyone seemed happy with this little sense of community. Only Gwynne slept apart from the group, though the extravagant master bedroom above everyone else suited her just fine.

During the trip, Gwynne spent most of her time in the workshop. The rickety landing craft had been left behind in the jungle, which didn't seem to bother Gwynne in the slightest. "It was on its last legs already. I can do better," she had said, working on a blueprint while Cassie toiled away at her studies. She couldn't make heads or tails of the document, but trusted Gwynne's engineering knowledge at least somewhat.

Cassie herself was busy learning illusion magic, a subject with which she was hitherto struggling.

"I don't see what the problem is," Gwynne said, being very unhelpful. "It's just creating an image. All you have to do is picture the image in your head and command the magic to reproduce that image."

"Yes, I've got the core concepts, thanks," Cassie retorted. "I guess it's just maintaining that mental image that's difficult? My brain has trouble focusing."

"Ah yes, that makes sense. Perhaps if it helps, you could try to reproduce an image that you can already see. Try making an illusory duplicate of myself, perhaps."

"Are you sure?"

"Of course! I'm the best one to tell if you're doing it wrong."

Cassie just shrugged. She started the incantation anew, instructing the magic to create a three-dimensional image of the object of her focus within a prescribed area. There was a flash and a form appeared. Suddenly there were two Gwynnes in the room. The proper Gwynne looked over the image and studied its form.

"Hmm, you made my breasts a bit too big."

Cassie blushed, but continued to focus. "No I didn't! That's just what they look like."

"Odd, perhaps they've grown a bit. Hard to tell from so close," Gwynne said, examining herself. "You know what, you're right, Cassie. I think I've grown a bit."

"Well la-di-da for you. Spare a little titty growth for your best friend?" Cassie was teasing, but she was intensely bitter about this one insecurity.

"You know Granny offered to give you a full makeover," Gwynne said.

"Yes, I know, and I definitely appreciate her work," Cassie looked at Gwynne's shapely body and began to feel that undefined sadness again. "But we've got more important things right now. And besides, it's kind of scary, even if I do want it."

"Why is it scary? Don't you hate the body with which you were born just as much as I do?"

"I mean, yeah. It's just… I dunno. I guess I'm just anxious that I might not be myself anymore afterward. Or that it might go horribly wrong and I'll be ugly."

Gwynne clasped Cassie's hand and shook it to reassure her. "Nonsense, you'll always be my dearest friend Cassie to me, no matter what."

Cassie was blushing intensely at the hand contact now, and the illusory double vanished. They stayed like that for a few seconds before Gwynne switched back into practical mode. "At any rate, Cassie. You should really start making yourself a spellbook. What kind of self-respecting wizard doesn't have one? That's what I say, anyway."

"Well I *was* using that one you lent me, but it kind of got ruined in the jungle."

"Right, which is why you need a proper book that you can enchant with waterproofing and whatnot. Which reminds me, I actually picked something up back in Abaddon for you but completely forgot about it. I'll be right back."

Gwynne, ever a whirlwind of activity, dashed from the workshop. She returned a few minutes later with a book in her hand. It was a black leather-bound tome with bright pink accents.

"Here it is! The color was inspired by your hairstyle back then, so I apologize if it's no longer your thing, but the book is the real deal. Proper leather binding, high-quality parchment pages that don't bleed through, and a suede bookmark. I hope you enjoy it, Cass."

Cassie took the book and ran her fingers over it. Her very own spellbook. She had been teleporting, throwing fire, and flying all this time, but it wasn't until this moment that she felt like a proper wizard and not some wannabe trainee. The color scheme, while garish at first blush, resonated with Cassie and made her feel like a kickass female wizard. *Like Gwynne,* she allowed herself to think at last.

"I'll give you time to fill its pages, though I'm sure the very first spell you're going to scribe is teleportation since it seems to be your specialty. The most important thing, though, is that a wizard's spellbook is her lifeline. It's where she keeps all her most important spells, particularly general-use ones. Make sure you keep it on your person at all times."

"Thank you, Gwynne. I love it."

For the rest of the day, Gwynne instructed Cassie about how to scribe spells in her spellbook. She even taught her some spells to place on the spellbook itself. The first of these allowed the tome to shrink down to the size of Cassie's palm or back again with a gesture for easier toting. Another allowed the book to hover in front of her as long as it was open if she willed it. The last was a warding spell that prevented incidental to moderate damage to the book and prevented unwanted eyes from opening it or viewing its contents.

At the end of all this, Cassie was worn out from successive spell-casting. "Gwynne, I don't know if I've ever seen your spellbook. May I?"

Gwynne shook her head. "Oh, I don't have one right now."

"What happened to 'every self-respecting wizard'?"

"Oh, I didn't mean *me*. I've completely memorized all my most important spells, so I've no further need to lug around a book. Anything outside of the spells I've memorized I just look up."

Cassie rolled her eyes. "I bow down to the all-powerful Gwynne Brandwyck who has every spell memorized because she is Very Smart."

Gwynne laughed, a loud and honest laugh that was very different from her usual smug chuckle. "I *am* very smart, thank you! And if you had actual experience around other wizards, you'd know just how amazing I actually am."

"Let's just say I reserve the right to judge."

"At any rate, smartass, I will need your help with the new craft I am constructing."

"Oh, the all-powerful Lady Brandwyck needs the help of one as lowly as me?"

"Seriously, Cassie. I'm still cursed and I have, as the young ones say, 'hella spells' to put on this 'sick puppy'."

Cassie grimaced. "Please do not ever do that again."

"Only if you promise to help me."

"Okay, Cringe Queen, but not until I've rested. I've used a ton of energy putting enchantments on my spellbook. Maybe tomorrow?"

"That works. We'll be arriving at Bixton overmorrow, so I want you rested before you go down there. There's no telling what the King is up to since my fiasco at Ackerman's party, and I have a sneaking suspicion that he means to act sooner rather than later."

"I can use a disguise. Maybe I can get that illusion spell to work."

"We'll see."

* * *

The following day, Cassie was summoned to the hangar, where Gwynne had completed her blueprint. From what Cassie could tell, it depicted a single- or double-occupancy winged craft, shaped like a miniature version of the *Moon* itself. There was a domed cockpit in the front that wrapped up over the top along wide steel wings in each of which was set a chain gun. The craft had a slender body leading to an elegant tail with flaps to finely control inclinations. A set of retractable landing gear was built into the bottom. Gwynne stood proudly over a heap of raw steel, aluminum, wire, leather, brass, glass, rubber, and other various materials.

"Okay, Cassie, you ready to make this thing?"

"No, you haven't taught me the spell yet."

"Of course not, I'm asking if you're *feeling* ready."

"Still no, this looks way too complicated for me."

"Don't worry, I've written down the incantation. All you have to do is recite it verbatim and picture the blueprint in your head. Once you're done, we can go over the additional enchantments."

"I'm excited for you to get your magic back, if only so that you stop using me to do your grunt work."

"Selfless as always, Cassie. Now, can we get started?" Gwynne was lucky she was so pretty.

Cassie spent the next half hour learning and reciting the spell from the scrolls that Gwynne had prescribed. Once she had completed, she felt her vision swim for a second. She then opened her eyes and steadied her breathing to see a fully manifested fighter plane in the hangar of the *Pale Moon*. The engineers had shown up to watch the performance, and the Ranklin boys hooted and hollered at the magic.

"Yer gonna pu' us ou' ov a job, miss!" Bimmy cried.

"Assembling a blueprint is simple," Gwynne explained, "but maintaining it is a completely different matter. As long as there are machines, there will be need for engineers."

Cassie sat down and took a deep swig of water from a canteen she had brought with her for this exact reason. "I hope I'm not making any more of these."

"Of course not, but you will need to help me with some enchantments on the craft."

After letting her rest for a minute, Gwynne helped Cassie to her feet and the two completed a number of complex enchantments on the new plane. Some of the spells were so long that Cassie completely lost focus on what exactly they did, but Gwynne just assured her to follow what was on the scrolls. Once they were finished, Cassie felt like she could go to bed right then and there.

"Excellent work, Cass. You really are a most helpful friend."

Cassie was breathing deeply with fatigue. "I've always said that was one of my defining traits. Not my looks or smarts, but how useful I am to others." She meant it sarcastically, but found that there was a ring of truth to the statement.

"Have you decided what to name her?" Gwynne asked.

"I get to name it?"

"Not an 'it', she's a 'she'. And yes, you constructed her, so you get first dibs on the name."

Cassie contemplated for a moment. "Well, if this is the *Pale Moon*, perhaps she could be something related. How about… the *Morning Star?*"

"I love it, darling. Has an air of elegance and mystery to it. Very well, *Morning Star* it is."

* * *

That evening at dinner, Gwynne was discussing the plan for the next day with the others over bowls of beef stew. It had been Havershank's turn to cook, and while the dish left much to be desired in terms of depth of flavor, it was much better than Cassie had been dreading. It seemed everyone here had at least a rudimentary knowledge of cooking, even if Horatio's idea of dinner usually consisted of roasted meats and little else. Cassie herself had only cooked casually throughout her life, mostly preparing simple meals at times when her mother couldn't be bothered to feed her and she had to provide for herself. She found herself thinking again about Feckalia's off-handed comment some weeks back about getting a cook for the House. While they were unlikely to find such a person in Bixton, Cassie decided that if she were to recruit another member to the house, they'd have to be a cook.

"Cassie, you there?"

She realized that Gwynne was calling her name. "Oh, sorry, I was a little lost in thought."

"I was wondering if you were okay with getting a werewolf fang. We can send someone else instead if you're afraid."

"Oh 'ell no, miss!" Jimmy cried. "I ain' goin' nea' one o' 'em fings! I got'a protec' me 'andsome face, I do."

"'Ow nice of ye t'be finkin' o' me, mate," Bimmy joked.

"Wot? Why would I be finkin' o' you, Bim?"

"Because you said… never mind, ye oaf."

Havershank just shook his head and stole a piece of beef from Bimmy's bowl.

"Oi, givvit back, ye wee blighter!"

The brothers tussled for a bit over the stolen chunk of meat and Horatio guffawed at their antics. Gwynne redirected the attention back onto herself, where she liked it. "As you can see, despite their mechanical talent, our engineers are completely hopeless for much else. Really, you're the best woman for the job, Cassie."

"Do I have to… kill the werewolf to get its fang?"

Gwynne did not meet her eye. "Unless you can think of a way to extract a sharp tooth from the mouth of a bloodthirsty killing machine."

"But… isn't it a person? I'd be killing them, too."

"You're a smart girl, I'm sure you can figure something out. And besides, if the legends are to be believed, a loose werewolf will just go on killing to satiate its animal urges, despite the best intentions of the host. You'd really be doing the townsfolk a service by getting rid of it for them."

Cassie was extremely uncomfortable at the idea of killing a living creature, especially one that was actually a human. Sensing the tension, Feckalia spoke up.

"I could just go. I could whip up a Zonan disguise in an instant and blast the damn thing straight to the fifth hell before it has a chance to hurt anyone."

Gwynne shook her head. "While I have no doubt that you are strong enough, Miss Feck, I worry firstly that you may go overboard and destroy the fang along with the beast, or that you might spend the whole night getting entirely too friendly with the local lads and maidens."

Feckalia rolled her eyes. "Oh, c'mon, I'm not *that* much of a trollop. I know how to stop after one or two."

"My point precisely. No, you'll be much more useful here at the House. There's another matter that's been concerning me. Without my magic, I haven't been able to cast my usual wards against scrying. Even without Ackerman's tracking spell, there's no reason that the King isn't monitoring my position as we speak. The only reason I hadn't worried about it up 'til now is because we've been out of the country. Now that we're waltzing back into Zona, and to a town as close to New Ozion as Bixton, we're sure to attract the attention of the royal army who, need I remind you all, is still very much after my head. We'll need our most powerful combatants aboard should the army attempt a strike."

The rowdy Ranklins had ceased their squabble and were now looking at Gwynne with sober faces. Cassie could see Ollie's eyes widen in fear. Everyone here was scared of this possibility, and Gwynne could sense it.

"But don't worry. If things go according to plan, Cassie will return with the fang long before things turn for the worse."

"Right, and that will require me to kill," Cassie murmured.

"Sometimes that's just how it is in this bitch of a world," Gwynne said, not allaying Cassie's concerns in the slightest.

* * *

Cassie had trouble sleeping that night. She kept envisioning that she killed the werewolf, only for it to shapeshift back into someone she knew. While she wasn't fond of some from her past, namely Hardden or her mother, she certainly didn't wish them dead. Or worse, what if it was someone who had a family at home? She couldn't be responsible for that. In the middle of the night, realizing she wasn't falling asleep any time soon, she left her bedroom and went to the library.

Tibberwyx was awake, which didn't surprise her, and ze buzzed over to greet her with entirely too much gusto for this late at night.

"Cassie! What an odd time for you to visit. Are you okay? Couldn't you 'sleep'? Or whatever it is you humans do at night? Need a good book to put you to sleep? I recommend Newern's *Treatises on Zonan Agricultural Demographics*. Puts me to sleep just reading the table of contents!"

"Actually, Tibb, do you have anything on werewolves?"

"Werewolves? Now that's a funny topic. I've heard of them, but never seen one myself. Wasn't sure they were real, to be honest. Do you believe in them? Are you afraid of them? Is that why you can't sleep? Oh! Are *you* a werewolf, Cassie? Is that what you've been hiding from me all this time? Because I know there's *something*, I just can't tell what. Human emotions are so bizarre and hard to read."

"I'll just go search for myself, thanks."

The magical library directory returned but a single result for 'werewolf', an omnibus tome called *Encyclopaedia of Monsters and Magical Beasts*. The title sounded a bit fanciful and Cassie feared it might be prone to hyperbole, but there wasn't much choice. The book itself was a massive tome, and must have been over a thousand pages in length. Fortunately, the article on were-beasts was easy to find near the end of the book.

According to the author, were-beasts came in many varieties, each taking the shape of specific animals, though wolves are by far the most common. The author claims that they may only be killed by use of silver weaponry, as anything less will simply allow them to heal their wounds. Lastly, the bite of a were-beast is enough to spread the curse to other individuals. It made no mention of their fangs, aside from describing how particularly brutal and terrifying they are, nor how one might acquire one without resorting to violence. This book was completely useless to her.

"How's it going there, miss werewolf?" Tibb asked, making Cassie jump.

"I'm not a werewolf! But anyway, Tibb, do you mind if I ask your opinion on something?"

"I suppose you may do so. I am nothing if not absolutely full to bursting with opinions. I could give you my opinion on the paltry human concept of courtship, if you like, since you seem to be struggling with the process yourself."

"Tibb, please, just answer my question, okay?"

"Okay, no problem, certainly, can do, righty-o, affirmative."

Cassie had to rub her temples to stop herself swatting Tibb right on zir alien babydoll face to make zir stop talking. The lack of sleep was really trying on her nerves.

"Have you… ever had to kill something? Or… someone?"

"Oh yes, of course," Tibb responded instantly. "I kill bugs all the time and put them in my jar. Love having a nice jar full of little dry buggies for snacky times. Crunchy crunchy! Oh, I love the little spindly legs."

"Okay, less about the bugs. Have you ever had to kill someone… you know, sentient?"

Tibb was silent for a second, which was a miracle in and of itself. "Yes. My life before entering into the service of the Mistress was most tumultuous. I was the youngest of three, my older brother being Pytt, and my older sister being Mirkle. Only one of us could take over the Silver Stream, and fey law dictates that any means are fair to decide this contest. I didn't want the responsibility, myself, as that place drives me crazy."

This was saying a lot for Tibb. "Yeah, we went there, actually. I'm pretty sure we met Pytt, though the memory is a little hazy now."

"Yes, your feeble human minds could not even begin to comprehend its majesty. Anyway, Pytt was so kind and strong, but Mirkle was a selfish-" Tibb made a clicking noise, which Cassie could only assume meant something obscene in the fey tongue. "So I killed her. Found poison in her room and switched it out with her honey. She was planning to kill me anyway, so I could prevent my own murder and avoid sullying my dainty brother's hands with the deed. He never knew I did it, and don't you dare tell him."

"Don't worry, I'm not going back there anytime soon. Do you regret it, though?"

"If you absolutely must know, human, I do, in a way. There was little to be done in that situation, and I don't regret protecting myself and Pytt, but I do regret that there were no other options. Keep in mind, fey don't experience emotional turmoil to the same extent as humans, and we live much much much longer lives, so it doesn't keep me up at night. Not that I need to sleep anyway. But I will carry that weight with me until I become but fodder for the fungus that grows upon the great trees."

"I see." There was clearly much more to Tibb than there seemed.

"Anyway, human," Tibb said, brushing the subject off as easily as if she had asked zir about the weather. "Would you like a cookie? The lovely demon made me some."

Cassie was feeling a bit peckish, and felt a cookie would cheer her up. Tibb flitted off and came back holding a cookie in both hands, making it look massive by comparison. The cookie contained little bits of dried fruit that paired well with the sweetness of the dough. After a few bites, Cassie's eyelids began to feel heavy. She excused herself from the library and made her way back to bed, just barely arriving in her room and getting into bed before she fell asleep.

247

18

Flying and Festivities

That Cookie! - No Joy in Worker Abuse! - Thieving Crow Special - Wanted Dead or Alive

Cassie rose late the next day, afraid that she had missed the mission. Looking out her wide bedroom window, she could see familiar alpine steppe pass beneath the *Moon*, and a small town coming into view. She dressed in a hurry and dashed from her room.

In the hallway, she bumped into Ollie, who was leaving the bathroom, his hair bearing the dew of a recent shower. He was fully dressed, thankfully, but also had a damp bath towel around his neck. He was whistling some tune that Cassie couldn't recognize. And by 'bumped', she nearly bowled the man over in her haste.

"Oh gods, sorry about that, Ollie. Are you okay?"

"Sorry! Yeah... I'm... I'm fine, Cassie."

"Are you getting used to the House okay?"

"I... yeah. It's good. Sorry, no, it's great actually."

"Oh, glad to hear it. I figured you'd like being here, what with fellow magic users."

"Yeah. It's different from when I was in the military. There were tons of mages there, of course, but like… not nearly as much life. Not as much heart, ya know? It's all orders and protocol and salutes and stuff. Didn't feel like I could really express myself there."

Cassie didn't know much about military life, but imagined it was every bit as gray and cold as she had read in books. "Well if there's anything you need, let me or Gwynne know, okay?"

"Oh, okay, thanks. To be honest, Gwynne is kinda intimidating."

Cassie laughed. "Yes, she is. But that's kind of what I like about her."

Ollie just looked Cassie up and down and nodded to himself, as if that explained something. "I see."

"If you think she's scary now, wait until she gets her magic back. She's the most powerful mage I've ever seen."

"Yeah, I wasn't exactly buying the line she told us when we met about being your apprentice."

What was that supposed to mean?

"Yeah… Anyway, do you have any regrets about leaving the army? Seemed like you were pretty eager to be out of there."

"Yeah, like I said. I couldn't really be myself, ya know? And like… they want you to like… live and die for your fellow soldiers, but they don't bother to actually connect with you. It's like… you want me to die for someone I barely know? I dunno… Plus I never really liked the violence. Kinda made me upset a lot."

"I understand." Cassie felt bad for him. She doubted she could cope with the death and dismemberment that came with being a member of the military. It seemed Ollie had only been there to fulfill his end of the government scholarship and saw his first opportunity to bail. "Anyway, I'm glad you're here, at least. I hope you'll be able to really feel at home and express yourself fully."

"Haha yeah," Ollie said. "I've had a lot of fun playing music for everyone, and I hope I can be of use in a scrap as well."

With this, Cassie remembered that she was late. She bid farewell to Ollie and rushed downstairs to find no one about. She searched the House and found Gwynne in the hangar, briefing some function of the *Moon*'s features to the Ranklins.

"...and after that, it will need another five minutes to recharge- Oh, hello Cassie. Nice of you to join us."

Cassie, out of breath from her mad search, leaned on her knees. "Sorry, must've overslept a bit."

"That's fine. Tibb said ze knocked you out with a sleeping spell so you'd be well-rested. I wasn't expecting you for another hour or so."

That cookie! Cassie thought.

"At any rate," Gwynne continued. "I was just explaining the *Moon*'s shield generator to the engineers here. You're welcome to take the *Star* down to Bixton whenever you're prepared, Cass."

"Where's Horatio?"

"He knows all this already, seeing as how he and I designed these features together. Currently he's in the gunner's cockpit keeping an eye out for hostile air traffic."

"Okay. Can you show me how to fly this thing?"

Gwynne spent the next fifteen minutes briefing Cassie on the workings of the *Morning Star*. The cockpit glass opened up, allowing Cassie to climb directly into the pilot's seat. Glass dials, bronze levers, and a leather-covered steering stick lined up in front of Cassie, dazzling her with the amount of feedback. By the end of everything, she felt she had a passable grip on how to fly the craft, but was still nervous that she would just plummet out of the sky as soon as she left the hangar.

"Just trust in my design and your magic, Cassie." Gwynne said to reassure her. "The *Star* has stabilizers and guidance spells that make it so even a child could fly her. You'll do great!"

Cassie strapped herself into the leather seat with thick fabric buckles that fit her form like a glove. Gwynne lowered the cockpit glass and gave her a thumbs-up. Cassie breathed deeply to calm her nerves as the hangar bay rolled open and wind rushed in. Gwynne's hair was swept about on the outside of the craft, but Cassie was perfectly insulated. She turned the ignition key and the machine roared to life. Twin propellers on the wings began to spin, pulling the craft inexorably closer to that precarious lip of the launch ramp. Remembering her instructions, she thrust the throttle up to maximum and the propellers became shredding discs, launching the craft forward and out into the sky. Immediately there was a sharp drop that made Cassie's stomach crawl up into her chest cavity, but just when she thought she was going to die, the plane righted itself and soared straight ahead through the bright midday sky.

What had started as the icy grip of fear gave way into a rush of exhilaration as Cassie could feel herself moving at quite the clip. Easing back on the throttle, she attempted some practice steering. It was somewhat counter-intuitive that in order to execute a turn she had to roll the craft and pull up on the nose, but within a few minutes she had gotten the hang of it. The *Pale Moon* looked like a great bird gliding along, and she swooped by its underside, catching a glimpse of Gwynne and the Ranklins waving to her from the hangar, and the mounted gun turrets on the ship's underwings rotating to follow her trajectory. She waved back at everyone, hoping they could see her. She hoped that Gwynne's fears were unfounded and that she would not have to resort to using those turrets to kill.

Once she felt comfortable in the pilot's seat, Cassie set off towards Bixton, which was only a few miles away from where the *Moon* glided in a holding pattern. She could see the town as a dark spot on the mountainside, and as she got closer the buildings, fields, and roads of the town appeared like miniatures beneath her. She slowly nosed the plane down and found a remote field in which to land. Her technique was a bit rough, but the craft touched down without damage.

After locking up the *Star*, Cassie cast her disguise spell. She tried to make herself look as much like a nondescript Zonan woman as possible, though she had not brought a mirror to check the disguise's efficacy. At the very least, she had gotten the skin color, hair color, and outfit correct, and saw that she had dirty blonde hair, pale white skin, and a boring gray dress.

The field itself was only about half a mile outside of town, so Cassie was able to get there without too far of a walk. As she approached the familiar outskirts buildings, she could hear the sounds of crowds and music echoing across the mountainsides. Cassie had forgotten the exact date, but it seemed the harvest festival was in full swing. This would make it much easier to slip through unnoticed in the throngs of celebrators.

Cassie walked through the town's outskirts, remembering the last time she was here, fleeing from the Peace Officers aside Gwynne, whom she had barely known at the time. Funny how things turned out. The streets here were largely bare, as the majority of the populace would be near the town's center for the main festivities. She decided for old times' sake to go through the industrial district, since it was on her way. All the factories were closed for the day, and their smokestacks sat quiet and disused. Before long, she found the Jones & Sons factory, and she couldn't help but sneer at the building. Thinking back to her former daydreams of blasting Hardden to smithereens, she decided to do something a bit more humane. She pulled out her spellbook and opened it to a page about arcane markings. Casting the spell, she waved her finger over the side of the building, spelling out the word 'MANLET' in tall red capitals. The spell would wear off in a few days, but otherwise would be impossible to remove by mundane means and would give Hardden the embarrassment of a lifetime.

Satisfied with her act of civil disobedience, Cassie carried on towards the festival. She hadn't noticed before, but the moon was out in the day, barely visible amongst the sparse cirrus clouds. Perhaps this meant the Wolf was active in the daytime?

She passed through the commercial district, noticing that an entire block of shops had been demolished. This hurt her soul, and she worried about Mr. Burton's shop before realizing he was one block over. Still, she recalled visiting these very establishments all her life, and had even patronized them when she was last in town. It gave her a haunting feel of impermanence, worsened considerably by the sign erected upon the temporary fencing that surrounded the block, advertising that a Joy Mart was soon to be built. Cassie's disgust was alleviated slightly by the *other* signs stuck at haphazard angles around the fence.

"Say NO to Joy Mart!"

"No Joy in Worker Abuse!"

"Protect Bixton! Boycott Joy Mart!"

It seemed some amongst the townsfolk rebelled against the capitalist exploitation, and Cassie hoped that it would make a difference, remembering the callous nonchalance of Hector Joilen himself when discussing the matter of civil protests. She couldn't help but feel that without a top-down system reform, things would only continue to worsen. She remembered Mr. Burton's tenuous competitive edge and how much longer he'd be able to maintain it with the economy's rapid inflation and the impending Joy Mart set to undercut his and everyone else's prices.

To take her mind off the sorry state of the kingdom, Cassie found herself down at the water's edge where she had first seen Gwynne. How little she knew then! There was a sort of nostalgic feeling that pervaded the town, but one less of the joy of a bygone era and more of the residual ache of a lifetime of misery.

As she stood by the Mellius down the canal, she heard the voices of soldiers from nearby. She slipped under the nearby bridge, pressing herself against the cold stones of the underarch. Boots thudded above her and voices echoed into the short tunnel.

"…unidentified flying craft. Owl may have sent the Crow back to its hometown for something."

Who's the Crow? Cassie wondered before realizing they must have been talking about her. She *had* been seen aiding Owl on numerous occasions, and between Mordecai's stalking and her mother's treachery, the royal army probably knew all about her now. Still, it was funny that they had taken to calling her Crow. She assumed it was meant to be a pejorative name based on her skin color, but she thought it was rather badass.

Guess I'm a proper phantom thief now, she thought, and smiled, practicing calling herself The Crow in her head.

"Spread out and search the town," a soldier continued. "Question anyone suspicious." The footsteps faded away into the distance and Cassie emerged from her hiding spot. It seemed she would have company, and needed to complete her business as swiftly as possible. She had made the *Star* invisible, one of its many arcane enhancements, but she worried about being found out herself. She had memorized a few spells that might help her out in a pinch for just such an occasion, but she hoped she wouldn't need to use them. She made doubly sure the soldiers were gone and headed towards the town center.

The sound of crowds grew to a roar as she approached the festival grounds. People milled about every which way, and it wasn't long before Cassie found herself amidst throngs of booths manned by local chefs, artisans, farmers, and artists. People crammed themselves together to wait in line at the more popular booths, and others still walked the streets in between with bags full of purchased goods or hands filled with street food. Cassie was pleased to see that there was a sandwich stand belonging to Mr. Burton. People nearby were raving about his top-quality ingredients and his almost supernatural sense for ingredient pairing.

Cassie got in line and eventually approached the counter. Mr. Burton seemed incredibly busy, and paid her little notice.

"'Ello Miss, wot can I get ye?"

Cassie grinned. "It's so good to see you again, Mr. Burton. Got any of that spicy mayo for a customer for life?"

Mr. Burton shook his head and blinked at her. "Well blimey, 'ardly recognized ye there. Tha's a real makeover ye gave yerself."

"Oh don't worry, it's only temporary." Cassie appreciated Mr. Burton's attempt at subtlety.

"Very well, one Thieving Crow Special coming right up. That'll be five crowns."

"I see you've had to maintain your competitive edge." Cassie reached into her pocket and pulled out a five-hundred-crown note and handed it to Mr. Burton. "Oops, I seem to have given you the wrong banknote! Oh well, feel free to keep the change as an investment into Burton's Butchery and Delicatessen." It was a large chunk of Cassie's cash, but figured it did more good for Mr. Burton than for her anyway.

Mr. Burton picked his jaw up off the floor and stammered out his sincere gratitude, handing her a large sandwich wrapped in newsprint alongside a heaping helping of fries. Cassie felt good about herself, but wondered if what she had done was really for Mr. Burton's sake or it was more to make herself feel good. She ultimately decided that it mattered little, as a good deed was a good deed regardless of intention.

She spent a few hours just visiting the other booths and buying local foodstuffs and artisan creations that caught her eye. There was even a makeshift barn on the far side of the town square where various farm animals were on display for children of all ages to touch. Cassie had a soft spot for the animals, and found herself petting cows, goats, chickens, and pigs.

She had spent nearly all her money and had just about filled the wondrous bag by the time the sun began to creep lower in the sky, threatening an imminent evening. The moon only continued to rise in the sky, nearing its zenith. The already cool fall climes began to drop in temperature, and mountain winds swept over Bixton, chilling the air even further. Cassie pulled a jacket from the wondrous bag and threw it over her shoulders. As she did so, she nearly dropped it at the sight of a familiar face in the crowd.

Walking through the mass of people was a face that Cassie knew all too well. This person wore a casual dress, but their face was the unmistakable lightly creased countenance of Cassie's mother, Corrine Mott. Despite the surrounding merriment, Corrine was not smiling, instead bearing a faraway look in her eyes. Behind her, holding her hand, was someone that Cassie did not recognize at first. This person had white skin that was so bright she swore it would glow in the dark. Atop their head were tight blonde curls, and Cassie's stomach dropped.

The girl pouted. "Mommy! I want to play the games!"

Please, gods, don't let this be Ophelia! Cassie prayed to herself.

Corrine just shook her head. "Be patient, Feelie, Mommy's hungry."

Cassie felt simultaneously disgusted and sympathetic for her sister. She knew Ophelia suffered from delusions of grandeur, but Cassie had hoped she would grow out of it. Unfortunately, Corrine had done nothing but encourage this behavior, which now led to Ophelia bleaching her hair and skin. But Ophelia was an adult now. Despite how Corrine had botched her upbringing, she was responsible for her own decisions, and there was nothing that Cassie could say that would change their minds. She wanted desperately to step up to them and give them a solid piece of her mind. The Cassie of months ago would likely have done just that, but she knew that she needed to maintain her cover. Besides, would they even listen? She doubted it. No, they'd just find some way to make themselves the victims.

Cassie decided to remove herself from the situation and retreated to the outskirts of the crowd. She passed a bulletin board near the town hall that contained two wanted posters, each bearing an artist's rendition of a familiar woman. One was clearly Gwynne, as she had looked at Black Eagle Keep. The poster read "Wanted Alive, Prince Quintus, 'Owl of the Pale Moon', 1,000,000 Crown Reward". Beside it, another poster portrayed what was clearly Cassie, though the artist's rendition was not flattering. The poster read, "Wanted Dead or Alive, Cassandra Mott, 'Crow', 50,000 Crown Reward". It was no surprise that Gwynne was worth twenty times as much as Cassie, but the numbers still made her head spin.

"At least I'm wanted by *someone*," she joked to herself, doing little to alleviate the fear she felt seeing her face on a wanted poster as a heinous criminal.

A flash of movement from a nearby rooftop caught her eye and she saw two tiny humanoid figures just sitting on the edge of a roof and watching the proceedings. These figures had little butterfly wings and were dressed only in loose loincloths. Cassie wondered why she had never seen fey in Bixton before, but judging from the fact that nobody else in the crowd seemed to notice them, they were likely invisible to the average person. The two faeries waved to her and she nodded back, content to keep her distance after her ordeal in the fey world.

19

Fang and Friendship

Desperately Needing Closure - Put the Rabid Dog Down - You Live Like This? - Something Precious that You Want to Protect

Seeing that her family was out at the moment, Cassie realized it would be the perfect opportunity to visit her old home and collect some of her belongings. She had left before without realizing that she wouldn't be back and didn't have time to pack. Besides, she wanted to give a proper goodbye to the house in which she had grown up. It just felt right.

Making her way through the streets, she eventually arrived in the residential district unhindered. The streets were empty here, and she made her way to the Mott household with ease. The house looked exactly the same as ever and that nostalgic feeling was stronger than ever within Cassie's heart. The lights were naturally all off as the only two occupants were out at the moment. In lieu of her key, which she had long ago misplaced, she used a spell to unlock the front door, probing with arcane words to find the right configuration of the lock. In only a few seconds the door was open and the dark house loomed beyond. Despite the familiar feeling, the house seemed ominous.

Cassie knew that this was likely a trap, but was desperately needing closure.

She stepped into her former home and cast a dim directional light spell to find her way up to her old room, making sure to keep the beam away from windows. Everything looked more or less as she had left it, as if she had never even gone away. The door to her old room was closed, and she was surprised when she opened it that her room was immaculate. Again, it was like she hadn't even left. She thought for sure that Ophelia would have loaded boxes of old clothes that didn't even fit her anymore into the room, but there was no trace of such a thing.

Cassie took some time to look over her old possessions. She started with the wardrobe but found that each of the outfits therein were far too plain and tacky for her tastes now. She wondered how she had ever settled for wearing them. Likewise, the keepsakes and mementos around her room elicited no emotion in her. The only thing that resonated with her at all was her book collection. She was particularly fond of the *Great Detective Grimsby* series, of which she owned every volume. There was just enough room in the wondrous bag for her books, which she hoped to at least add to the House's library.

With that, there was nothing more for her in the Mott household. An idea struck her, as she left her room, however. She found a pen and parchment downstairs in the kitchen and began writing a letter to her mother and sister, explaining all the ways they had wronged her over the years, and that she was happy now with the woman she loved and was now a very accomplished criminal.

That ought to make Mom's head spin, she thought, as she placed the note upon Corrine's pillow and proudly walked down the stairs. She left the house again, not bothering to lock the door behind herself, when suddenly something collided with her and grabbed her hard. Looking around, she saw that a whole group of soldiers had caught her, and a familiar face strutted up to her with saber in hand.

"Miss Cassandra Mott, I presume? We really need to stop running into each other like this."

Cassie found herself quickly gagged with a thick cloth before she could begin casting. A smart move on the soldiers' part, which meant she was at their mercy until she could physically break free.

The soldier captain that seemed to accost Cassie at every turn leaned down to her to gloat. "I suppose it's only right that I offer my name. I am Captain Michael Ross, and I am the leader of His Majesty's special cases task force. It is our job to track down renegade criminals such as Owl and yourself. But really, who could have predicted that Owl would really be the Princ-"

Captain Ross's wind was knocked from his lungs as Cassie kicked him as hard as she could. Her boot impacted his midriff and he staggered back to catch his breath. She struggled against the soldiers' grips, but was unable to break free. Ross was furious now. He charged up to her.

"Oh you've done it now, dog. I'm going to make you regret that before you die!"

As the Captain raised his saber to strike, a howl filled the early evening air.

"It's the Wolf!" a few soldiers cried, looking around for the source of the sound.

Ross's blade stopped. "Shut up, you fools. There are no wolves in the Brachius! They were hunted to extinction decades ago. No doubt it's just some neighborhood hounds." He then turned his attention back to Cassie, fury now tempered. "Now then, dog, I'll give you one chance to talk. If you attempt to cast a spell, I'll slit your throat before you can utter a single incantation."

He removed the gag from Cassie's mouth and she coughed and sputtered now that her mouth was clear.

"Don't you ever... misgender my best friend."

Ross slapped her. It wasn't terribly hard, but it still stung.

"You're in no position to be making demands. Now, tell me, and you may just live, what is Owl planning next? How do they intend to harm His Majesty?"

"I thought I made it clear last we met, even if I knew, I wouldn't tell you pigs."

"Very well, I figured I'd at least give you the chance to beg. His Majesty will be taking care of matters on his own soon, anyway. You're clearly no use to us, so I will put the rabid dog down."

The gag was placed in Cassie's mouth once more, and Captain Ross took up his striking stance. Cassie closed her eyes, still struggling in vain against her bonds, but it was no use. All she knew was the soldier's saber rushing down towards her neck.

But there was no impact. Instead, an ungraceful "Huunghh" came from somewhere in front of Cassie. She opened her eyes to see that something had struck Captain Ross, a shaggy and gangly form that was now tearing into the man's shoulder with jagged teeth. Blood sprayed out, flecking Cassie's face with hot crimson. The Captain was screaming from where the creature had knocked him to the ground. Everything erupted into panic. Soldiers began aiming their guns at the beast, struggling not to catch their captain in the crossfire.

Bang! Bang b-bang! Bang bang!

Rifles erupted, unloading lead straight into the creature and making Cassie's ears ring. Smoke from the rifle muzzles filled the air, partially obscuring the melee and making Cassie cough. The soldiers holding her were unsure what to do, and she was able to break free from their uneasy grip. She was about to make a break for it when a shape loomed upwards in the smoke, threw its blood-soaked mouth back and howled. Everyone froze for a split second before the soldiers turned and fled. Cassie was too terrified to speak or even move. The creature looked around at her and raised a clawed hand towards her. She screamed, but the sound died in her throat as the hand resolved itself into... a thumbs-up?

The Wolf howled again, the gunsmoke clearing. Cassie could see its body peppered with bullet wounds, but each hole steamed and started to close, expelling the lead bullets onto the flagstones with clinking sounds. Once the healing process was finished, the werewolf kneeled down and its form shrank and twisted back into a more recognizably humanoid shape. This person was wearing brown slacks and a brown waistcoat over a white shirt. Their messy close-cut hairstyle seemed familiar to Cassie, and her suspicions were confirmed when they turned around to reveal Jax Dennin.

"Jax? *You're* the Wolf of Bixton?"

"Hey there, Cass. Looks like I've got some explaining to do, huh?"

Cassie dropped the illusion spell and hugged Jax. "I'm so sorry I left without saying goodbye! I had no idea what was going on at the time."

Jax requited the embrace, and they patted her on the back. "I figured it was something like that. I thought you had skipped town after getting fired, and I felt so bad that I didn't try to come check on you or anything. I really should have been there for you."

Cassie pulled away from them, only just now realizing she was standing in a pool of Captain Ross's blood.

"Umm, you didn't kill him, did you?"

"What, the army asshole? He'll live. The soldiers will come back for him soon, I bet. Let's make ourselves scarce."

The two reunited friends fled from the scene of the battle, returning to Jax's apartment a few blocks away. The building in which they lived was an unassuming three-story affair with brick walls that were slightly crumbling and cracking with age. Jax unlocked a rickety plywood door and let Cassie into their studio flat. The entire unit was but a single room, barely bigger than the living room and kitchen of the Mott household. Along one wall was a standalone sink, a toilet, a pitiable stained washbasin and a flimsy wooden table. On the opposite wall was a small bed that barely had enough room for one person, with patched sheets and ripped mattress. Overall, it was quite pitiable indeed.

"Jax, you live like this?" Cassie asked, aghast.

"Yeah, yeah, I know, it's kind of a mess. And it's not exactly ritzy, but it's pretty much all I can afford on a factory worker's salary. You know how it is."

Jax pulled out a battered folding chair and sat it down on the floor. Cassie took the seat and Jax sat on the bed. Cassie immediately launched into her tale of leaving Bixton with Gwynne, traveling all over the world, getting involved with a heist, nearly dying multiple times over in the rainforest, and back again.

"You know, Cass, if I hadn't seen the wanted signs for myself, I'd have found your story hard to believe. But we're friends, and you never were good at lying. As for myself, well… Honestly not much has changed for me. I've still been working in the factory day in and day out, but I guess you already know about my moonlighting. Yeah, I'm a werewolf. It runs in my family, so I've been like this since I was a kid. My parents kept me locked away inside when the moon was at its strongest, but when I grew up I learned to control my power. Then I left my parents to make a life for myself and ended up here. I managed to keep a low profile until one day I was seen by who else but Cathy Bateman. Before I could do anything, the rumors started flying. I've never actually killed anyone, of course."

"That's a relief to hear."

"Yeah, it turns out that were-beasts aren't mindless killing machines like the rumors say. Though I admit I'm pretty terrifying." Jax flexed their arms, revealing a distinct lack of muscle in their human form. "I decided to lay low for a while at night, but the rumors wouldn't go away, and I got restless. Wolf nature, I guess. I decided I needed to go explain everything to Cathy, and that's when I bumped into you. You caught me in the middle of scavenging a roast from the bins-"

"Oh gods, Jax, that's disgusting!"

Jax gave a wan smile. "A nasty habit, I know, but wolf brain says Meat Good and I find indulging it from time to time keeps the instincts in check. Anyway, I wanted to explain everything to you then, but you ran away. Can't blame you, I guess."

"And you chased me?"

"I mean, a *bit*, but only so I could explain, you know? But I realized that would probably be bad, so I stopped pretty quickly, especially when I heard dogs barking. Dogs hate me, apparently. Gotten into my fair share of scraps in my time." Jax hung their head in shame. "Then you came to work the next day and I wanted to explain, but you were hiding it, so I didn't want to pry... I dunno, I guess I'm just awkward like that. I was also afraid that... that you wouldn't want to be my friend anymore."

"Oh, Jax, no, honey. You're still my friend. I don't care if you're a werewolf or a were-bear or a were-cricket. You've still been nothing but kind to me, and I'd like us to still be friends."

They lifted their head and looked at Cassie. "Pinky promise?"

The two linked pinkies and swore on it.

"Oh, by the way, Cass, have you seen the Joy Mart lot?"

"Yeah, makes me sick. I've been to Ultan, and their economy is in shambles there because of it. I even sorta met Hector Joilen himself. Wish I had slugged the bastard, in hindsight."

Jax laughed. "That's amazing. Next time you see him, give him one for me, as well. You'll be pleased to know that I'm working with the protesters here in town to fight the Joy Mart construction."

"Oh yeah, I saw the signs!"

"Oh good!" Jax beamed. "I helped work on those. It's not much, but

I've been doing what I can. Plus, I've decided to spend my wolf hours keeping an eye out for soldiers and Peace Officers and scaring the crap out of them. Seems to make them a lot more tame. It's nothing world-changing, but I hope that we can make a difference here.

"By the way, your mom came by a few weeks ago. Seemed to think I was hiding you here! I told her the truth, which is that I had no idea what you were up to and hadn't seen you since your last day of work."

"Did she seem upset?"

"Nervous, more like. Not sure exactly what she was thinking about the situation, but I imagine she was worried to a degree."

"Good."

"Cassie, she's your mother. I know she's been pretty shitty to you, but she's family. You should go check on her."

Cassie shook her head. "Sorry, but you're wrong about one thing. While she may be my mother, she's not my family. I have a new family now, and they're more important to me."

"Fair enough. Hey, why did you come back to Bixton anyway? Surely it wasn't just to see little ol' me?"

"Actually, in a way, it is. Gwynne is under a curse, and she needs a werewolf fang in order to break it. I don't really know how this works, but would you be able to spare one? I'm so glad the Wolf turned out to be you, I didn't want to have to kill someone for just one fang."

Jax thought about it for a minute. "I think I left a fang in that soldier's shoulder, so you should be able to grab it if you're quick-," the sound of a distant explosion rocked the small apartment.

Jax looked over towards a shuttered window. "Uh, Cassie, do they normally do fireworks at the festival?"

Cassie scrambled to her feet and made her way out of the door, a cold dread sinking into her stomach. "No, they don't."

Outside, something lit up the evening sky in the distance. There were thunderous *booms*, flashes of light and a *brap-brap-brap-brap* that could only be machine gun fire. In the flashing light, Cassie could see two gunships locked in aerial combat. She could just barely make out tiny shapes between them filling the air, occasionally bursting into flames and careening towards the earth.

"What's going on out there?" Jax asked, following Cassie outside.

Cassie didn't say anything, her mind kicking into a panic. One of those ships was definitely the *Pale Moon*, and that meant Gwynne was in danger. Without her magic, she was a sitting duck, helpless before the Royal Army's might.

"What are those ships doing? Is… is one of those yours?"

"I… I'm afraid so. Jax, I gotta go."

Jax gave Cassie another hug. "I understand. Do whatcha gotta do, girl."

Cassie felt sad, knowing she likely wouldn't see Jax for a while. "You could come with us. I'm sure you'd be welcome on our ship."

Jax just shook their head. "I'm needed here, Cass. Despite everything, I love this town, and I want to do all I can to protect it."

"You want to protect Bixton? Why? I hate this place."

"Well, you grew up here, so I can understand that, but I'm used to being on the run and being rejected for what I am, so this was the first place I felt like I belonged and that I had someone who cared about me. Plus, I've come to get to know so many people in the community as part of the protest committee and I think I can make a real change here."

Cannon fire drowned out anything else that might have been said.

"I understand, Jax. I… I'll miss you. I'll send you postcards, okay? And I promise I'll be back someday."

"I know you will, hon. Don't worry about me. Now go! Don't you also have something precious to you that you want to protect?"

20

Canyon Run

Shut Up, I'm A Princess! - How to Tell a Girl Goodbye - Sparks of Arcane Energy - A Gut-Wrenching Creaking Sound

Cassie dashed as fast as she could back to the area where Captain Ross's body was last seen in front of the Mott household. To her dismay, the body was nowhere to be found. She fumbled around in the pool of blood to see if she could find the object she sought. Her hands were covered in blood, but she found a long ivory object in the middle of the pool. It was about two to three inches long and curved elegantly into a sharp point. It glistened slightly in the moonlight. She wiped it off and placed it in her pocket. She didn't know what she would have done if it had been missing.

With the target of her entire visit to Bixton in hand, she took off for the other side of town and the field where she parked the *Morning Star*. In any other circumstance, she would have just teleported, but she needed to bring back the *Star*, and it looked like the *Moon* could use the air support. Plus, who knew what awaited her on the ship, and she felt it would be prudent to save her magic. Of course, the shortest path was through the middle of town. Within a few minutes, Cassie found herself at the wall of people once more. The crowd were all watching the military spectacle in disconcerted earnestness like one might watch a fireworks display.

Cassie elbowed her way through the crowd, but it was slow going. Right around sundown was when the festival typically picked up in terms of traffic and activity, with its dancing, music, contests, and stage shows entertaining guests into the evening. As a consequence, the town square was even more jam-packed than earlier in the day. As she forced her way through, Cassie could see the tips of soldiers' rifles as they tried to contain the crowd.

"Do not be alarmed, good citizens. The Royal Army is just taking care of a terrorist who has invaded our fair soil!"

"Do your patriotic duty and cheer on His Majesty and the Army!"

This was, of course, a gross oversimplification for propaganda's sake. Cassie ignored the soldiers and tried to stay out of their line of sight. They knew she was here now, and the slightest glance could give her away. She didn't have time to cast the disguise spell again, and she especially did not dare now that there were so many people around. Fortunately, this thick of a crowd provided excellent cover.

"Get 'em, Your Majesty!" Someone cried, and many others yelled their support. This made Cassie sad, knowing the full gravity of the situation. It just wasn't fair what had happened to Gwynne, and though she was truly a thief, she had only done what she needed to do to survive and maintain her autonomy.

Before she knew it, Cassie had bumped straight into a young blonde woman, and to her surprise and disgust, realized it was Ophelia.

Ophelia turned around with a flick of her curls. "Sorry about tha- Oh my gods, Cassie, is that you?"

Cassie tried to get away, but she was penned in by the crowd. Realizing a confrontation was inevitable, she tried to get through to her sister.

"Ophelia, what in the world have you done to yourself?"

"I'm pretty now, Cass-Cass. Not like *you* could understand." This comment stung, but Cassie resolved to be the bigger person. She knew Ophelia was just trying to goad her into a fight.

"As much as I hate to admit it, you were pretty before all this. Now you just look like… someone you're not."

"Shut up, I'm a princess! Once they catch that rogue prince, I'm going to marry him and be his bride! And then you'll be sorry that you weren't nicer to me."

"I really don't have time to explain to you the many *many* reasons why that won't happen. Plus, just because I didn't fawn over you like Mom did doesn't mean I didn't try to be reasonable with you. Perhaps one day *you'll* understand *that.*"

Speaking of her mother, the crowd parted and Corrine stepped through, holding a roasted turkey leg in one hand.

"Feelie, dear, don't be afraid- Oh my gods, Cassie, is that you?"

Like mother like daughter, I guess, Cassie thought. "*Hi,* Mom. Didn't expect to run into you like this. I see you've finally learned my name. How nice of you to wait until I'm a wanted criminal to finally get that straight."

"I can't believe what you have been doing! Gallivanting across the kingdom with that terrorist and getting involved with high crimes! You've worried me sick. You will come home this instant and let me straighten you out. I'm going to get you a new, respectable job somewhere and we'll work on smoothing this whole thing over with the government."

Cassie rolled her eyes. Nobody here was going to listen to her. Clearly nothing had changed. "Yeah, that's not gonna happen. I finally found somewhere I'm wanted and I belong, so with any luck you'll never see me again."

"Guards! Help!" Corrine began to shout. A pair of soldiers some fifteen feet away turned around, and their rifle tips bobbed as they tried to make their way through the crowd towards the woman's cries.

"Really, Mom?" Ophelia said, who clearly thought that this much, at least, was beneath her.

Corrine continued anyway. "The Crow is here! Help!"

"Sorry, Mom, you had your chance. And Feelie? You don't need all this nonsense to be loved." With that, Cassie finished her memorized teleportation spell and disappeared from the gap in the crowd, appearing on the far side of the town square. A few people were startled, but most didn't even notice her appearance. They were too busy watching the dogfight or looking over to see who was shouting. Cassie didn't wait around to see what happened, and carried on once more towards the edge of town.

As she neared it, she could see that there was a makeshift barricade on all the roads out, manned by five members of the Peace Officers. This was exactly like what had happened in Ultan, but this time Cassie was at full capacity. She approached the barricade with a swagger that startled the waiting officers.

Cassie retrieved her spellbook, willed it back up to its normal size and opened it in front of her. "Good evening, Officers. Looking for me?"

Each of the men struggled to load their rifles. Cassie was surprised they hadn't already done so, but they must not have anticipated her egress from this side of town.

"It's Crow!" one of the officers shouted.

"You're a disgrace to this town!" another jeered.

Cassie laughed. "Oh, *I'm* the disgrace, am I? Priceless. We'll see how much of a disgrace I am after I've rescued this country from its greed and corruption." This was not a goal she had hitherto realized she had, but it sounded right in the moment. And who knew, maybe after all this was said and done she could actually make some kind of change.

The men just sneered at her. "You're a thief *and* a terrorist! We'll be rewarded handsomely by taking you down, Changer."

The officers finished loading their guns and aimed them at Cassie's chest. She just smiled. With a few quick words, she completed a second spell she had memorized. When the men fired, their bullets ricocheted off an invisible force field around Cassie's body, causing tessellating patterns to appear across the field's surface. This was a physical ward that she had learned after the trip to the jungle, rightly assuming it would come in handy during this excursion.

"You know, boys, this isn't the first time I've been shot at while simply trying to leave town. You sure do know how to tell a girl goodbye." Cassie was giddy with power now. The officers blanched, realizing their big masculine power sticks had no effect on this strong and independent woman.

"Dammit, it's no use!" the officer who seemed to be in charge shouted. "All personnel, fall back!" The men turned to run, retreating away from Cassie and out of the town.

Cassie just shook her head. "Aww, where are you going? We're just getting started."

With a wave of her hand, an arc of force whipped out at the men, knocking them off their feet to the ground. They each groaned and nursed bruised knees and elbows, winded but relatively unharmed. The blow to their morale, however, was extremely potent. As they scrambled to their feet to flee again, Cassie gave another wave. This time, each of the officers' belt buckles burst, causing their trousers to drop around their ankles, revealing unflattering white underwear.

"You're a monster!" One of the men shouted as he hopped away, trying desperately to pull up his pants.

"Oh no no no. I've seen plenty of monsters in my time. I'm no monster, I'm just a wizard. Apprentice to the most powerful mage in the world, to boot, and don't you forget it!"

* * *

Cassie allowed the Peace Officers to flee properly after that, deciding they had had enough humiliation. She jogged out of town towards the field from before, hoping she hadn't used too much energy during that power trip. After about twenty minutes, she was back at the location of the *Morning Star* and had dismissed its invisibility. With a strain of effort, she opened the cockpit and clambered in. Remembering Gwynne's instructions, she turned on the craft's engine and thrust it forward, using the short grassy field as a runway. By the end of the field, she had gotten up to speed and had attained lift, brushing the landing gear on nearby hedges.

She was then up in the air, shooting over the town of Bixton. A few soldiers from down below attempted to fire their rifles at her, but the bullets whizzed by, unable to hit her at speed. She thought she saw her mother's enraged face from down in the crowd, but that may have just been wishful thinking. Regardless, she pushed the plane's engine as fast as it could go towards the roiling aerial battle in the distance.

She was so focused on her destination that she didn't even notice that she was being tailed. She spared a glance in one of her mirrors to see that there were two fighters closing in on her tail, emblazoned with the crest of Zona. They must have been outriders surveying the surrounding area in case the *Moon* called in reinforcements. With a flash of muzzle fire, the Zonan fighters let loose on her. Cassie thrust the stick to a sharp angle and began evasive maneuvers, bullets ricocheting off the *Star*'s magical wards, sending sparks of arcane energy flying. The wards prevented direct damage to the *Star*'s hull, but only to a certain extent. There was only a set amount of energy imbued into them. Too much punishment and they'd shatter, leaving Cassie completely vulnerable.

She'd have to lose these chasers before she joined the battle proper, though, and they were gaining on her by the second. Surveying the landscape, she came up with an idea and dove her plane down into a pass between mountain peaks, rushing by densely packed forests and trickling creeks glistening in the moonlight. The very tip of her wing clipped a copse of trees on a particularly sharp turn, scattering needles and traumatizing a small flock of birds.

What she lacked in speed, she made up for in endurance and maneuverability and she needed to take advantage of that. The valley was quite narrow, and required pinpoint maneuvering in order to avoid contact with the claustrophobic slopes that formed walls on either side. The valley she flew into quickly turned into a ravine, grasses and trees giving way to craggy cliffs and then a fully-fledged canyon, rock walls jutting out at sharp angles. This was an extremely risky maneuver but there was no other way to get the pursuing fighters off her tail.

The canyon floor below was home to a snaking river that slowly bored this channel into the rock. This was the Myers Canyon. Cassie had been here once before on a school trip, but had never seen it like this. Geological records indicated that this canyon was formed over millennia of erosion, and under any other circumstance the sheer size of the natural wonder paired with the visual magnificence of its multi-colored strata would have been a picturesque sight, but it was all a brown blur from the cockpit of the *Star*.

Cassie was terrified, but she had entered a kind of adrenaline trance in which she couldn't think about her fear and could only react on instinct. The noise of the plane's engine was deafening, and various pipes vented steam into the chamber, making the cockpit a whirlwind of sensory overload. She knew that without all the magical assistance placed on the craft she would likely be dead already, but didn't have time to think about that now. All she could think about was taking the turns as they came and anticipating what might follow.

One of the fighters' guns flashed past the *Star*, impacting the canyon wall and sending a shower of dust and debris onto Cassie's cockpit. She was blinded for a split second and scraped a wing against the rock, but fortunately the warding held and she was able to right her course. The other planes were not quite as lucky, scraping their bellies across the rough surface.

Ahead of her a rock pillar rose up to meet her and she whipped the craft around it and through a tight passage. She just barely managed to avoid scratching the cockpit glass, but one of the trailing fighters failed to evade in time and damaged one of its wings. It shook in the air, but remained aloft for now. The fighters let loose another spray of bullets, this time nearly nicking Cassie's landing gear. She flicked her gaze to a gauge on the plane's dashboard. The arcane wards were holding at around 50% power, meaning she couldn't take too many more hits before needing to recharge. She'd need to make a move soon.

Up ahead in the canyon, maybe a mile down, the river dropped into a dark cave. Cassie had an idea but it might exhaust a good deal of her strength. Using the disguise spell from earlier as a basis, she simultaneously conjured an illusion of her plane while making the *Star* itself invisible. She sent the illusion down into the cave while pulling back on the stick and soaring upwards herself. Just as she planned, one of the two tailing fighters didn't notice her trick and dove into the cave to pursue, the other veering up at the last second. Once it was inside, Cassie dropped the spell. Unfortunately, the second fighter caught sight of her and began to follow once more. Not knowing what else to do, Cassie pulled the nose back and climbed higher and higher, veering only to dodge sprays of machine gun fire from behind.

As the *Star* climbed, threatening to join its namesakes in the heavens, the air temperature began to drop sharply. Cassie could see ice crystals begin to form on the cockpit glass and she heard a gut-wrenching creaking sound of the craft's hull begin to contract in the cold. More worrying still, the plane's engine began to sputter and slow. Cassie, who was not a trained pilot and did not know about stalling, began to panic. Out of instinct, she jerked the flight stick back, causing the *Star* to flip. It seemed she realized the danger just a second before whoever or whatever was flying the remaining fighter, and due to her better maneuverability, she was able to flip around in time to loose her own volley of gunfire, tearing apart her assailant's starboard wing. The other plane erupted into flames and began to plummet to the ground. She felt bad for the person she assumed was piloting it, but surely they had parachutes for just such an occasion?

At any rate, there were no traces of enemy planes up here among the clouds, so she pointed the nose of the *Star* towards the *Moon* and charged forward at top speed. The actual moon was either full or quite close to and its baleful gaze reminded Cassie that with each second Gwynne's life could be inching closer to an unglamorous end. She pushed the thoughts out of her head for now. She feared the engine would give out, but the small plane dutifully bore her back towards its home, though the state of said home remained to be seen.

VI

House Brandwyck

21

Homecoming

A Necklace of White-Hot Beads - A Particularly Disgusting Grub - Need a Hand, Bruv? - A Blisteringly Fast Classical Concerto

Thunder rolled across the sky, though the evening clouds were sparse. Up ahead in the distance, Cassie could see the two battleships locked in combat. The familiar avian shape of the *Pale Moon* flew along beside a hulking mass of ugly black metal, more beetle than bird. It was oblong, thicker at its bow, with a round shielded chamber on top that looked like it may be full of gas. Judging by the shape, this was an armored combat dirigible. It was bedecked all over with golden filigree, and the Zonan royal crest was emblazoned across the front of its hull. Along its side were towering gold letters that spelled the ship's name, the *Crowning Glory*. It was easily twice the size of the *Moon*, though most of its bulk could be attributed to its gas tank. Nonetheless, a row of cannon bays lined the belly of the steel beast, each one belching out in turn to harass the *Pale Moon* with heavy fire.

The *Moon*, to its credit, was taking it like a champ. Each cannonball shattered into bits of shrapnel on a colossal force field around the ship's form, like the one Cassie had used earlier but a thousand times bigger. She had no idea where the power source for this shield came from, but decided she'd have to ask Horatio when this was all over. The *Moon* had two gigantic Gauss cannons beneath its wings that took a few seconds to charge, but when activated fired blinding beams of plasma out towards the *Glory*, obliterating any fighters in its wake and leaving searing melted spots on the dirigible's hull.

But the cannons weren't fast enough. In addition to its onboard artillery, the *Glory* had come bearing a swarm of fighter craft, like the ones that had tailed Cassie back from Bixton. At first she thought that the fighters were unopposed, but a blast of fire filled the windy night air, burning a formation of fighters to a crisp. There in the center of the melee was Feckalia, transformed from mischievous maid to terrifying demon. Cassie could barely make her out, but it seemed Feck's eyes were glowing red, and even inside the cockpit in the midst of an all-out battle, Cassie could hear Feck's screams of rage as she pelted the enemy fighters with every ounce of her magic. A necklace of white-hot beads appeared in the sky before each exploded with concussive force, reducing immediate fighters to ash and unbalancing those caught in its shockwave.

The battle must have been going on for almost an hour before Cassie arrived on the scene in the *Moon*'s only deployable craft. She felt guilty that she had taken so long, and was amazed that everyone had lasted. It was truly a testament to Gwynne's years of preparation for just such a battle that the *Moon* was still standing at all, despite the battering it was taking from both the *Glory* and its fighters. Still, it seemed the thing the *Moon* lacked most of all was offensive firepower. She wasn't meant to be able to take down a full-scale battleship like this and mostly relied on speed and defenses to escape sticky situations. If there was an hour in which Cassie's help was ever needed, it was now.

"Cassie! Thank the devils you're back!" Feckalia's voice sounded in

Cassie's head. "I've established a telepathic link. You can reply by just thinking back what you want to say. Did you get the thing?"

"If you mean the fang, yes."

"Oh hells bless. You've gotta get in there! A docking craft boarded the *Moon* right before you showed up. I tried my best to down it, but it was shielded from magic. I suspect there's a powerful mage on that thing."

"But what about you?"

Somehow, Feck laughed into Cassie's head. "Oh, I'm fine. It's pretty rare I get to cut loose like this, especially in the human world. By the way, I know you're a squeamish baby, but don't worry. All these gnats out here are unmanned. They're basically robotic planes. No need to moralize about shooting them down."

This was certainly a relief to Cassie. She had felt a nagging guilt about shooting down that craft before, but all doubts were now erased. "Thanks, Feck. Keep up the good work. Over and out."

"Yeah yeah, go kiss your girlfriend already so she can get her magic back!"

"She is not-" Cassie felt the psychic link terminate.

Under normal circumstances Cassie would have blushed and flustered, but she compartmentalized her useless lesbian brain and decided to deal with that later. There sure were a lot of things she was putting off at this point.

With renewed vigor, she pushed the *Star* forward into the combat, firing free with the plane's guns. The first volley alone took out two autonomous craft that hadn't seen her coming, but now they were onto her. A three-unit formation broke off from harrying the *Moon* and turned their attention to Cassie. As one, they fired upon her, but she was able to dip down underneath them and roll around to their sides to dodge. While the *Star* had built-in g-force dampeners, she couldn't help but feel flung around its cockpit. She considered herself lucky that she didn't get motion sick.

As she righted herself from this maneuver, she was able to catch the tail rudders of the attacking craft with her bullets and they spun out of control down through the clouds and out of sight. Before she could find her next target, a spray of fire impacted the top of her craft, traveling from port to starboard along the wings. The magical wards absorbed these shots, but her power was low, down to 10%. She needed to land soon or else she'd be shot from the sky.

Turning her craft up again, she caught sight of the *Moon*'s hangar bay, laying open to the sky. She could almost make out an ugly black lump inside, matching the scaled hide of the *Glory*. She set the engine to full throttle towards the hole, weaving between gunfire and smoke as she approached. But a fighter was on her tail. She couldn't lead this thing through the *Moon*'s shields, so she banked and rolled, trying to get away from it. A *brap-brap-brap* of gunfire impacted on the *Star*, and a warning siren alerted her that the shields had been depleted and the landing gear had been damaged. Realizing she didn't have room to maneuver or time to deliberate, she instead dropped the throttle down to low and activated the *Star*'s airbrake. She jolted as she came to an abrupt slowdown in the air, and her assailant flew past her. She had just enough time to fill the machine with daylight before it scraped off the *Moon*'s shields and careened towards the ground.

Her path now clear for the moment, she activated the engines again, coming in for a crash landing. The landing gear wouldn't deploy, the hatches stuck closed from the damage. Fortunately, that seemed to be the extent of the issue, and Cassie was able to maneuver inside the shields of the *Moon*, which parted specifically for her craft's signature, and pointed the nose of the *Star* towards the hangar. She tried to reduce her speed as much as possible, but she misjudged with no real landmarks and the *Morning Star* screamed into the *Pale Moon*'s hangar bay and scraped against the floor, screeching to a halt inches before it would have impacted the far wall.

Cassie hurried to unbuckle herself and open the cockpit. She kicked the glass to the fully open position and launched herself out onto the floor. The *Morning Star* was tilted to the right, leaning precariously on its starboard wing. The chassis groaned a little as the craft settled, clearly upset at its treatment by Cassie's hands.

"Sorry about that, girl," Cassie said to the plane. "I'll have you fixed up in no time after all this." She patted the riveted steel by way of apology, knowing the inanimate object couldn't understand her feelings anyway.

Looking around the hangar, she could see flaming skid marks where the *Star* had landed, as well as the combat still roiling outside. Fortunately, the enemy's numbers seemed to be thinned from when she arrived, but she could see Feck still hovering in the middle distance, looking exhausted. Cassie wondered how much more energy Feckalia had left. She was their only hope at the moment, at least until Cassie could make it to Gwynne. Cassie prayed that Gwynne would be able to salvage the situation, though the limits of her magic were still unknown. Gwynne always considered herself the strongest wizard in the world, but who knew how far that went, exactly. Could Gwynne do anything to the armored dirigible that threatened to blow down their front door?

The hulking black boarding craft didn't inspire confidence. If the *Glory* was a gigantic beetle, this thing was a particularly disgusting grub. It sat on a number of steel struts that propped the thing up, and she wondered how exactly it was able to take off without propellers. The body was one lumpy black shape with a thin cockpit at the fore. It didn't seem to bear any weapons, and likely its intended purpose was to get into tough situations and deposit ground troops. There was a hatch, now closed, at the craft's aft that might allow soldiers to deploy.

As if to confirm, Cassie could hear the sounds of combat coming from deeper within the ship. She rounded the landing craft and ran into the hallway. Amidst the steaming pipeworks like a spider's web of iron, a group of soldiers were brawling with the *Moon*'s engineers. The Ranklin brothers weaved between the inner structures that they had come to know like the backs of their hands since their hiring and brandished heavy pipes and wrenches like clubs at the soldiers, who were having difficulty using their rifles and sabers in these cramped quarters.

Bimmy swung a pipe deftly through a gap in the plumbing, cracking it down on the helm of a Zonan man in front of him. The man crumpled to the ground, unconscious. "Cassie, me ol' mate! It's a rummy bloomin' miracle t'see yer!"

Nearby, Jimmy held a soldier in a chokehold. The soldier flailed in vain to break the muscular man's vice, but eventually collapsed into unconsciousness beside the man Bimmy had felled. He smiled at Cassie. "Lookin' right stunnin', me ol' gal!"

"Izzat you, lass?" Horatio called from further in. "Ye better get ye up t' the main decks sharpish. The bloody king 'imself is 'ere! Also some 'orrible scarred bloke wit' even more 'orrible spells."

This sounded like Mordecai, though Cassie had yet to see the full extent of the man's scarring.

"What about you all? Are you okay?"

"It's right bloody distractin' tryin' t'man both the cannons while this lot 'ave their wrestlin' match right in me ear!"

Bimmy charged toward another soldier, who attempted to shoot him with his rifle, but the bullet hit a pipe, sending steam pouring into the maintenance ducts and ricocheting off into the depths of the ship. "Leave this lovely maiden alone, you buggers!" Bimmy shouted. The soldier, who had no time to draw his blade, turned his rifle around and used its butt as a club. Wood met lead as the two men's weapons clashed. "We're doin' th' bes' we can, innat roight, bruv?"

Havershank, who had an advantage of smaller size, let loose a bare-knuckle haymaker into the stomach of another man, then followed up with a kick to the jaw, sending the soldier staggering back into a pile of loose bolts, where he did not stir. Havershank gave two thumbs up.

Bimmy's soldier knocked back the pipe and brought his rifle butt crashing down on the man's head. Bimmy staggered for a second, and Jimmy rushed over and knocked the soldier to the floor with a charging lariat. "Need a hand, bruv?"

Jimmy extended a hand and hoisted Bimmy back to a proper stance. There were only about five soldiers left. Cassie was confident in the brothers' teamwork and decided to press on.

"Give 'em hell!" Bimmy called to Cassie as she pressed on towards the stairs to the House. The other men cheered in unison, and Cassie felt invincible.

She made her way through the dark piping and grated floors. Despite the support of everyone else, she couldn't help but feel a bit nervous. Every step took her closer to Gwynne, and she could only hope that she could make it in time. Around a corner, she found the wooden staircase that led up into the hallways of the House proper. As soon as she took her first step on the wood, however, a sickly green sigil appeared beneath her feet. Its shape and symbols were unfamiliar to her, and a screeching pain shot over her brain. Someone, though there was little doubt who, had laid a trap on the staircase, and an insidious one at that. White hot pain was all that Cassie could feel, and she buckled over, as if the material world was merely a distant and far away viewpoint.

Through the pain, a cold terror began to grip Cassie's mind. She felt physically and metaphysically minuscule against the vastness of time and space. She perceived her birth, life, and death as mere blips on the cosmic timeline, a bare fraction of a second on the clock of the universe. She was nothing. Nothing she could ever do would matter. Even if she achieved fame in her lifetime, all achievements faded when faced with eternity. This was a familiar feeling to when Cassie had beheld the oozing green eyeball octopus that was Mordecai's patron.

Whatever this spell was, it forced Cassie to relive every moment of failure throughout her life with painful clarity. She saw herself as a kid being scolded by her mother for wanting to wear a dress instead of starchy pants. She saw herself getting fired by Hardden, face screwed up with rage. She saw herself shouting at Gwynne, knowing that in hindsight this was a comparatively minor issue. But the thing was, Cassie was used to the feelings of shame from these moments, and while going back through them was painful, it did not make her despair, at least not more than usual.

After a few minutes, the pain subsided and Cassie could see again.

"Was that it?" she said to no one in particular. It seemed that Mordecai had once again underestimated his opponents. If this was the worst he could do, she had little to fear. But then again, Cassie had no idea how long she had been stuck in this psychic prison. If the trap's intention was not to harm but instead to buy time...

Cassie dashed up the stairs again and onto wooden floors. There didn't seem to be signs of anyone else around, and the House was suspiciously quiet.

"What would Gwynne do here?" Cassie thought out loud. Even though Gwynne had sequestered herself inside the house, there was no telling where she would be. It seemed uncharacteristic of the bombastic wizard to simply hide away and wait to be found. Cassie jogged through the halls, thinking it would at least be prudent to start her search in a centralized location like the foyer. As she got closer, she could hear the sound of frantic guitar music. Ollie must be ahead.

Whipping around a corner and skidding on the polished floor, Cassie looked into the sitting room where she saw the buzzed fade of

Ollie's hair backed up against the fireplace and playing a blisteringly fast classical concerto on his guitar. Standing opposite from him and looking very much in control of the situation was a man that Cassie had only seen before in glimpses. He still wore that fancy black suit, but it seemed his mask was removed. Mordecai was a Zonan man that appeared to be in his late twenties, which made sense given his past with Gwynne. He had ragged brown hair, giving him a bog-standard Zonan appearance, if a bit more disheveled and unhinged. However, what set him apart most was the multitude of twisted scars across his face. It was as if something caustic had splashed all over the man, corroding and contorting his skin into grisly patterns. Cassie didn't know enough about him to know when he had contracted this macabre injury, but couldn't help but conflate it with the acquisition of his mind-rending patron.

Ollie looked quite out of his league, and with a forceful strum he deflected a bolt of sickly green energy from Mordecai's hands. Gwynne and the King were nowhere in sight, though the sounds of muffled voices came from the kitchen, the next room over.

"Cassie!" Ollie shouted. "Help!"

"Mordecai!" Cassie shouted, hoping to redirect the warlock's attention. "Why don't you pick on someone your own size?"

The grim man turned leisurely on his heel and grinned at Cassie, sending waves of fear down her spine. "Oh good, the Crow has shown its miserable face," he intoned in his voice like whiskey. "Finally a main course. I was tiring of toying with this paltry appetizer."

"Leave the bard alone. I'm taking you out here and now. There's no way I'm letting you anywhere near Gwynne again!"

With a shout in Elder from both parties, they clashed in the entrance to the sitting room from the foyer, placing Cassie in the midst of her first ever mages' duel.

22

Mages' Duel

This Was Just Her Color Now - No Sensations At All - We'll Always Be Best Friends - Mad Fits of Grief

Lights flashed in chromatic aberration as the two mages' fury impacted on one another. Both Cassie and Mordecai had magical wards that protected them from direct damage so their battle was an arcane sword fight of attacking with spells, parrying the opponent's attacks, or dodging out of the way of blasts.

Mordecai's energy was that same enervated green color as before in Black Eagle Keep and Cassie feared what it might do to her should it connect with flesh. Judging by the trap the man had set earlier, psychic torture was likely involved. Cassie, on the other hand, found that her emanations were of a bright pink color, which would have surprised her had she not spent a week with hair of the same hue due to Gwynne's concoction. She guessed this was just her color now.

Where the pink and green collided, bright white flashes twisted and swirled as if reality itself were being warped, sending shockwaves across the room. Cassie's teeth chattered and grated with the force, but she continued to stand her ground.

Mordecai gave a cartoonishly evil laugh. "I see you've picked up a few tricks since our last dance, Cassandra!"

Cassie flung a bolt of pink energy at him, which he deflected with a glowing hand. "I learned a thing or two from my best friend."

Mordecai gritted his teeth in an exaggerated snarl. "No! He's *my* best friend. You didn't grow up with him! You don't know him like I do!"

Normally, blatant misgendering like this would have provoked Cassie further, but she only smiled. "Sounds like you don't know Gwynne very well at all, then, if you can't even gender her correctly."

"Stop saying that name! I will never accept that my brother is a woman!"

"Oh yeah? Well if she's your 'brother', then what's her name?"

"What kind of question is that? It's Ab… A… Godsdammit, why can't I remember his name? What kind of devilry did you concoct, you Changie 'baxer?"

Cassie dashed in close, cloaked her fist in arcane energy, and threw a full body punch at Mordecai's face. Her fist impacted on the man's shielding, but let off a crackling sound as the force field dissipated the bright feminine energy across its surface. "I'll thank you to refrain from using slurs in my presence, bleach boy. Besides, I'm not the one responsible for removing Gwynne's deadname. You've the Butterfly King to thank for that." Mordecai's face was gripped by shock and confusion. Cassie didn't bother to explain further.

"No matter. All I need do is kill you and I can rejoin His Majesty in taking back the prodigal son."

"I think you'll find that no small undertaking. Besides, if you really cared about Gwynne like you say you do, maybe you'd actually listen to her instead of swallowing the lies that the king has fed you."

This must have struck a chord, because Mordecai screamed and lunged forward towards Cassie with hands open in a grasping pose.

She tried to dodge back, but he was too quick. His hands locked onto her shoulders and she could feel the life draining out of her as her brain began to contort in pain. She screamed and felt her knees begin to buckle. Doubts began to enter her head. She was a fool for thinking she could take on Mordecai all alone. This must be where she died.

As her eyes began to feel heavy and she thought she might pass out, she began to hear the sound of music. A sweeping allegro gently rose and fell, and Cassie could feel her energy pulse back up, countering Mordecai's drain. She looked around and saw Ollie crouching behind a chair in the wrecked sitting room, sweeping over his guitar strings.

"C'mon Cassie! Don't give up! You can beat this lunatic!" Ollie was looking terrified, his eyes wider than Cassie had ever seen them, but he didn't give up. He didn't abandon her.

She could remember now. She wasn't alone after all. Feckalia was outside using all of her energy to protect the *Pale Moon*. Horatio was manning the cannons to keep the *Crowning Glory* at bay. The Ranklin brothers were knocking down the royal soldiers that had infiltrated the belly of the *Moon*. Gwynne was currently engaged with the king to some extent. And poor Ollie had been all alone with Mordecai until Cassie had shown up, and even now was using his bardic spells to support her. That also reminded her of something Feckalia had said. The landing craft had deflected her magic.

Wait a minute, Cassie thought, *that means that Mordecai has already used up some of his energy. And probably not an insignificant amount, to boot. Plus, he's had to maintain that curse on Gwynne all this time. He must be exhausted!*

True to her estimation, Mordecai was breathing heavily. "Heh… A lunatic, am I? That's fine. I'll be a lunatic if that's what I have to be for His Majesty."

Cassie began to push back on the man, reversing the grapple. "Give it up Mordecai. Why are you so in love with the king anyway? From what I've heard, he's a pretty shitty person, and an even worse father."

Was it just Cassie's imagination or did Mordecai blush slightly?

"I am *not* in love with *His Majesty!*"

She thought he emphasized 'His Majesty' a bit too much. Suddenly everything clicked into place. Cassie pushed Mordecai away and began to laugh.

"Wait a minute, wait a minute. I think I've figured it out. You're actually in love with Gwynne, aren't you?"

Mordecai was definitely blushing now. "No, I am in love with Prince Ab… A… Fuck! Why can't I say the name of the man I love? Curse your foul Abaxian magics!"

Everything made sense now. No wonder Mordecai was so obsessed with delusions of capturing and detransitioning Gwynne. Cassie felt a twinge of an emotion she could only identify as jealousy, but it didn't last long.

"Well I'm sorry to break it to you, but Gwynne is a woman. Always has been and always will be. And more than that, she's the woman *I* love. I won't let a crazy Change-phobe like you near her."

Mordecai was so furious he began to cry now. He let loose a flurry of energy blasts, many of which went wide and left scorch marks on the walls and furniture. Cassie was able to deflect the few that were true to their target, but her energy was running low. She'd need to end this soon.

She was too busy dodging attacks to notice that there was a change coming over her opponent. Mordecai's eyes were fading to a deep black, more like pools of deep space than actual eyeballs. She just barely had enough time to look before he rushed at her with supernatural speed and grabbed her around the throat, the scars on his hand and face pulsating with a blackish green power. In an instant the world went dark. Cassie thought she might be passing out, but her consciousness endured in the blackness.

She looked around. Mordecai's hands were no longer on her neck. She was standing alone in a pitch black void. No sounds or other sensations from the House could be felt. There were no sensations at all, even. She couldn't even see herself, but she knew she was there.

Am I dead? She wondered. She had often thought about death, being hopelessly depressed for a long time, but this didn't seem like it.

After a stretch of time that felt like an eternity, Cassie could see infinitesimal pinpricks of light fill the globe of her perception. They offered no illumination at her immediate vicinity, but they were at least visual landmarks.

She could now make out something moving against the starry backdrop. Something enormous. No, 'enormous' wasn't the right word. The thing was massive beyond comprehension and seemed to stretch forever and all around her. It was hard to make out details, but Cassie could swear she saw writhing masses of tentacles. Her mind struggled to comprehend this colossal entity, and she felt minuscule, like a paramecium before a planet.

It was then she realized that there was a sound here, a rumbling deep bass that was deafeningly loud, but so low-pitched that she could barely hear it. Through this aural avalanche she could hear something else swelling up. It was the sound of a human voice. Or something that approximated a human voice. It sounded more like a deep demonic chant layered with a screeching high-pitched double tone. She recognized the words as being in the Elder tongue, but the nature of the voice made it difficult to make out exactly what was said. She thought she heard bits of 'I beseech thee', and 'o gods of creation and destruction', and other supplications.

As the voice rose to a more audible volume, Cassie saw a shape begin to form. It was a humanoid shape floating with legs pinned together, arms outstretched, and head lolling back. The nude body was glowing an effervescent white, as if it was merely a projection of a soul that could scatter apart at any second were it not for the tentacles made out of black space itself that swathed the body and squeezed it as it spoke, causing its voice to waver in tone with each contraction.

The body finished its incantation and became motionless. The rumbling of space rose in pitch, becoming an audible crashing in Cassie's ears. As this happened, something began to change about the space around her. Where the pinprick stars dotted the surroundings, bright yellow eyes began to appear, glowing sinister amber light onto the space where Cassie and the body inhabited. At first it was just a few eyes, but slowly more and more opened up into an uncountable number of ocular organs just floating in space like asteroids with slit-like pupils and no irises to speak of.

For a moment, nothing happened. The eyes just watched and the body remained motionless. Finally the body spoke again, this time in human tongue.

"What is wrong, o infinite ones? Why do you not do as I command? Why do you not obliterate the existence of this mere mortal?" Cassie recognized the voice now as Mordecai.

Nothing happened. Whatever he was trying to do wasn't working.

Cassie found that she could speak for the first time, and by the light of the infinite eyes discovered that her body was visible. "Yeah, that's the problem with being a warlock, Mordy. Your magic is at the whims of the creature to whom you've bound yourself. Seems like your patron isn't willing to do what you order. Perhaps you've forgotten who owns whom in this relationship?"

"TRUTH", a deafening word rang out in Elder.

"No, this is impossible! I am the Scion of Nonexistence! I should be able to erase anyone who stands in my way!"

"QUARK COMMANDS UNIVERSE NOT" the same voice screamed again in Elder.

"You recalcitrant squid! What is your purpose if not to do what I say! I am the Royal Magician of His Majesty's Kingdom of Zona!"

"WALLS CRUMBLE, KINGDOMS FADE, LIFE EXPIRES; SEC-ONDS PASS"

"Give it up, Mordy. I think it's trying to say that you're too insignificant to command an Elder God."

"TRUTH"

Mordecai just screamed, the chthonic double-tone making his cries sound like audio interference.

"It's time you gave up all these delusions. You are not a cosmic entity, you'll never take Gwynne, she'll never be the person you want her to be, and she'll never love you like you want her to."

Images began to flash through Cassie's mind. It was like when she had absorbed Ackerman's curse from the crystal, but from a completely different viewpoint. She saw the same or a similar scene of practice swords in a castle clearing. This time, she saw everything from a shorter perspective grasping one of the wooden swords in front of them. In front of her view was Gwynne as a child.

Child Gwynne spoke, looking quite upset. "I don't get it, Mordy. Why are you so much better at this than me? It isn't fair!"

"Don't worry, ######. You'll get better, all you have to do is practice!" Gwynne's deadname, now erased, sounded like static in the memory.

"But as I improve, you improve as well. How am I supposed to surpass you?"

"My lord, you're only eleven years old. You'll grow and become more magnificent as you become a man." This didn't seem to reassure Gwynne, for reasons that were obvious in hindsight.

This memory faded, being replaced with a new one. In this vision, a young adult Gwynne was standing on a moonlit balcony, looking listlessly at a starry sky. Cassie's view was from behind and inside an open bay window. Loose curtains flowed gently in the night breeze. The viewpoint stepped out onto the balcony and beside Young

Gwynne before speaking.

"My Lord, are you truly going to be leaving in the morning?"

Young Gwynne turned to face the speaker, looking exasperated. "Mordecai, I've told you a thousand times to just address me by name. I hate these stuffy titles. And yes, I am leaving. You know just as well as I that studying magic is my life's goal. Plus I'm craving some independence for once. I've barely even been outside of the palace, what for father treating me like a porcelain doll."

"Will you at least visit?"

Young Gwynne looked confused. "What's the matter, Mordy? Missing me already?"

"Of course, ######. Days without you here are barely worth living."

"No need to be so morose. I swear, sometimes it feels like you treat me with a bit too much reverence. Take me down from your pedestal. I'm just a person, after all, albeit a stunningly good-looking and mind-blowingly talented person."

"That's what I like about you. You're not like everyone else here. You aren't afraid to buck tradition and tell your father when he's being an ass."

Young Gwynne laughed. "Somebody has to keep his ego in check. Everyone else around here is too afraid of losing their job and being thrown out on their asses to disagree with him. It's pathetic, really. If I was in charge, things would be different. Not just in the palace, but this country as a whole."

"I dream of the day that your ambitions come to fruition, my prince."

"Okay, can we relax a bit? The last thing I want to do is spend my last night at home feeling sad and sappy. Let's party, already!"

Mordecai gave a tired laugh. "Of course. Just promise me that no matter what happens when you're away, you'll always be my brother."

Young Gwynne gave a look of someone who was uncomfortable with the manner of address, but had spent a long time learning to hide that feeling. "Yes, I promise that we'll always be best friends."

There was a shock of emotion in this memory that was all too familiar to Cassie. 'Best friends' wasn't enough. Cassie almost felt bad for Mordecai, but then remembered how much of an ass he was.

A final memory crystallized now. Gwynne was not present in this one, and it seemed this was a memory Mordecai had of talking to the king. Cassie had never actually seen King Quintus before, and his long beard and thin nose gave him a proper imperious look.

"What happened to ######?" Mordecai shouted to the king.

"Calm thy fury, Sir Drake. It seems ###### has vanished, leaving behind only this letter."

The king extended a piece of unfolded parchment to Mordecai, who snatched it and read it over. The words were a blur to Cassie, but their meaning went without saying.

"What does he mean?" Mordecai asked, voice wavering. "About being a woman?"

The king just shook his head. "I understand not. Some foul Abaxian magics no doubt. I knew sending that boy to the dark country was a mistake. Someone has ensorcelled him into thinking he is something he is not."

Fiery feelings of rage, betrayal, loss, and heartache permeated Mordecai's perspective. "Please, Your Majesty, allow me to bring him back. I can make him see reason."

King Quintus gazed into the middle distance, a sad but steely expression on his face. "A wild horse, that one, just like his mother. No, that boy is dead to me now. You will make preparations for war. I will make Abaxia pay for what it has done to me."

"Your wish is my command."

"Thank you, Sir Drake. You're like the real son I never had. I'm so proud of the man you've become."

Cassie could take no more of this. Mustering up all her energy, she began to push back against Mordecai's mental influence. With an explosion, everything went white. There was a sound like shattering glass and Mordecai, the one from the present, screamed anew. With a flash of light, Cassie found herself back in the sitting room of the House. Mordecai was curled up on the floor in front of her, convulsing in mad fits of grief. Clearly he would pose no further threat.

Ollie stood up from his hiding place behind the now ruined armchair. "Is… is it over? You guys kinda blipped out for a few seconds."

Had it only been a few seconds? Her time in that strange void felt like forever. What's more, she felt almost fully drained of energy, and it was all she could do to stand.

Any retort she could have mustered was silenced by a voice from the next room.

"Cassie, is that you? Whenever you're done, I would appreciate your help here."

23

Heartbare

Right Now You're Just Confused - Butterflies the Size of Fey - A Crash Course on Spatial Recursion - Anything?

Cassie's exhaustion was forgotten in a moment, at least by her mind. She staggered into the kitchen and dining area to find Gwynne locked in armed combat with a man that Cassie now recognized as King Aberforth Quintus. Gwynne had her rapier drawn and was fending off the king's strikes, he himself wielding a shortsword in his right hand and a magnificent gilded shield in his left. The kitchen table was overturned in the corner, giving the two fighters a cramped arena for their duel.

Despite his age, the king was still a formidable fighter, the same old master that had taught Gwynne everything she knew. He deflected Gwynne's thrusts with his shield as easily as one might bat away a mosquito in their face. Then when he retaliated, his sword crashed down like an avalanche despite its short length. It was all Gwynne could do to parry.

"Foolish child! You have relied too much on that fickle and useless magic and let your sword arm grow weak!"

"If it weren't for your idiot lapdog's stupid curse, I'd show you just how *useless* my magic really is!"

"Hah! Sir Drake may be a fool, but I'll give him one thing, he's devoted. Nothing you can do shy of killing him will make him let go of that curse, and I know you won't do that."

Gwynne grunted as she deflected another hammering blow. "Of course not. I may be a thief, but I'm not a damn murderer."

"That's right, and I'll make you come home and face charges for that, *boy*!"

Taking advantage of her father's gloating, Gwynne kicked out at the man's shield, sending him staggering back against the wall. Before he could recover, Gwynne slammed the basket of her silver rapier into the man's face. Cassie expected his nose to shatter, but he only seemed bruised. Either Gwynne was pulling her punches or the king had some kind of warding. Possibly a bit of both. "How many times must I tell you, you senile old man? I'm a woman, and you will address me as such."

The king chuckled and stood back into his fighting stance. "Poppy-cock. I raised you by myself for your entire life. I know you better than you know yourself, and right now you're just confused. Come home and be the man I know you are."

Gwynne stood back, holding her rapier at the ready, but not advancing. "Clearly you know nothing. You have never once listened to me or valued anything I had to say. You can't even respect my own determination of my gender."

"Yeah!" Cassie found herself chiming in, before she could stop herself. "Gwynne's obviously a woman. Are you blind?"

Gwynne smiled a little, and strafed around to place herself between Cassie and the king. "Thanks for that, dear."

The King narrowed his eyes and wrinkled his nose a bit at Cassie. "So this is that Abaxian I've heard so much about. They call you The

Crow. Tell me, Crow, are you the one that put these ideas into my son's head? And is it you who has magicked his name from my mind?"

"I only had the pleasure of meeting Gwynne a few months ago, but that was enough time for me to get to know her. It's a shame you're too self absorbed to celebrate who she truly is."

"Oh, and who is this person you think you know?"

"Gwynne is the most precious thing in the world, and is the woman I love."

Gwynne was broadsided by this, and looked back at her. "C-Cassie, what? Truly?"

Before Cassie could affirm, the king spoke once more. "What smoke and mirrors did you perform to make this poor girl enamored with you? You do know that you are not deserving of such rapture."

Gwynne grimaced and turned back to her father. "Just because you didn't love me doesn't mean others cannot. I know I'm not a perfect person. I know I've hurt people. I know I'm selfish and foolish and stupid. But plenty of people care about me anyway. The only one who can't is you."

"You lie. I have loved you since you were born. You were my son! How could I not love you?"

"Because you didn't love *me*, you loved the idea of a perfect son that would be your mini-me and follow in your footsteps. Once you realized I was not that trophy son, you considered me dead while continuing to hang onto that fantasy. Never once did you stop to care about my feelings or what was important to me."

The king snarled, slashing forward with his sword. Gwynne ducked under the blade's arc and swept at the king's legs. He did not trip, but staggered back. "I'm not done talking, father. All of that could possibly have been excused with a simple apology if you hadn't done the worst thing of all. You killed my mother."

Cassie gasped. She didn't know much about Gwynne's mother, but had surmised that she was dead. This was big news, however.

"I didn't kill her! I sent her away, as I could not stand the sight of her anymore for bearing me a disgusting effeminate son."

"Yes, where she died in poverty and ignominy. Can't you see that this kingdom is crumbling around you? No, you can't, you're too busy playing war with the lives of your citizens to pay attention to the fact that you're allowing vampiric corporations to run the economy and thus everyone's lives into the ground."

"Do not criticize my ability to rule when you yourself abandoned the throne!"

"I'll criticize all I please!"

"Very well. I had hoped that I might be able to talk some sense into my poor, foolish child. I see that there is nothing left but to eliminate you. As my divine right as King of Zona, I hereby sentence the terrorist Owl and his partner The Crow to execution."

The king had entered a righteous fury now. He charged at Gwynne and pummeled her with a flurry of sword swings. The man may have been in his fifties but he was still extremely muscular and well-toned. Gwynne stepped back as she deflected blow after blow, but her strength was waning. It wouldn't be long before her guard was broken and she had no defenses left. With a final cry, the king threw his shield to the ground, gripped his sword with both hands, and began hammering down on Gwynne's rapier, outstretched to block the blows. But the thin rod of a blade could not withstand such punishment. With one final heavy blow, the rapier cracked and shattered, sending shards of silver metal flying around the room. Gwynne herself fell to the ground at the impact. King Quintus breathed heavily and raised his sword once more.

But Cassie was ready. Drawing the werewolf fang from her pocket, she pounced into the melee and over Gwynne. She poured all of her remaining magic into a shield which blocked the King's execution blow.

"Cassie! What are you doing?"

Cassie found herself straddled over Gwynne's legs, hands on the floor by her hips and looking directly into her eyes. She had never before noticed this level of infinite detail in Gwynne's eyes, nor did she realize how arresting her gaze could be. Cassie held the fang up between the faces of the two women, which were now only inches away.

"Gwynne, I don't want to be best friends anymore."

Clang! Clank! Clang! The King was trying his best to break Cassie's shield, but the miserable shank of steel could not breach. Cassie had thought all her energy was spent, but there was something else powering this shield. It was as if her love for Gwynne opened a new reservoir of energy.

"W-what do you mean? Didn't we have such a touching moment where-"

"I don't want to be best friends anymore because I care about you too much! I can't just be friends. Gwynne, I love you! I love you so much. You changed my life and you've given me the power to finally take charge of my own destiny. You're gorgeous and funny and *so* smart. You're more confident than I could ever hope to be." Cassie found that she was crying now, but didn't care. Nothing existed in the world except for Gwynne. "I can't help but spend every waking minute thinking of you. Seeing your smile makes me melt. All I want to do is spend my life by your side and do everything I can to make your dreams come true." At this point, Cassie could no longer speak, her emotions were too raw and potent. She only cried her gay little heart out.

Gwynne didn't speak for a second and just took the werewolf fang from Cassie's outstretched hand. "Cassie, I... I've never truly known what it means to be loved. I'm afraid I might hurt you. You're the only person who's really ever been there for me when I was hurting. You're the only person who I feel like really *gets* me. You stick by me through all my bullshit and still support me. Despite what I know you think about yourself, I find you to be absolutely gorgeous. Your eyes... gods, your eyes. An eternity could find itself lost in those charcoal pools, as I also find myself. I find myself always wanting to make you smile and to protect you from harm. That's why I can't bring myself to love you, because I know I'm not worthy and I'll just hurt you."

Cassie shook her head, speaking through the tears. "Stupid! Hurting someone is part of loving them! I've no doubt we'll fight and quarrel, but that's just who we are! And you know what? I'll love you even still. I don't care that you're flawed. In my eyes, you're perfect. Just tell me you love me, you idiot!"

Gwynne, for once in her life, looked quite flustered. She was definitely blushing now, but wouldn't look away from Cassie's eyes. "Cassie... I..."

Cassie laughed. "C'mon, you big baby. You can do it."

Gwynne began to cry now, herself. Thick streams of water flew from her eyes. "Cassie! I love you so much!"

Before either of them knew what was happening, Cassie had, purely on instinct, launched herself onto Gwynne. Their lips met and fireworks exploded around them, though Cassie could not tell if these were magical manifestations or just in her head. Gwynne's lips were every bit as soft and luscious as she had imagined, staying up at night to dare to fantasize about this exact moment. Wrapping her arms around Gwynne felt right, as if her appendages were made to fit perfectly around her lover's torso. Gwynne wrapped one arm around Cassie's waist and placed the other on the back of her head as the two embraced. Cassie could feel her heart rate, already elevated from the tense combat, skyrocketing to where she feared it might stop. She wished she could live in this moment forever as butterflies the size of fey danced in her stomach. For just a moment everything was right in the world.

But something else was happening in the moment. An electrical energy that Cassie had dismissed as pure adrenaline and desire started to spark between the two women. After a moment, Gwynne drew away and Cassie could see that Gwynne was glowing. All of a sudden, the reality of the situation rushed back to her and she whipped around to see the King of Zona crash down his sword on her feeble magic shield. The shield shattered, but before the king could land a killing blow Gwynne jumped to her feet and thrust a hand out. A *boom* of magical force erupted from her palm, sending the king rocketing back across the kitchen and out the opening into the side hallway. The curse was broken. Gwynne's magic was back.

Gwynne leaned down and extended a hand to Cassie, who felt woozy both from the drain of magical energy and the rush of emotions. She took Gwynne's hand and was pulled to her feet, leaning on Gwynne.

"You okay there, baby?" Gwynne asked, sending the butterflies for another set of loop-de-loops. Cassie was breathless and could only nod.

From the hallway, the king groaned as he stirred from where he had landed. "Impossible!" he said to himself. "Mordecai assured me that the curse could only be broken if the boy was captured!"

Gwynne looked down at Cassie with a wry smile. "What do you say we go give the old man a talking to?"

Cassie would even have jumped out of the hangar bay that very moment had Gwynne asked, and just clung onto her love as Gwynne went to accost her father. Before long, she was standing over the heap of a man, who was clutching the small of his back and struggling to rise.

"I suppose you're going to kill me now, boy?"

Gwynne just looked at the king, her face distant and impassive. "No,

I'm going to get some catharsis whether you like it or not."

Gwynne raised a hand to the king, ostensibly to cast a spell, but before anything could happen, the king sprang to his feet and ran off down the hallway.

"Mordecai!" he shouted, in vain. "Protect me, you useless lout!" But Mordecai could not answer him, still wracked by mental anguish on the sitting room floor. The king quickly realized that his attack dog was not coming and blanched. He fled further off into the house.

Gwynne just shook her head and followed after him at a leisurely pace, Cassie hanging onto her arm. "You forget, *Your Majesty*, this is *my* house!"

With no incantation at all, the shape of the house began to twist and contort. Wood creaked and splintered as every room and hallway in the House folded over on itself to form a single straight path. "I think it's time for a crash course in Spatial Recursion: one of the most difficult magics, and my specialty."

The king tried a door and threw himself through, only to find himself back in the same hallway, closer to his wrathful daughter than when he started. He shrieked an undignified and cowardly squeal and just ran full speed down the passage. Much like in the fey world, gravity meant nothing here, and Gwynne just walked inexorably forward, not worried at all about the possibility of the king escaping. Cassie thought she saw a glimpse of a door above her that opened into the sitting room, and she could see Ollie hanging onto the leg of a chair for dear life and looking quite sick indeed.

As much as Aberforth tried to run, escape was impossible. The hallway felt like it went on forever, but eventually terminated in a single door. He threw open the door and slammed it shut behind him. Cassie could hear the sound of a lock turning, but Gwynne's expression did not change. With a mere wave of her hand, the door flew off its hinges and careened into the room. Cassie could see that beyond the now open threshold was the theatre room that Feckalia had found only recently. As the two women entered, Aberforth collapsed on the stage in a deep bow.

"P-please don't kill me!" He sniveled.

Gwynne walked up to the stage in front of him. The house lights dimmed, leaving the three people on the stage in a bright spotlight.

"I told you, you idiot man. I'm not going to kill you. I'm going to do something far worse to you."

The cowardly king could only whimper and cry. Gwynne extended a hand, now cloaked with swirling purple magic, and touched the back of Aberforth's head. At her touch, the purple energy dissipated and the man began to scream.

"What did you do to him?" Cassie asked, afraid Gwynne was torturing him.

"Oh you'll see."

The king cried ever the harder, but was now speaking through the anguish. "Everything's wrong! It's all wrong! Ugh, get me out of this body! It's wrong it's wrong it's wrong! I'm going to die! I'm so lonely. Why didn't you love me? Why can't you love meeeee? Gods, I hate myself so much!" The king began to scratch at his own skin, as if he could peel it away and reveal a more correct form beneath.

Gwynne looked down on the writhing man with no pity. "Aberforth Quintus, I have just transferred the memory of all the negative emotions I have felt over my life due to my gender dysphoria and your abuse and neglect. This is not a curse, and the feelings will pass, but you will always remember how it feels to be me and you will always bear the shame of how you treated me."

"Please…" the king gasped. "Make it stop! Have mercy on your poor stupid father, I beg of you!"

"Hmm, I dunno. I don't know if you deserve it. Maybe if you called me by my name?"

"A- Ab-… son please…"

Gwynne shook her head and clenched her hand. The sorrow seemed to redouble and the king gave shrieking wails anew. "That's not my name. I am a woman and my name is Gwynne Circe Brandwyck."

"G-Gwynne… please. I'll do anything!"

"Anything?"

"Yes, of course. You want money? The throne? It's yours. Just please, make the emotions stop!"

Gwynne's stoic facade broke, revealing a terrifying face of raw fury. She exploded. "Then call me your daughter, you son of a bitch!"

"Gwynne… My daughter… Please, help me."

"No." With a snap of her fingers, the king disappeared. Gwynne's emotional fever broke and she bawled openly, hugging Cassie tight. Cassie completely empathized with Gwynne, having only recently gone through something similar herself. The two women embraced, letting their sorrows out and finding solace in one another's arms.

A sharp *crack!* rang out across the theatre. The embrace was cut short.

"What was that?" Cassie asked.

Gwynne looked grim once more. "Nothing much. I'm afraid the *Pale Moon* is falling apart."

24

Unclear Futures

Splinters of Wood Flew Like Shrapnel - This Might Get A Little Bumpy - More Important Than Gold - One Last Heist, For Old Times' Sake

Cassie was panicking. "Falling apart? What do you mean? Has the ship been hit?"

Gwynne gave her a forlorn smile of someone resigned to their fate. "I'm afraid she's been hit many times up 'til now. It was only my magic of inertial dampening that keeps us from feeling the motions of the *Moon* inside the House. The ship is so heavily damaged at this point that the magic is unraveling."

"What can we do? How can we fix her?"

Gwynne just grasped Cassie's hand. "We can't. All we can do is get everyone clear."

In an instant, the dark theatre vanished and Gwynne and Cassie were back in the sitting room. Gwynne's spatial manipulation seemed to have been reversed, and the room was back to normal. Everyone was as Cassie had left them. Letting go of Cassie's hand, Gwynne kneeled down and touched Mordecai's shivering form. In a flash, he disappeared.

"What did you do to him and the king?"

"I merely sent them back to their ship. They've lost the will to fight."

Ollie stood up from the floor and grabbed his guitar. "What in the hells is going on here? Did we win?"

"Sort of," Cassie said.

Gwynne turned to him. "Come along, Mister Retzel, we're abandoning ship."

Ollie looked flabbergasted. "Wh- oh… okay then."

The three dashed through the now crumbling hallways, Gwynne and Cassie refusing to unlink hands. Ollie gave their contact awkward looks, but Cassie didn't care. If he couldn't figure it out on his own, she wasn't about to tell him. Planks of wood crashed to the ground around them, and doorframes cracked and shattered. Splinters of wood flew like shrapnel, but Gwynne used a shielding spell to protect the party from danger.

Whipping around a corner, the stairs to the basement came into view. The three mages trotted down single-file immediately before the doorway collapsed.

"I've released the magic on the House!" Gwynne shouted. "It will collapse in on itself, easing the burden on the *Moon* and buying us a bit more time."

Cassie was sad to bid such a sharp and immediate farewell to her new home, but reassured herself that wherever Gwynne was would always be her home.

They came down at last into the mechanical passages of the ship. The Ranklin brothers had taken care of the last remaining soldiers, and they rushed about trying to repair busted pipes and gears within the ship's inner workings. Gwynne touched each of the soldiers in turn, causing them to vanish back to their ship just as the other Zonan forces.

"C'mon, lads, give 'er all ye got!" Horatio urged. He himself had gotten up from the gunnery seat and was assisting Havershank in patching up a steaming pipe. Altogether, the men looked beaten and exhausted, but still they carried on to save the ship.

"Give it up, boys," Gwynne said. "I'm officially giving the order to abandon ship. We're getting out of here."

"Ye bloody *what*?" Horatio shouted, over the cacophony of failing airship.

"C'mon, Horatio, she's had a good run, but it's time to go."

"Oh 'ells no, lass. Ye ain't gettin' me oot o' this baby if its th' las' thing I do! I can still fix 'er!"

Gwynne shook her head. "Oh faithful Horatio, you foolish man. She's already dead. I'm just as sad about it as you, but I couldn't allow myself to leave you behind to die. You're a good friend and too valuable of an engineer besides."

Cassie was shocked. Horatio began to cry. "Ah kno', I jus' love this ship so much, ye ken?"

Gwynne ran over and hugged the short man. "It will be okay, my good man. We'll build a *Pale Moon Mk.II*. But I can't do it without your help."

Horatio wiggled his way out of Gwynne's grasp. "Ah, quit th' theatrics. I'll go, I'll go. Jus' don' touch me no more."

The Ranklin brothers were likewise crestfallen. Jimmy was weeping openly, trying and failing to staunch the tears on the hairy back of his arm. Bimmy just turned to him, also trying to hold back tears. "C'mon, mate. Ge' it togevva'. An airsman knows when t' let the ship go down. No tears, now, you lot." But it was too late, Bimmy was also crying. Havershank's bottom lip was clenched with herculean strength into a reserved frown, but he couldn't help but tear up a bit.

"Well, now that we're in agreement, let us not dilly-dally. Quick, men (and Cassie), to the hangar!"

Everyone stampeded through the steaming pipes and cramped quarters, but were stopped in their tracks by a fire that engulfed the passage.

"One o' the gas lines musta burst!" Horatio shouted. "Lemme go get a fire extinguisher!"

"No need! I can take care of this," Gwynne said, never missing a chance to show off. With a quick muttering and wave of her hand, a wave of ice swept over the piping, extinguishing the fire and freezing the gas leak shut. Gwynne led the way again, and before long everyone had come out and into the hangar of the now sinking *Pale Moon*. The wind was whipping into the room, blowing everyone's hair about and testing Cassie's balance. She could barely hear anything at all, however a harmony of meows greeted them. She looked down to see Baal and Belial the cats running up to Gwynne and hollering at her feet.

Gwynne knelt down and scooped up her cats, kissing them profusely. "Oh Baal! Oh Belial! My babies! Mommy was so worried about you!"

Cassie was not particularly close with either cat, but was still relieved that they were not in danger. Gwynne would have been inconsolable, and Cassie would have felt guilty.

"Alright everyone!" Gwynne said, taking charge of the situation. "Cassie and Ollie, you take the *Star*. Everyone else, load up into this Zonan landing craft. I should be able to fly it."

Gwynne pressed a hidden button on the rear of the landing craft and its hatch sprung open, turning into a small gangway up into the belly of the grub. The men needed no second bidding and trotted up the ramp, buckling themselves into rows of seats along the inner walls of the craft. Gwynne herself stepped towards the craft, but turned to look back at Cassie.

"Cassie, I'm sorry I couldn't protect the House. I know it was your home and how precious that was to you."

"It's okay! Buildings can be replaced, but people can't, least of all you! Let's go already!"

Gwynne smiled and retreated back into the landing craft with her cats, closing the hatch behind her.

The *Star* was slightly damaged from its earlier crash landing, but it still looked operable. Cassie turned to Ollie. "Okay, let's go."

"I... don't really like aircraft," Ollie grumbled.

"Are you kidding me? Jump, then, for all I care!"

Cassie pushed open the cockpit glass and clambered in. Ollie deliberated for a second, clearly trying to overcome an anxiety that Cassie hadn't realized he had.

"Seriously, Ollie, c'mon. I know it's scary, but your other option is literal death."

"O-okay," he stammered, climbing up into the second seat, shaking the entire time. Cassie instructed him how to buckle himself in and closed the cockpit.

The Zonan landing craft had already taken off and Cassie could see Gwynne looking very competent (and pretty) in the pilot's chair. She had strapped both of her cats into the co-pilot's seat and they looked very upset about this arrangement, but couldn't break free. The black grub trundled its way out of the hangar and out into the open air as Cassie was booting up the *Star*'s engine.

An explosion racked the hangar. The *Star* tumbled and flipped, landing upside-down on the hangar floor. Ollie screamed and began to hyperventilate, having a panic attack. Cassie wanted to help him, but had no idea what to say and had more important things to worry about. She couldn't roll the *Star* out of the hangar in this position, though it mattered little as she knew the landing gear was still malfunctioning. All she could see beneath her was the cold steel of the hangar floor. She'd have to get creative.

"Okay, Ollie, hold on tight. This might get a little bumpy. Close your eyes if you gotta."

She had recovered a small fragment of magical energy since her confession to Gwynne, and she had to leverage it carefully to get the plane out into the air without using too much stamina and blacking out. Speaking the incantation she now knew well, she conjured a force vector on the *Star*, pushing from the tail and causing the plane to rocket out into open air. The plane's propellers roared to life, and with a few acrobatic flips and rolls, Cassie was able to right the *Star* before she blacked out.

But it was only for a few seconds, and she came to with Ollie screaming and the nose of the *Star* approaching the ground at high velocity. She regained her senses and pulled up on the flight stick at the last moment, swerving the *Star* out of the dive and onto the ground, causing it to skid to a bumpy halt on the grassy steppe.

"See Ollie, what'd I say? Nothing to fear."

"I think I'm gonna be sick…"

* * *

After Cassie and Ollie exited the crashed plane and Ollie had emptied the contents of his stomach in a nearby brush, she looked around for a glimpse of the others.

A red shape was shooting towards her on the ground, and she quickly recognized it as Feckalia. The demon flew up to Cassie and touched down before collapsing into her arms.

"I'm… so sorry… *cough* Cassie. I did… *gasp* my best…"

Cassie squeezed Feck tight, the tall woman looking comical in Cassie's arms.

"Oh Feck, please don't blame yourself! You were wonderful! Gods, I could stand to learn a thing or two from you. We only made it as long as we did because of you."

Feck gave a coughing laugh. "Yeah, I guess I'm pretty awesome, huh?"

Cassie rolled her eyes. Clearly Feck would be fine.

"Where's Gwynne and the others? They were in that boxy Zonan plane."

Feckalia stood up again and calmed her breathing. "I dunno. I passed them on the way down, but Gwynne told me to come make sure you were okay when she saw you nosedive like that. What in the hells were you thinking, Cass?"

"Sorry… I… uh… blacked out for a few seconds."

Ollie, who had just returned from cleaning himself up, looked at Cassie with an expression of shock and concern. "I'm never flying with you again, you're crazy."

"Yeah, well, we made it out, didn't we?"

The cold late fall air made Cassie shiver. It was properly night now and the moon itself wasn't even out, though there was light from the small localized fires lit by the *Star*'s emergency landing. As if to punctuate, the plane's landing gear popped out.

It was impossible to see the commandeered black steel grub against the darkness of the sky, but she could see the two warring airships in the distance. The *Crowning Glory* was moving away in the direction of New Ozion, making a hasty retreat. The *Pale Moon* on the other hand, was on fire and listing at a worrying angle. It picked up more and more speed before it slammed into a mountainside, mirroring the airship crash that had started this whole adventure for Cassie so long ago. She bowed her head and gave silent words of thanks to the *Moon* for her service to the House. Like before, she knew the ship couldn't hear or understand her, but it just felt right.

"Damn, that sucks," Feckalia said, tactlessly. "I was really starting to like that place."

A few minutes later, the black grub flew up at a crawling pace and touched down. Clearly this thing was built for endurance and not speed. With a hiss of depressurizing air, the hatch door opened and Gwynne and the boys rushed out. Everyone met in a big group hug, though some (namely Feck), were less than thrilled about this embrace. Once everyone let go, Cassie pounced on Gwynne and the two kissed again, this time more passionately than before, the flames of destruction lighting them from behind.

Everyone else looked awkward, and Horatio coughed to break the tension. Cassie pulled away, bashfully, but still held the hand of her love.

"Ah take it ye broke tha' there curse, eh?"

Everyone laughed, despite the situation.

"Yes, my magic has returned in full, and then some. I feel like I could move the planet by will alone."

"And… wha' about th' Zonans, miss? An' the ship, too," Bimmy asked, clearly fearing for his job security.

"I don't think the king will be bothering us or anyone else for a while. He's seen the error of his ways, I made sure of that."

The men exchanged looks, afraid of what Gwynne was capable of.

"Don't worry, he is unharmed. There are going to be some big changes in Zona, I think."

"Is the war over?" Ollie asked, sheepishly.

Gwynne just shrugged. "Only time may tell, though I hope so. I think our two nations have done each other enough damage."

Gwynne's cats sat close to her feet, not used to this many people around. To Cassie's delight, Belial rubbed on her legs a bit before going back to Gwynne. It seemed the grumpy cat had accepted her at last.

Suddenly, a cold wave of dread swept through Cassie. "Oh gods, we're missing someone!"

Gwynne cocked an eyebrow. "Hmm? Let me see. Me, you, Horatio, Ranklins One, Two, and Three, Feckalia, Mr. Retzel. Everyone seems accounted for."

"But what about Tibb?"

Gwynne just laughed. "Oh, Cassie. I thought you would have figured it out by now. Tibberwyx's library exists only in the fey world. It was never physically in the House to begin with. Only the entrance was destroyed. I fear this may mean that Tibb's contract is broken, but I hope to see zir again someday."

Cassie felt relief that gave way into sadness. The only real home she had ever known was gone, exploded on the side of a mountain. "So… what's gonna happen to us?"

"What do you mean, dear?"

"I mean the House, and all of us here. We don't have anywhere to go."

"I suppose not, but a house can be rebuilt as long as its family still lives."

"*Family is more important than gold,*" Cassie whispered, remembering her mother's mantra.

"What was that, Cassie?" Gwynne asked.

"Oh, nothing. I guess this means the Owl's thieving days are over? That's a shame, I was just getting used to my role as their dashing sidekick Crow."

Gwynne laughed. "Oh I don't know about that. We'll certainly need gold to finance a new House Brandwyck. You know, I've heard rumors lately about a magical gem called the Orb of Dreams. Apparently looking into it will send you into a world of dreams beyond your wildest imagination. Could probably fetch a pretty penny. What do you all say? One last heist for old times' sake?" Everyone gave a hearty cheer, even Ollie, who was still looking quite terrified by everything that had happened.

Cassie gave Gwynne's hand a squeeze. The future was more uncertain than it had ever been, but she knew that as long as she was here with Gwynne and the rest of her dearest friends whom she considered family, she would always be home.

Author's Note

If you've made it this far, thank you so much for reading my book! I've put a ton of the ol' blood-sweat-'n'-tears into this novel and it touches on many topics that are very personal to me. I hope the story was able to entertain you, make you laugh, maybe even make you cry a little? I know I cry every time I read the last couple chapters, but maybe I'm just a big softie. At any rate, I hope you are able to find something to enjoy in the story. If you did, please consider helping to spread the word. Some great ways to do so are to tell your friends and family who may enjoy the story to check it out. Word of mouth goes a long way! Also, a positive review on whichever website you used to purchase the book helps to sway potential new readers and gives me a warm and fuzzy feeling in my sad gay heart. Lastly, if you would like to discuss the book, please consider visiting my Discord server, a link to which can be found on the next page.

That's enough ingratiation from me, though. I hope this story is well loved enough to warrant a sequel, as I have tons of ideas for future escapades for Cassie and company, and I hope you'll look forward to it!

Thanks,
Sarah Hawthorne

About the Author

Sarah Hawthorne is an author, game developer, artist, and all-around storyteller. She loves fantasy, sci-fi, horror, and mystery stories. She lives with her partner Abigail and two cats Miles and Cammy.

You can connect with me on:
- https://baph.xyz
- https://twitter.com/baph_xyz
- https://baph.xyz/discord

www.ingramcontent.com/pod-product-compliance
Lightning Source LLC
Chambersburg PA
CBHW051136130726
47988CB00005B/1857